THE DOCTOR

When he takes over a small-town practice in Vermont, Matt Chapin falls in love with Cissie, a young widow. His impetuous unfaithfulness ends the affair and Cissie marries Matt's best friend.

But their destinies are intertwined, and in this crowded and adventurous story they will have other chances to realize their happiness will be found only with each other....

Avon Books by
Agatha Young

THE TOWN AND DR. MOORE   21923 $1.75
I SWEAR BY APOLLO   22608 $1.75

I Swear by Apollo
Agatha Young

AVON
PUBLISHERS OF BARD, CAMELOT, DISCUS, EQUINOX AND FLARE BOOKS

AVON BOOKS
A division of
The Hearst Corporation
959 Eighth Avenue
New York, New York 10019

Copyright © 1968 by Agatha Young.
Published by arrangement with Simon & Schuster.
Library of Congress Catalog Card Number: 68-22975.

ISBN: 0-380-00274-4

All rights reserved, which includes the right
to reproduce this book or portions thereof in
any form whatsoever. For information address
Simon & Schuster, 630 Fifth Avenue
New York, N.Y. 10020.

First Avon Printing, June, 1970.
Third Printing

AVON TRADEMARK REG. U.S. PAT. OFF. AND
FOREIGN COUNTRIES, REGISTERED TRADEMARK—
MARCA REGISTRADA, HECHO EN CHICAGO, U.S.A.

Printed in the U.S.A.

I swear by Apollo . . . that according to my ability and judgment . . . I will keep this oath . . . according to the law of medicine. I will follow that system and regimen which, according to my ability and judgment, I consider for the benefit of my patients, and abstain from whatever is deleterious and mischievous. . . . While I continue to keep this oath unviolated, may it be granted to me to enjoy life and the practice of the healing art, respected by all men in all times. But should I trespass and violate this oath, may the reverse be my lot.

—Hippocratic Oath

I
City Point, Virginia

CHAPTER ONE

The war was over. The big encampment at the joining of the James and the Appomattox, that had been a triumph of organized men and materiel, was well along toward being abandoned. June sunlight, pure and sparkling, and at this early hour without heat, struck levelly across the empty parade ground. It reached the long rows of deserted, gray hospital barracks, transforming them, and touched a small colony of neatly aligned tents, intensifying their whiteness.

There was no one to see the morning's high glory that would be gone in a few more minutes, when the sun rose higher. There was, however, a sign of the day's beginning, for above a low building across the parade ground from the tent colony a thin spiral of pale blue wood smoke was languidly rising. Then, from a higher part of the camp, at a distance from the tents, there came the jarring thud of the morning gun, and a flag, hanging limp in the still air, jerkily climbed upward on a tall pole. As it came to rest a bugle sounded, the urgency of the notes softened by the humidity that had been rising all night from the river.

At the same moment a flap of one of the tents was pushed forcefully aside and a young man, ducking through the opening, straightened himself and stood surveying the scene. He wore a white shirt, open at the neck, and the blue uniform trousers of the Northern army. The sleeves of the shirt were rolled up the well-muscled arms as far as they could be made to go, as though the wearer was too energetic, too impatient of restraint, to stop at the elbow. He stood with his legs wide apart, his head thrown back, sun glinting from his disordered brown curls and from the russet-gold hairs on his forearms. The pose suggested that he was actively curious about, and ready for, whatever the new day might bring.

He turned his head from side to side, apparently in the hope of finding something either new or challenging in the familiar scene. Seeing nothing that had not been there before, he permitted a yawn to overtake him. He indulged it generously, expanding his chest and stretching his arms, luxuriating in the well-being of his fine body. Then, as though even this had not dispelled sleep, he ran the fingers of both hands through his brown curls with a scrubbing motion. In the midst of this he stopped, his conscious mind belatedly aware of the now silent bugle. He lowered his hands, turned in that direction and grinned. With mockery and great enjoyment, he imitated the sound.

"Ta ta ti-ti-ta, ta ta, ti-ti-ta, ta ta ti-ti-ta, ti *taa* ta."

Pleased with himself and the world, he stooped to tie the tent flap open. When he straightened up he saw, coming around from the back of the next tent, a most unsoldierly-looking soldier who was wearing nothing at all above the waist and clutching his unfastened trousers with both hands. This unhappy-looking individual said, "Hullo, Matt. Gotta see the doc," and he started toward the closed flap of the next tent.

"*Hey,* you can't go in there. Doc Hurd's not up yet. He's got to have his rest. What you want him for, Ben?"

"I got me a risin' right where the top of me pants goes."

"See him at sick call."

"Can't. Look here, Matt." Ben approached, shuffling through the dust, the backs of his trouser legs dragging. "I gotta go on guard duty. So I can't go to sick call. And I can't wear my pants. Got so goldarn bad in the night that—"

"Come in here and let me look at it." Matthew turned and went into his tent. The soldier Ben reluctantly followed, saying, "You ain't no doctor, Matt. You're nothin' but Doc Hurd's orderly. I want Doc Hurd."

"I'm a surgical orderly and I'm doctor enough to fix a

boil, if that's what you've got. Sit on that stool and face the flap."

Reluctantly, with a heavy sigh, Ben sat down as he was told, facing the open flap of the tent, and let his trousers drop. A couple of inches from the spine, just where the waistband of the trousers would lie, was an angry, fulminating boil. Matthew stooped to examine it and said, "You been a soldier long enough, Ben, to know you've got to wear drawers, or at least a shirttail, to keep your pants from rubbing."

"It's this goddam climate. When you think they're goin' to disband us, Matt?"

"Couldn't say. Soon, I should think."

Matthew moved swiftly to the back of the tent and returned carrying an open razor and a handful of lint, holding them so that if Ben turned around he could not see them. Ben said querulously, "I don't mind your lookin', Matt, but I want Doc Hurd—"

"Say, what sort of boat's that on the river?"

Ben craned his neck. "Can't see the river from here, you fool. *Jumping Jehosophat!*"

Ben leaped off the stool but he was too late, for the sharp edge of Matthew's razor had cut a neat cross on the head of the boil and the contents were streaming out.

"Shut up and let me clean up this mess, will you?"

"But I told you—"

"It's all done. Sit down and keep still."

Muttering resentfully, Ben sat, and in a moment there was a neat patch over the boil. Matthew poured water into a tin basin, washed his hands, and said, "Now I'll write you a certificate to get you off guard duty." He wrote rapidly with a pencil on a page torn out of a notebook, signed "Hurd" with a flourish, and gave it to Ben. "See Dr. Hurd tomorrow."

Ben took the paper, found a trouser pocket, and shoved it in. Then holding the trousers in both hands as before, he made for the tent opening, saying over his shoulder, "You're a bastard, Matt, but I gotta say it feels better already. Thanks."

When Ben had gone, Matthew left the tent and set out across the hard-beaten dirt of the parade ground toward the building from which the curling wood smoke rose. A path made of sun-warped boards led from the margin of the parade ground to three board steps and a closed door. He mounted the steps, which bent a little under his weight, and slammed the door open with the palm of his hand, saying loudly, "First come, first served. Morning, all!"

The room he entered was long and low, with hooks in the ceiling from which hung a double line of very large pots and pans. Two huge black wood-burning ranges stood side by side, and in front of them, their backs to the room, stood five women. There was a loud sound of frying and the women were in a flurry of activity; nevertheless they all turned heat-reddened, sweaty but smiling faces toward the young man standing in the doorway. Through a partly open sliding panel there was a view of a mess hall with long tables set for breakfast at which a few early risers were already seated. The oldest of the women, who was holding a long-handled spoon, said a brisk "Mornin', Matthew." She was thin and gray-haired, with bright black eyes like a bird's, and she pronounced "Morning" through her nose in the Vermont way, so that it sounded like *"More*-nin."

Matthew let the door shut behind him and came into the room. "I guess I'll eat in here with you girls, Mrs. Bascomb," he said.

"That you will not. You'll eat in the mess hall with the others, like where you belong. What makes you think you're so special anyway, I'd like to know? Now git out of here." She raised the spoon and threatened him with it as she might brandish a stick at a cow in a pasture. "Now *git.*"

Laughing, he advanced on her, crouching a little, arms outspread to catch her. She shrieked at him, "Oh my land. Matthew, you *stop*," but he caught her and began to waltz her over the bare boards of the kitchen floor. The girls by the ranges watched, giggling, and Mrs. Bascomb shouted, "Let me go, you . . . Let *go.*" Managing to free the hand that held the long spoon, she whacked him smartly on his lean, tight-muscled behind. He said, *"So!"* in mock menace, drew her tightly against him, bent over her and spanked her once, soundly. The watching girls screamed with pleased horror. He released her, went to a deal table by a window, pulled out a chair and sat down, saying in a parade-ground voice to the girls by the ranges, "All right —bring on the grub." The girls giggled louder.

Matthew beat the tabletop smartly with his fist, and one of the girls gave him a startled look over her shoulder, then came to the table where he was sitting. The girl had a broad-cheekboned, pleasantly homely face and a strong, stocky figure. She gave a reliable, no-nonsense impression that was her best qualification for life with the troops. Before she spoke she wiped glistening beads of sweat from her upper lip, using the sleeveless part of her arm.

"What you want to eat, Matt?"

"The usual—ham, eggs, cakes and 'lasses. Fries if you got 'em. Thanks, Isobel."

"Someday you come up our way and taste the maple syrup we got, you never put molasses on cakes again. And I ain't Isobel. I'm Ruth. Which you should know good and well by this time. From a New York feller in a Vermont regiment—can't expect no better, seems like."

Matthew made a sudden grab for her, but she moved with swift adroitness out of his reach. From a safe distance she glanced out of the window beside Matthew and said, "Here comes Dr. Hurd. Lookin' for you, likely, though why he keeps the likes of you around beats me."

"Because I'm the best damn surgical orderly in the Northern armies, that's why."

Ruth made a sound of derision and went back to join the other women. Matthew turned to look through the window at the man who was coming slowly along the duckboard path. He was big, stoop-shouldered and gray, and his clothes hung on him as though he had lost a good deal of weight since they were new. A stained and shabby uniform coat, on which the tarnished insignia of a major was visible, had been draped over his shoulders. On his head he wore, pushed well back, a battered forage cap with a cracked visor that, to judge by the small size, had not originally been his own. But though his clothing had the appearance of tired sloppiness, the man himself gave the impression of being notably clean. He wore no beard. His big knuckled hands, which hung from shirt-sleeves a little too short, were red from frequent scrubbing, and the fingers, though misshapen, looked capable of precise, delicate movements.

Once Matthew, in the early days of his service, had remarked on their suppleness and Dr. Hurd had replied, "You get them that way by practice. You want to be a surgeon someday, maybe, you better start limbering them."

"How?"

"You take an egg cup and a piece of suture silk. You put the three middle fingers down inside the cup and tie a suture knot without getting any of your fingers above the rim of the cup."

"My Lord—I could never do that."

11

In secret, Matthew tried it and found it even harder than he thought. He went on trying, and though he began to hate the cup, his fingers, and the suture silk, achieving this skill became the focal point of his days. When he succeeded the first time, he was panting from the effort and there was sweat on his forehead. He kept trying, and very slowly it got easier. Then one day, when he was sitting at a table alone in the medical tent, tying and retying knots inside the cup, he was startled to hear Dr. Hurd's voice behind him.

"So you finally got it. Good. Next thing is—get so you can do it without moving the egg cup the least little bit. Without touching the sides, even. After that, work for speed. You don't want your patient to bleed to death while you're getting a knot tied."

The odd thing about all this effort to acquire a skill was that Matthew had not the slightest intention of becoming a surgeon. He had never even considered it. What kept him tying knots in suture silk was not ambition but a very strong dislike for having anyone do anything involving dexterity better than he could do it.

Dr. Hurd kept watch of Matthew's progress (little went on near him those heavy-lidded eyes did not see), and in time he let Matthew practice his new accomplishment on a living patient. The problem was a fairly simple one—the clamping and ligation of an artery that had been well exposed—but doing it gave Matthew the surprise of his life. Feeling the pulsation of the living artery under his fingers was a strange, exciting, and at the same time a disturbing experience. For days he kept the memory of it, not so much in his mind as in his fingertips. It made him restless, and for a while he was moody and discontented with his surroundings, though he had no idea why this should be so. Dr. Hurd never suggested he try it again, and shortly, being kept very busy on routine work, Matt more or less forgot about it. When he did remember, he felt again momentarily the lift of spirit, and also the restlessness.

It occurred to Matthew to wonder if Hurd ever had such feelings as these. If so, he showed no sign of it, though perhaps he had once had them, long ago. Hurd at work was businesslike and intensely concentrated, though he had the curious, not uncommon surgeon's knack of knowing all the time what those around him were doing.

The door of the big kitchen opened and Dr. Hurd entered. A wave of heat from the now fully risen and merciless sun entered with him. He blinked because of the change of light, and said to the cluster of busy women, "Morning, girls." Receiving their chorus of good-mornings, he dropped his head a little to one side and gave them a wide-mouthed, faintly diffident smile that, along with the twinkle in his eyes, produced an effect of unexpected charm. Seeing this, Matthew thought, not for the first time, that the old boy must have been considerable of a heller in his youth. Hurd half turned to Matthew.

"Hullo, Matt. Thought I'd find you where the girls are." With his hand on the back of a chair, drawing it out, he raised his voice a little. "Ruth—you got a nice-looking steak there, and some fries?" He sat down opposite Matthew, put his elbows on the table, scrubbed his hands over his face and said, "It's going to be hotter than the hinges today."

"Same like all the other days."

"Worse."

"Well, there's not much work these days with the regiment under strength and no more fighting."

"Excepting the fights the boys get into among themselves. Seems like if they haven't got an enemy to fight, they just got to fight each other. I thought, after doctor's call, I'd ride over and have a look at that sick kid in the shanty, other side of the river. Want to come along?"

"Sure. But there ain't anything in regulations says you got to do free doctoring for enemy brats over half the countryside."

"There's not, but . . . what would you do, Matt?"

Matthew, accustomed to taking himself for granted unless shocked out of it, regarded this question with surprise. "I don't know. If I were on my own, maybe I would, maybe I wouldn't. I don't know."

Dr. Hurd turned to watch Mrs. Bascomb and the girls standing over the two huge ranges. They were working almost frantically now, speaking to each other in low, tense voices. Oven doors banged, pot lids rattled and every few minutes one of them would step back from a cloud of steam and, raising her arm, push back her damp hair. A sliding panel in the wall was open, showing a room filled with long tables and groups of soldiers standing or sitting around them. Mrs. Bascomb was pushing platters heaped with food through the opening onto a counter beyond. "Fine bunch of women," Dr. Hurd said. "Back on the farm again, the younger ones are going to find it mighty dull. Made up your mind where you're going to go when we're disbanded, Matt?"

"No, I haven't. I'd like to find me another war, but there isn't any."

"Got any money?"

"Only what back pay's coming to me."

"We'll talk about it sometime soon. Here's our grub."

Ruth stood beside them with a crowded tray, which she began to unload deftly. Dr. Hurd, his hands hanging down beside him, gazed at the steak and fried potatoes on the thick white plate in front of him. The steak still sizzled faintly, as though talking to itself, and beside the mound of fried potatoes a little lake of pale grease had begun to form. "Jesus," he said, "I can't eat all that. It's too goddam hot to eat anything. I guess I just thought I ought to be hungry."

He pushed the plate petulantly away from him, broke a doughnut in half, dipped it in his milky coffee, and began to munch thoughtfully. With his mouth still full, he said, "I haven't been really hungry, seems like, since we got to this damn unhealthy place. At my age, you don't eat, you lose some tissue you never do get back again, no matter what. You get tired, and every day there's a little bit of you that doesn't rest. Fact is, I'm getting old, Matt."

He picked up the rest of his doughnut and started to eat it without bothering to dip it in his coffee. Matt, his knife in his fist (while he ate he never put it down), paused to gaze at him with the faintly embarrassed, faintly bewildered air of youth perplexed by problems of the old which are beyond their knowledge. Hurd's thin, slightly grayish face was turned toward the window. His sad, passive gaze traveled over the sun-drenched scene, where groups of men, listless in the mounting heat, were slouching toward the mess hall. Across the parade ground the little cluster of tents gleamed with a whiteness that hurt the eyes. In contrast to them, the long low barracks, unused since the war's end, had a shabby look, paint peeling, debris collecting in their doorways. A field piece with a broken wheel rested lopsidedly in a patch of weeds; old packing boxes that had been abandoned before they were opened lay scattered about. The docks along the river were empty and already beginning to warp and fall apart in the burning, tropical heat. He turned the calm but troubled gaze on Matt.

"Ah, withered is the garland of the war."

"What?"

"Shakespeare. If you're through, let's get the hell out of here, Matt."

The horses that Matthew brought around to Hurd's tent after doctor's call were borrowed from the adjutant of a cavalry regiment that, like Matthew's own, was waiting to be ordered home. The two beasts were tough-looking veterans, wise in ways of war, and one of them had a long scar on his brown flank where a rifle bullet had grazed him. Matthew, already in the saddle, watched through the folded back tent flap as Dr. Hurd made ready for departure. The doctor both worked and slept in this tent, and though it was a large one, the cot, a big table, three folding armchairs, a low field trunk and various smaller paraphernalia left little free space in which to move around.

Dr. Hurd was stacking bottles full of pills on the shelves of a traveling medicine chest that was open, like a book standing up, at one end of the table. His motions were mechanical, as though he were bored by the familiarity of this task, but he was precise and thorough, and when he had closed the case he locked it with a key on a very long chain that he took out of his pocket. A revolver in a holster belt was hanging, with a number of other articles, from a nail driven into the central tent pole. He took it down and strapped it loosely around his waist. There was a campaign hat with a wide brim hanging beside the revolver. Hurd took it down and clapped it on his head, picked up a worn saddlebag and came out, squinting into the sunlight. The hat brim threw a deep shadow on his face, giving it a gaunt, remote look.

"Got the necessary here," he said, holding up the saddlebag, then hanging it to the much used, discolored saddle. He mounted with the heaviness of a man who rides infrequently and is hampered by the stiffness of his aging muscles. "You get us some lunch?"

"Yeah. Meat and bread the girls gave me."

"Where did you get that thing?" Hurd pointed to a cavalry carbine hanging from Matthew's saddle. It was a short, one-shot gun, better suited than the long, curved saber or even the longer rifle for fighting on horseback in woods and underbrush.

"Borrowed it from a fellow up the line. I thought I might get in a little practice while we're halted for lunch."

He said it with a smile and Dr. Hurd laughed outright. "Can't bear to have anybody do anything better than you, can you?" Dr. Hurd, who before the war had hunted in the Vermont mountains whenever he got the chance, was a sure and deadly shot.

"Better than sitting on my duff, Doc. You all set? Let's go."

Deep blue shadows had crept close to the buildings, for the sun was almost overhead. As they crossed the parade ground and went down the slope to the river, little puffy spurts of dust rose from under their horses' hoofs. When they reached the long pontoon bridge, both men slacked their reins, letting the horses pick their own cautious, finicking way. The bridge was a ragged structure of planks of uneven lengths, laid on a line of miscellaneously shaped boats that had been placed side by side from one bank to the other. It was wide enough for the two men to ride abreast, but there were no railings, and the whole structure moved uneasily under the horses' nervously thudding hoofs. Below the bridge the river flowed sluggishly, without currents, a solidly moving brown mass. From the prow of each boat a V-shaped patch of ripples had formed, always in motion, never changing form.

The sound of the uneven hoofbeats echoed dully from the banks and empty wooden wharves. Toward the middle of the stream, three of the boats had partly broken loose. Here the planking shook and swayed, and in one place dipped some inches below the surface of the stream. The horses, splashing water and not liking the treacherous feel of the moving planks, advanced with tossing heads and distended nostrils, bit chains rattling. When they reached firmer footing, Hurd said irritably, "They should keep this damn thing in better repair. Come a good rain, the whole works is likely to take off downstream."

"I suppose they think it doesn't matter since the encampment's going to be abandoned pretty soon, anyway."

"I suppose. It's a funny thing—I never thought I'd pull through this war. I always felt in my bones I was going to get mine somewhere along. And now here we are at the end. It's all over, and by God, I'm still alive. It astonishes me. Matt, when they finally let us get away from this Godforsaken place, how would you like to come up north to Haddon and read medicine with me? A degree from a good school's a lot better, but I stand pretty good in the town, and you've learned quite a bit already. The town would be glad to have you. So would I.

"I'd have to think about it, Doc. I'm not so sure I'd like life in a small town."

"Not enough doing to suit you, you're afraid? You might be surprised." The horses, with a return of confidence, came clattering off the bridge and climbed the bank. "Here, Matt, let's halt a minute."

They reined in under the meager shade of some scraggly sand pines, and the horses, bothered by flies, began to stamp and swish their tails. Dark patches of sweat stood out on their brown flanks. The heat brought out a warm, resiny odor from the pine trees. Dr. Hurd raised the flap of his saddlebag and drew out a bottle. "It's pretty raw stuff you get around here, but it's better than nothing." He raised the bottle to his lips, then, wiping his mouth with the back of his hand, he held the bottle out to Matthew. "Here."

"You drink too much of that, Doc." Matthew raised the bottle, swallowed and shook his head as the liquor burned its way down his throat.

"Here, you impudent young bastard, give it back. Time you're my age you'll find there's virtues in this stuff you don't know now are there." Hurd drank again and let the bottle slide back into the saddlebag. "That's all I got until tomorrow, but that's not what we were talking about. Hold old are you now? Twenty-one, isn't it?"

"Yeah—just."

"Seventeen and a half when you joined the regiment. So you might say you've grown up in the war."

"You grow up pretty young on the streets of New York."

"Maybe, in a limited sense. What I'm getting at is, war's a pretty limited environment to grow up in, too. You work hard, sure. But you don't have to worry about where your food's coming from. Unless you're an officer, most of the time you just stay around waiting for someone to tell you what to do next. You, for example. You don't have any responsibility but to do what I tell you to. You don't have to do any thinking for yourself. About girls, maybe—not about work."

Matthew gave a quick smile that lit his handsome face with good-natured enjoyment of this comment on himself. "What are you getting at?" Matthew said. Hurd did not answer the smile, but his manner did not quite disregard it.

"What I'm getting at is, once you're out of the army you're going to find yourself with problems you didn't know existed. Things like earning a living and looking after yourself in other ways. You're smart—smart-alec smart, sometimes. You've got to tone that down a bit, Matt. I think you're better than smart. I think you've got a good head on your shoulders. People like you. You're a worker. You're strong. My guess is that when you do run into responsibility, you'll meet it all right. Thing is, you need experience—the experience of being on your own."

Getting no reply, Hurd glanced at Matt and his eyes, slits under their drooping lids, were bright and hot with a momentary jealousy of age for youth. He said gruffly, "Let's get going, shall we?"

They turned into a sandy road that ran straight, with pines on either side. On Dr. Hurd there settled a hazy state in which, relaxed, he let himself be carried along. It was a way of resting, of restoring himself when opportunity offered, that, like the horses, he had learned from experience. He let his mind, without hindrance, slowly form pictures out of the substance of the past. At his side, riding effortlessly, Matthew began to sing in a fine, true baritone, and Hurd, half listening, found himself reliving a scene that had taken place more than three years past. With odd detachment he saw himself, not so thin or weary then, his movements quicker, standing beside an operating table that was one of a row set up in a barn. Mote-filled sunlight came a little way into the barn from the wide, open double doors, and when Hurd stopped to listen he could still hear the distant sound of firing. The operating tables were doors that had been taken off their hinges and set up on trestles, and on all of them wounded men were lying. Outside many more wounded were sitting or lying, waiting their turns. Hurd had been operating since the first of them had been brought in by the stretcher-bearers, many hours before. His nostrils were puckered from the heavy smell of blood and his throat was dry from breathing the dusty air inside the barn.

Because the supply of chloroform was getting low, it was being used sparingly, and the groans and screams of the men had worn Hurd down more than the long hours of hard and bloody work. The boards under his feet were slippery with blood; sweat ran continually into the corners of his eyes, making them smart so that he had to blink continually. The contrast between the square of brilliant sun in the open doors and the dim light inside the barn made his head ache.

On his operating table there was an old fellow who shouldn't, in Hurd's opinion, be in the war. He had obviously been lying out somewhere for quite a while before the stretcher-bearers had found him and brought him in, for gray stubble had sprouted on his hollow cheeks and the blood-caked flesh around his wound had hardened. Hurd thought that probably the old fellow wasn't worth saving. Still, the big hip wound had maggots in it, and maggots, he had observed, tended to keep infection from taking hold. This was an unconventional piece of medical lore, but he was growing more and more sure it was sound. The creatures seemed to eat only dead tissue, doing a better job of cleaning up a wound than a surgeon could do with a knife, and doing it frequently before medical help could be had. Hurd watched the plunging mass of white worms thoughtfully for a moment, planning his work. Then he said with assumed briskness, "All right, Pop. We'll fix you up now."

"Give me a whiff of chloroform, Doc. Just a whiff or two . . ." His voice was hoarse and rasping, which made Hurd think the old boy, lying out on the field, must have shouted for help a lot before the stretcher men got him.

Hurd turned his head and met the old man's eyes. They looked back at him with hopeless pleading, straight at him without wavering; then his stubble-covered cheeks quivered and his lips began to tremble. "Just a whiff, Pop," Hurd said.

He was holding the chloroform-soaked rag to the old man's nose when he chanced to look toward the open doors. A skinny lad of seventeen or eighteen, half hiding himself, was peering in. His face was pale, his head a mat of loose, chestnut-colored curls, and he was staring with intense fascination at what was going on inside the barn.

Half an hour later, as two orderlies were carrying the old fellow away, Hurd was surprised to see that the lad was still there. Boldly, he had come inside the barn and he was standing very still, watching with the same fixed intensity.

"What you doing here?" Hurd said.

As though this were an invitation, the boy walked up to the table. "I came to enlist."

"What's your name?"

"Matt."

"Short for Matthew?"

"Yeah, Matthew Chapin."

"Want to work in here for a bit?"

"Sure. What you want me to do?"

"Take that bucket over there with the sponge in it and clean up this table before they bring the next one in. Sight of blood disturb you?"

Matthew shook his head, perhaps not quite truthfully.

This daydream of Dr. Hurd's had become curiously vivid when he was startled out of it by a suddenly louder burst of song from Matthew. "For Christ sake," he said irritably. Matthew had dropped the reins and was sitting with his head thrown back, his fists against his hips. His body, so different from that of the skinny lad who had stood peering into the barn, was swaying with the motion of the horse. He sang as though the vitality in him were too great to contain and must burst out of him:

The strife is o'er, the ba-til's done;
The vic-to-ree of life is won;
The song of triumph has begun.
Hall-i-lu-yah!

The last syllable was a shout of sheer animal spirits. Annoyed by the jar his nerves received, Hurd said, "Shut up, will you? It's too damn hot to yell like that. Anyway, here's where we turn off, and when we get into the scrub, we ought to go kind of quiet. No point in letting the whole countryside know we're here. They don't love us any. You've never been over the river before, or you'd know it's not the inhabitants you have to look out for, but the drifters, the bummers, as they call 'em. Horses are pretty scarce here on the Southern side. Ours might just tempt somebody. . . . Watch out for branches now."

They turned onto what might have been a fairly good road before the war, but now it was a sandy, weed-grown track narrowed by encroaching underbrush. They made their way along it in silence except for the soft thud of their horses' hoofs and the occasional tinkle of a bit ring. After perhaps a quarter of a mile they came into a clearing with grass and some rotting boards where a shanty had once stood.

Dr. Hurd said, "It's not much farther. What say we stop here and eat, though maybe we better keep the horses kind of out of sight."

He dropped the rein and the horse lowered his head and began to crop grass. Hurd sighed and started to swing out of the saddle. At that instant there were two shots, two almost simultaneous reports, and Matthew knew, by instinct rather than by any sensation, that a bullet had passed close to him. He heard the doctor grunt and swear, and knew that he was in the saddle again. The carbine was in Matthew's hands before he had time to think about it. His horse had raised his head and, ears forward, was intently watching the underbrush. Matthew, watching too, thought he saw something that moved a little. Then for an instant he saw clearly. There were two men, both peering at him through the bushes. One was half hidden, but as the other moved again Matthew saw first a red shirt, then a face with a long scar running upward from the corner of the mouth, which it had pulled out of shape, and above it very black hair that hung down over the forehead.

The man in the red shirt evidently saw him also for he turned and ran. Matthew raised his gun and fired but the blur of red kept moving, and the sounds told him the other man was running too.

He kicked his horse as a signal to advance, struggling to reload his gun. They were in the underbrush and a branch lashed like a whip across his face. His eyes stinging and watering, he tried to see, but he could only hear crashing noises. He raised his gun again and, without much hope, fired in that direction, and the continuing but diminishing sounds in the underbrush told him that he had missed once more.

He swore and turned his horse back to the clearing, calling out to Hurd, "I missed them—two of them, but I scared them good . . ."

Hurd was on the same spot, sitting with bowed head, holding with both hands the front of the saddle.

"You all right, Doc? Jesus, they didn't get you, did they?"

The doctor began to sway, and Matthew, reining in beside him, caught him with a hard grip on his upper arm. Hurd turned his head. His eyes were blank, his lips blue and his face gray-pale.

"Where did they get you?"

Hurd's lips moved, but no sound came. He roused himself and said, "Leg. Other side. I'm all right now, but for a minute . . ."

Matthew guided his horse to the other side and saw that the doctor's foot was out of the hooded stirrup and hanging down. There was a small, bloody hole in the trouser leg below the knee. Dismounting, Matthew put his fingers in the hole and ripped it wider. The wound was much bigger than the hole in the trousers would indicate. He knew, because he had seen this kind of wound often, that it had been made by a soft-nosed bullet which, when it strikes, flattens, making a ragged wound in the flesh many times its own size. This one had hit the bone and, without any doubt, smashed it into splinters for a distance of three inches or more.

Matthew stared at the wound thoughtfully for a moment. A trickle of sweat ran down the back of his neck and he slapped at it with sudden anger. Then he ripped the trouser all the way down, pulled a handkerchief out of his pocket and bandaged the leg with it. There was not much blood, but he felt in Hurd's pocket for another handkerchief and tied it loosely over the first one. Hurd sat silent and passive, not watching what Matthew was doing. Matthew said, "We'd better get this shoe off before your foot swells."

Hurd nodded vaguely, but as the shoe came off he groaned and clutched the saddle in front of him. A big spot of bright red appeared on the handkerchief.

Matthew dropped the shoe on the ground. "Let me get your holster belt, Doc. I'll make a sling out of it that will hold till we get back to the main road, then I'll fix you up a splint out of tree bark or some sticks."

Docilely, and as though he did not quite know what was happening to him, Hurd moved a little to let Matthew get at the belt buckle. With the belt and the stirrup strap he constructed a support that would hold the foot without weight. Dr. Hurd, his brain and feelings still numbed by shock, watched as though all this had little to do with himself, but Matthew, glancing up, saw that his lips were not so blue and his eyes less dull. He said, "If you think you can sit in the saddle all right, we'd better get the hell out of here before those two bums decide to come back."

Dr. Hurd drew a long, quavering breath and his trembling hands moved gropingly. "Just pull that whiskey bottle out, Matt, and give me a little drink. . . ."

CHAPTER TWO

Night had come and the tent was lighted by a lantern hung from the center pole. Matthew was sitting in Dr. Hurd's folding camp chair which he had drawn up to the side of the cot on which Dr. Hurd lay. He was sitting relaxed, knees crossed, but with an unconscious grace in the pose, a suggestion of activity merely suspended that belongs only to a youthful body in its prime. His clothes were still powdered with dust from the ride, and the odor of horse still clung to him.

"Perhaps you'll feel differently about it in the morning," he said.

"No, I won't. You know better than that. The leg's got to come off."

Dr. Hurd spoke with asperity, but his words were thickened and blurred by the opium pill he had taken. He shut his eyes and leaned back against the pillows—his own and the one from Matthew's cot—that were propped up against a rolled uniform overcoat. He drew a long, sighing breath and shut his eyes, Matthew regarded him with a steady, troubled gaze, seeing how thin the worn-out frame looked. The arms, exposed all the way by the sleeveless undershirt he was wearing, were little more than bones, muscles and tendons. Below the arch of the rib cage the abdomen was sunken, even hollow. Matthew let his gaze travel downward over the long body to the wound below the cut-off trouser leg. The splint, made of a piece of tree bark stuffed with grass, came up to the wound on either side. There was a dressing over the top through which a little blood had seeped, and a piece of mosquito netting had been spread over the whole leg. Flies had settled on the netting, and Matthew, leaning forward, waved his hand to chase them away. Then, frowning, he again studied the doctor's face.

In the past three and a half years Matthew had seen hundreds of wounded men, but these were men he knew either slightly or not at all. He had never before seen what pain will do to the outward aspects of a familiar personality. To Matthew, Dr. Hurd's face surrounded by white pillows was that of a stranger. The thin features had become since morning a gray, gaunt mask, deeply lined by thoughts and sufferings of years long past. Without animation, without any of its usual surface reflections of the present, it seemed to Matthew stripped to its essentials. And these essentials, not being what he would have expected to find if he had ever thought about it, troubled him.

Like a great many healthy, non-introspective young men of his age, Matthew thought about other people only in relation to himself, and being for the first time forced out of this point of view, he was feeling—of all things in the world—lonely. He was feeling deserted and helpless. He had no idea that this is commom among those who stand by when someone close retreats into the circumference of his own suffering. But from this he was rescued by Dr. Hurd himself. Opening his eyes and turning his head toward Matthew—and so ceasing to be a stranger—he spoke.

"You realize, don't you, Matt, that you'll have to do it?"

"Do what, Doc?"

"Cut off my leg, you damn fool."

"Jesus, no. Not me."

"Who else is there to do it?"

"There's that doctor with the cavalry outfit . . ."

"Dr. Tully? Not for me. I've seen some of his amputations—you have too. He leaves a cone-shaped stump so a man with a wooden leg suffers misery every step he takes all the rest of his life. I'm talking kind of blurred, ain't I? You understand all right?"

"Yeah. But good God Almighty . . ."

"You've seen me do it God knows how many times. Do you think I didn't know you were itching to get your hands on it?"

"This is different."

"No, it's not. Minute you get to work, you'll forget it's me."

Matthew lowered his eyes and frowned at the board floor in front of his feet. After a while, his shoulders drawn in tensely, he began to clasp and unclasp his fingers on his bent knee. Once he looked up sharply and, encountering a steady gaze from under the heavy lids, looked down again. Sounds of the summer night invaded the tent. Matthew was no longer aware of being watched. He was breathing faster and the fingers were clasped tightly now, but the hands made small, twitching motions, as though faintly responding to steps in a sequence of thought. When Dr. Hurd spoke again, he started and stared with his mouth open, as though these thoughts had been too concentrated to be easily dispelled.

"First thing in the morning, Matt. Soon as it's light enough to see well."

Matthew made no reply and Dr. Hurd, turning away his head, shut his eyes again. Matthew got up and quietly moved around the tent, stopping a moment to stare thoughtfully at the long table on which the medicine case still stood. After a moment he picked up the case by its metal handle and carried it over to a corner. The bottles it contained rattled faintly and the sound roused Dr. Hurd. He said, his voice thicker now because his mind felt no urgency, "What you doing, Matt?"

"Arranging a few things."

"Better get some sleep."

"I'm going to get my cot in here."

"No room."

"I'll make some room."

His hand was on the tent flap to pull it back when Dr. Hurd said with sudden strength in his voice, "Matthew." The tone, the use of his full name, made Matthew turn and go to stand by the cot. Dr. Hurd tipped his head back and looked up with an expression of deep anxiety.

"I want to know, Matt, are you afraid?"

Matthew thought about this for a minute, then he said seriously, "No, Doc. Not in the way I think you mean. I'm not afraid to *do* it. I'm just a bit afraid I may not get some little things just right."

Dr. Hurd turned his head toward the tent wall, and Matthew saw that his chin was trembling. Eyes squeezed shut, frowning, Hurd said fiercely, "Get the hell out of here, will you? Get some sleep."

Morning had come, but though Matthew had been moving around the tent, Dr. Hurd had made no sign of having heard him. Matthew was not sure that he was asleep but with such a wound he thought that sleep was not likely. He went to stand by the side of the cot. Hurd was lying so still and he seemed to have sunken in, as though some inner support had given way. Matthew stood with his hand on a chair back and watched him anxiously for a moment, assured himself that Hurd was breathing evenly, and then he carried the chair to one end of the long deal table.

He put it down at a calculated distance, its back toward the table. He hung a length of cord over the chair where it would be ready, when the time came, to tie Hurd's foot to the chair back. That done, he squatted in front of the open medicine case, took out a bottle labeled CHLOROFORM and held it up to the light. There was very little liquid in the bottle and he drew in his lips, grimaced at it, and put it in his pocket. He shut the case, and, getting up, he lifted it by its brass handle, carried it over to the chair, and settled it on the chair's canvas seat. It would hold the chair steady when the chair back would have to take the sudden weight of the severed leg. He surveyed this arrangement rapidly and tested it with his hand, though he was already sure of it from having gone over it again and again in his mind during the night.

After that he stood frowning in thought, the frown making prominent two small muscle bunches, like horn buds, on his forehead. He was thinking about something that had been in his mind a great deal during the wakeful hours of the night. It was the question of what to do about getting someone to help him, to do for him the things that, during an operation, he did for Hurd. Nothing had been said about the need for an assistant, and Matthew was wondering, as he had on and off during the night, whether Hurd had forgotten it or simply assumed that Matthew could find someone.

The alternative was to do the operation alone, and the more he thought about it the more certain he was that this was what he wanted. He decided not to bring the matter up.

The decision brought him a surprising amount of contentment, and even a sense of freedom. Without knowing it, he smiled. Briskly, moving with easy assurance, he carried a small stand to the foot of the table and opened out on it the government-issue kit of amputation instruments. During his years as Dr. Hurd's orderly, he had cleaned these instruments many times and he liked them. Handling the long artery forceps, the bone saw, the knives kept so carefully sharpened and the long lengths of ligature silk gave him a special, even a sensual, pleasure. Now as he lifted them from their blue plush bed and laid them out on the stand, he was aware of a prickling in his fingertips—a sign, though he did not recognize it, that his nerves, his blood vessels, his adrenal glands were ready for action. Then Dr. Hurd spoke his name and Matthew's head came up with a jerk.

"Yes, sir."

He left the instruments and went to stand by the cot. Dr. Hurd was obviously suffering, but in spite of that he looked better than he had a few minutes before, not so gray or so remote. Matthew, noting these things with satisfaction, almost as though he took credit for them, said, "I hoped you were sleeping. I'm all ready. We better get on with the job."

"Just a minute. Just a minute, now."

Matthew smiled at him. "Not scared, are you, Doc? I've gone over it in my mind again and again. I know I got it right."

"No, I'm not scared. Or maybe I am. I don't like this

business. First time a knife's been laid to any part of me, and I don't like it, but I got some things I want to say. A good stiff drink would make them easier to put into words."

"There isn't any more. You emptied the bottle, Doc."

"Must have had so damn much opium in me I didn't know what I was doing. Oh, well . . . Draw up a chair, Matt."

"We shouldn't put this off."

Suddenly angry, Hurd shouted, "Draw up a chair!"

When Matt was seated, Hurd watched him for a moment through narrowed eyes. Then he moved his shoulders restlessly. "You've got confidence in yourself, haven't you?"

"Maybe."

"You've outgrown this job of doctor's orderly, Matt."

Matthew nodded, not troubling, it seemed, to affirm more strongly a fact that was self-evident.

"I want to have some more talk with you about your future soon as I'm able after this. What I've got on my mind is, have you got all the points—the fine points—of anatomy straight in your mind? I mean, you're cutting down, and you expect to find the femoral vein lying in the same channel as the femoral artery, but sometimes it isn't there at all. Sometimes you come on it when you don't expect to. Now you go easy till you've got it and the femoral artery located. I haven't got so much blood I can afford to lose any I don't have to."

Matthew's bold, open face was easy to read. His pride was hurt.

"Now the sciatic nerve. You want to get a good hold on it with the forceps and pull it down—"

Matthew was on his feet. "Now look here, Doc, I think I can understand how you feel about this operation. But the thing is—do you think I can do it, or don't you? Yesterday you thought I could. If you've changed your mind, I want to know it. If you have any doubt—any doubt at all—I'm not going to do it."

Hurd sighed and closed his eyes. Matthew stood looking down on him, his hands resting on his hips. After a moment of silence Hurd said without opening his eyes, "You can give me the chloroform right here, Matt, and move me to the table after I'm under."

"*No*, sir. I've heard you say, plenty of times, never move a man who's well under les' something happens to his airways. Now, we're not going to talk about it any more." He bent over the cot and slid his arms under Dr. Hurd.

"For Christ sake, Matt . . "

Dr. Hurd's body felt unexpectedly light and bony in Matthew's arms. As he was lifted, Dr. Hurd grunted, then, mouth open, lips drawn back from his discolored teeth, and his eyes wide and staring, he began to pant. The mosquito netting, still caught on the rough bark splint that came up to the edge of the wound on either side, suddenly showed a bright stain of red. Matthew said, "All right, Doc. I'm being as quick and gentle as I can."

He laid Hurd on the table in such a way that his legs, bent at the knee, hung over the bottom edge. Hurd turned his head away and wrapped his arms around himself. Matthew, resting his hands on the table, bent over him.

"You think you can stand just a bit more? We haven't got so much chloroform and I want to be a bit saving with it. I want to tie your foot to the chair. I won't pull on it any."

Hurd nodded, his head still turned away, and Matthew, bending over him, saw his lips shaking and a tear squeeze out of his eye. Matthew hesitated, sighed, and went back to the foot of the table. In one quick motion he raised the injured leg, and with one hand wrapped the length of cord around the ankle and around the chair back, then used both hands to tie a double knot. When he turned around he saw Hurd propped up tensely on his elbows, his scrawny neck stretched, and the glassy stare of agony in his eyes. Matthew put his hands under Hurd's shoulders and with a shuddering sigh Hurd let himself be eased down flat on the table.

There was less than an inch of chloroform in the bottle, and Matthew, taking a handkerchief out of his pocket, wadded it up and poured all of the chloroform on it. "All right," he said, "here we go," and he was not aware that he had used a phrase that Dr. Hurd used always at the start of an operation. He put the handkerchief down over Dr. Hurd's nose, holding it there lightly at first, and then more firmly. The other hand he held under Hurd's chin, holding his head back. The thick odor of chloroform spread out in the warm air of the tent.

The sun was fully up now and, shining on the canvas, made a full but eerie light inside the tent. A small swarm of flies, drawn upward by the warmth, circled overhead, their buzzing loud in the stillness. Once a horse and rider went past the tent at a gallop, the horse's hoofs thudding dully on the hard, dusty earth of the parade ground. Once Dr. Hurd moved, partly raising his arms in a purposeful but meaningless way. Matthew reached out and pressed them down again and absently the thought came to him that he was hungry. They'd started this business too early to get anything at the mess, and with all that talk . . . He was getting damn hungry. Also, the heat and the chloroform smell were making him feel sleepy . . . He took away the handkerchief and studied Hurd. He was breathing tranquilly. Against the taut skin of his neck a little pulse was beating, not evenly but in little irregular jumps, with now and then a longer pause between. Matthew, pondering, watched this for a moment, then he raised one of Hurd's eyelids. What he saw satisfied him. He pushed the balled-up handkerchief under Hurd's shoulder to keep it out of the air in case what little that was left of the chloroform was needed later.

He could begin now and he'd better, he thought, get at it because that amount of chloroform wasn't going to last forever. The tips of his fingers were tingling again and he cursed the stifling heat, feeling that he was not getting enough air in his lungs, but knowing that his own nerves, and not the heat, were to blame. He felt strangely alone. Wiping the sweat off his forehead with the back of his arm, he went down to the foot of the table in a way that he tried to make brisk and businesslike, stood between the doctor's bent leg and the outstretched one and frowned at the instrument stand. Moving swiftly, he reached across the injured leg and touched the instruments one by one, making sure he could reach them easily. After that, he turned the leg as far toward him as he could, making sure he had not tied it to the chair so tightly that he could not get at the underside. Then he pushed the doctor's cut trouser leg farther up out of the way, and tightened the tourniquet that circled the leg high in the groin. The skin around it was blue and puffy, but he was satisfied. There was nothing else to do before beginning. The lonely feeling came back to him strongly, but he wasted no time thinking about it. He put out his hand for the knife and as he picked it up a wave of red suffused his face. The knife that he had handled so many times to clean and put away felt strange in his hand.

This was not the first time that, holding a sharp knife, he had cut through skin, but he had done it seldom enough to be surprised at the skin's toughness. He was not cutting deeply. He was no more than outlining where the cut would be, the skin barely parting. A thin red line followed the point of the knife, and as this lengthened, Matthew's attention focused on it more and more until, fulfilling the doctor's prophecy, he was not aware of anything else at all.

Feeling with every nerve in his own body the drag of the knife and the live quality of the skin's resistance, he drew on the underside of the leg the downward curve of a half arc, making its base at the side of the leg. From that point he drew another, larger arc over the top of the leg to the other side. Then, turning the leg away from him, he made the other half of the arc on the underside, joining it precisely. He put the knife back on the stand and picked up another. He did this because the toughness of the skin seemed to have dulled the knife, and he was so absorbed in what he was doing that he was unaware that he had seen Dr. Hurd do this same thing many times and for the same reason.

He was working swiftly now, following the line he had drawn, through subcutaneous tissue, down to the fascia that covered the muscle, then into the muscle, his alert tactile perceptions, as though functioning apart from his brain, taking note of these muscles' varying density and texture. As the walls divided behind his knife, bleeding points appeared, and he touched them with a piece of gauze in his left hand, but he did nothing more, knowing that they would retract into the leg's tissue and be sealed off. But though he was working swiftly, he was also working with exceeding care, for he was nearing the great saphenous vein which carried so much blood that it must be tied before it could be cut. He knew where the vein ought to be, but he also knew that it sometimes was found a surprising distance to one side or the other.

The knife moved in quick, short strokes. Matthew stood with feet apart, bending over, watching intently, the whole of himself so concentrated on what he was doing that the knife had become an extension of himself, its point his focal point. Overhead, the circling flies, attracted by the smell of blood, were coming lower. Two of them lit on the leg and began to crawl toward the open wound. Matthew blew at them and they flew away. Then he found the vein, or what, after a second's thought, he felt sure must be the vein. It appeared to be no more than a dark streak, a blood clot flattened by the action of the tourniquet. To make sure, he dissected downward a little way and saw that he was right, but that vein was varicosed and its walls weakened. Hoping it would be strong enough to hold a ligature, he began to cut around it, clearing the way to slip the ligature silk underneath.

A voice spoke from the open tent flap and he jumped, some instinct in him that was quicker than thought jerking the knife away from the vein. The soldier who had the boil on his back slouched in the entrance, his shirt unbuttoned, his forage cap on the back of his head.

"Say, ain't there going to be no doctor's call today? I got . . . Sweet Jesus, what's going on here?"

"Get out."

Suddenly Matthew was filled with fury such as he had seldom felt. "Get out of here." The knife was in his hand. He threw it.

He missed because the soldier was too quick for him. Matthew saw him jump aside and heard the pound of his running feet on the hard earth. For a second Matthew stood there looking after him, one hand on the leg above the knee, the other, that had held the knife, opening and closing. He was feeling the heavy beat of his own heart in his chest and in his throat, shaking him. Then he imagined he felt a slight movement of the leg under his hand. Instantly recalled, he faced around and looked with sharp attention at Dr. Hurd.

If consciousness was returning, it had not yet returned. Thankful, and reminded of the urgent need not to waste time, Matthew reached for another knife. The only remaining one was the one he had discarded earlier. With a grunt of dissatisfaction he took it up and went to work.

The concentration, the extreme of attention, did not fully return. He kept an awareness of Dr. Hurd, and of the state of his own metabolism. He began to think farther ahead and to complete each step in his mind before his knife reached that point, but at the same time, on another highly active plane of his mind, he was acutely aware of what he was at that instant doing. This state of superconsciousness, of intensified clarity of the mind, was like a new dimension of the thought. It filled him with a triumphant sense of rightness, of having found the exact state of mental being best suited to the work in hand. Most of all, it gave him a sense of power.

A feeling of triumphant power was by no means unknown to Matthew. On the contrary, he experienced it every time he came the victor out of a fight or made love to a woman. To find it with a knife in his hand cutting through living flesh was unexpected. To find it related to the processes of his mind was new, invigorating and enthralling beyond anything he had ever imagined.

He was working now with confidence, and very fast, as though he had done these things many times before. The saphenous vein was tied, with long ends of silk dangling, the femoral artery and vein found and tied together. He found the sciatic nerve, caught it in a clamp, cut it and, pulling it down as far as he could with his left hand, he crushed it quickly with another clamp held in his right hand, took that clamp away, and dexterously, with the fingers of his right hand only, he tied a double knot. He took intense pleasure in doing these things exactly right, for this procedure was a specialty of Dr. Hurd's. Most surgeons merely cut the nerve and let it retract upward, with the result that for a long time afterward there would be sensations in a leg and foot that were no longer there.

He was down now to the bone itself all the way around, and he began to push back muscle and skin flaps, for the bone must be cut two inches higher than the skin incision so that there would be no straining when the flesh was reunited. This was the point at which he usually helped Dr. Hurd, holding the muscle back in the loop of a towel. Now, when he had to work alone, he tied it back with gauze, took up the saw and cut through the periosteum—the membrane covering the bone—and the bone together.

Though he was prepared for the fall of the leg, the sound of the bark splint hitting the chair back startled him. Flies that had gathered around the edges of the pools of blood on the floor rose buzzing. Matthew straightened up, aware that his back felt stiff and that perspiration was making his skin prickle on the back of his neck and behind his ears. Then he untied the bandage and watched with critical interest as the flesh and muscle came down over the bone. In his mind he heard Dr. Hurd saying, "The cut parts have got to come together naturally, as though they loved each other—else your work isn't good." They were coming together naturally. Dr. Hurd groaned and Matthew glanced swiftly at him, saw that he was nearing the level of consciousness, but not there yet, and went back to work.

He finished swiftly, loosened the tourniquet before he stitched the flaps in place, watching with pleasure the normal color sweeping downward through the leg. When he had finished, he lifted the doctor's thin body back on the cot and put one of the pillows under the stump. Dr. Hurd turned his head and muttered something unintelligible, but without opening his eyes. Matthew straightened and stood looking down at him. The doctor was gray-pale and the stubble on his cheeks and chin seemed more prominent than ever. The pulse in his throat was no longer making the skin jump, and after watching a moment Matthew put two fingers on it. The beats were light and had the feel of being surface only. They ran a little together, "thready," like beads on a string, and Matthew, turning away to get the cleaning up done before the old doctor regained enough consciousness to feel pain, decided it would be a good idea to get a stimulant into him as soon as he could swallow.

He cleaned up in the shortest way possible and dumped the splinted lower leg in a covered can outside the tent, too tired to open up the wound to see what the bullet had done to the bone, as he had intended. Then he sluiced a bucket of water over the floorboards and decided to let it go at that for the present. He dragged the stand and table back in place and folded up the chair. Then he poured water out of a tall pitcher into a basin and, bending over, carried some of it in his cupped hands to his face. The water was warm and he imagined he could smell blood in it. He swore, picked up the basin and, carrying it to the tent opening, flung the water angrily on the ground outside. He took the basin back and filled it again, but the water still felt warm and he still thought he was smelling blood in it. He looked around for a towel and saw none. He thought, to hell with it. He remembered that he hadn't eaten and thought to hell with that too. He leaned over the table that the basin was on, supporting himself with his hands, too completely dead tired to straighten up. Then Dr. Hurd said something indistinct but in a louder voice and something in it sounded like "Matt," so he did straighten up and went back to stand by the cot.

CHAPTER THREE

Colonel Bouget's tent was no different from any other, except that a sentry slouched outside at a spot sufficiently removed from the open flap so that his unmilitary attitude could not be observed from within. Matthew spoke to him without slowing his walk, that was too rapid and purposeful for the heat of the day.

"Colonel Bouget in there?"

"Yeah, he's signing papers. . . . Hey, Matt, you can't walk in like that!"

But Matthew was already inside the tent. He came to a halt, breathing hard, before a paper-littered table behind which Colonel Bouget was sitting. The colonel was a vigorous man who felt his position as commander of a volunteer militia regiment, made up largely of his neighbors, to be a hopeless one. He tried to counteract this by strict insistence on the outward forms of the military life; but his efforts had, from the start, met with good-natured disregard. The colonel lived up to his own precepts, however. Though the tent, with the sun on it, was stiflingly hot, he was wearing his uniform coat, buttoned up, disregarding the sweat that stood out on his face in glistening beads. He looked up from his papers, saw Matthew standing before him in rumpled shirt with sleeves rolled up, and open nearly to the waist, and he flushed angrily.

"You know better than to come in here like that, Private Chapin."

Matthew put his fists on his hips, rocked back on his heels, and stared at the colonel, but he made no reply.

"Well? What do you want? Dr. Hurd send you? He shouldn't have let you come looking like that."

Matthew let his hands drop to his sides and, with his eyes fixed on the canvas wall back of the colonel, said in a flat tone, without expression, "Dr. Hurd is dead."

"Dead!"

Matthew made no attempt to answer, for his thoughts were turned inward. The belligerency of his attitude had vanished and he had almost forgotten where he was. A change had come over Colonel Bouget also, which Matthew did not see. He was leaning back, his hands lying on the chair's arms, staring at Matthew with eyes that had lost their light while his lips moved indeterminately, as though his mind was failing to supply him with words he wanted to use. He had a stricken look. The false front of military authority was gone and there sat the Bouget whom his neighbors in the Vermont town of Haddon knew—old "Fussbudget" who ran the feedstore and was always glad to lend a hand loading feed bags into a friend's wagon. Finally he made an effort, his hands curved around the chair arms, and he said in a hushed voice, "What happened, Matthew?"

Sweat had begun to run down Matthew's face and he raised an arm and wiped it. Then he pulled out of his pocket a meager packet of papers and a small bundle knotted in a handkerchief and laid them on the table. "These are his. I brought them along. They're all he has that matters, I guess."

Colonel Bouget sat up and put a hand on them, looking up at Matthew. "But what happened?"

"It was sometime in the night—just before sunrise. I was sleeping in the tent with him and I found him like that just about as it was getting light."

"But what . . . He's not been looking too good lately. I noticed it two, three times, but what—" Suddenly the muscles of Bouget's face bunched up under the yellowed skin, making it look like apples in a bag, and he struck the table with his fist. "Hurd! We can't spare him. The whole town . . ."

He stopped, dismayed by his own thoughts, and they were both silent. The heat and the smell of dust weighed on them, and somewhere in the suffocating tent a cricket began to shrill. Matthew jerked himself up and said, "I guess I better tell you the rest of what happened. He didn't just die."

"Tell me," Colonel Bouget said simply, leaning against the canvas back of his chair.

"We went across the river. Doc wanted to go see some sick child he was looking after. A couple of bummers shot at us and they got him in the leg. That was day before yesterday. I should have reported to you then, I guess . . ."

Bouget nodded "Go on," he said.

"The leg had to be amputated. Yesterday morning I took it off."

"*You* did! You had no business . . ." Bouget hitched his chair forward and stared up at Matthew with a look of shocked horror.

"He asked me to. Said he wouldn't trust that surgeon the cavalry's got, and there's nobody else. I didn't have any trouble doing it. He came out of it weak, but not too bad. There wasn't any hemorrhage and I thought he'd be all right. He *was* all right every time I looked at him during the night, until just before dawn. Maybe his heart was weak and it just stopped."

Colonel Bouget leaned over the table again. He picked

up the little packet and put it down. He sorted through Dr. Hurd's papers, making a pile of them, but absently, without really seeing what they were. Then he looked up at Matthew as though an idea had occurred to him, momentarily lifting him out of his grief. Abruptly he got up, came around the table and took Matthew by the arm.

"I'm forgetting, boy. I was knocked so hard by this I didn't think. You've worked with him—you were close to him. You must be feeling pretty bad."

Matthew released his arm by stepping back, and stared at the colonel with a return of the belligerency. Bouget said, "He didn't have any family. Wife died years ago. No relatives at all, so far's I know, but the whole town . . ."

"I know all that."

Matthew turned away and started to leave the tent, but just as he was ducking under the flap Bouget spoke. "Wait a minute, Matthew. That reminds me of something. Those papers . . one of them's for you, I'm almost sure. It's a matter I know about. Just wait a minute and I'll have a look."

He went behind the desk and began laying Hurd's papers aside, one by one, until he came to a long envelope which he held out to Matthew.

"Here it is. It's got my name on it, but it's for you."

Matthew took it, crammed it into his pocket and left the tent without a word.

He had no clear idea where he was going, but instinctively he turned away from the direction of Dr. Hurd's tent and his own. Walking rapidly, he crossed the empty space of the parade ground, a solitary figure moving with the unconscious grace of youth.

Near the long, low building that housed the kitchen and mess, he smelled roasting meat and was reminded by it that he had not eaten for a long time. And with that came a sharp longing for the return of the common day, for the noise and bustle of the women working and for the feeling of being among people once more. At the same time another part of him rejected the thought of normal life so violently that a feeling of nausea almost overcame him. As quickly as he could he moved out of range of the rich, heavy odor, taking a path that led him into a narrow space between two of the deserted hospital buildings. Here, in shadow, the cooler, fresher air of night still lingered, and when he came to some plank steps he sat down on them.

For a moment he sat there without stirring, elbows on knees, his head in his hands, fighting to regain a lost sense of himself in relation to the shattering of his familiar way of life. This was not thought, for his mind was very nearly a blank. He had reached, and was standing in, a dead space in his existence between the old and familiar and the new and unknown. He sought to move forward, to acquire a feeling of being part of a known pattern; but since he had not the least idea what was to happen to him next, this was impossible. Still hopelessly in the void between his own past and future, he drew a long, sighing breath and let his hands drop down to hang between his spread knees.

He continued to sit there numbly, weighted with weariness. He was feeling nothing at all. Sometimes his eyes were shut, but he was nowhere near sleep. Sometimes they were open, staring at the litter that had gathered around the steps, but without seeing anything. After a while the discomfort of his plank seat began to invade his consciousness, and when this became too strong he shifted his weight a little. When he did this, the envelope in his pocket crackled. He sighed again with reluctance at being brought out of his hypnotic state, rolled himself on one hip, pulled the envelope out of his pocket and tore it open.

Inside was a folded piece of ruled paper from a notebook. He unfolded it and saw one brief paragraph in Dr. Hurd's writing. Still a little numb and without conviction that this had any relation to himself, he began to read. The strong, familiar writing said to him, "This is my last will and testament." Startled, he straightened up and read on with closer attention. After a formal phrase or two concerning the doctor's lack of legal heirs, the will indicated that "all of which I die possessed is to go to my orderly, Matthew Chapin, to be used to get a medical education because he seems to me to have the makings of a good medical man, if he wants to be one." The date was March 1, 1865, and Hurd must have written it in the cookhouse, sitting at the deal table, for in one corner there was a circular stain that looked as though a coffee cup had been put down on it. The two witnesses that Vermont law requires were Colonel Ovander Bouget and, surprisingly, Mrs. Bascomb, head of the women.

After sitting with the will in his hand for a while, Matthew slowly and carefully put it in his pocket. Then he tore the envelope into pieces and dropped them among the litter on the ground. When he rose he discovered that he was stiff and that the back of his neck ached as it sometimes did after long hours of standing beside an operating table with Hurd. His mind simply did not grasp the provision of the will. It had as yet no reality for him.

The first step he took was almost uncertain, but by the time he came out from between the buildings into the sunshine all trace of uncertainty had vanished. Anyone watching him cross the parade ground would have seen him walking rapidly—not joyously but with an urgently compelling purpose.

The horse that Matthew rode that afternoon was the one that Dr. Hurd had ridden, the experienced veteran with the long scar where the rifle bullet had creased his flank. He went along at a businesslike pace with an air of philosophic contentment and of minding his own affairs that kept him from intruding on Matthew's thoughts. These thoughts were crowding in so fast that he could not follow through any one of them and he made no attempt to. He rode leaning forward, the visor of his cap pulled down to shade his eyes, and in place of the carbine he carried a long rifle cradled with one hand across the saddlebow.

When he came to the overgrown road that led to the clearing, he dismounted, and leading the horse, carrying his rifle couched against his side, he went on as quietly as he could. Every little while he stopped to listen, but he heard only the faint, random sounds of the heat-enduring woods. The smell of the pines was thick and astringent in his nostrils. When he judged himself to be near the clearing, he led the horse off the road, behind a tangled growth of underbrush, and tethered him to a sapling pine. Then he went back to the road, and, the rifle held now in both hands, ready to raise and fire with the least waste of motion, he went on more cautiously than before.

The clearing lay empty and sun-filled. Matthew stood in shadow on the edge of it and listened intently, and in the woods he felt the nearness of unseen life. A bird gave a raucous cry and he tensed and listened to the flapping of heavy wings. Gradually he grew accustomed to the quiet, grew into it, became part of it. Then he thought he heard a faint, continuing thread of sound. He focused all his attention on it and was not sure he heard it at all, but his nerves held the impression of it, as though they, and not his hearing, had detected it. The sound, he thought, could be talking, as of someone telling a long tale. He crept cautiously a little way around the edge of the clearing and again stood still to listen.

From this place he thought the sound was stronger. It was not unlike the continuous murmur of a running brook, and he thought he might be hearing two voices in low, earnest talk, though no differences in tone and no separation between words were distinguishable. Then unmistakably he heard the clink of metal. He raised his head, every sense alert.

He did not hear it again, but he was sure now that the sound had meaning, and he was sure of the direction from which it had come. Still listening, but with part of his attention diverted, he studied the trees and bushes on the far side of the clearing. Through these he thought he saw the contour of a small sandy mound, such as might have been thrown up from the digging of a ditch or pit when this deserted spot was active farming land. He thought it possible that on the other side two men were sitting. And as he watched, a faint, blue haze of wood smoke began to drift upward. Lightly, with the tips of his fingers, Matthew felt over the firing mechanism of the rifle. Then he began to move slowly forward, keeping to the edge of the clearing.

He could hear the voices much more clearly now, though he did not try to distinguish the words. There followed the sudden sizzle and spit of something dropped into a hot frying pan, and the smell of bacon came to him. Crouching now, he crept forward. The men were still hidden from him by the mound, and as he was thinking how to proceed and at the same time keep cover, he stepped on a piece of twig that snapped under his foot. Instantly the voices on the other side stopped and the sound of frying grew fainter as the pan moved away from the fire.

A long moment of tense quiet followed. Then a voice said distinctly, "Ain't nothin'. Get on with it, Jeb," and the frying noise resumed, but Matthew felt that both these unseen men were still listening.

After a while they began to talk again. Matthew took his forage cap off and laid it on the ground. Then on all fours, moving his rifle ahead of him, he began to crawl up the mound, the sandy soil moving loosely under him as he advanced. Near the top he knelt and brought the rifle up into firing position. Then he stretched himself upward, inch by inch, until he could see over the crown of the mound.

The two men were not so close as he had thought, but

they were no more than twenty yards away. One was sitting with his back against a tree, a long stick in his hand with which he was poking at the fire. He was idly intent on what he was doing, but if he raised his head he would be looking straight at Matthew. The other squatted, holding the frying pan over the flames, his head tipped back and sideways away from the smoke. The one leaning against the tree was the man in the red shirt. Matthew shot him first.

He shot him unhurriedly, taking time to aim with care, but the next man he shot swiftly, as fast as he could bring the rifle around. The body of the man in the red shirt jerked forward as though he were starting up, the mouth opened and a bright red stream of blood came down from his forehead over his face. Then, slowly, he fell sidewise and his body hit the ground with a soft thud. The other, dropping the frying pan on the fire, fell backward, rolled to his side, drew his legs up and wrapped his arms around his body. He quivered once all over, his head jerked spasmodically backward, and he lay still. Yellow flames from the spilled grease in the frying pan leaped hissing upward.

Matthew continued to kneel on the mound, the lowered rifle held in both hands slantwise in front of him. The tall yellow flames died quickly down, leaving only the red glow of burned-out sticks. The bird Matthew had heard earlier cried again overhead and he tipped his head back, trying to see it, as though this were important. He did not see it or even actually search for it, and the woods were still again.

He laid his rifle aside and let himself slip backward down the slope of the mound until he lay full length, his head turned sidewise, cheek against the warm sand. He lay in that position a long time, his mind slowly emptying of thought until he was aware only of the isolation of this place, his own weariness, and the two dead men out of sight on the other side of the mound. But he was aware of them only as objects, different and more important than other objects around him.

After a while he was no more than conscious that they were there, for his thoughts had turned to the camp and the necessity to go back there and go on with a life that would now be different. He thought about the ways in which it would be different, separately, one by one. He did not dwell on any of them, his mind simply recognizing each one and letting it go, like beads slipping through his fingers. Then he rolled over on his back and lay, his elbows in the sand, arms bent, hands closed into fists in the air above him. In a moment or two he felt a smarting in his eyes and he realized with detached astonishment that they were filled with tears.

II
Haddon

CHAPTER FOUR

The march from the railroad station to Haddon was long. The road ran in a narrow valley between steep hills, but the tramping feet raised little dust from the stony soil, and the men, exhilarated by the return to this familar land, moved briskly and without fatigue. Matthew, marching toward the end of the column with his blanket roll on his back, thought he had never breathed air so pure or seen a sky so blue. He marched in silence, trying to take in all he saw in this strange land, but among the men around him there was much shouting and talking as familiar landmarks came into view, and their voices were loud with the excitement of this return. At the end of the column was a light wagon in which the women, who had been with the regiment to care for the men all through the war, were riding home. Unlike the men, they rode almost in silence, sitting on the floor of the wagon, holding on to the low sides. Matthew turned from time to time to look at them for their quiet impressed him, and he saw that some of them were crying for joy, some frantically waving handkerchiefs at anyone they saw.

Whenever they came on groups of white houses that clustered at a crossroads, the band began to play, then dogs barked and people ran out of houses and barns to wave and call out to the passing men. When the women from these houses saw someone in the column they knew, they would jump up and down and shout his name and children ran into the road to march a little way beside the soldiers. Sometimes they gathered tight bunches of black-eyed Susans and Indian paintbrush from the roadsides, and men, smiling, tied them to the barrels of their guns.

After a while the man marching next to Matthew, who had been looking around with bright, smiling eyes, enjoying himself, said, "Ain't far now. Just around that bend. Look! By God, here they come to meet us."

Up ahead Matthew saw them, women and children and a few men who were too old for soldiering, running toward the column, and when they met this charge the women broke the column up as effectively as any rebel charge. The man next to Matthew had a black-haired girl in his arms and she was kissing him, laughing and crying at the same time. For a moment Matthew's legs were entangled in her flying skirts and he felt the aura of her warm, eager body. He moved a little way out of line to give these two what privacy he could, and for an instant, but only an instant, he was sorry for himself because there was no warm, pretty creature throwing her arms around his neck. After a moment a yellow dog appeared and trotted contentedly along beside him. Matthew said, "Hullo, fella," and grinning, stooped to pat him.

By the time they came to an arch of hemlock boughs over the village street some of the column had melted away, but Colonel Bouget drew the rest of them up in parade-ground style as best he could. These stood in lines facing a long village green and a white church at the far end of it, the thin spire with the dark slope of a mountain behind it so intensely white as to seem to have a dimension beyond reality. As Matthew shuffled sidewise with the other men in response to the command to trim the line, he looked about him at the village buildings of red brick and white wood, at the flags and great, spreading trees, and felt an energy behind it all of which he had never been aware in the sleepy, dusty, sun-dried settlements of the South, and he felt vitality in himself as though body and mind were absorbing the stimulus of this strong, bright land.

Colonel Bouget held them in formation only long enough to dismiss them with proper formality, and then the ranks broke and the men ran to the green where long trestle tables, covered with white cloths and loaded with food, were set up under the maple trees. In a moment most of the men had women and children clinging to them on both sides, laughing and dragging them toward the tables. Though most of the women wore skirts without hoops, some were in their Sunday best, and when these were embraced, the hoops lifted their skirts up behind in a way that amused Matthew greatly, for these swinging bells sometimes revealed much that was not meant to be seen. Matthew followed the crowd at a leisurely walk, finding all this pleasant but, like a small boy who knows nobody at a party, feeling a little out of it.

He stopped under a maple tree at a little distance from one of the tables, unfastened the blanket roll he carried slung over his shoulder and let it drop to the grass. As he was about to let the strap by which he was holding it slip out of his fingers, the thought came to him that he had taken the roll off his back for the last time. It seemed, in a way, an ending, so that the next thing he did, whatever it might be, would belong to a wholly new and unknown way of life. Still holding the strap, suddenly reluctant to let it go, he considered this for a while, oblivious to the noise and laughter around him. But he found his feelings too complicated to analyze and he lost interest in them, so he let go of the strap without giving it any more thought, and looked around to see what there was to do to amuse him.

Everyone near him had mugs of coffee and sandwiches or pieces of cake, and pretty girls behind the tables were handing out more. There were three or four behind each table working together, all of them having a wonderful time and twittering like flocks of sparrows. But at the table nearest him there was only one girl with pots of coffee and pyramids of doughnuts in front of her, and Matthew stared at her idly. She was a plump girl with warm, rich coloring, thick red-brown hair, large brown eyes and full red lips. Her dress looked like an old one and she wore it without hoops, but it had been freshly washed. Her low-cut bodice was not tight, like the other women's, and when she shifted her position he could see her unsupported breasts moving freely under it. She was watching the girls at the other tables with a bold, sullen expression in which there was not so much resentment as detachment, as though these noisy girls belonged to another world. Seeing the look, he grew curious about her and why she seemed to be avoided by the other women, though about that he thought he could make a pretty good guess.

She seemed to feel his look, for she turned toward him and their eyes met. She looked him over boldly and seemed to like what she saw, for something in the brown depths of her eyes took fire, the red lips parted, color flooded into her tanned face, and with what seemed to him an instinctive and unconscious motion she straightened herself so that her full breasts pressed against the bodice of her dress. She was a pretty and stimulating sight, and he grinned at her.

She turned away at once with a little toss of her head and busied herself moving the coffee mugs this way and that. He waited and, just as he expected, she glanced at him again, slyly, with lowered head and half-shut eyes. He straightened from his leaning position against the tree and strolled toward her with a slightly swinging stride. She pretended not to know that he was standing in front of her. She had lifted a fold of her skirt and was making a great business of brushing at an imaginary spot, but awareness of him fairly radiated from her. He continued to stand there waiting, and after a moment, being elaborately casual, she turned back and saw him.

"Oh," she said, and her hand went to her breast in a gesture of simulated surprise that was too crudely done to fool anybody, and he roared with laughter. She stared at him with an injured look, then delighted good spirits welled up in her and she joined in the laughter.

After that they appeared to have advanced enormously in liking and in understanding of each other. "Hullo," he said, pleased with himself and her, and took two steps that brought him right up to the edge of the table.

"Hullo."

The quality of his gaze made the color rise to her face again. She lowered her head and put one stubby finger with a not very clean nail on the tablecloth and moved it around as though to bore a hole right through.

"Got some coffee for a soldier, sister?"

"Could be." She made a sudden show of efficiency. "You want milk in it?"

"Sure. Anything you got."

She filled a mug and handed it to him and pushed a plate of doughnuts toward him. He took a swallow of coffee and a bite of doughnut, watching her with a bright predatory look of which there was no mistaking the meaning. Then he said, with his mouth full, "What's your name?"

"Sue. Sue Diggle."

"Short for Susan?"

"No, just Sue. Say! You ain't from Vermont, be you?"

"Never been here before. I'm from New York."

She pouted at him, thrusting out her full red underlip. "We don't like 'em from New York—nor from New Hampshire neither."

No more than she, did he know of Vermont's ancient enmities, of which at this time only a tradition remained. Smiling, he said, "Don't you think you could learn to like me just a little bit?"

She looked him over, pretending a critical appraisal, her eyes shining with merriment. They were both enjoying themselves immensely.

"Maybe I could. I like the way your hair curls."

They both laughed again, and the shared laughter, as before, heightened their excitement.

"Your hair's most the same color as mine."

"It is, isn't it?"

This they both recognized as the end of the preliminaries, and they lapsed into silence. He helped himself to another doughnut to fill the pause, and when he had eaten half of it he said, "Where do you live?"

"Out the road a piece—quite a piece."

"What road?"

"Why do you want to know?"

"I might feel like going out that way sometime."

"I'm not going to tell you. Want some more coffee?"

"Maybe I better get it at some other table."

"Theirs ain't so good as this."

"How do you know?"

"I just know, that's all. Here . . ."

She reached for the cup, but before she could fill it Matthew felt a hand laid on his shoulder. He turned to see an elderly man standing there. He was sparse and gray, but he stood very straight and there was an authority in his manner that told Matthew he was someone out of the ordinary.

"Your name's Matthew Chapin, isn't it? Mine's Stoner. Edward Stoner. I was an old friend of Dr. Hurd's." Stoner held out his hand, but he did not so much shake Matthew's as wrap his long fingers around it. His hand was cold to touch and he released Matthew's quickly. "Let's step over this way, shall we? I'd like a few words with you in private."

Stoner glanced at Sue, a sharp, unmistakably disapproving look, and said perfunctorily, "Excuse us, Sue," his manner making perfectly plain Sue's status in the town. Stoner led the way along the fringes of the crowd to a spot by the railing that was comparatively isolated, and Matthew, glancing back at Sue, saw her standing there, his coffee cup still in her hand, gazing after them with large, disappointed eyes that made him think of a dog that has been told to stay home. Matthew moved so that his back was toward her and gave his attention to Stoner, who was saying, "I have the bank here in Haddon. Dr. Hurd, of course, did his banking with me. Your colonel tells me you have a document of Hurd's concerning his money affairs. That right?"

"Yes, his will. He left me his money."

"That's what Bouget told me. You have it with you, I suppose. Want to let me see it?"

"Sure." Matthew's hand went toward his pocket and Stoner stopped him.

"Not here. You can bring it into the bank or . . . you got any place in town you're planning to stay?"

"No. I haven't even thought about it."

"There's no real reason why you shouldn't stay at Hurd's if you want to. He kept two, three rooms in the Hulls' place up the street—had his office there and took his board with the Hulls. We could go there now and I could explain you to Alice Hull, though my guess would be she's already heard and maybe is even expecting you."

The muscles of Stoner's face were briefly involved in a slight motion that Matthew took to be a smile. Suddenly self-conscious, Matthew smiled too, said, "Sure," felt this to be inadequate and added, "Sounds like a good idea."

Matthew went back to the tree and retrieved his blanket roll, which contained his few possessions, but, loath to sling it on his back ever again, he carried it in his hand. He and Stoner left the green and walked up a tree-shaded street behind the church at the end of the green and stopped in front of a white house that stood just below the steep rise of the mountain. Stoner said, "Alice Hull will be back at the green making coffee. The side door here is Doc Hurd's office entrance. It's hard to think he's not coming back."

They went through a gate in the white picket fence and up a short path to a door that opened into a tiny vestibule cluttered with boots on the floor and snowshoes hanging from nails. Matthew glanced at these curiously and dropped his blanket roll on top of the boots. Stoner opened a second door without using a key, and Matthew, following him inside, wondered if the office had been left unlocked for all the years of the war or whether Mrs. Hull had left it that way thinking they might come.

Over his shoulder Stoner said, "This was Hurd's waiting room and his sitting room too, when there weren't any patients." He stood back to let Matthew look around the shabby, comfortable, book-lined room. "Hurd was a great reader—but I suppose you know things like that about him."

Matthew had shut the door behind him but he neither heard what Stoner was saying nor advanced farther into the room. A wholly unaccustomed feeling of diffidence had taken possession of him as though he had discovered a dimension in the doctor's life that he had failed to realize and in which he had no place. He felt almost like a trespasser here, and in dismay he turned toward Stoner with an impulse to appeal to him, though he could not have put his feelings into words. He found Stoner watching him with a look of understanding, compassion so unexpected as to be unnerving.

The effect of this was fortifying and he looked resolutely around him, at once forgetting himself in amazement at the shelves of books which covered two walls of the room from floor to ceiling. He felt that his surprise was evident and that he ought to say something, which he did in a voice that sounded not quite like his own.

"He used to quote things out of books a lot. Shakespeare mostly. He seemed to enjoy doing it, but there wasn't much chance to read during the war."

"Come and sit down, boy." Stoner indicated two shabby armchairs that faced each other on either side of a Franklin stove. "Many's the time . . . well, we won't go into that. This chair's the one Hurd always used. I'll sit in it, if you don't mind."

The stove had been swept clean of ashes, and the empty, discolored grate looked peculiarly cheerless. Matthew sat down, and as he did so he caught sight of an old medical bag standing on the floor beside the stove where, perhaps, Hurd had left it when he went off with the regiment to war. Matthew looked quickly away.

There was a moment of silence, then Stoner said slowly, "He used to sit here evenings. You'd always find him reading with the lamp table pulled up close. Winters, he had big boots on because this part of the house—he built it for himself—has no cellar under it and there's a kind of a draft on the floor. Hurd used to say, 'A draft's a breath of fresh air somebody objects to,' but cold nights he always wore those boots."

Matthew found nothing to say to this, and after a while Stoner said in a different tone, "Well, may as well have a look at that will, if you're agreeable." Matthew reached inside his coat for the will and Stoner took a pair of spectacles out of a case. The strong spring shut the case with a vicious snap that seemed to disturb him, for he sighed as he put the case back in his pocket and took the will that Matthew held out to him. He read it carefully, folded it and handed it back.

"Seems all right to me. But you'll have to see lawyer Bradley about it soon as you can. You'd like to get it settled up, I suppose."

He gave Matthew a look of elderly shrewdness, studying him, seeming to draw pleasure from his youth and good looks without overestimating their importance. "How long were you with Dr. Hurd, boy?"

"Three and a half years, give or take a little."

"And you're how old now?"

"Twenty-one."

"Then you grew up in the war, so to speak. Got your maturity in it. That's not a normal environment—makes for a warped viewpoint, I suppose, but it should make you strong and self-reliant. Can't see that it's done you any visible harm. Did you try to learn from Dr. Hurd?"

"Not just at first. There was too much to get used to. After that I did. He helped me too."

"What Bradley and I and some of the rest of us figure is, that's like an apprenticeship. You been reading medicine with Hurd, you might say. Nowadays, there's beginning to be a feeling a man should have a degree before he practices. I'm not so sure. Plenty of good men here in the country don't. Depends on the school, maybe. Anyway, you've got the money for an education and you're more or less obliged to use it for that purpose, I should think."

Stoner stopped speaking but Matthew neither moved nor spoke. The banker drew a deep breath and continued in a slightly more emphatic tone.

"What I'm getting at is this. There's nothing in that will says *when* you use the money. You're young—a year or more wouldn't matter. We need a doctor here in Haddon pretty bad. With Doc Hurd away we've been having it hard, for the nearest man's almost twenty miles from here, over the other side of the mountain. We've got somebody says he'll come—a doctor named Greer. He's young like yourself, but he can't get here for a while because his wife's having a baby, and he's got property to sell, and he feels he can't leave till he's got somebody to take his place. Things like that. May be a year before he gets here. We've been thinking we'd ask you if you'd stay and doctor us till then."

Matthew pulled in his legs and sat up straighter in his chair. "I'd have to think about it," he said.

"You could get a degree in two years, I suppose. Then, if you wanted to come back here and settle, there'd be room for both you and Greer, I should think, especially if you both did a little farming on the side."

"I'm no farmer."

"Neither was Hurd, and since his wife died years ago, along with the first baby, what he made was a bit more than enough, as you can see by that will you have. We're going to miss Ed Hurd pretty bad—have been missing him. We were all counting on his coming back to us."

Stoner shifted his thin body enough to pull a handkerchief out of his trouser pocket. He began to wipe his glasses with it, slowly and with care, as an old man does to whom, through years of habitude, glasses have come to have more significance than glass and wire, as though they were a part of himself. Matthew watched him thoughtfully, with neutral eyes. Stoner put his glasses in the case, using his thumb to deaden the snap. He dropped the case in his pocket and moved around to face Matthew squarely. The sallow face had softened, the faded eyes had lost their spark. Stoner was again in the act of producing what he clearly felt to be a smile.

"Well, young fellow?"

"Like I say, I'll have to think about it. All right if I camp here a bit?"

"Belongs to you, so far as I can see. Well . . ." Stoner slapped the arms of the chair, then pushed himself out of it. "Mrs. Hull will feed you, same as she did Ed Hurd. I'll speak to her about it as I go back through the green. You got enough money to get on with? Excuse my asking."

"Some back pay—enough, I guess." Matthew let his

gaze travel around the small room, over the books, the stove, the armchairs, the worn Turkey rug. Then his eyes returned to Stoner. "Thanks," he said gravely.

When Stoner had gone, Matthew stood still until he heard the outer door of the vestibule shut, then he went slowly into the room that Dr. Hurd had used as an office. He found it was smaller than the book-lined room, and it was dark, for the two windows were close to the wall of the house next door. There were only two wooden chairs here, a table desk, and a long, high object covered with a sheet. Curious about this, he pulled the sheet off and saw an examining table with a black leather top that looked to him expensive and little used. He had never seen one before and he stood beside it for some minutes, studying it with interest. Then he put the sheet back carefully and went to look at the desk. Here he found some steel pens resting on the arms of a fancy inkwell, a blotter pad, a small bowl, and a pile of medical journals. He lifted the journals and saw that the first one was the May issue of 1861 and the last of September of that same year when, presumably, Dr. Hurd's subscription had run out. The blotting pad still held lines of the reverse impression of Dr. Hurd's slanting script, and Matthew turned quickly away from it to pick up the bowl and hold it between his hands. He thought perhaps it had once held ashes from Dr. Hurd's cigar, and then it seemed to him that the whole room smelled faintly of cigar, as though the odor had permeated the rug, the curtains, perhaps the walls. He put the bowl down and went into the next room.

This too was small, but it was light, for the windows looked toward the back. Standing at one of them, he saw a small yard of mowed grass ending in the steep, tree-grown slope of the mountain. On the far side of the yard there was a barn that had an unused look. He turned away to examine the room, which seemed to him austere and very clean. The bed, which was covered with what his aunt in New York would have called a "crazy quilt," looked as puffy as a pan of risen dough. He went to it and pressed his fist down on it, grinning as half his arm sank into the feather tick beneath.

The quilt made him remember his aunt and her spinsterish ways with curious vividness. She had died, and, as a strange and not very friendly lawyer had explained to him, her small income had died with her, leaving Matthew with no money but the little that the lawyer handed him as the proceeds of the sale of her shabby household goods.

At the time Matthew had felt only bewilderment and a sense of being on his own that did not so much disturb him as surprise him. Then the idea of enlisting had occurred to him and he acted on it enthusiastically without delay. At the moment, all this seemed so remote to him as not to have any reality, but he sighed as a tribute to the past, punched the quilt again, and turned away to examine the rest of the room.

There was a commode by the bed with a lamp on it and a book which he assumed to be a Bible until he picked it up and saw that it was a collection of Shakespeare's plays. There was nothing but a washstand, a chair, and a darkened painting on the wall opposite the bed. He crossed the room to look at this and saw that it was a portrait of a young woman dressed in a fashion that to him seemed strange. The grim look of the young face he took to be the artist's rendering of what, in life, might have been only a decorous reserve, but beyond that the unskilled work conveyed nothing. He gazed at it solemnly for a moment, while a feeling of aimlessness grew on him. With his hands in his pockets, whistling softly, he wandered back into the front room. Then he remembered his blanket roll and dragged it in from the vestibule and unpacked the belongings that he had stowed inside.

When he had finished, Dr. Hurd's old bag caught his eye and he dragged it out, sat down and opened it on the floor between his feet. He found it was filled with bottles, neatly labeled, and packets of powder papers. On an impulse he got up to get the field instruments and amputation kit that he had brought to Haddon in his blanket roll, dropped them in the bag and put the bag back beside the stove. This seemed the right thing to do and he was glad he had thought of it. After that he pulled a book off one of the shelves without even looking at the title, but the medical language it was written in meant nothing to him and he put it back. Before very long he was thoroughly bored.

He was beginning to be hungry when, from the direction of the church on the green, he heard the slow notes of a bell, clear and lovely in the stillness. He counted six, and continued to listen, for the sound seemed to hang in the air after the last note had struck, compelling attention, holding the mind away from other thoughts until memory lost it. This he thought must be the time for supper, and he rose, went out, and walked slowly down the path to the gate. He pushed it open and stood still a moment, aware of the special quiet in the streets of a village at this hour when the inhabitants are occupied indoors.

Being city-bred, he was accustomed to going in and out of houses by their front doors, but the front door of the Hulls' house had so unused a look that he chose a well-worn path at the side. This led him to a back door that had for a step the largest piece of quarried stone he had ever seen, a piece that must have taken a team of oxen and several men to move into place. Not having been in Vermont before, he had never seen anything like it, and he was admiring it when the screen door opened and he looked up to see a man standing there. He had the thin, bony figure of a man in late middle age who is still doing hard manual work. He wore loose trousers dusted with patches of sawdust and a shirt open at his scrawny neck, and he regarded Matthew with bright, inquisitive eyes but an utterly impassive face. Matthew grinned at him with easy friendliness and said, "Hullo. You're Mr. Hull, I suppose."

"Yes, I be, but nobody hereabouts says the mister." He spoke without even a suggestion of a smile, but he held the door open. "You be the young fella Stoner was aspeakin' of, I presume. Come in, Doc." Then, speaking to someone behind him, he said, "Ma, here's the new doc."

Matthew found himself in a kitchen with a big wood stove and a set table with three chairs placed around it. A large gray-haired woman, who was heavy rather than fat, had turned away from the stove as Matthew entered. She greeted him as solemnly as Hull had done. "Evenin'," she said, making two words of it, as the women in the regiment pronounced "morning." "Eve-*nin*." Matthew gave her the same warm smile that he had given Hull, and this seemed to confuse her for she flushed slightly, as though some sort of rule had been broken, and said, "Set you."

Hull was already in a chair at the end of the table and Matthew took the one in the middle. Hull took a thick slice of bread in his carpenter's gnarled hand and pushed the plate toward Matthew. The bread made a lump in his cheek like a quid of tobacco. Mrs. Hull left the stove carrying a coffeepot and took the vacant chair, glancing at Matthew under thick gray eyelashes that looked as though they had dust on their tips. The meal was cold boiled meat, bread, coffee and cold pie, but there was plenty of it. The Hulls seemed to have nothing at all to say and they watched every move Matthew made, but he thought their unsmiling manner was reserve rather than unfriendliness, for they both continually pushed platters and plates of food in his direction. Toward the end of the meal he realized with astonishment that they were both shy of a stranger, and trying to keep up their dignity in spite of this feeling. No one had ever been shy in his presence before and it pleased him, but at the same time it set him apart in a way that made him uncomfortable.

When he was back again in the part of the house that he could not yet think of as his, he discovered that he was completely tired out. He dropped down in one of the armchairs and let his thoughts wander back over the day's events, but the fact that he had this very morning been a soldier marching with a column of men, most of whom had been his companions for the last three and a half years, seemed as unreal to him as that he was now in a strange town in rooms that had unbelievably become his own.

After some time spent in aimless brooding that carried him into loneliness and right to the edge of depression, he made an effort of will that brought him wearily to his feet. Longing for sleep, he undressed, but when he was in bed he found that the feather tick was too soft for muscles accustomed to the hard ground, or at best a canvas cot. For a while he lay awake wondering if he would do better to get out of bed and sleep on the floor, but he was too tired to make the effort, and presently, in the midst of vague, discontented thoughts, he slept.

Some time later he was awakened by a loud racket that brought him out of bed, standing, before his brain cleared, and he realized that this was not a call to arms in the night but someone pounding on the inner vestibule door. Swaying with sleep, putting both hands on the commode to steady himself, he shouted, "I'm coming."

He groped his way to the front room, barked his shin on a chair, swore, found the door and pulled it open. A small boy holding a smoking lantern was standing there, looking up at him with a pale, frightened face.

"Hullo," Matthew said.

"Are you Doc Chapin, mister?"

Startled, Matthew hesitated, said, "Well, yes," and added with more firmness, "Yes, I'm Dr. Chapin. Who wants to know?"

"My pop. He's out in the street with the rig. He says will you please come quick? It's Peter next door to us.

He's real bad. He's choking, so will you please come quick?"

"What's the matter with him? Why is he choking?"

"It's the diphtheria. Mrs. Ward—that's his ma—says won't you please come fast as you can."

For a moment Matthew found no answer; then he said in a voice that again did not sound to him quite like his own, "Sure. Soon's I get dressed."

Diphtheria was no new thing to him. Dr. Hurd's habit of looking after sick children wherever the regiment might be had taught him what there was to know about the disease, but that was little enough. Many times Dr. Hurd had told him, "The kids get it, and more often than not that's the end. Maybe five or six in a family, all gone in two, three weeks, and it's even worse if older people come down with it."

As he lit the lamp and began to pull on his clothes, Matthew tried to remember anything useful that Hurd had told him, but could recall very little. Hurd had seemed to have an instinct about the disease. One look at a sick child and he knew what the outcome would be. "Sometimes they die of the poison the disease puts in their system, and there's not a thing you can do about it. Sometimes the false membrane grows down around their windpipe and they smother if you can't help them. Sometimes they just get well, no thanks to you."

The boy with the lantern was waiting just inside the door. Matthew suddenly remembered Dr. Hurd's bag and stopped to pick it up, hoping that what he might need was in it. As they went out he said, "What's your dad's name?"

"Tenney. We got the next farm to Mrs. Ward."

"Then she doesn't live in town?"

"No. Out a piece."

Tenney was waiting with the wheel of the buggy already warped around so that Matthew need waste no time in getting in.

Tenney said, "Evenin', Doc. We'll put the boy between us." Matthew settled Hurd's heavy bag at his feet and they drove off. Tenney appeared to think he had said all that was necessary, and they went through the dark town in silence. Matthew considered explaining that he was not a doctor, thought, hell, sure I'm a doctor—why not? And said in a tone he tried to make weighty, "Tell me what you can about this, Mr. Tenney."

He learned in sparse words, and Vermont turns of

phrase he sometimes followed with difficulty, that Mrs. Ward was a war widow with one child named Peter. They lived about four miles out, though she was "goin' about to sell" and move back into town. There had been an outbreak of diphtheria in the neighborhood that spring that had resulted in as many deaths as cases.

The small boy beside Matthew wriggled and said shrilly, "I didn't get it."

Matthew said, "Good for you, kid," and put an arm around him, liking the feel of the small, warm body against his own.

His father turned on him. "You shet up, you. Don't you never say nothin' like that again. It's bad luck. So you shet up good."

The fright in the man's tone was unmistakable. With a change of tone that was an attempt to disguise this sudden outburst of panic, he said to Matthew, "We didn't let him out of the house whole time, that's why. Some folks say it's catching like, and I'm one thinks it is. Didn't go to none of the funerals. Didn't make us popular hereabout, but there was others felt as I did." And Matthew saw a picture of a terrified countryside, not knowing what to do or where the disease would strike next.

Tenney was saying, "Kid's all I've got, and the wife's past the age for more. We lost three of typhoid time this one was a baby. Then the wife come down with it. Doc Hurd sat by her bed most of the night, time she was at her worst, sponging her to keep the fever down. Most other doctors would thought that woman's work."

"And this boy Peter is the only case around you now?"

The last case had been two months ago, and people, thinking the epidemic was over, had begun to feel safe again. Up until today Mrs. Ward thought Peter's sickness was going to be mild; then Tenney and his wife had been awakened to find Mrs. Ward with a lantern in her hand, standing on the grass under their window. She said Peter was strangling and to get the new doctor quick. Then she bunched up her skirts in her free hand and, the lantern swinging, ran back to her own house a quarter of a mile away.

After that recital they drove in silence, the slim wheels of the buggy crunching the gravel of the road. The light of the lantern swinging from the dash illumined the steady rhythmic motion of the horse's flanks. Once a deer leaped into the road in front of them and, with a flick of his white tail, vanished. The small boy slept.

Matthew himself was growing drowsy when Tenney said, "That light up ahead's where we're goin'. Reckon she put it in the window for us." They stopped by a hitching post at the side of a small house and Tenney moved the wheel to make space for Matthew to get down. "You'll excuse me if I don't come in on account of the boy here? I plan to leave the rig here so's you can drive back to town when you're ready. Leave the horse in Hull's barn and I'll send the boy in after him tomorrow. If I put the lantern out, reckon you kin see by sky-shine?"

"Sure. Thanks." Matthew jumped to the ground and turned to retrieve his bag. As he started up the path to the door, Tenney called after him, "Good luck, Doc."

CHAPTER FIVE

Matthew knocked and without waiting pressed down the latch and went in. And at once, before any other impressions reached him, he was aware of an odor, not strong but pervasive and so in possession of the place that he was shocked by it. Then he realized that he had smelled it a few times before in his life and that he should have been expecting it here, for Dr. Hurd had said, "You can tell diphtheria by the smell, always. Even if it's a mild case with no special symptoms but the fever, remember the smell will tell you. And a child smells different from a grown person that's got it. An older person smells old, like a trunk full of old unwashed clothes, but the smell in a child is active, like the smell itself is alive. You'll learn all that in time."

The room was big and lighted only by a lamp at the far end near a window, the light they had seen from the road. It shone on a narrow bed and on a woman sitting on a chair beside the bed. She was young, with pale blond hair drawn into a knot low at the back. She had turned her head when he came in, but that was all, and she was staring at him as though dazed by fright and anxiety. Beyond her, half hidden, Matthew could see the form of a child on the bed. He came toward her briskly, bag in hand, listening with the larger part of his mind to the harsh sounds that told him the little body on the bed was fighting to draw air through a passage that was being swiftly closed. With his attention focused on those dreadful sounds, Matthew nevertheless spoke to the woman with heartiness, not knowing that his tone and his choice of words were an unconscious imitation of Dr. Hurd.

"I'm Dr. Chapin. Have we got some trouble here?"

And as Dr. Hurd would have done, he approached the bed with confidence, letting his bag drop with a thud to the floor. She got to her feet and backed away to give him room.

"Oh, Doctor, he's so bad."

Matthew stood by the bed looking down. The child was a boy perhaps five years old. He was lying rigid, his small body arched in his effort to drag air into his lungs past the false membrane that was filling up his throat, compressing his windpipe. He was far gone and barely conscious, his face a dark, bluish color, his lips almost black, his eyes wide, staring sightlessly.

Matthew said sharply, "Bring the lamp here."

She moved at once to obey him, picked up the glass lamp from the table and held it high so that light fell on the boy's face.

"Please help him, Doctor. Please."

Matthew bent over the bed, not answering her, his mind struggling to recall what Dr. Hurd had said on those occasions when Matthew had held the lamp and Hurd bent over a sick child: "Matt, remember this, if you ever have to do this sort of thing yourself. If the membrane has spread up into the nose, there's nothing you or anybody else can do. But if it's spread downward and it's compressing the windpipe, there's just a chance that if you make a hole in the windpipe to let in the air . . ."

He watched the struggle that drew painfully scant breaths into the tense body, and without his knowing it his self-awareness slipped away. He forgot to play the part of the brisk, confidence-inspiring young doctor. He was no longer pretending to be anything he was not, or concerned about himself in any way at all, for he was wholly lost in an effort to understand what was happening in this little boy.

With each fighting breath the child's nostrils flared, but he could not tell whether air was actually being drawn through them. He put out his hand and held the side of his finger in front of the child's nose and he thought—he was almost sure—he felt the air stir. He was a little more certain of it when the scant breath went out. He would have liked to feel still more sure, but the decision had to be a firm one. He made it. The membrane had not spread upward into the nasal passages.

He straightened up and realized that he had been holding his own breath. He filled his lungs deeply and felt his heart beating hard. Then he realized that the woman was standing close behind him, holding the lamp, and that she was saying over and over in a high, strained voice, "Please help him, oh please, please help him."

Matthew turned on her and spoke sharply because the agonized voice tightened his nerves. "What's your name?"

She stared at him in blank surprise, not able to adjust her mind to answer. A lock of her colorless hair had slipped down and was touching the corner of her mouth. She did not seem to know it was there. Matthew, feeling the urgency in the child's harsh breathing, said with anger, "Quick. What's your name?"

"Cissie."

"All right, Cissie. I'm going to try to do something for Peter. I don't know if I can or not, but I've got to have your help. You'll have to hold the lamp and do just as I tell you. Do you think you're up to it?"

"Yes."

She spoke more firmly than he had expected and he felt a momentary relief.

"All right, then. Hold the light so I can see to get things out of this bag."

"It's Dr. Hurd's bag, isn't it?" she said as though she found comfort in this. He did not answer her. Squatting beside the open bag, he drew out a bottle of chloroform, held it in his hand, hesitating, and dropped it back. The child, he thought, was too far gone to feel anything, and from the look there was very little time. He rose with the familiar case of instruments in his hand.

"Cissie, get me a towel, a dish towel—anything of the sort."

The retreating light in her hand made strange, moving shadows. With his eyes on the child he opened the case on the bed. The breaths were coming in short, agonized gasps, the lungs fighting harder for air, the airway growing narrower even while he watched, and he had to fight against a feeling of panic that was making his own breath come short. He picked up a corner of the sheet and wiped the palms of his hands on it.

Cissie came back and silently held out a towel to him. He made a roll out of it as he had seen Dr. Hurd do. Then he pulled the pillow out from under the boy's head, thinking he should have done this earlier, and slipped the rolled towel under the thin shoulders. The child's head was pressed against the palm of his hand, the neck muscles drawn tight, and as he lowered the head to the bed, tipping it backward, he felt a convulsive tightening of the whole small frame. He put his hand on the child's chest, shocked by the rigidity of the straining body. The skin felt cold and damp.

Making a careful effort to control his voice, he said, "Cissie, bring the lamp close so I can see without any shadows, and hold it steady. That's right. He won't feel this—remember that. But be ready to do what I say."

She did as she was told in silence. He drew a deep, fortifying breath, bent over the bed and touched the child's throat with the fingertips of his left hand. He knew nothing about what lay under the skin. He was trying to make himself see in his mind what he had seen Dr. Hurd do, to visualize the location, the length of the cut he was about to make that should expose the windpipe for a second incision. His other hand groped in the instrument case, found a small retractor and laid it on the boy's chest where he would be able to get it quickly. Then he picked up a knife.

He must do this now, at once, or not at all. Without giving himself any more time, he made a quick, transverse cut, guessing at the depth. The top layers of skin parted and the cricothyroid membrane lay right at the point of the knife. Behind him, he heard Cissie draw in her breath sharply, but the lamplight did not waver. He took up the retractor, spread the incision and jerked his head to bring her closer beside him.

"Cissie, take hold of this handle and hold it steady— and hold the lamp steady. I'm going right through into his windpipe now, and when I do he can breathe."

The circle of lamplight in which he was working swayed and he said, *"Cissie!"* The light quavered and steadied and he said urgently as he sopped at the bleeding with a piece of lint, "This depends on you as much as on me. Do you understand? It will be all over in a minute. But when he gets air through the hole in his windpipe he'll cough, and bits of what's choking him will fly out. It may sort of explode. It's dangerous stuff that you might get the disease from, so try not to let it hit your face. All right—steady now."

When he took the lint away he could see clearly what he felt sure was the windpipe and though he knew the danger of a mistake his next move was quick. The incision in the windpipe was little more than a stab, and he leaned back and away. He heard the air whistle in and felt the child's body rise as though to meet it. Then the cough came and bits of the evil membrane flew from the opening in the boy's throat. Matthew said sharply, "Keep hold of the retractor," and he reversed the knife, as he had seen Dr. Hurd do, to hold the airway open with the handle. The small form trembled and the chest rose as the lungs filled with air. Matthew watched a moment, then he took the retractor away from Cissie. He slipped it out of the incision, letting the cut partially close against the oblong handle of the knife, and dropped the retractor on the bed.

A wave of heat went through Matthew's body and sweat broke out all over him. There were more coughs, more lung-filling breaths. Matthew tried to speak, found he could not, and cleared his throat instead. The strained arch of Peter's back, the tension of all the child's muscles, had relaxed and he was lying naturally. Without looking at Cissie, Matthew nodded his satisfaction, and the circle of light from the lamp she was holding shifted so that he knew she was moving away. The boy's face was losing its dark, bluish color with every breath he drew, and Matthew, still holding the knife just below the blade, feeling the exhaled breaths against his hand, watched with intense satisfaction but with a sudden consciousness of his own fatigue.

The light receded farther and wavered. He said, "Here, don't go away, Cissie. I still want to see. You did fine, Cissie."

He glanced at her over his shoulder and saw her begin to sway. He shouted, "Hey!" just as Cissie and the lamp fell to the floor. Then the lamp broke with a crash and the room was in darkness.

He said, *"Christ,"* and thought that at least the lamp had put itself out instead of igniting the spilled oil on the floor. Then he thought about the knife in his hand that was still holding the wound open. If he let go, the airway he had made would close itself in a few minutes if not right away. He considered this. There was no sound from

Cissie and he indulged himself in a surge of bitter hatred for her.

Slowly he drew the knife handle out, keeping the index finger of the other hand beside the wound so that he could find it again quickly if he had to. Once more the boy coughed and Matthew swore again and wiped the back of his hand on the sheet. He listened intently and was sure the boy was breathing smoothly and soundlessly. He laid the knife on the bed out of harm's way.

The next problem was light, and as Matthew moved away from the bed, trying to avoid the spot where he thought Cissie was lying, he felt pieces of the lamp chimney crunch under his shoes. With arms held out in front of him, he groped for and found a table near the window where he had seen the lamp standing when he first came in the house. He ran his hand over the top, hoping that there might be some matches, but he found none. He stood still, helpless in the darkness, and not knowing what to do. After a moment he called loudly, "Hey, Cissie." There was no reply and the silence gave him the sensation of being alone and miles from anywhere. He listened for any sound of the boy's breathing, and he could hear nothing, which he realized could be either good or bad. There was nothing he could do but keep on groping through the blackness until he found matches.

The most likely place for them would, he thought, be somewhere near the stove, and he began to feel his way along the wall in an effort to locate it, angry with himself for failing to notice it on his way in. He found a door that led, he supposed, into some other room, then a sink with a pump and something that felt like a kneading board. He hit the top of his instep painfully against a rocker, and found the stove at last by bruising his hip against it. His groping hands found that it was cold, which probably meant that neither Cissie nor the boy had eaten for some time. He felt upward for the stove's shelf and there he found the matches in an open box. He struck one and by its feeble light he saw a mantel with a steeple clock and two brass candlesticks beside it. To his relief there were half-burned candles in the sticks. Husbanding his match flame, he lit one of them and picked it up, then, on second thought, he helped himself to a handful of matches and dropped them in his pocket.

He carried the candle back to the bed, held to a slow walk by the fluttering of the flame, barely glancing at Cissie lying on the floor as he passed her. He saw at once that Peter was breathing well; in fact he seemed to be sleeping, and his color was nearly normal. Matthew put the candlestick on the floor, gathered up the instruments that were lying on the sheet, put them in their case and dropped the case into the open bag. The wound was bleeding again, though not very much, and he wiped it with a piece of lint. Then, frowning, he went to look at Cissie.

She was sprawled at his feet in an ungainly attitude, arms flung out, her legs wide apart. Her hair had come loose and an end of it lay in a pool of oil from the lamp. He moved it with his foot and sighed, wondering what he should do for her, and not having any idea, for in all his years with Dr. Hurd he had never had to deal with a fainting woman. The only thing he could think of was to get her off the floor. Along the wall was a long, wooden settle, and he thought vaguely that he might put her on that though he did not think it would be any great improvement over the floor, except that he could feel that he was doing something.

He was bending over her, about to pick her up, when she sighed softly, stirred a little and opened her eyes, looking up at him with the remote peacefulness, the sensation of physical luxury, of the mind that has not yet made the whole journey back to consciousness. Matthew had seen this look before in the eyes of men who had fainted from their wounds, and not understanding it, his impulse had always been to recall them fully to consciousness. He felt the same impulse now and so he said, "Cissie" in the firm tone of the rational world. He was at once vaguely sorry, for her eyes immediately showed first recollection, then fear. But not all her faculties were fully awake, for when she spoke her words were slowed and thickened. "What happened?"

"You fainted—lamp and all."

"Peter!" The word was a sharp cry. Memory had returned to her and she moved in an effort to sit up. He pushed her back again and squatted beside her, keeping a hand on her shoulder.

"Lie still. He's all right. He's sleeping."

She stared at him with troubled eyes, trying to read his thoughts, making up her mind whether to believe him or not. "Really," he said. "Listen."

She raised her head, listening, and when she had convinced herself that Peter was no longer fighting for breath, she lay back again. Her mouth began to tremble and a tear came out from under her closed lids to run down the side of her face. She moved a little and whispered, "I think I'm going to be sick."

"No you're not," he said decisively, and saw that she was beginning to fight against her own weakness. She moved a little as though she were again considering trying to get up, then suddenly she opened her eyes and stared with a startled look.

"I'm on the floor!"

She sounded weakly indignant, and he laughed. "I was just going to pick you up when you came to."

"I want to get up."

She struggled to rise and he helped her to her feet. She wavered and leaned against him for support. Her body felt frail and light, and in the dim glow of the candle, with her hair falling loose down her back, she looked almost like a child. She straightened up, however, and he thought with approval that there was plenty of determination in her slight form. Nevertheless, he kept a supporting arm around her waist.

"Come and lie down on the settle," he said.

"I'm going to look at Peter."

He did not argue with her, but he kept his arm around her and she seemed glad of its support. They stood beside the bed and she bent over the sleeping boy. He tried to draw her back. "Don't get too close, Cissie."

She pushed him away, but when she had satisfied herself that Peter was sleeping normally, she straightened up and gave him a smile, uncertain but full of sweetness. At the same time bright tears filled her eyes, glistening in the candlelight.

"That's enough," he said severely, and, laughing, picked her up and carried her to the settle. He put her down awkwardly and she tucked her skirts under her, leaning back against the settle's wooden arm. She did not look comfortable, and he said, "You need a pillow. Where will I find one?"

"In my room, through that door."

In the light of the match he struck he saw a small, neat room and, on the bed table, a lamp. He lifted the chimney and held the match to the wick. When he came back he was carrying both a pillow and the lamp. He put the lamp on a table where the light would not shine in her eyes, made her as comfortable as he could with the pillow at her back, and drew an armchair close by for himself.

She lay for a while with her eyes closed and he sat comfortably, resting and studying her face. She was pale and she looked worn and tired from the strain of the child's illness, but there were signs of character underlying the fatigue, and this set him thinking about how she had handled herself through the ordeal of the night. She had, he acknowledged with a strong surge of admiration, handled herself very well indeed. There had been no flinching when her child's throat had been cut open before her eyes, and by an untried doctor who was a stranger to her, about whom she knew nothing at all. And if physical weakness had made her faint, it was not until the emergency had passed. Even then, the moment she was fully conscious she had struggled hard to master the weakness and to regain her self-possession. He had never seen any woman show so much fortitude—in fact, fortitude was not one of the traits he associated with women. The thought of it stirred him in a curious way, and he spoke her name to himself, not quite aloud: "Cissie Ward."

She could not have heard him, but she turned her head on the pillow, opened her eyes and gave him her sweet smile. He was astonished to see how the smile took away the look of tiredness and how pretty she was.

"I was nearly asleep," she said in a soft, drowsy voice.

"You probably haven't been sleeping much the last few nights."

"Not much."

"Sleep some more, if you want to."

"You won't go? You won't leave us?"

The anxiety in her words, and behind them the confidence in himself, touched him and at the same time troubled him, and he felt to his dismay that his face was growing red. He said a little gruffly, in what he hoped sounded like the tone a doctor would take, "No, I won't leave. Not for a while. Not till I'm sure you're both all right."

She made a sound like a sleepy bird and shut her eyes, but she opened them again at once.

"You promise you won't go?"

"I promise—not for a while."

With her eyes shut she gave him the lovely smile and almost at once she was asleep. He waited for a while to make sure, then he rose and walked as quietly as he could. He crossed the room toward Peter's bed. He glanced at the broken lamp and the pool of oil on the floor as he passed and thought he should do something about cleaning them up; then he thought about how tired he was and decided to leave them alone for a while. Peter was sleeping quietly, one hand half open on the pillow beside his cheek. Matthew watched for a few moments, unconsciously conforming the rhythm of his breathing to the sleeping child's. Then he went back to his armchair, tried to adjust himself so as to find a little comfort within its rigid lines, leaned his head back, shut his eyes, and in a moment he too was sleeping.

CHAPTER SIX

The barn behind the Hull house contained, Matthew discovered, a buggy that had belonged to Dr. Hurd. He spent a contented morning washing it, saddle-soaping the harness he found hanging on a nail, and rubbing Dr. Hurd's old bag with shoe polish. The livery stable supplied him with a horse, and a much better one than he had hoped for. "He's young," the stableman said. "Won't stand without hitching, but he'll git yer where you're goin' in good time. And yer don't never need to use a whip to him—just rattle the whip handle in the socket as a sort of reminder, like."

Surprisingly, all this turned out to be true, and by the end of the week Matthew would have looked the part of a respectable country doctor but that his mail-order clothes had not arrived and he had nothing but his uniform to wear.

Patients began to come to him and to send for him, though not in any great numbers. Sometimes they were truly ill, sometimes the victims of accidents, or merely those who found enjoyment in challenging a new doctor with an old and stubborn complaint. That patients were not crowding his office did not trouble him, for the weather was too fine to produce sickness in so hardy a people, and in any event he was only marking time until he could go away to some as yet undesignated medical school. Except in caring for accident cases, he was unsure of himself to such an extent that he often felt like an impostor, and he would not have tried to do many of the things he did if there had been another doctor in the town.

In spite of these worries and responsibilities he was enjoying himself, for he found himself, by right of his profession, one of the small group of the town's elite. He would have been less than human and more mature than his years if he had not shortly begun to regard his good fortune not as the result of chance but as his due, owing to him because of personal qualifications that it did not occur to him to doubt he had. To be greeted as an equal by such men as Stoner and Colonel Bouget might have gone to his head more than it did were it not for those troubled moments when he groped in Dr. Hurd's bag for medicine he hoped would not harm a patient ill with he did not know what ailment.

He tried, and very hard, to make up for his lack of knowledge by reading, but the books he pulled down from Dr. Hurd's shelves more or less at random were little help to him, for he did not know the meanings of the technical terms they contained. Then one evening he happened to open one of a long row of notebooks he found on a shelf behind the desk in the consulting room. It was filled with Dr. Hurd's hurried script and contained careful records of his cases. All the other notebooks were similar, and they covered many years of practice.

At the beginning of each new case, under the date, Hurd had set down the symptoms, followed by his diagnosis. Sometimes this diagnosis would be a single word, like "Pneumonia," set down in a firm hand, or "Fever having some resemblance to typhoid" would appear in writing that conveyed an impression of thoughtfulness. There followed, in each instance, a notation of the medicine and dosage. By turning the pages, and following one case through to its conclusion, Matthew could learn the whole course of an illness and its treatment.

Sometimes, when a treatment had failed and the patient died, Hurd had ended his record with some lines of self-criticism. Matthew came across one case, entered as "Acute inflammation of the intestines" under which Hurd had written after entering the patient's death, "Feel that a purge in this case, though indicated, precipitated death. Must consider this and try to discover distinctions that will indicate when purges are safe, when not."

For Matthew, bending over the notebook open on the desk, the words brought vivid memories of Dr. Hurd, and sitting there in the lamplight he dreamed for a while of himself finding the answer to the problem that had bothered the doctor.

Because Matthew's patients were few, he was able to take the time to drive out to Cissie's house each day, which he continued to do long after Peter ceased to need this attention. Perhaps he was lonely without realizing it, for he greatly enjoyed Cissie's joyful welcome, and he thought she grew prettier each day. Flushed and smiling, she would leave whatever she was doing with an alacrity that did not fail to flatter him.

"Oh, Doctor," she would say with shining eyes, "I'm so glad you've come."

"Is everything all right?"

"Oh, yes, but it's such a comfort to have you come. It's lonely sometimes way out here and I feel so out of things, not being in the town. Your coming makes me feel—well, safe."

And this in turn produced in him a sense of being a fine, strong fellow, the kind that people could rely on. The role was a new one and it pleased him. She made him think well of himself.

Peter too liked him. Once he got over being a wan, sick little lump of misery, he began showing signs of a personality that was robust though not naturally very playful. To encourage him, Matthew, sitting on a chair beside the bed, would pretend to shadowbox with him, and Peter, squealing with delight, would strike back with small fists until his face grew flushed and Matthew said, "There now, that's enough, young fellow."

Always he would find that while he was playing with Peter, Cissie had busied herself making coffee and setting out cups and a plate of cake or doughnuts on a little table. She would bring Peter something for himself and say, "Come, Matthew," as though he too were a small boy whom it pleased her to look after. Then he would pull the armchair close to the little table, opposite the settle on which she had seated herself, and watch her pour the coffee, enjoying the curve of her wrist as she held the pot over the cups and feeling a deep sense of peace and contentment. Sometimes they would sit together like this almost in silence, communicating without words; sometimes they would talk a little. She was utterly without coquetry, which fascinated him; and to his surprise, because this was so unaccustomed, it pleased him. He was sure that she enjoyed his visits, and he guessed that she felt warmly toward him, but she always maintained toward him an attitude of reserve. He wondered at first if this came from her consciousness of the difference in their ages and of her widowhood, but finally he decided that these things were only partly the case, for as they learned to know each other she seemed to him to glow with new youthfulness. All this had the effect on him of making him feel more mature than he had ever before felt in any relationship with a woman.

He acknowledged to himself quite freely that he had never known anyone like her. The women who had been with the regiment had been strong, self-reliant, busy, and had treated him more as an impudent boy than as a man. The other women he had known, those with whom he had discovered and proved his manhood, he could now, in memory, scarcely distinguish, the one from the other. Before the war there had been only the old aunt who had raised him and regarded him with vague bewilderment, and various leggy young girls whom he and the other boys used occasionally to chase down the street. None of all these had Cissie's charm—or in retrospect, any charm at all. None had her delicate, almost fragile grace, or the quality that seemed to permeate her and that he was just experienced enough to recognize as the attribute of being a lady.

He grew to love the little house and to feel pleasantly at home in it as he never had in the home of his childhood. He took delight in all its details, in the plants blooming in the windowsills, in the braided rugs on the floor, in the blue-and-white china in the corner cupboard and in the way the sunlight lay in a long streak of brilliance across the floor. He even came to have a sense of guardianship about all this that led him to seek out small chores, such as filling the kindling box or emptying the ashes from the stove; and each day, just before he left, he filled three buckets with water that Cissie might be spared the labor of working the pump handle up and down.

His curiosity about her remained unsatisfied for he had very little success when he tried to draw her into talking about herself. He felt shy about questioning her too directly, preferring to put his probings into the form of statements about his impressions of her. Once he said, "You don't seem like a country girl, Cissie," and waited in an absurd state of expectancy for her to give him a glimpse of herself.

"But I am a country girl," she said, and smiled in a self-deprecating way that he found utterly charming. "I was born right here in Haddon."

"Then how did you . . ." Appalled by his own boldness, he left the rest of the sentence unfinished, but she was quick to catch his meaning and she flushed with the compliment it implied.

"Oh, my mother and father were both from Boston and I still have relatives there. Mother was abroad once. In Italy. She knew a great deal which she tried to teach me, but she died when I was fifteen. My father was the Congregational minister here, but he died a year later and Mr. Stoner—I call him Uncle Ed—was my guardian until I married. Now you know all about me. Tell me about you, Matthew."

He did not in the least consider that he knew all about her, but he felt he should not question her further, and so he replied to her. "There's nothing to tell," he said, honestly convinced that this was true, and to his annoyance felt himself growing red when she laughed at him.

Once, as she reached forward to refill his cup with coffee, she said, "You're going away to study medicine, aren't you, Matthew?" and he thought he heard a tone of anxiety in her voice that encouraged him greatly. "When are you going?"

He laughed and said, "Ask me something I know the answer to, will you?" and would have said much more except for Peter, who was in his bed ten feet away, playing with the toys that were strewn over the counterpane.

Peter was always with them, even after he was well enough to be out of bed. Though he was a likeable little fellow, Matthew cursed him for his presence, for there was never any chance to see Cissie alone. He tried to convince himself that a five-year-old did not matter, but when he attempted to take Cissie's hand she would draw it away with a warning shake of her head, or if Matthew resorted to words she would whisper, "No, Matthew. Little pitchers have big ears." However, he felt that he would not yet be allowed liberties even if they were alone, which did not in the lease reduce his longing to try, and he had great hope for the future.

Peter was getting well very nicely and needed no more doctoring. Nevertheless, Matthew continued to come. Then he hit on the happy idea that it would be good for the child to be taken for a drive, and was pleased with himself for inventing this excuse to continue his daily visits. The drives grew longer and longer. With Peter sitting between them, they headed up the narrow valleys between hayfields that Cissie called "mowings," or turned into some steep, rutted side track beside a turbulent mountain stream, where hemlock boughs made twilight over moss-grown rocks. They talked together over Peter's head and gradually he learned much about her that she had not told him. For one thing, she was better educated than he.

And he discovered that she had a little musical skill, enough, at least, to play the treadle organ in church on Sundays. They sang together, choosing songs that Peter liked, for they both made much of the boy as though to justify their being so much together. Her voice was high and true, if a little thin, and he, singing with her, held his strong baritone down.

Gradually he became aware of a vein of conventionality in her that he felt was not to his best interest, though he had not so far troubled to examine himself as to just what his interests might be. He wanted to make love to her; of that he was entirely certain. Her smile, the light touch of her hand, her graceful, swaying body seemed to him full of promise—if only they could be alone without Peter. He suspected that she might be at least thinking about marriage, for he thought he knew that women did this with or without cause. However, he felt that she should be perceptive enough to sense that he was not, for how could he even consider such a thing with medical school and the beginning of professional life ahead of him? How he might feel in the future, when these aims were realized, it was not in his nature to trouble himself to reflect on.

He was looking forward to medical school, the thought challenged and excited him. and he tried to tell her how he felt, dwelling on it a little so that she should not mistake him. He soon discovered that it was a subject she did not want to discuss. She shut her mind against it, and when he brought it into their talk she deftly turned to other matters. Then one day, when he was more than usually persistent, she cried out, "Oh, why do you keep talking about that old school all the time?" He stared at her in surprise, and as though, having once spoken her mind, she could no longer contain herself, she said with a vehemence that was new to him, "I simply don't understand you, Matthew. I don't see why you want to go and give up a year or two of your life when it isn't necessary. I can't see one single reason for your going."

"Why, I *want* to go, Cissie."

This conversation was taking place in the buggy, over Peter's head, and when she heard his reply, she flushed and said with some force, "But that's very silly of you, Matthew. You can have a good practice right here, without leaving at all. If you go away for a year or two, Dr. Greer, who's coming, will have all the patients by the time you get back."

"I have to go, Cissie, to get the money Dr. Hurd left me. Anyway, I'm not sure I want to live in Haddon for the rest of my life. But the main thing is I *want* to go to a medical school. I wish I could make you understand."

Indeed, it seemed very important to him that she should not only understand but sympathize with his desire to leave Haddon, and it never occurred to him that this might be asking a good deal of her. She said no more on the subject at this time, and she kept her head turned away from him while he sat in silence wondering what he should construe from the unusual spirit she had shown. Peter, aware of tensions, squirmed unhappily and said, "Mommy, are you crying?"

"No, darling." She bent down to lay her cheek on the boy's blond head. "It's just that . . . never mind, Peter, please."

After that, for some days, though she was not less friendly, she seemed more withdrawn and, most of the time, preoccupied. He knew that her thoughts were filled with what he had said about medical school, and after some troubled consideration he decided if he left her and the subject alone she would shortly get used to the idea of his leaving. He did not mention it again, and as little by little her mood seemed to lighten, he assumed that she had begun to understand. It was September now, and with it came Peter's sixth birthday, after which he would begin to go to school. Matthew brought him a pencil box and some colored crayons; Cissie gave him a schoolbag and baked him a special cake with frosting. The day was glorious, warm but clear, with sudden brief breezes that rustled the leaves and warned that the fine weather would not last forever. Matthew suggested that they pack a picnic and take it to a clearing in a high valley that they had seen on one of their rides.

They went on their picnic and warm sun shone down on the little clearing; evergreens walled it closely about and the air was filled with the sound of the rushing water of a brook hidden from sight at the bottom of a steep, ferny bank. They got out, Cissie holding her skirts away from the wheel with one hand while she gave Matthew the other with more outgoing friendliness than she had shown him for some time. Peter, with a shout of joy, ran toward the brook and they heard him scrambling down the bank. Cissie looked after him anxiously, but Matthew said, "He'll be all right," and started to unhitch. He fastened the half-round cement drag to the horse's bridle by its long leather strap and left him to graze.

While Matthew was making these preparations he kept his eyes on Cissie, for it had come over him that with Peter out of sight playing in the brook, he and Cissie were alone at last. He lifted the picnic basket out of the buggy and set it on the grass at a spot she showed him. She knelt in a billow of skirts to unpack it and he sat on a fallen log at the edge of the woods to watch her. He found that he was strangely moved, almost trembling, and after a moment he spoke to her in a voice that sounded to him not like his own.

"Cissie, come over here and sit down a while."

She gave him a bright, preoccupied, housewife's glance, but she put the forks she was holding back in the basket and, impeded by her skirts, scrambled to her feet. He made room for her on the log and she sat, hands folded in her lap, a happy smile on her face that somehow touchingly resembled Peter's. He longed for her; he had every intention of shortly taking her into his arms, and yet he wished to prolong the almost enervating sweetness of the moment. He wanted to talk to her and have her talk to him, to have their minds come close before their bodies touched.

"Cissie."

"What, Matthew?"

He reached down beside the log, found a stiff spear of grass, broke it off and twirled it in his fingers. Looking not at her but at the twirling grass, he said, "Cissie, did you love your husband?"

"Why yes, Matthew, of course."

"Is that why you married him?"

"Yes, certainly. You can't think . . ."

He threw the piece of grass away from him and turned to face her. "It's you I want to know about. I want to know everything about you, Cissie. Were you happy with him?"

"Yes, I was. It was hard at first and there were only about two years before he went to war."

"Why was it hard? Wasn't he good to you?"

"Yes, he meant to be. We lived with his father on a big farm on the other side of the mountain. Father Ward is a stern man with old-fashioned ideas about the family living together, and he had a sister there who I think hated me because my folks came from Boston. That didn't make things very pleasant around the house, and then when I was carrying Peter I wasn't very well."

She stopped and stared at the ground, made suddenly disconsolate by these memories, and he said gently, "Go on, Cissie. These are the things about you that I've always wanted to know, but somehow I never felt I could ask you about them till now. Was Peter born there?"

"Yes, after John—my husband—went to war. He went with the regiment from over the mountain and he was killed at Bull Run without ever having a chance to fire a shot at the enemy, they say."

"So then you came back to Haddon?"

"Yes. The Wards' is a great big house, but having a baby in it upset Miss Ward, so after I got the news about John we—the baby and I—came back to Haddon to the little house we're in now that Uncle Ed found for us."

They were silent for a while, Cissie lost in memories of days gone by, Matthew in his awareness of her. She appeared to feel that she had reached the end of her story, but after a moment, not looking at her, he asked, "Are you still in love with your husband, Cissie?"

"Why yes, of course."

"I mean really, actively. If he were to come back would you feel the same as when you married him? Tell me truly, Cissie."

She considered for a moment, and then he thought a little shiver went through her. "I suppose the way one person feels about another is always changing, at least if you're young, don't you, Matthew? I didn't feel the same way about him when he went to war as I did when we were first married, and I don't imagine he did about me either. We loved each other, but in a different way. And now—I just don't know how I'd feel. Sometimes I can't even remember how he looked, and I feel so bad about it. Matthew, don't let's talk about it any more. Listen and see if you can hear Peter. Maybe I should go after him."

"Peter's all right. You told me once you get lonely

sometimes. With just you and Peter in the little house alone."

She nodded her head without speaking.

"So do I, for that matter," he said.

After that they were silent. They had reached a point of tension when it seemed to both of them that everything hung on the next word that either of them might speak. He moved along the log close to her and put his arm around her waist.

"Cissie, I need you and I think you need me."

Again she nodded without speaking, and she inclined a little toward him, leaning against him slightly.

"Then why shouldn't we be everything to each other?"

She looked up at him sharply. "What do you mean, Matthew? What are you trying to say?"

"I mean, I love you and why shouldn't we live together? Nobody need know—"

She was on her feet before he had finished speaking. *"Matthew!"*

He too jumped up and he gave her time to say no more. He put his arms around her and pulled her close to him, feeling her gasp and struggle, overpowering her as easily as though she had no strength at all. He bent over her to kiss her and she said, "Don't, don't!" in a voice that sounded like a low moan. She tried to pull away and to turn her face, but her efforts to free herself had reduced him to a frenzy. He had gone beyond reason and restraint. He felt a fierce joy in overpowering her.

The kiss was long, and before he had finished he felt her go limp, not in yielding, but in helpless despair. Feeling this despair in her, his pleasure drained away and he let her go. He was hurt and angry now, and surprised that she had not responded to him for he had been so sure of her. She covered her face with her hands and stumbled away from him to sit down on the log, collapsed on it as though she could not stand. Her head was bowed in her hands and he knew that she was weeping. Irritably he thought that she was behaving like a girl who had never known what love was, and a prudish one at that. He felt put upon and cheated by her unexpected behavior.

He came nearer to her, intending to say something of this, and stopped, for her weeping had become heartbroken and pitiful, and watching her, some of his anger went out of him. He moved close to her and looking down at her bent, disheveled head, he said, "Cissie . . ."

He stooped over her and put a hand on her shoulder. She drew away from him and through her tears she said, "Don't touch me."

He straightened up and stood looking down at her, thinking about his injured feelings. After a moment he said, "Please, Cissie," meaning he wished that she would stop her tears, and he did not know what else besides. Her face was hidden for she had turned away from him as far as she was able.

"I didn't know you could be so cruel."

"Cruel!"

"Yes, cruel. We've been such friends, and I thought . . . oh!"

She began to weep again and he sat down on the log beside her. "What did you think, Cissie? Tell me."

"I thought—oh, never mind. Take me home. I'll go find Peter."

She started to rise and he took her arm to prevent her. "Wait a minute. Did you think I was going to talk about our getting married? Was that it?"

She made no answer, but neither did she attempt to get up again, and he took away his hand.

"You know I can't think of getting married as things are. I've got years of work ahead of me. I'll be frank and say I never considered such a thing. But I think we love each other and I think we could make each other happy, and I don't see any reason why we shouldn't."

"I don't want to talk about it, Matthew."

"Do you think it would be wrong? Is that what you're trying to say?"

"Yes. But I don't want to talk about it. I want to go home."

"And spoil Peter's birthday?"

"Oh!" She began to tidy herself, to pull the bodice of her dress straight and to smooth her hair. He said, "Don't spoil the kid's good time."

She stood up. "Very well. But this has to be the end of everything between us."

She started to move away, and he said to her retreating back, "Don't take what I said as insulting to you. It wasn't, because I didn't intend it that way."

She made no reply to this and he sat on the log, his arms folded on his knees, and watched her go to the picnic basket and begin to set out the lunch. He felt tired and listless and, now that he thought about it in the light of her refusal of him, somewhat amazed at himself for failing to realize how strong a hold her background and her training had on her. After that he just sat there, not thinking of anything very much but feeling miserable.

Cissie finished laying out the lunch and went away across the clearing; then she disappeared down the bank of the stream, calling Peter. He sat on, emptied of every feeling but his sense of loss of her. He could hear her walking among the stones beside the brook, and then those sounds died away as she went farther upstream. The clearing grew very still except for the rushing of the brook and for the faint, disturbing sound of light wind stirring overhead in the tops of the trees. He became more and more aware of the solitude and of the deep forest that surrounded this place. He felt at his back the cool air that breathed out from among the trees. His forehead felt damp and clammy after the heat of his emotions, but he made no move to wipe it. He sat on for what seemed to him a long time.

After a while he drew a deep breath that was meant to fortify him and rose from the log. He crossed the clearing slowly until he reached the helter-skelter of the picnic littering the grass. The lid of the picnic basket was open and he bent to close it. When he dropped it the small sound, nothing in itself, seemed in the mountain stillness to fill all his consciousness even after there was no sound, as though echoing in hollow places within his head.

After a time, he sighed again, not so much because of Cissie but because of the way a bright hope can vanish in a moment. He felt desolate and aimless, as if all the progress he had recently made into life had been wiped out, and he was back, with nothing gained, in the emptiness that had followed the death of Dr. Hurd. Then he discovered that he wanted Cissie still but that he felt a great sorrow for her and for himself that was so diffuse and so wholly without pain that it was almost peace. He went patiently back to his log and sat down to wait for her.

CHAPTER SEVEN

The meal on the grass was thoroughly difficult for both Cissie and Matthew, though they both did their best for Peter's sake. Matthew made much of him, joking with him good-naturedly. Cissie was indulgent, but she did not have it in her to be gay. Matthew knew they were not quite succeeding and that the boy's subtle instincts told him that something was wrong, for now and again the child would glance quickly from one to the other with a veiled, puzzled look. This touched Matthew and he tried the harder, for it seemed to him that Peter had taken his cue from his elders and was doing his best to help cover up a situation he did not comprehend.

On the drive home the child, overcome by food and fresh air, and perhaps a little by the strain of the false gaiety of the meal, slept nestled against Matthew's side. Cissie sat with her head turned away and Matthew's heart ached for her for it seemed to him that, by allowing Peter to sleep against him, he had stolen a comfort from her and left her singularly alone. Still, he did not dare to speak to her and after a time he realized that she had taken out her handkerchief and was crying quietly into it. Once he ventured to whisper, "Cissie," in a tone of soft pleading, but she only shook her head without turning so that he could see her face.

When they reached her house, she made it clear by the way she gathered up her skirts and took up the picnic basket that she wanted no help from him, so he did no more for her than to warp the wheel around to give her room to get out. This she did quickly, setting the basket on the grass and reaching back for Peter, not looking at Matthew, but burying her face in Peter's coat as she lifted him out.

Matthew did not wait for them to reach the door, but slapped the reins on the horse's back, rattled the whip in the socket and was away without a backward look. The truth was that he was getting angry. He felt that he had

79

done all he could to explain himself and to make peace and that she had refused even to listen to him, much less to permit him to state his case. In this mood, giving his resentment full scope, he drove off toward Haddon, a soft cloud of tawny dust following behind the buggy's black top.

Thinking about it all in retrospect, he regarded with amazement the fact that, all this time, Cissie had been thinking solely of marriage when marriage was so palpably impossible for a man of his ambitions, at present or for some time to come. It seemed to him, as he brooded about it, quite incredible that she could have deluded herself into believing that he had such an end in view, and he exonerated himself emphatically for any blame for this. In fact the more he thought about it the clearer it became to him that she herself was not free from blame for not understanding him better; he assured himself of this with great emphasis. He even extended the blame to include all women who were, he now perceived, incapable of any emotion that would not lead them into the safety of marriage. Their singleness of purpose, as he now saw it, almost awed him. He told himself that he was lucky to have kept his wits about him and so avoid the trap.

All this accomplished, however, was to lead him into a terrible depression. Abruptly he gave up all the arguments with which he had been trying to justify and reassure himself, and quite without restraint he began to suffer from Cissie's loss. He writhed with the torture of his misery. He kicked at the dashboard, he slapped the reins and roused the horse into an unhappy trot. He said *"Oh Christ!"* in a terrible whisper. And while this was going on, another and more remote part of his mind was observing these feelings with astonishment in view of the fact that in all that had happened up to now he had not thought of himself as deeply involved with Cissie, or of this affair as being of a different pattern from any other.

When the acute phase of his misery had passed, he sat with the reins held loosely in his hands, the sun warming him, and gave thought to how he could find ways to support the intolerable burden of his life. The best plan, he thought, would be to see Stoner at once and tell him that a longer stay in Haddon was out of the question. Haddon had looked after itself without a doctor for all the years of the war and they could go on doing it a while longer. Medical school for him! And as soon as possible.

Having reached this decision, he felt a degree of satisfaction, if not of comfort. He looked around him, surprised to see that the day was still bright, the distant hills still clothed in their blue mist. And then, on the road ahead, he saw a woman walking toward him. She was walking with a determined air, her skirts swinging with each step. Her sunbonnet had slipped backward off her head and was hanging by the strings, letting loose a mass of auburn hair. She carried a large basket on her arm as though the weight of it bothered her. He watched her idly for a moment, glad of the sight of anything that would break into his mood. Then he recognized her, and sat up straight. "Sue, by God!" He slapped the reins on the horse's rump and when he caught up with her he was leaning out on her side of the buggy, smiling broadly.

"Hullo, Sue."

She looked up at him blankly. Her face was flushed from walking and not very clean, and there were beads of sweat above the curve of her full, red upper lip, but there was a healthy, earthy, full-blown look to her that surmounted these blemishes. She looked as though she belonged to the good, rich soil, as though she had the sun in her veins. "Oh," she said, and answered his smile, her look of weariness vanishing and a flood of warm color rising to her cheeks. "It's the man from New York, isn't it? Dr.—Dr. Something. I forget."

"I said to call me Matt—remember? What are you doing way out here?"

"Goin' home, that's what I'm doin'. I live up this road a piece. Quite a piece." She sighed, obviously thinking of the distance, and jounced the laden basket so that Matthew glanced at it.

"Been to town?"

"Doin' the tradin' for me and Pa."

"Want a lift home?"

"But you're goin' the other way, Matt."

"I can turn around, can't I?"

"Oh my God, would you? I'm beat. I'm really beat."

She handed the basket up to him with alacrity and he put it by his feet and fixed the wheel for her. She put her foot on the step and gave a little jounce to push herself up. The jounce made her full breasts jump and he grabbed her arm and pulled her in so hard that she landed against him with a yelp of laughter. The red lips were parted just below his own and she lay sprawled against him. He bent his head and kissed her.

"Hey," she said when he let her go. "Hey, you—what do you think you're doing?"

"I think you're a damn pretty girl who likes to be kissed. Made for it."

"Oh, *you!*"

She threw herself into her corner of the buggy seat, but she was obviously not displeased. "Folks is sayin' there's goin' to be trouble with a young, good-lookin' doctor in town. I guess folks is right."

"You like to be the trouble?"

"Oh, *you!*" she said again, and he laughed. Her words sounded like a standard, almost automatic response to a situation that was certainly not unfamiliar to her. She raised her arms to tidy her thick hair and he saw that her dress was wet with patches of sweat at the armpits. She seemed to his alerted senses to be surrounded by an aura of body warmth that was not perceptibly an odor, though it carried suggestions of barn and field, but rather an emanation of healthy vitality, of her sex declaring its readiness as naturally and freely as a flower opening its petals wide.

He felt his body making its response on its own volition and without the sanction of his mind. This pleased him greatly for it seemed to him the best, the most appropriate answer to Cissie that could possibly be found. Exultantly he rattled the whip in the socket and the horse jerked himself into activity.

When they were turned around he glanced at her with half-shut, gleaming eyes. She was leaning back in her corner, watching him eagerly, he thought, full lips parted, the pleased speculation so plain on her face that he almost laughed. To tease her and to keep the situation from ripening too fast, he decided to speak to her in an impersonal, though friendly tone.

"Do you always walk when you go to town? Doesn't your family have a horse?"

"Sure we got a horse. And a good wagon too. I git to use 'em, or leastwise to ride the horse, if Pa ain't workin' or sleepin' one off."

"Which is your pa doing today—working or sleeping?"

"Sleepin' one off. A good one." She giggled and gave Matthew a look of mischief. "I like to git the eggs to town when he ain't noticin' to count how many I got, or ain't around so's he won't git the money away from me before I git a chance to hide some of it. I got a good price today." She slapped a pocket in her skirt that was sagging from the weight of a purse, and he heard the jingle of coins.

"Your pa all the family you've got?"

"That's all. Just me and Pa."

"Aren't you afraid he's sobered up and is waiting for you to come home?"

"Maybe. But likely if he woke up he's took the horse and gone to work. That's why I didn't take him—so Pa could if he woke up. I hope that's the way it is." She sighed windily.

"Does he often have to sleep one off?"

"Sure. Once, twice a week, maybe, if he's just got paid for clearing a piece of land."

More questions brought out the fact that Sue's mother was dead, that three brothers had died in an epidemic of typhoid while they were all children, and that Sue had kept house, raised chickens, done the milking and countless other chores from the time she was twelve, at which age she had stopped going to school.

Her home, which she referred to as the "place," was a half mile nearer town than Cissie's house, in the same narrow valley. There were a few acres of stony pastureland on which the junipers and hemlocks were steadily encroaching, and a few more acres of wet bottomland that Pa was going to drain and turn into fields someday when "he had a mind to." Pa's living, such as it was, came from pulling stumps on the land of more ambitious neighbors, a work he accomplished by digging up to the point that a chain and the horse could be brought into play. Matthew gathered that the chain was the most valuable article that Sue and her father possessed, and that on a basis of daily hire the horse was worth more than Pa. The economics here involved did not seem to strike Sue as out of the normal.

Another thing he noticed about Sue, because it formed a contrast to Cissie, was that she seemed quite willing to talk about herself, and did it with perfect frankness. Cissie, while not exactly holding anything back, had always shown a certain reticence, and this Matthew had put down, without really giving it consideration, to that quality she had which he vaguely associated with being a lady. As he thought about it now, under cover of Sue's garrulity, it dawned on him that Cissie's reticence might have a source still more remote in her incessant and ever-present desire to improve herself. She strove for what she herself called "right thinking"; she read good books when she could get them even though they bored her; she was constantly watchful of her manners and behavior. She strove hard to be the sort of person she thought she ought to be. Matthew felt fairly certain Sue never tried to be other than she was, and he thought that she pushed truth in front of her like a wheelbarrow. Under the circumstances he was finding these characteristics refreshing. With Sue he felt himself expanding, and if it was what Cissie would call the baser part of his nature and the lower part of him generally that was doing the expanding, the feeling was pleasing and comfortable.

He came out of this reverie to realize that Sue had asked him a question. "What?" he said, grinning and blinking his gold-brown eyes at her like a cat enjoying the warmth of the sun.

"You weren't listening to a thing I've been saying."

"I was thinking about you." He put a hand on her knee and she clamped her knees together on his fingers. Again he was aware of his body's responsiveness, but he took his hand away.

"What *did* you say?"

"I said, you go to Cissie Ward's house every day, don't you?"

"How do you know that?"

"Oh, I see you pass."

"Peter's been sick, you know."

"He ain't sick now."

"Jealous?"

"Cissie's a stuck-up bitch. The grand minister's daughter who takes Sunday dinner at the banker's house and won't have nothin' to do with Pa and me less she wants Pa to do a chore for her. Then she comes to our door holdin' up her skirts in both hands as though the dirt in our yard would poison her. And she stands there smilin' with her head a little on one side as though that would most likely get her what she's after. She says, 'Mr. Diggle'—*Mr.* Diggle, when nobody calls Pa nothin' but always Joe. '*Mr.* Diggle, a hinge has pulled out on the shed door. Would you please be so good as to step over and fix it for me, *Mr.* Diggle?'"

Sue's imitation of Cissie's manner and careful voice, though crude, seemed funny to Matthew in his present mood, and he laughed. Sue giggled with him.

"I was standin' right there back of Pa, but do you think she could see me? She could not. I says, 'What's the matter with you, Cissie, you can't pound a couple nails back in? Your arm broke?' Pa says, 'Shut up, Sue.' All that airy-fairy-queen manner of hers sort of gits him. Makes him randy, I guess. She just looked through me like I wasn't there, but that old fool Pa gits his hammer and traipses back to her place with her. You think she's pretty, don't you?"

"Not so pretty as you." Matthew put an arm around her, drew her to him roughly and kissed her. She squealed and slapped at the hand he was pressing under her breast, but she was obviously delighted. After that they drove in silence for a long time, both moody. Sue let her body sway with the motion of the buggy and once Matthew came out of his reverie to watch her covertly. He rather imagined that Sue's body ruled her, that she gave precedence to its demands in most things. Whatever he might think of that as a way of life, it certainly had its attractions. Feeling those attractions, he rather hastily retreated into the gloom of his thoughts about Cissie and, so to speak, shut the door.

A little farther along Sue pointed a finger that had a semicircle of black under the nail at a small house set near the road. "There's the place."

Though he had passed it many times going and coming from Cissie's, he had never looked at it with curiosity before. Everything about it was far gone in decay. The squat house had never seen paint, and the weathered siding was curled by the heat of the sun. Around the foundations last winter's protection of tar paper-and-manure was still in place. The roof was patched with pieces of rusted tin, one broken windowpane had a rag stuffed in it, and missing pickets gave the fence a toothless look. Debris littered the yard: a broken plow, an earthen milk pan with a piece broken out of it, bottles left where they had been thrown. The doors of a small barn stood open, as did the door of a narrow, slanting outhouse.

Sue sat up straight and cried with surprised delight, "Pa ain't t' hum. He's gone. You hitch and come in. I got some pie and I can make us some coffee iffen the fire's not gone out."

"How do you know your pa's gone?"

"Wagon ain't here. Chain ain't hangin' on the apple tree. Matt, you come on in and set and have some pie."

"Well . . . won't he be coming home pretty soon?"

"Come on, now." She looked at him sidewise through lashes that seemed to be made of delicate wires of gold and bronze. Her full red lips parted in a smile. "I ain't like Cissie," she said with so much confidence that he wondered, slightly shocked, if she could possibly know about the strained relations between himself and Cissie. He hesitated and in that moment his desire to express, positively and defiantly, his resentment at Cissie's behavior got the better of him.

"Is there a place to hitch around back?" he said.

"Yes—only . . ." She hesitated, then said with a wistfulness that in a less selfish mood he might have found touching, "The doctor's rig—you don't have to hide it. You kin leave it right out front for people to see."

"I'll hitch in back."

He turned the horse into a rutted drive where some hens were squatting with their feathers fluffed out in the dust holes they had made. A mongrel dog came out from behind the barn and barked at them. He had wiry yellow hair and a stiff ridge of it was standing up on his neck and back in the way that Matthew thought a wild boar's did. Sue yelled, "You shet," and he stopped his barking and trotted contentedly along beside them, long, dripping tongue hanging down.

Sue flounced herself around on the seat to face Matthew. "You don't hitch out back at Cissie's. I seen you."

"That's different."

"Oh."

He smiled at her to ease what sting she might feel in his words and saw that her face had grown deeply and painfully red. So she was not as coarse and insensitive as he had thought. The discovery disconcerted and burdened him, rather as though he had been given some object to hold that he didn't know how to dispose of. Feeling far less confident in this casual relationship than he had a moment ago, he hitched and took Sue's basket out of the buggy while she watched him in silence.

In silence they went into the small, untidy kitchen where he put the basket on a table and pulled out a chair for himself while she untied the strings of her sunbonnet and hung it on a peg. Still without speaking to him or looking in his direction, she went to the stove, raised a lid, saw that the fire was out and slammed the lid down again.

"Never mind the coffee," he said. "Sue . . ."

"What?"

"Why don't you like Cissie?"

She looked at him then and he saw to his surprise that she was near to tears. Quickly, she turned her back on him and said, "She's stuck-up. I told you that. She thinks Pa and me is common trash."

"Even if it's true that she thinks that"—he thought it well might be—"why should you care?"

Sue had taken a pie out of a cupboard, and she set it down on a shelf with a bang. Still with her back to him she said, "Because she's always had everything I wanted —that's why. Way back in school she was teacher's pet because she'd learned to talk in that refined way she has and all that pale yellow hair. She finished schooling and I didn't. She's somebody in the town—she goes with all the best people—and I—I'm just Pa's daughter." She picked up a knife to cut the pie, and put it down again with force. "And now everybody's sayin' she's goin' to marry you, and she'll be the doctor's lady, and have fine clothes and everthing."

Matthew, staring at her bent back, felt the shock of her words as though someone had pressed a cold, wet sponge to the back of her neck. After a moment Sue began to cut the pie with vicious jabs and to slide the pieces onto plates that she took out of the cupboard. He rose and went to her, took the knife out of her hand and turned her around. She made a sound like a stifled sob and looked up at him with eyes that were swimming with tears.

He said, "You're prettier than Cissie," and he kissed her. When the kiss was finished, she whispered, "Oh, Matt," and pressed herself tightly against him. Before the next kiss he looked past her to find a place to take her and saw through an open door a small room largely filled by an unmade bed. That satisfied him and he gave his whole attention to the kiss.

CHAPTER EIGHT

All this time the weather had, in the Vermont phrase, "held." Golden day had followed golden day, but though the sun shone, it had lost its midsummer redundancy and become thin as though with much wear, and the moment it sank behind the black mass of the mountain a chill took possession of the land. Then one day wind rushing through the pale, stagnant sky tore the thin veil of sunshine and swept it away, making place for torrents of gusty rain. The rain beat and lashed, driving tormented cattle to the woods. Every stream was loud with water, the river's voice was a roar, downspouts gushed and tin roofs drummed. Fires smoked, washings would not dry, bread rose lopsidedly or not at all.

The result of all this noisy fury was much sickness, and Matthew's pleasant leisure was ruined. Every chair in the waiting room was filled with coughing and sniffling citizens whose damp clothing in the heat of the fire in the Franklin stove made the room as steamy as a kitchen on washday. Matthew could do little other than say "Go home and keep out of the wet," but he knew they expected more of him than that, so he gave them pills or powders that he felt fairly sure would do them no harm.

He did not see Cissie and he did not dare to knock on her door. But he drove past her house every day, hoping for a chance meeting that he could make use of to re-establish himself. On these wet expeditions, when the horse splashed through liquid mud, he sat in the middle of the buggy seat to avoid the cold trickles of water that penetrated at the sides, a rubber sheet covering him from dashboard to chin. In this sheet there was a flap-covered slit for the reins to come through, which allowed him to drive with dry hands, but dampness coming in under the buggy's hood blurred his sight when he peered at Cissie's little house as he drove slowly past.

Because of the weather he felt sure she would be at home, but he never saw her, and the door and windows were tightly closed. Once he thought he saw a corner of a curtain move, and he pulled up and waited, rain drumming loudly on the buggy top and water gurgling in the ditches at the side of the road; but nothing more happened and he drove glumly on, only to turn around and come past again. He knew she would see through this performance, and felt that she was probably laughing at him. He did not care. The picture he carried in his mind of her pretty pale face under the cloud of flaxen hair tormented him. Driving along, his brown curls glistening with damp, his amber eyes drawn into slits, he ached for her. He knew, or thought he knew, that she was not really suited to him, that the longing he felt for her was purely physical, but this knowledge did nothing to assuage his feelings. He was in torment.

And when he had passed Cissie's house, turned around and passed it a second time, when he had gone down the road and around the bend, he began to look for Sue's signal that would tell him that Pa had taken refuge from the weather in the town's only tavern, leaving her alone.

The signal they had agreed on was a lamp chimney slipped over the point of a picket in the dilapidated fence —an arrangement that was reasonable in bright weather, for women often put their newly washed chimneys in such a place to dry. In the rain, Sue's one chimney looked forgotten and forlorn.

Sue's house was warm, the windows fogged and steamy, which gave a pleasant sense of the world excluded. Sue herself, Matthew felt, was the perfect antidote for Cissie's heartlessness. Perhaps she suspected, when she lay in his arms on the tumbled bed, that in his mind it was Cissie whom he was holding, for she would often say, "It's me you love, Matt, isn't it? It's really me, isn't it?"

He never answered these importunate questions quite directly, but said, "What do you think?" or gave her some other evasive answer that he hoped would satisfy her and leave him clinging to the tatters of truth.

The signal was there every day during this week of streaming skies. Sometimes, when they were sure that Sue's pa would not soon return, they lay for hours on her bed, loving until they were both exhausted. Sometimes they took risks and indulged in a quick and messy tumble. Once Matthew found her in the barn gathering eggs and took her basket away from her, threw her down on the hay and made love to her in a tangle of skirts. Afterward she lay on her back, her strong, rounded arm raised to reach a shaft of mote-filled sunlight that came through a crack between the boards, amusing herself by making the dust particles swirl and dance. But when she was bored with this she sighed and said with sadness, "I love you, Matt."

He knew she meant it, and he suspected that he was her most intense, most gratifying experience of love. He was vaguely flattered by this feeling of hers, but he felt careless toward it in spite of the savage satisfaction he derived from their lovemaking. He did not think her capable of a deep attachment. He guessed that part of his attraction for her was to be attributed to her pride in the fact that as the town doctor he was one of the elite who would not ordinarily look twice at Joe Diggle's daughter, for she had her own way of being a snob.

After a week of the bad weather, when it began to seem as though there was no other existence but this damp, restricted one, the storm began to break up. First the rain stopped; the downspouts gurgled for a while, and were silent. Then a west wind swept the gray rain clouds away over the mountaintops, and it all happened very swiftly, so that in less than an hour the skies were clear. After that the air grew still and very cold, so that Matthew, walking in the village street, heard people saying to each other, "Black frost tonight."

On the corner, where Main Street makes an L with Maple Street, Matthew met Stoner, whom he had not seen since he had dropped into the bank to add a few dollars of earnings to Dr. Hurd's legacy that lay to his credit there. The banker was wearing red mittens, his rather long nose was blue with cold, and his breath made small bursts of vapor in front of his face when he talked.

"Hullo, Matthew. Black frost tonight, looks like."

"Sure to be," Matthew replied, though he had no knowledge of the subject.

"You got a minute? Want to drop into the bank with me?"

"Glad to."

The bank was a small, almost new building of red brick with tall, stone-capped windows. When Matthew and Stoner went in, the place was empty except for a teller in a cagelike enclosure who was coughing and breaking open rolls of coins by hitting them against the edge of the counter. The cough, the "thwack" of the coin rolls and the clatter of coins cascading into the coin drawer were loud in the stillness. Matthew nodded to the teller, who looked at him with the absent expression of one who is carrying figures in his head.

Stoner led the way to a back room and, shutting the door behind them, motioned to a chair and said, "Sit down, Matthew. Take your coat off, if you like, but this won't take a minute. I have something here that will interest you." He himself sat down before his rolltop desk and began to pull folded papers out of pigeonholes.

In a moment he said, "Here it is," and held one of them out to Matthew. "It's the prospectus of a medical school in Toledo, Ohio. Plenty of schools nearer home, of course— even right here in Vermont—but I happened to hear about this place, so I wrote them, thinking you might be interested. Naturally, I'm not expecting you to leave until Greer gets here, but it's not too soon to begin to look around."

Matthew said, "Thanks," and put it in his pocket without unfolding it. He started to rise but Stoner motioned him down again and tipped his swivel chair back until the spring twanged. He cupped the ends of the chair's arms in his hands and smiled pleasantly.

"Lots of sickness in town, I expect?"

"Quite a bit."

"This cold snap will take care of it. People mostly will be all right now until the spring thaw. Then we'll get it again. Some years the spring thaw used to run Hurd pretty near ragged."

Matthew made no reply. These were preliminaries and he wanted to get them over, for he found to his surprise that he was apprehensive about the unknown subject of this interview. There was a twinkle of amusement in Stoner's eyes when he asked the next question.

"I take it you've never lived in a small town before?"

"No."

"Well, there's things about a small town that don't apply to any other place. I've been wondering if you fully appreciate that yet. For one thing, people always know what's going on, and a doctor especially is sort of in the public eye."

With Sue suddenly uppermost in his mind, Matthew spoke shortly. "What are you getting at?"

Stoner's air of kindly amusement richened. "Matthew, my boy, we all know that you've been seeing a good deal of Cissie Ward." He brought it out with an air of triumph and with a widening of his smile that left Matthew slightly embarrassed and on the defensive.

"Peter has been a very sick kid."

At this Stoner laughed aloud. "Peter's back in school, but every day folks see the doctor's rig heading out that way."

"I haven't been going to the Wards' house lately."

"I know that too. Cissie told me."

Matthew's impulse was to shout, "What business is it of yours?" and to fling himself out of the room. He jerked forward in his chair, grasping the arms in a way that made his elbows protrude in sharp angles. But then his habitual good temper, which usually made him feel that an argument was simply too much bother, came to his rescue. He sighed, settled back and said in an emotionless tone, "We had a quarrel. I'm sorry about it, of course."

"She let me know there was something. In fact I would

say she was both hurt and angry, but she wouldn't talk about it, so I don't know what you quarreled about. I pressed her because I tell you, Matthew, I don't like to see trouble between you two, but perhaps you've discovered Cissie can be a very strong-minded young woman sometimes for all her delicate look."

For a moment Stoner brooded in silence; then he sighed and gave Matthew a look that seemed to confirm the brotherhood of man between them in the face of the trying business of women when they made themselves difficult. "I don't suppose you'd want to tell me what the trouble is, would you, Matthew?"

"No."

"Well. . . . Forgive my asking, but as I say, I hate to see trouble between you two. I'm very fond of Cissie. She's my ward, you know."

"I did know that." For some reason, perhaps because Matthew thought of Cissie solely in relation to himself, he was not altogether pleased to be reminded of this.

"Yes, her father left her in my care before she married. He was my closest friend. Then when young Ward died, I became executor. He didn't leave much, but one day when Ward's father—Peter's grandfather—dies, Cissie will be a rich woman by our standards—or Peter will, which amounts to the same thing."

These confidences embarrassed Matthew, not because nicety of feeling made him regard himself as not entitled to them, but because Cissie had never seen fit to tell him herself. Stoner said, "I am as fond of Cissie as though she were my own child," and waited for Matthew to make some appropriate reply.

Matthew, however, maintained a rather sullen silence, and after a moment Stoner slapped the arms of his chair, the classic and with him habitual way of indicating that an interview was at an end. "Well—I wanted to give you that prospectus. That particular school may not suit you, but it may give you a basis for comparing others."

Stoner rose and Matthew, saying "Thank you, I'll look it over," rose also. They moved, with slight constraint between them, slowly toward the door. With his hand on the doorknob Stoner paused and appeared to consider. Then he gave Matthew a look of such positive satisfaction that it was evident his thoughts pleased him.

"Matthew, my boy, I don't think you've met my family. Wouldn't you like to come and dine with us after church on Sunday?"

Matthew accepted with good grace, though he felt it would require his going to church himself and might interfere with the drive, that had become a ritual, past Cissie's unwelcoming house. Then he was in the banking room under the teller's curious stare and with a feeling of release let himself out and hurried down the steps to the street.

The Stoner house was the largest in the town, and though it had been standing for close to half a century, it could still rate as architecturally the most pretentious. The bricks of which it was made were of the delicate rose color lost by later builders, the trim was gleaming white, and in front of the paneled door with its intricate fanlight was a portico with four white columns in the classic manner. The house stood well back from the street, shaded by elms, and the land at one side sloped down to the Little Torrent River. This land, which was neatly kept lawn, contrasted oddly with the ragged, stony bed of the impetuous little river, and on the lawn there stood a rustic summerhouse or gazebo, which no one ever used, designed in the worst of current taste.

When the heavy latch of the white gate clicked behind Matthew, he paused to survey all this, not because it was new to him since it could all be plainly seen from the street, but in a kind of amused appreciation at finding himself here inside the fence. Then, with a half smile on his good-looking face, and transferring his appreciation to himself as he saw himself in the better of his two new mail-order suits, he went briskly up the walk, lifted the well-polished knocker and let it fall once.

Stoner himself opened the front door, wearing a smile that seemed to say, "Now you see me as I really am, a simple, home man." What he actually did say was "Glad to see you, Matthew. Come in. Come in."

"I hope I'm not late?" Matthew said, though he knew quite well he was not, and entered a hall nearly as chilly as the outdoors, for it was the custom in large houses not to heat rooms in which nobody lingered. Stoner seemed to bear him forward on a wave of good will.

"Not late at all. Here, let me hang up your coat. Cissie is already here."

"Cissie!"

"Yes, a little surprise for you both. She doesn't yet know you are coming. I felt she would find herself not

93

able to maintain the attitude she has taken toward you while she is with us. I very much want to see an end to the misunderstanding between you. Come."

Stoner moved toward a closed door to one of the front rooms, but Matthew continued to stand where he was beside the coat rack. The thought of facing Cissie, after what had passed between them, filled him with acute diffidence, and to gain himself a little time he pretended to look around him admiringly. There was reason enough for it though he was hardly aware of this. The hall was finely proportioned, and from it a curving stairway rose as lightly and airily as a curl of smoke. Light from the fan and the two leaded strips beside the door made the mahogany of a fine pair of tables gleam with warm color. A tall clock near the stairs ticked quietly.

"Nice place you've got here."

Stoner, deflected from his purpose, came back a few steps and surveyed the hall with much the same air of appreciation that Matthew was showing.

"I like it, though I take no credit for it. My father built it in 1820 when there was still good money in merino sheep. My wife thinks it's old-fashioned—keeps fussing at me because it's too plain—not fancy enough, she means. You know how women are. But let's not stand here talking. Mrs. Stoner's in the kitchen overlooking the hired girl, but Cissie and Peter and my son Timothy are all in the parlor, this way."

Cissie was standing beside a center table, turning over the pages of a large album, but it was Cissie in a new guise. The gingham dress, without hoops, in which he was accustomed to see her had been replaced with black, wide and flowing, and banded with widow's crepe. On the back of her head was fastened a cap with a cascade of lace and little bows of black velvet, and under it her pale hair was parted and smoothed.

In the first moment of surprise at her appearance it seemed to Matthew that she had purposely transformed herself into a stranger, that she was deliberately flaunting her widowhood at him, and though almost at the same time he remembered that she had not known she would see him, he felt his face growing red with hurt resentment.

He saw the startled widening of her eyes, the sudden jerk of her shoulders, and then, lips parted, eyes bright with anger, she turned to Stoner. She said nothing, but she could not more plainly have demanded an explanation of him. He gave her none. He merely stood there looking from one to the other with pleased benevolence as though he expected them then and there to rush together in mutual delight.

Her turning to Stoner gave Matthew a second or two in which to recover himself and to be shaken all over again by her loveliness and beyond that by a quality which he had never realized she possessed. Perhaps then he was thinking for the first time of her, and not of himself, and when she turned back to him, her eyes still lit by anger, no resentment was left in him. He took a step toward her and when he spoke to her he was unaware of the desperate earnestness in his voice.

"Cissie."

She turned to the table and carefully shut the album she had been looking at; then she moved away toward the fireplace. Her skirt rustled slightly as she walked. Matthew followed her with hungry eyes, watching her sink into an armchair, her black skirts ballooning around her. He saw, without really seeing, the bright fire of birch logs and Peter, sitting cross-legged on the hearth rug, begin to work himself crabwise closer to his mother's chair. Then Matthew was recalled by Stoner, who touched his arm and said, in a voice made slightly heavy by disappointment at the failure of his scheme, "This is my son Timothy."

Matthew found himself unwillingly shaking the limp hand of a skinny youth of seventeen, or thereabout, who seemed to be having some trouble with his Adam's apple. Young Stoner mumbled something, shoved back a lock of blond hair with the V of his thumb and finger, looked wildly around and departed to a corner of the room where he sat down and stared sternly at the fire as though he disapproved of its exuberant crackling. Matthew watched this not without sympathy, then realized that Stoner was moving away toward a table that held a decanter and small glasses and that he had just asked Matthew if he would have some sherry.

Matthew said "Thanks" hurriedly and Stoner, holding out two glasses said, "Just give one of those to Cissie, will you?"

The glasses were delicate and very full and he carried them across the room with some apprehension. Reflections of the firelight leaped and glowed in the amber liquid. Stepping around Peter, who looked up at him resentfully, as though he half understood what his mother felt, Mat-

95

thew held one of the glasses out to Cissie. "Will you?" he said, his tone sounding of solicitude and trouble.

She took it without a word, but she looked up at him and he thought, though he could not be sure, that the brightness of her eyes might be from tears. It came to him then that recently she had wept a good deal because of him and he was sorry. He was more than sorry—he was appalled—that he had done such a thing to Cissie, who seemed to him so lovely and suddenly so dear. It was a selfless emotion and he was weakened by it, physically weakened, as he had been when he lay on his back on the mound of sand grieving for Dr. Hurd. Moments of this sort of selflessness had been few in his young life, and he had not the skill to cope with them, so that some of what he was feeling, his compunction and self-blame, showed in his face as he held the glass out to Cissie.

She took it with a hand that trembled slightly for she saw and understood what he was feeling and it took away from her the support of her resentment. For a moment they were completely vulnerable, the one toward the other. Then, in an attempt to retreat into less disturbing, more normal feelings, she made a pretense of composure and raised the glass to sip from it. A drop spilled on her skirt. He quickly set his own glass on the mantelshelf and bent over her.

"Cissie..."

She rubbed the spot with the heel of her left hand and said as though she had scarcely enough breath to form the words, "You shouldn't have come here, Matthew."

"I didn't know you were here, but I'd have come anyway, you know that. Cissie, I've got to talk to you. Can I drive you home?"

"Timothy is going to drive me."

The instant when they had defenselessly confronted one another was over, and he could almost see the memory of the hurt and anger of their last meeting flooding back on her. A moment ago she had been close to him; now she was hopelessly far away with all the barriers between them once more. He sighed and straightened up, took his glass and leaned against the mantelshelf. Peter, on the floor at his feet, regarded him with a steady, thoughtful stare. "Hullo," Matthew said, trying to sound friendly. Peter turned his head away with a child's proud reserve that can be so disconcerting to a grownup, and Matthew was hurt unreasonably.

From across the room Stoner, who was making imaginary business at a side table, seemed to be aware of silence, glanced at them over his shoulder, and frowned at what he saw. Mercifully at that moment the door opened and Mrs. Stoner came in, and Stoner said heartily, "Well, well, I hope you've come to tell us dinner's ready. That was an extraordinarily hungry sermon we had this morning. Matilda, this is Dr. Chapin. Matthew, my wife."

Mrs. Stoner was a short and dumpy woman, her face set, like a molded pudding, into folds of worried preoccupation. She answered Matthew's greeting inaudibly, without quite looking at him, and he realized to his astonishment that, like the Hulls, she was shy of strangers and ill at ease. He had no time for further impressions for there was a general movement in the room, everyone standing and going toward the door.

CHAPTER NINE

They went together into the chilly hall, then into the warmth of the dining room at the back of the house. This was a sullen room, composed of dark greens and dismal browns, a room so placed that the sunlight stopped at the windows, never entering through the panes. It depressed still further Matthew's already gloomy spirits. Cissie seemed to take a hold on herself and to walk with a degree of self-possession that he envied and could not for the life of him imitate. Again and again he searched his mind for something to say, and when he did succeed in bringing out a remark, the talk had either moved on to something else or what he said sounded to him extraordinarily puerile. He ended by keeping silent, suffering from a self-consciousness that was a new experience to him and that made him thoroughly miserable. He could not take his eyes off Cissie and her charm, her unfamiliar dress. Her air of being at home in this household added to his unhappiness. She was like a stranger to him. All this time she never turned to him, or spoke to him directly. He might not have been there for any notice that she took of him, and yet he felt that she was deeply aware of him and underneath her easy talk she was continually thinking about him with a troubled mind. It was as though they both struggled to communicate in this silent way, and his feeling that she wanted to reach him grew more and more urgent until it was almost unendurable.

The long, slow dinner grew to be a nightmare to him. Stoner's heavy sprightliness, Mrs. Stoner's whispered conferences with the hired girl, young Timothy's self-conscious pose of boredom and Peter's shrill interjections grew to be something like torture. His suffering became so settled a state that the end of the meal came as a shock of surprise and he felt a panic unreadiness for what might happen next.

"Well," Stoner said, slapping the arms of his chair and pushing himself away from the table. He rose, giving them all in turn his benevolent smile. Young Timothy mumbled something and fled. Mrs. Stoner led Peter toward the kitchen, promising a second plate of pudding. Slowly and in silence Stoner and Cissie and Matthew moved out into the hall and down its chilly length, Cissie still rustling gently and, it seemed to Matthew, reproachfully. He followed close behind her, in the grip of a paralyzing conviction that his whole life was hanging in the balance.

Then they were in the parlor and Matthew stood near the door, as preoccupied as though he were alone. Stoner went to the fireplace, threw a birch log on the embers, watched the sparks for a moment and went back to Cissie.

"Cecilia . . ."

Matthew, startled, gaped at him, his mind, made sluggish by food and trouble, failing to connect this name, which he had never heard, with Cissie.

"Cecilia, my dear, I have some letters to write. Will you forgive me if I leave you for a little while?"

It was, of course, a conspiracy of the Stoners. Matthew recognized that. He heard her say, "Yes, Uncle Ed," in a faint, breathy voice that betrayed to Matthew that she was perturbed, as unprepared to be alone with him as he with her. Then the door closed behind Stoner, and Matthew's uncertainties vanished. He could hold his feelings in check no longer. With arms held out to her he cried, *"Cissie!"*

All that he knew he felt for her, and a great deal that was so deep inside of him that he was just discovering it was there, burst out of him with the cry. But Cissie's back was already turned to him and she was moving, with that rustling of her skirts that was like the sound of a soft wind in dried leaves, toward the chair by the side of the fire. Instead of sitting in it, however, she stood behind it, her hands on its back. She spoke softly, in a voice that neither pleaded nor ordered, with a word that was only the beginning of a sentence, and stopped there.

"Matthew . . ."

He came to stand in front of her, the chair between them. All his unhappiness was in his face, and his feelings were busy trying to join the Cissie he thought he knew, the little country girl in her gingham dress and gentle, appealing ways, with this altogether different, silk-clad, self-possessed young woman, and he could find nothing to say. He kept silent, watching the firelight making shifting lights and shadows on her, the graceful curve of her bent head under the lace of her cap, the delicate, almost fragile-looking hands gripping the chair's back.

She seemed to be searching for words to express what she had clearly made up her mind to say. After a pause she raised her head and gave him a direct, candid look. Her gray eyes were not soft and misty, as he had so often seen them, but clear with purpose.

"Matthew, I want you to understand that this is Uncle Ed's doing. I didn't know that you were going to be here."

"I suppose you wouldn't have come if you had!"

She thought about this with more seriousness than the petulance of the remark called for; then her thoughts made her flush. "No, I think not."

He shoved his hands in his pockets and kicked at the edge of the hearth rug. Then he took his hands out again and came a step nearer her.

"Cissie, I was out of my head about you. I still am. I'm beginning to think I always will be. I didn't mean any 'disrespect,' as you called it, by what I said to you, or did, that last time we were together. I wasn't thinking about that at all. I just knew that I was crazy about you, that I'd never felt like that about any woman before, and I thought—I was sure—you loved me too. I didn't think about anything else. I didn't realize that you wanted . . ."

He knew he was growing incoherent and he felt entirely unable to put his feelings into words. He gave up trying and stared at her with darkened, brooding eyes in which there showed a good deal of hurt resentment. Her hands on the chair back tightened and the flush deepened.

"I did love you, Matthew. I wasn't ashamed of it."

"Are you now?" he said miserably.

"I don't want to be." She drew herself up and looked at him fairly. "No, I'm not. There was nothing wrong about the way I loved you and I won't blame myself for it. But I blame myself for not realizing . . . I'm older than you are, Matthew, and I should have understood—though I never knew anyone like you. When people are in love they are married. I thought we were in love and that you were going to ask me to marry you, Matthew."

"Cissie, we were in love. I still am—I'm just beginning to realize now how much. But does love always have to mean marriage?"

She made a small movement of distress and he answered it as though she had spoken.

"Yes, I suppose for you it does. The way you've been brought up—the way Haddon looks at those things. But, Cissie, I thought you understood that I have two years of medical school ahead of me and then I have to find some place to practice and get established there."

She cried out in surprise, "I thought you were going to practice here in Haddon."

"I never said so. I don't think I'd want to live all my life in a small town. But that's not what we're talking about."

"No, that's not what we're talking about." She sighed and seemed to give the chair back more of her weight to support.

"I thought you knew I wasn't in any position to think about getting married. And I'll be honest—I wasn't thinking about it. I don't think it ever occurred to me, because I couldn't marry with all that ahead of me. But we loved each other, and I didn't see any reason why we couldn't be together to any extent that loving each other made us want to be. I'm damned if I do now."

"Oh, Matthew!"

"Listen, Cissie, there's nothing in a thing like that that either of us would need to be ashamed of. Quite the contrary. I've had women before, but . . ."

She bent over the chair back so that he was not able to see her face. After a moment she began to stroke the pile of the material, concentrating on it as though it took thought. He watched her, fretting inwardly, until she again gripped the edges of the chair back and looked at him directly.

"You expected us to be lovers until you went away, but

you didn't expect it to last beyond that, did you, Matthew? Answer me truthfully. It was just to last until you left, wasn't it?"

He moved away from her to the fireplace, where he put his arm on the mantelshelf and his forehead on his arm. After a pause he said, speaking to the fire at his feet, "I'm afraid that's true, Cissie. I'm beginning to think differently now."

They were silent then for a long time, both of them standing very still. When she spoke it was with a gentleness that made him turn and look at her.

"You think I'm a prude, Matthew, and perhaps I am. I couldn't live with you as a lover and keep my self-respect or the kind of standing I value in Haddon, and I wouldn't do it anyway because of Peter. You don't shock me by the way you feel about it, or at least you don't shock me any more now that I've had time to think about it. But there's a good deal more than prudery involved. The kind of relationship you wanted just isn't good enough. If there isn't to be a lasting, durable love, with tenderness and consideration for each other, in which we would share everything that happens in life—if we aren't to have that, I don't want anything at all."

Suddenly she clenched her hand and began to strike the chair back, and her voice rose. "Do you hear me? If we're not to have that, I don't want anything at all. I love you, I'm not afraid to tell you so. I love you. And I don't want anything second best. I never want to see you again, do you hear? Never, never!" She turned her back on him, covered her face with her hands and burst into stormy weeping.

He came away from the fire and stood near her, not speaking to her or watching her but standing with his head down, scarcely aware of the weeping but lost in a tremendous upheaval of thought. Her tears slackened to heartbroken sobs. She sought blindly in her sleeve for a handkerchief and turned away, wiping at her eyes. Still he did not raise his head. Finally in a stifled voice she said, "Why don't you go away?"

He started as though he had forgotten her presence, glanced at her with eyes clouded by trouble, and walked away to the far side of the room. He stayed there a long time. When he came back he was walking purposefully, his clenched hands swinging at his sides.

He found her bent over, giving elaborate attention to

arranging the folds of her skirt that needed no arranging, and keeping her face hidden from him. He spoke to her with all the strength of a new decision, so that without intending it he sounded stern.

"Cissie, when I finish medical school, will you marry me?"

She made a sound, inarticulate and not at all romantic, an ugly little sound midway between a gulp and a choke. Then she turned her back on him completely. He went to her and not very gently took her in his arms. He put his hand on the side of her face and turned it up to him. She gave him one frantic, frightened look, then she shut her eyes. Her long lashes were lying on her cheeks stuck together in points by her tears, her face was smeared and puffy from weeping, her mouth still trembled. He kissed her.

CHAPTER TEN

During the morning office hours there had been few patients, but, as was always the case, they had left behind them a disturbance of the room's atmosphere. Over the arm of a chair still hung someone's forgotten muffler, a dismal, knitted brown thing. A little girl, wearing an asafoetida bag on a string around her neck, had kicked her heels here for half an hour and the bag's outrageous odor still haunted the senses. Dusty footprints on the rug, chairs out of place, cigar ash spilled on a tabletop—the influence of these things would not be dissipated until later in the day when Mrs. Hull had swept, dusted, tidied and aired. Even then the room would seem to keep a trace of its public use until evening came and lamps were lighted. Now not one thing or the other—between its two employments, so to speak—it was at its very worst.

On the off chance that another patient might arrive, Matthew was still there. He had drawn a chair close to the Franklin stove to catch the warmth of the dying fire. He was sitting with his feet on the fender to keep them above the floor draft that, though the trees had not yet lost their leaves to the winter winds, or snows turned the tops of the mountains white, was nevertheless uncomfortably noticeable. He was reading with care the prospectus of the Toledo medical school, a flimsy thing, printed in poor type, and because he had no experience of such things, the lengthy, ornate phrases, that seemed to him fine and informative, were telling him less than he realized.

He discovered that before he could be permitted to join what the prospectus called the "select group of high-principled and dedicated young men that form the student body," he would have to meet three requirements. He must have a letter of recommendation from a clergyman, a hundred dollars for each of the two years of the course, and a reading and writing knowledge of English. This seemed surprisingly easy, almost disappointingly so. He felt that to join such a company, something as difficult as a needle's eye would be more suitable.

In smaller type it was explained that of the hundred dollars, five was for matriculation, and presumably went to the owner of the school, a Dr. Burnett. The rest was to be paid in small and varying amounts to the professors. There was a graduation fee, twenty dollars; a fee for a diploma, ten dollars; and six dollars for something called a hospital ticket. Room and board were not included but Matthew, shutting his eyes and leaning his head back as an aid to mental arithmetic, thought the cost of that might be somewhere near twenty-five dollars a month. He took a pencil out of his pocket and did some figuring on the margin of the prospectus, adding everything together, and the result pleased him.

On the second page, in fancy lettering, was a list of the subjects to be taught, and though they were few, they sounded formidable enough to make him uneasy. They were surgery, medicine, materia medica, chemistry, therapeutics, biology, anatomy, and diseases of women and children. All these subjects would be taught by lecture, and the lectures on anatomy would be supplemented by work in the dissecting room. There were, it stated, "hospital connections," though what that meant was not clear to Matthew.

The second year appeared to be an exact repetition of the first, though this was not fully stated. At the end, students who passed their examinations would receive their degrees and could practice—subject to the licensing laws, if any, of their chosen states.

The rest of the prospectus was given to an encomium of the school, flowery in phrasing and worthless in content. Matthew read it conscientiously. The last line was printed in bold type, and read: **"Students!!! The School Year opens the third Monday in October and ends the first Monday in March. Welcome All!!"**

Below this was a sort of footnote, an afterthought in type so small and blurred that Matthew got up and took it to the window to read. It stated that ordinarily a small charge would be made for a body used in the dissecting room, but under certain circumstances students could avoid payment. This was vague enough to be intriguing. The paragraph went on to say that anxious parents need have no concern about the source of the bodies. "They come from afar, from the dregs of society, the criminals and paupers. In our dissecting room these poor wretches vindicate their existence by contributing to science, a fact that no doubt counts in their favor when they stand for Judgment before the throne of the Almighty."

On this pious note the prospectus ended. Matthew put it away in a drawer, and then he sighed, for during the reading of it he had left behind the problems and limitations of his life in Haddon. They were now with him once more. He pulled out his watch, saw that it was close to noon when no more patients need be expected. He went into the bedroom, poured water in the bowl and washed his face and hands, sniffing at his fingers afterward because of a nervous notion that the smell of asafoetida might still be clinging to them. Then he went around to the Hulls' back door and in to dinner.

The Hulls were, as usual, silent, but there was a suppressed liveliness in Hull's manner, and Mrs. Hull's eyes were so bright when she glanced at him from under her dusty lashes that he wondered if news of his engagement to Cissie could have reached them so soon. He thought he saw the same knowledge in the faces of those he passed in the street on his way to the livery stable, and it made him uncomfortable but at the same time elated, so that he went along with a buoyant, heel-ringing stride.

The day was fine; the sun where it touched the frozen grass was just warm enough to melt the hoarfrost that, in shadow, still cloaked it in silvery, shimmering white. Thin patches of ice on the road, that would be puddles later in the day when the sun reached them, shattered under the wheels into sharp, glasslike splinters. The water under the bridge, that was black with cold, sounded loudly in the bodiless air, and close to the banks where the current was quieter ice had begun to form. The iron rims of the wheels rattled on the loose planks of the bridge, exciting the horse into a brisk trot, and white vapor streamed back from his distended red nostrils.

Beyond the bridge, where the voice of the river could no longer be heard, the fields and woods were quiet with cold, still and waiting. The bare branches of the maple trees, from which the sap had retreated into the roots, were black and brittle; the yellow larch spires burned like slim, tall flames. Here the horse slowed to a walk, and Matthew, himself affected by the frozen stillness, was content with the torpid pace. A rabbit bounded across the road in front of them and plunged into the weeds, from where it watched with palpitating sides. The strokes of a distant church bell struck like beating wings at the clear air.

Sue's house came into sight, shabby and squat but sparkling with hoarfrost, a cottage in a fairy tale. And there, on a picket of the broken fence, was the lamp chimney. It gave Matthew a strange feeling to see it, for in the turmoil of his thoughts since dining at the Stoners' the day before, he had not once remembered Sue.

He found that he could think about her now with kindly willingness to make allowances for all that had taken place, and in this he included himself. Their transgressions seemed to him remote, and he felt only forgiveness toward them. He would not be seeing Sue again. Smiling reminiscently, he studied the house as he might a picture in an album that stirred amusing memories of events that had no bearing on today. This benevolent detachment from his own actions was a new experience for him and it gave him a pleasing impression of his own maturity. He felt he would always look back on Sue with tolerant good will and that this was right, and praiseworthy, and freed him from blame.

It was then that he saw a curtain at a front window move a little, and it brought him back to the present with uncomfortable suddenness. For the first time it occurred to him that she might have been watching for him, might be expecting him to turn the horse in through the gate. There was also the possibility, which he had not so far considered, that she might somehow have heard the news about himself and Cissie, in which case she would be harboring all sorts of bitter thoughts about him. In any circumstances a meeting with her was the last thing he wanted. Tingling with nervous discomfort at the mere thought of it, he slapped the reins on the horse's back and left the scene at a brisk trot.

Down a side road he caught sight of a small brick schoolhouse, a curl of woodsmoke rising from the chimney, and saw in his imagination the closely seated, wriggling young bodies, a fat stove sending out waves of heat, steamed windows and an atmosphere thick with many odors. Peter would be among the children trapped in there. The thought was a pleasing one and he lolled in the corner of the buggy, enjoying the prospect of Cissie alone. The sun, risen higher, gave an illusion of warmth; the day, still and clear, was of the sort that frees the mind to range far, so that the illusion of activity is there without disturbance of the body's tranquility. Matthew, immobile in his corner, was leading in his thoughts so energetic and constructive a future life that when Cissie's house came into view, recalling him to the present, he discovered that he was actually fatigued, his muscles cramped and stiff.

Cissie's house too wore a plume of smoke, and he turned into the drive feeling a sense of satisfaction as strong as though the ending of their quarrel were all his doing. Youth and his own temperament served to sustain in him, for the greater part of the time, a conviction of the world's rightness, and as he stretched his cramped legs, leaping over the buggy's side, he was on the very crest.

He half expected Cissie to run out joyfully to meet him, but the door remained shut. He announced himself by pounding on it thunderously, in an excess of good spirits, and without waiting for an answer, he depressed the latch and threw it open. A wave of warm air, damp and smelling of soapy water, met him and enveloped him as he went inside. Cissie, wearing an old cotton dress with the sleeves rolled up, was standing in front of the sink with her hands in a dishpan while near her a black iron teakettle on the stove was sending up a jet of steam from its spout. She cried out when she saw him, "Why, Matthew!" and a warm color came into her face.

In the old gray dress, its skirt hanging limply close to her body, her hair in an undisciplined pale cloud, she presented a picture so unlike the Cissie he had last seen that when he had shut the door, he leaned against it and laughed aloud. She seized a dish towel and began quickly drying her hands and he straightened himself, went to her, took the towel out of her hands and drew her into his arms. "You knew I'd come, didn't you?" he said, holding her close to him. She was not wearing stays, and under her clothing her body felt so slight and warm, her bones so small and fragile, that it was like holding a live bird. He bent and kissed her gently. Then inspired, he held her close and kissed her hungrily. She struggled to free herself, pushing at his chest with her hands.

"No, Matthew, please. Not like that."

"Be good, will you?"

"Please let me go."

"Don't you love me?"

"Yes, but . . ."

"All right, then, behave."

He forced her to let him kiss her again. It was a long, demanding kiss and after a moment she gave up struggling and went limp in his arms as though the kiss had drawn all the vitality out of her. He loosened his hold on her and she almost fell.

"I want you, Cissie."

"No, no."

"Why not?"

She stepped back from him, raised her arms and began to pin up her loosened hair. He watched her, eyes half shut, with brooding intensity. In a moment she let her arms fall as though their weight burdened her. A look of sadness darkened the gray of her eyes, and she sighed.

"You're not really going to medical school, are you, Matthew?"

"Certainly I am."

"But—oh, come and sit down and let's talk about it. Do you want some coffee? I think it's still hot."

"Please."

He sat in an armchair with a woven seat and, legs thrust out in front of him, watched her take a cup and saucer off a cupboard shelf, dip some cream from the top of the milk in a tin pail with a long-handled ladle, and fill the cup with coffee. She brought it to him with a bowl of crushed loaf sugar.

"Thanks," he said, drawing in his legs and taking it from her. He smiled because she was enjoying this little domestic scene and because he was finding it pleasant to be waited on. She tipped the sugar bowl toward him and he helped himself liberally. As she carried the bowl back to the cupboard she said over her shoulder, "There isn't any real need for you to go at all, you know."

"If I don't I have to give up the money that's being held for me, the money Dr. Hurd left me."

"That wouldn't matter. We'd get on all right. I doubt if any of the doctors in this part of the state have degrees, and anyway, nobody ever even thinks about whether they have or not."

She came back and stood looking down at his big body, sprawled sidewise in the chair, as gracefully relaxed as a large animal's. He gave her an upward glance from his glowing yellow eyes, which were so like a cat's when a bird is near that she laughed a little nervously, backed away from his dangerous vicinity and sat herself in a chair facing his, demurely eyeing him. He drained his cup, and with a grunt because he had to reach so far, he put it on the seat of the wooden settle.

"Oh, we'd get along. It isn't that." He spoke carelessly, but his tomcat look was taking in her feminine consciousness of herself. Then, deliberately ignoring it, he straightened himself up and spoke seriously. "I *want* to go, Cissie."

"Oh." She kept silent for a moment and then she said a trifle plaintively, "Why, Matthew?"

"Because, my God, it's an opportunity that shouldn't be missed. It's a chance to learn something about something I really like. Surgery. You don't think I'd be content to be a country doctor all my life, do you? Setting broken arms or sewing up some fool that's let his hatchet slip, or draining abscesses on smelly old women? Not on your life. I want to be somewhere where real surgery is being done. I want to do it myself—and not on a kitchen table. I want to work in a real operating amphitheater and get to be so damn good at it that I'm one of the best."

He stopped speaking and sat gripping the arms of his chair, his mind filled with the future. Cissie made no attempt to reply, and gradually it was borne in on him by her silence that what he had said had been a shock to her. She had, it seemed to him, a stricken look. She sat so straight and still, her hands pressed together between her knees, her wide eyes darkened to the color of rain-filled skies, that he was touched by compunction.

"I'm sorry, Cissie."

"I hadn't thought of it like that, Matthew. I didn't know it meant so much to you."

"Does it matter that it does?"

She thought about this for a moment, sitting bent over with an invisible load on her shoulders; then she shook her head. "No, it doesn't. It just takes a little getting used to, that's all, and I hadn't thought about not living in Haddon. But, Matthew, I want you to be like that." Her voice rose a little. "I love you to be like that." Suddenly she jumped up and came to him and dropped to her knees in front of him. She laid her hands on his knees and looked up at him. "I just hope I can live up to you, that's all. I'll try. Oh, Matthew, I'll try. I love you so."

"Then prove it." He spread his knees and drew her between them close to him.

She came willingly. "I'll do the very best I possibly can, always, always."

"No, I mean prove it now, Cissie."

Startled, she sat back on her heels and stared at him.

"If I'm not going to waste a year, I'll have to start school right away. I'll have to leave very soon. And I'm going to be away a long time. I want you now, before I go. I want you right now." He reached for her and took her by the shoulders to pull her back to him.

She grasped his wrists tightly. "No, no. It wouldn't be right."

"Why not, if you love me?"

"It would spoil our married life together, can't you see?"

"No, I can't."

"But it's true, Matthew. I know it is."

"How do you know?"

"I just know, that's all. We'd always have the knowledge that we did wrong. We'd never escape that knowledge."

"Oh, ———." He used a word that made her close her eyes in pain. "The trouble with you is, you don't trust me."

"I do. You know I do. I wouldn't be marrying you if I didn't."

"It's how we feel about each other that counts, Cissie. Nothing else matters at all. Can't you understand that? I'm going away for a long time. I want to be sure of you."

"Then marry me and I'll go with you."

"That wouldn't be fair to you, or to me. Or to Peter," he added as an afterthought. She looked as though she might be going to cry and he said, "Cissie, do you want me to come back again?"

"Why, of course. What do you mean?"

"I mean you're not fair to me, that's what I mean. You're not fair to me and you don't trust me."

Even as he said these words, he had an uneasy half-memory of having said them before on other occasions. "You don't love me," he finished sullenly. He had begun to dislike this scene.

But she was deeply moved, and spoke with a desperate anxiety to be believed. "I do, Matthew," she cried. "You know I do."

"No you don't. If you did, you'd prove it." And having accomplished this age-old way of putting her in the wrong, he sat back and regarded her with gloomy austerity.

She was weeping, the tears running down her cheeks, while she clutched at him, her contorted face raised to him imploringly.

"Matthew, I love you more than I've ever loved anyone in the world. You must believe me, Matthew, you *must*."

He leaned forward and took her face between his hands. He said with fierce intensity, "Then show me. Show me."

She stopped weeping, a long shudder went through her body, and he took his hands away from her face. She shut her eyes and sat back on her heels. Her mouth was trembling and she was breathing in hurried little gasps. He watched her, smiling, a gleam of triumph in his eyes. It was a shoddy scene, redeemed only by her earnestness, and he half knew he should feel ashamed of it. He watched her now with growing gentleness. She drew a long sigh and straightened herself. Her eyes were still tightly closed but her face was shining with resolution and sacrifice as, head held high, she whispered, "All right, Matthew." Then she collapsed against him and held her lips to be kissed.

He made the kiss light and tender, and when it ended he brushed back her pale hair with a gentle touch. Then he felt for the buttons on the back of her dress and began fumblingly to unfasten them.

He had loosened her dress to the waist when there was a sound outside, the scratch of a foot on the slab of stone that served as a doorstep. Startled, they both looked in that direction, but before either one of them could change position the door burst open and Sue was standing there. Sue's red-bronze hair was in shining disorder, her eyes hot, her mouth wide-open as though she were about to scream.

For a moment she stood in the doorway taking them in, almost incandescent with anger. Then she laughed. It was a loud and ugly sound that tore at their nerves. Cissie clutched at Matthew, who closed his hand over her arm without taking his eyes off the girl in the doorway. Sue advanced farther into the room, breathing hard. *"You!"* she yelled, making a wide gesture with her arm that had the effect of sweeping Cissie away, and thrust the upper part of her body forward. *"You!"* she repeated, glaring at Cissie, and lowered her head as though she were about to launch a physical attack, her hands balled into fists. "You disgusting little bitch!"

Cissie struggled to her feet, hampered by her skirt, stepping on it and nearly falling. She began to retreat, and her dress, unbuttoned down the back, fell off her shoulder. She clutched at it. Sue tossed her head up in triumphant fury.

"I thought so! I thought this was what I'd find! Look at you with your clothes half off, and if I'd come a moment later I'd have found them all off, wouldn't I? Cissie Ward, who always pretended to be such a lady with such fine airs! Now you listen to me. I'm going to tell you something."

Matthew heaved himself out of his chair. "Shut up, Sue," he said in a tone that attempted reasonable patience.

"You shut up." Sue was screaming, using the full volume of her voice and more, so that her words rasped in her throat and almost choked her. "You shut right up, Matt Chapin, do you hear?"

She advanced on Cissie again, but Cissie had retreated as far as she could go and was standing now with the settle at her back, caught and forced to face her enemy. Sue went to stand in front of her and thrust her face close to Cissie's.

"Pa just come home and told me what he heard to the village. He heard you think you're getting married to *him.*" Sue jerked her head in Matthew's direction. "That's what *you* think, maybe, you stupid little fool. Letting him love you up and puttin' it out you're goin' to git married when it's me all the time, do you hear? It's me. It's my bed he's been in and I bin lovin' him like a real woman should, like a weak, washed-out little thing doesn't know how. I tell you, Cissie Ward—"

The slap was sudden, and the smacking sound it made stopped Sue and shocked her into silence. There was a moment of frozen stillness, an appalling vacuum without

111

thought or emotion. Out of it Sue emerged raging. She let out a yell that was like an animal's and plunged at Cissie.

What happened then happened fast and with so much action that Matthew saw only a blur of arms and thrashing bodies, a tangle of skirts and flying hair. And he yelled too: *"Hey!"*

The battle went right on with concentrated intensity and in grim silence except for thumps, sharp, hard blows on flesh, the sound of ripping cloth and the harsh rasping sound of desperate breathing. He yelled again: *"Hey, for Christ sake!"*

He advanced on this whirling melee and somehow managed to grab Sue in one hand, Cissie in the other, and to tear them apart. For a moment there was a respite and the two fighters stood still, panting. Then Sue recovered herself and made a lunge for Cissie. Matthew jerked her back roughly.

"Quit it, you two. That's enough. More than enough," he added, looking from one to the other. Their hair was down, the torn top of Cissie's dress had fallen to her waist. She was breathing in sharp, shallow gasps and Sue's full bosom was heaving.

"Let me go," Cissie said in a high, squeaky voice. Matthew released her but he kept a tight hold on Sue's upper arm and through her sleeve he felt the heat of her body and the *thud-thud* of her heart shaking her. Cissie took a step backward and with both hands pushed her fallen hair away from her face and gathered up her skirt which was torn out at the waist and trailing on the floor. Then she put her head up proudly and looked at Sue, her gray eyes cold with scorn.

"It's true I'm going to marry Matthew. I love him and he loves me. That other thing is all lies. It's every bit lies. He wouldn't have anything to do with a thing like you. The whole village knows about you, Sue Diggle. Matthew wouldn't touch you. Would you, Matthew? Tell her."

"Jesus," Matthew said. "Listen, I—"

Sue cut him short, glaring at Cissie, her underlip fiercely thrust out. "That's what you think, you stupid little fool. All right, *you* tell her, Matthew. Tell her how every day when you leave here you come to me. Tell her how I bin puttin' the lamp chimney out on the picket to signal when Pa ain't to home and you can have me all to yourself. Just tell her."

"Matthew!" Cissie's cry was pure agony.

Sue plunged ruthlessly on. "So you believe me now, do you? You'd better. Look at him. Just look at him."

This was exactly what Cissie was doing, and the look in her eyes, at first incredulous, was slowly changing to shocked horror. Matthew released Sue's arm and ran his fingers through his curls, clawing at them in desperation. He made a wide outward gesture with his arms.

"Listen, girls—"

Sue turned on him ferociously. "Listen nothing. I've had enough of you and your sneaking, underhand, deceitful ways. After what I seen when I come in here I wouldn't let you touch me with a ten-foot pole. I'm not one to take anybody's leavin's. I wouldn't dirty myself, Mr. fake-doctor Matthew Chapin."

Cissie had begun to tremble, her thin body jerking uncontrollably. She was obviously near the edge of a breakdown. Matthew turned to face her and she clutched at her torn dress as though to protect herself from his eyes. "You'd better go home," she said in a tight voice that had the beginnings of hysteria in it.

"Jesus, yes. I wish I was back in the war." He looked from one to the other, hunched his shoulders up in a shrug that was meant to salvage the remnants of his dignity, and turned away. *"Women!"* he said in a tone of concentrated bitterness, and made for the door in long strides. He went out and slammed the door with force, and at once was reminded by the cold air that struck him that he had left his coat behind. He jerked the door open again, and, careful not to look in the direction of the two women, he snatched it up and made a second ignominious exit, his ears filled with Sue's coarse, hateful laughter.

He was not to escape so easily. Halfway to the buggy he heard the door open again with a crash. He did not turn around. The sound itself told him that it was Sue who had done the opening, and he thought or imagined he heard from inside Cissie's loud weeping. Sue filled her lungs and shouted. "Bastard!" she yelled. "I'll see the whole town knows, you dirty, stinking bastard!"

III
Toledo

CHAPTER ELEVEN

Matthew arrived in Toledo the day before school opened, in time to find himself a room to live in and to have a look at the school building from the outside. The room was up four flights of wooden stairs, and he had not occupied it an hour before he realized that the constant clatter of other students going up and down would become the accompaniment of all his thoughts. There were two windows in the room that looked down on a flourishing ailanthus tree in the back yard. The bed, which was too short for him, was furnished with a lumpy straw mattress that rustled and a quilt that was soiled around the edges. There was a gas ring that, judging by the spots on the wall behind, had been much used for cooking, a washstand, a small chest of drawers, an ink-stained table, a chair, and a small stove. The table rocked when Matthew put his hand on it, so his first act in his new home was to fix it with a piece of cardboard torn from the top of a box of matches. That done, he opened his bag—or rather, one of Dr. Hurd's old bags—and his blanket roll, which were all he had brought with him in the haste of his departure from Haddon. He put his few possessions in the chest of drawers or hung them on pegs on the wall. Then he set out to locate the school.

He knew it was nearby and he found it two blocks away and a short block inward from the dreary expanse of Lake Erie. It was a square, two-story brick building, as plain as a prison and as ugly. There were no other buildings crowding it, for this was the outskirts of the town, and a medical school is always an unpopular neighbor. One entered the school by double doors at the top of a high flight of steps that cleared a large semibasement. The windows of this basement had been whitewashed on the inside to prevent anyone from looking through, and this gave rise to all sorts of rumors and macabre imaginings about what went on there. This and the school's comparative isolation made it, in people's minds, a place of dread and horror. The double doors above the steps were meant to be impressive, with their large brass handles and rounded tops. They had originally been painted white, but the contact of countless hands around the handles had dirtied them and spoiled their pretentiousness. At present they were shut, and the unoccupied look of the rest of the premises made Matthew abandon his intention of going inside to look around. Instead, he stood on the path that did duty for a sidewalk and looked up at all this.

Shoddy and ugly as this building was, he looked at it almost with awe, and felt that he was close to the heart of American medicine, though he had no idea what the past achievements and present standards of medicine might be. He knew nothing of the quality of the teaching he would find here and did not realize that he had no means of comparison and so could not judge if it were good or bad. He did not think to take into account that all of the impressions he had formed, of both the science and the art of medicine, had been given to him by one man. And so, feeling on the brink of great things, he stood there and solemn thoughts filled him.

Awe, however, is one of the least durable of the emotions. After a while it left him and he became aware of feeling rather flat and without any idea of what he should do next. He turned his back on what had so moved him and wandered over to the long pipe railing that stood by the side of the road and was intended for the hitching of horses. He sat down on this and put his hands in his pockets to keep them warm, though the air was more damp than chill. Across vacant lots on either side of the school building he could see the water of the lake, bleak and gray as the sky above, its surface heaving as though in restless discontent.

There was not another person in this dreary scene, but a yellow-and-black dog was sniffing around the base of a tree. He looked happy and busy and Matthew whistled to him, but the dog only raised his head, stared at him in a preoccupied way, and trotted off. Matthew sighed and rose, felt himself spat upon by a few malignant drops of rain, and raised his head to gaze resentfully at the sky. Then he too wandered off. He spent that evening in town, had a few drinks in a gloomy saloon, saw a burlesque show that bored him, had some more drinks and went back to his room at the top of the thunderous stairs. Throughout all this he was most careful not to think about anything at all, but Cissie and all that had happened between them crowded the spaces beyond his conscious mind.

The next morning he ate breakfast at the boardinghouse —about twenty other students seemed to be living there— but without making friends with anybody. Some were too noisy, others inclined to be reserved and silent, a difference which he assumed to be the distinction between newcomers and those who had already spent a year in the school. Most of them seemed younger than himself, though he suspected they were not, and that it was only his experience of the war that gave him this impression. Their seeming youthfulness contributed to his desire to hold himself aloof.

When, after breakfast, he went back to the school, the empty scene had come to life. Two or three horses hitched to buggies were tied to the rail; here and there windows in the school had been thrown up. The doors were open and young men were going up and down the steps or standing in groups below, talking in loud, cheerful voices. By and large they did not seem to Matthew a prepossessing lot. Some wore new but cheap and badly fitting clothes in which they appeared to be ill at ease, and Matthew took them to be first-year students, perhaps away from their homes for the first time and disturbed about what lay ahead of them. They made him feel experienced and scornful. Most of them had work-roughened hands and some the farmer's plodding walk, stepping high as though they were still among the furrows of a plowed field.

Matthew, a little depressed by the sight of those who would be his companions for the next two years, went up the steps and into the school. He found himself in a broad hall with stained mustard-colored walls above a varnished wood dado. There were doors on either side, all of them shut, and at the far end a stairway with massive banisters and handrail. This depressing place had only one other person in it: a thin, hollow-chested, black-haired young man who was standing in the middle of the floor, looking around with an expression that was a mixture of annoyed uncertainty and distaste. His clothes were good and well tailored, he wore them as though they were nothing unusual, and he had the air of feeling that something better than this emptiness was due him.

Matthew spoke to him politely. "Where do we go, do you have any idea?"

"I was wondering myself. They might put a sign up, don't you think? But there seems to be something going on upstairs. Shall we go and see?"

"Why not? We might as well."

"Stupid way to run things."

When this young man moved, Matthew saw with surprise that he was lame. The limp gave a slight pendulum swing to the upper part of his body, and Matthew had the impression that he was making a strong internal effort to control this in order to make his disability appear less than in fact it was. With the first step he took a deep breath, his thin black brows drew together in a frown that made a single, slanting, dartlike line between them, and the cords of his neck leaped into prominence. It occurred to Matthew that the extreme, hollowed-out thinness of frame might be the result of the labor of moving, and he was at once interested in a friendly, uninquisitive way. In the war, injuries and disabilities were so much of a commonplace that no one thought of being sensitive about them, and it did not occur to him that a disabled man not in uniform might have a different attitude. He slowed at the foot of the stairs in order not to hurry this stranger, and said with easy sociability, "You got that injury in the war, I suppose?"

"No, I fell out of an apple tree when I was a kid. It kept me out of the war—if it's any business of yours."

Matthew turned to look at him in astonishment and saw that the dark face had flushed a sullen red. He hesitated, aware of an emotional tension greater than seemed called for, and said, "Sorry. I didn't mean anything. I was a surgical orderly during the war, so . . . forget it, will you?"

They had come to a stop halfway up the stairs and were facing each other, the friendly look on Matthew's face unchanged, a nerve twitching under the skin of the other's cheek. They stood in silence, estimating each other, as though an important balance were being struck between them, until Matthew felt the absurdity of this. He smiled with a large and easy good nature that, however, made no concessions.

"My name's Matt Chapin."

"Mine's Edward Chisolm." His tone was not free of sullenness, but he put a hand on the banister rail and started once more to climb.

Matthew, looking at the hand, said, "You're new here too, I take it."

"Yes."

The hand was frail-looking with long, thin, but steady fingers, and it crossed Matthew's mind that it was a hand more fitted to use instruments than tools. It had, in fact, the appearance of being in itself a precision instrument.

"You come from around here?"

"Cleveland."

A group of students came clattering down with a reckless assurance that could come only from long familiarity with these stairs, and Matthew backed against the wall to let them pass. "Act like they own the place. Second year, I suppose. My God, where's that smell coming from? Smells like a battlefield on the third hot day."

An odor, not strong, but having body and thickness, had met them halfway up the stairs. Edward made a grimace of disgust.

"Bodies, I suppose, don't you? I hear some places try to preserve 'em, some don't. I'd say this place didn't. I guess we'll have to get used to it."

"Gosh Almighty, it's not going to be pleasant."

They continued their way up the stairs, and in the hall above they stopped by the open door of a large corner room. The room was crowded with zinc-covered oblong tables, the tops slightly canted toward a trough in one end. There were two stools by each table and by each stool a pail. Matthew went in and looked around him curiously. There was an odd shimmer in the light in the room that made a moving pattern on the ceiling, and looking for its source, he saw through a window the vast, troubled surface of the lake.

"Nice view," he said. "North light to work by. There's not a body here. Why do you suppose it stinks so?"

"I guess that they can't get rid of it. Let's get out of here."

Matthew left the window and they went out into the hall together.

"What the hell do we do now?"

"Register, I suppose. See the sign?"

At the other end of the hall, where some students had gathered, a white cardboard sign was fastened at a right angle to the wall above an open door. On it in bad lettering was the word REGISTRATION. They walked slowly toward it, Matthew accommodating his pace to Edward's limp. He was shortly to discover that Edward did most of his talking as he walked and that otherwise he seemed to prefer silence. This, Matthew had enough insight to perceive, was a trick, and a fairly successful one, to distract attention from his lameness. He used this technique now.

"Do you know what courses you're going to take? It has to be not less than five."

"I haven't thought. Surgery for sure, though."

"Everybody has to take it. And anatomy, medicine, of course, materia medica. Obstetrics I'm leaving out. It's not for me. Dissecting goes along with anatomy, I gather. I'm going in for chemistry and therapeutics too."

"What's therapeutics?"

"How you cure people."

"Then what's medicine?"

"How to find out what ails them, I guess. I'm not sure. Diagnosis."

"Well, for God's sake, why do they separate them?"

"Search me."

"Isn't there something about diseases of women and children? If anybody knows enough about women to teach about 'em, I gotta hear."

"Don't put yourself down for everything in the list. You might find yourself working harder than you'd like."

"Then I'll take everything you take except chemistry—to hell with chemistry—and add the women."

They turned into a room that seemed to be crowded with students, and were stopped by a man who was sitting behind a small table just inside the door. He beckoned them with his arm, as though he were scooping them in, and said through a scraggly reddish moustache, "Matriculation fees are paid here, gentlemen."

While Matthew and Edward were bent over the table, filling out the cards he pushed toward them, he stared at them with hard-eyed curiosity. He was a short, thickset man wearing a spotted frock coat hanging open and showing a gold chain looped across a firm little potbelly. Shoved back on his head was a top hat with the nap standing up in patches. His small eyes, which were too close to his nose and were slightly bloodshot, produced a calculating, predatory look that gave the impression that his first thought in any situation would be what there might be in it for him. Matthew, finishing his card, straightened up to find this look resting on him. He stared calmly back and the little pig eyes wavered and slid away. His red little lower lip pushed at his bristly moustache a couple of times and he announced in a surly way, as though it were a subject of dispute, "I'm Dr. Burnett."

Matthew gave him his largest smile. "You own this school? You're the Dr. Burnett in the prospectus?"

Dr. Burnett seemed to find Matthew's question gratifying. "I own the school. A good fact to bear in mind, gentlemen. That will be five dollars each. That is, if your application's been approved, and if you've complied with all what it says in the perspectus."

"I have a letter to that effect," Edward said coldly, not troubling to hide his dislike.

"Let's see, then." Dr. Burnett picked up a dog-eared copybook that was lying on the table and began to thumb awkwardly through it. "Chisolm, you say? Chisolm. Chisolm. Here it is, all in order. And you?" He turned the little eyes on Matthew.

"I've got the money here. I left in too much of a hurry to write in, or to get a letter from a clergyman. Sorry."

Dr. Burnett put the copybook down and stared at him. The stare was a mixture of hostility and cupidity, and after a moment of silence in which the wiry moustache moved up and down, combing the air, cupidity won out. "All right, seeing you're here. Five dollars each and I pass you in."

They put the money on the table and Burnett swept it toward him with a hand that had coarse reddish hair on the back, and ragged, dirty fingernails. He jerked his head to indicate that they were to move on to a large round table in the center of the room around which a number of men were sitting. The gesture was peremptory and dismissive.

Matthew touched Edward's sleeve as they moved away. "Wait a minute. Let's watch and see what's going on."

In front of each of the seated men was a sign with his name and the subject he taught lettered on it. Each had pen and ink, an open cash box, a notebook and stacks of cards. Students were slouching around the table, pausing to hand out money, have their names entered in the notebooks and to receive cards.

"Are those men at the table the professors, do you suppose?" Matthew said. "They're a battered-up-looking lot."

Edward examined them coldly. "They're worse than I thought they'd be, and I wasn't expecting much. They look like a lot of discards who can't make a living practicing. Come on—let's get this over."

"You go first. I'll follow you."

To each of the professors they paid five dollars to cover one term of instruction; had their names entered and were handed cards. Each card was differently designed, as though to suit individual fancy—some boldly printed, some decorated with scrolls, one in Gothic lettering, and one had been made with a rubber stamp, crookedly applied. These cards appeared in a way to match the personalities involved, as though in handing them out each man was giving a small sample of himself. Amused with this thought, Matthew looked at each of his future preceptors attentively. One or two had a defeated look, another seemed to possess little besides pointless bad temper, another seemed merely vague. All had the look of having been shoved into middle age as through the door of a prison, where they were surprised and pettishly discontented to find themselves. All looked as though their relation to life had somehow got slightly out of focus. All seemed wholly without interest in the students.

The effect of this on Matthew was depressing, and without realizing it he too began to slouch. Edward, however, appeared to be angered by what he was encountering, for his movements consisted of sharp jerks and he was taking no trouble to conceal his limp. He seemed, in fact, to exaggerate the unevenness of his steps, and perhaps it was the sound of this that made the last of the professors turn quickly to look at him. The face Matthew saw instantly wiped out all the impressions he had been receiving. It was both strange and startling—a white mask drawn over a face that had long ago been molded by suffering, and out of the mask there appeared two hot eyes, black and impenetrable as molten tar. Very black, straight hair hung down on each side of this mask almost to the cheekbones. Matthew, pulled into startled alertness, glanced at the sign on the table in front of this man and was not surprised to see a foreign name: DR. ALEX ZSOKAY—SURGERY & ANATOMY.

Edward's and Zsokay's eyes had caught and held. Matthew was behind Edward, and so could not see what part he was playing in this silent exchange, but Zsokay's burning look explored deeply and searchingly as though in it he were silently asking a question on the answer to which a relationship would depend. Then Matthew saw the cane, and at least partially understood. Two lame men were exchanging in this way God knew what of experience or comprehension or mutual support.

Whatever was passing between them seemed to satisfy both, for Matthew sensed a sudden ease in Edward's manner, the probing light died out of Zsokay's eyes, and a softening of the muscles of his face suggested an inner smile. He said, "Name, please," in a harsh but not unfriendly voice, and Edward, bending over and leaning on the table, gave it to him with an ease of manner that Matthew had not yet seen in him.

The little business was quickly done. Edward received his card and took it, laughing. Over his shoulder Matthew saw that he was holding a jack of diamonds on which Zsokay had scrawled his name in a bold hand. Then it was Matthew's turn and he was strangely disappointed that Zsokay did not so much as glance at him. He gave his name and watched Zsokay enter it in his notebook. Zsokay's hands were almost as bizarre as his countenance. The long fingers were slightly spatulate at the ends, the nails short and very clean. Odd bumps clustered around some of the knuckles, giving the fingers a distorted look. He was putting his hand out for a card when Matthew said, "Surgery is the subject that interests me most."

He said this partly because it was true, partly because it was instinctive with him to meet indifference with friendliness. Zsokay twisted sharply in his chair, looked briefly at his face and long and steadily at his hands.

"Ever done any?"

"A bit. I was a surgical orderly during the war."

"That probably means you'll have a lot to unlearn. Here's your card."

Matthew found himself holding a queen of hearts. He grinned at it and put it in his pocket.

They went back into the hall where some students who were standing about glanced at them incuriously, and where the dissecting-room smell was lying in wait for them. Matthew said, "Phew, let's get out of here," and they went on down the stairs as fast as Edward's limp would let them.

CHAPTER TWELVE

A pale but warmish Indian-summer sun was shining and the two young men sat on the horse rail, shielded by the school building from the lake breeze. There was no reason, now that they had registered, that they should stay in the vicinity of the school, but they did so unthinkingly, as though it had already become the core of their lives. Quite a few others appeared to feel the same gravitational pull, for there were twenty or more students idling on the steps or standing in groups on the weeds beside the boardwalk. Matthew and Edward had little to say to each other, a sense of what they were up against having produced a feeling of solemnity in them both. The school, with vacant lots on either side, seemed as isolated as a pesthouse, and these young men looked, and to themselves were beginning to seem, a group apart.

After some time Edward slid off the rail and said, "I'm hungry. Come on, let's find a place to eat."

The boardinghouse, which supplied breakfast and supper, found the cooking of a midday meal onerous and unprofitable and so left the boarders to rely on their own resources. Matthew said, "You know a place?"

"No, but one of those fellows could tell us." He nodded toward a small group of students that was showing by clannishness and boisterous assurance that they were second-year men. "I'll ask them."

He limped over to them and spoke to the nearest, a thickset fellow with heavily muscled shoulders and very large hands, whose loud, accented voice Matthew had heard at the breakfast table.

"Do you know someplace near where we could get a decent meal?" It seemed to Matthew that there was in Edward's manner the faintest suggestion of contempt toward these youths who were not so well dressed, and whose faces plainly showed that they were not so experienced in life as he. The big fellow seemed to be aware of this too, for he scowled as he gave Edward's thin form and well-cut clothes a brief, sweeping inspection. The others fell abruptly silent and for a fraction of time no one moved. The big fellow said in a thickly truculent voice, "Who the hell are you?"

"My name's Chisolm. I asked you a question."

The condescension in his bearing was plain enough now. The big brute of a young man lowered his head like a bull and one of the group said, "Take it easy, Preston." Matthew let himself slide off the horse rail. Preston came a step nearer Edward.

"Sure I know where there's a place to eat. I'm going there myself after a while. But you're not going there, see? It's for second-year men—not for dressy types like you. Now beat it, limpy, before I get a feeling I got to teach you manners."

Someone said, "Oh, put the lid on it, Pres, for heaven's sake. It's no skin off your ass."

Edward's face was darkly flushed and it was evident that he intended to stand his ground at whatever cost to himself. Matthew came quickly forward, stepped in front of him and confronted Preston. He was half a head taller and though not so powerfully built, his body was more supple, his movements quicker.

"My friend asked you a civil question. Are you going to give him a civil answer?"

Preston made no reply and the two stood tensely facing each other. Then one of the others, a personably young man who might be Norwegian or Swedish, detached himself from the group and came forward.

"Lay off, will you, Pres? We're all sick of you and your quarrels." He turned to Matthew and said pleasantly, "First- and second-year men don't fraternize much in this school and you'll make it easier for yourself if you don't try."

Preston gave a weighty shrug and moved away as though to make it plain that this scene no longer interested him.

Matthew turned his head to look after him. "What's eating him?"

"Oh, he fancies himself the big man of the school and that's his idea of the way to maintain his position. He's a Finn and his father's a laborer on an ore dock somewhere east of here, so Preston has to work his way. He's all the time trying to live it down. His real name was so outlandish he changed it to Steve Preston. There's a place you can get dinner over that way, just around the corner toward the lake. It's called Pete's. You can't miss it."

"Thanks." Matthew turned to Edward. "Let's go."

When they were partway to the corner, Matthew, about to make a remark, checked it, for he saw to his surprise that Edward's face was deeply flushed, his lips drawn tight, and it was plain he was angrily brooding on what had just taken place. Matthew himself, having dismissed the incident with large good nature, was disturbed by this sight. After a watchful moment during which Edward's dark mood grew no lighter, he said, "Look, take it easy. That guy's nothing but a regular-issue loudmouth. Common type in the war. Don't let him get you riled up."

"Mind your own business."

"Sorry!"

Matthew received the unexpected flare-up of anger without resentment. Edward, grim-faced and silent, lurched fiercely on as though he were fighting his way against a strong wind. And shortly they arrived at a shacklike wooden building that a crooked sign told them was Pete's. Unstable-looking wooden steps led up to a screen door that opened outward, making it necessary, after seizing the knob, to back down the steps again and swing the door wide before going in. The screen was full of rust holes and covered with flies that, when the door was opened, swooped dexterously inside.

Pete's was small, dark and smelled of frying fish. Sand tracked in from the road gritted underfoot. There were many voices and a great rattling of crockery. Matthew and Edward were hesitating just inside the door, looking around for an empty table, when a pleasant-faced young man near them attracted their attention by motioning to them, and when they went to his table he indicated two empty chairs opposite him.

"Sit there if you like. I'm leaving in a minute. My name's Odell."

They introduced themselves and when they were seated Matthew said, "You must be a first-year man."

Odell smiled. He had a round pink-and-white face and a short nose that suggested humor, on which was perched— rather unsteadily since the nose was not really shaped for them—a pair of silver-rimmed spectacles. As he was facing the only source of light, the lenses glittered, obscuring his eyes, but the effect was merry and one assumed the eyes themselves would appear much the same.

"As a matter of fact, I'm second-year. But pay no attention to that. I suppose you've run into a silly custom we have here. I don't believe in silly customs—or customs of any sort, for that matter. I'm here for a degree in medicine, which I have to get as fast and as cheaply as I can, and I don't have time for childish stuff."

"You know a big lunk, name of Preston?"

"Steve Preston? Sure. Hardest worker in the school. Paying his way as he goes by doing odd jobs, and in some of the courses he's really good. You'll see."

"What sort of jobs?"

"Oh, this and that. There's ways to make money if you want to bad enough." Constraint was noticeable in Odell's manner and he made obvious haste to get off the subject. "By the way, there's only two things to eat here—fish and stew. Take the stew. Always take the stew. You'd think with the whole lake outside the fish would be fresh, wouldn't you? It isn't. What you get from eating it the school calls Pete's disease."

A waiter in a dirty apron with some fish scales stuck to it came and stood beside the table. When he breathed and his stomach moved, the scales caught the light and gleamed. Matthew and Edward told him they wanted stew and coffee and he went away, walking as though his feet hurt. Odell took out a cigar and lighted it.

"Never smoked these things before I came here. If you don't smoke I advise you to take it up for reasons you'll soon appreciate. If you don't mind my asking, how did you two happen to pick this school?"

Odell looked to Edward for an answer to this, no doubt because his prosperous appearance consorted less well with these surroundings than Matthew's. Edward, preoccupied with his thoughts, had been turning a spoon he was holding over and over, studying it as he might something new and strange. He put it down contemptuously, as though it had suddenly become a thing he despised, and sighed in a way that made it fairly plain that he did not want to be drawn into this conversation, but he answered politely enough.

"Same reason as one of yours. It doesn't cost much."

Odell raised his eyebrows in disbelief, making his unstable spectacles leap upward, before he turned to Matthew with a questioning expression.

"I sort of decided in a hurry," Matthew said, recalling the circumstances of his departure with a smile. "It was the only school I knew about. I gather you don't think it's particularly good."

Edward gave a short laugh and Odell's glasses sparkled merrily at Matthew.

"Must be you have no basis for comparison. This is one of the worst. Old Top Hat—Dr. Burnett, that is—runs it for his own profit and spends just as little on quality as he thinks he can get by with. The professors are all part-time and second-raters, with dying private practice, and—"

Matthew interrupted in surprise, "Zsokay too?"

"Zsokay's different. He's a hell of a good surgeon, actually."

The stew, swimming on thick white plates, was set in front of Matthew and Edward, and without ceasing to give Odell their attention, they began to eat.

Matthew spoke with his mouth full. "If this place is like you say, what's he doing here?"

"Well, he's a Jew, for one thing. That and being a foreigner would be against him in getting a better teaching post, or in private practice. Besides, he's not exactly a lovable cuss. He got into some sort of political trouble in Hungary, supposedly. There's a story that he got the injury that made a cripple of him in some fracas connected with it. Maybe so, maybe not. He's a great teacher if he likes you and thinks you have ability, but if not he makes it hell for you. But to get back to the school—a place like this shouldn't be allowed to exist, and someday it won't be."

Matthew, who was chasing the last of the thin gravy around his plate with a piece of bread, looked up. "How do you mean?"

"In the past a lot of medical schools were owned by doctors, because that was the only practical way. A hundred years ago it was a self-sacrificing job to run a medical school, and a doctor was lucky to get a living out of it, let alone a profit, so most of them were reputable men doing the best they could. Times change, and it got so some money could be wrung out of a school if the doctor who owned it wasn't too scrupulous. That's when we began to see doctors of the type of Old Top Hat starting schools like this one. They're an abuse and worse, but they haven't been in existence long enough for a reform movement to get started. We're slow about getting around to reforming in this country, which is both good and bad."

"If it's like you say, something should be done about it."

"You're right there."

"Take me—I supposed all schools were more or less the same."

"There'll be a reform someday that will close up places like this. Or at least I hope there will be. Say, it's late. I got to get out of here."

He pushed his chair back but before he could get to his feet Matthew stopped him and he paused to listen, sitting on the chair's edge.

"That's interesting. How come you know so much about schools?"

"My grandfather was one of the good ones who started a backwoods school in Illinois. But I tell you one thing . . ." Odell hitched himself forward again and put his elbows on the table. "A school like this that isn't inspected or supervised, that's under the sole control of the owner who milks the students and turns them out worse doctors than if they'd just read medicine with some good practitioner . . . Where was I? I forgot where that sentence began. I mean to say, we'll get the reforms we need someday, though maybe not till we need 'em a lot worse, but we'll get 'em in time. Me, I'm not going to practice when I get out of here if I can help it. That's why I'm here instead of reading with a good man. I'll have a degree and I'll get me a job on a medical journal in the East if I can, and do my damnedest to give those reforms a start. Now I really have to stop gassing."

He rose smiling, his glasses glittered at them with enormous vitality, and before either of them could reply he was gone. But then unexpectedly he came bounding back again. "Will you fellows take a bit of advice?"

Edward nodded and Matthew said "Sure," but with a trace of caution in his voice.

"Zsokay's class—both years—meets in the dissecting room tomorrow morning. Get there good and early. Get yourselves a table near a window. North side is best, though they have to keep the windows open most of the time and it's damn breezy on the lake side. Write your names on the table in chalk. It'll be yours for the rest of the year. So long and good luck."

Odell was standing now at the table's end where the light no longer shone directly on him, and Matthew, looking up, saw his eyes for the first time. They were a darkish gray, very serious, tired and, surprisingly, a little sad. They were eyes belonging to a man of far more depth than he had supposed. The next minute, and before either could thank him for his good counsel, he was gone, and the battered screen door slammed behind him.

Matthew turned to Edward, who was running his finger around and around the rim of his empty coffee cup, and for a moment he, who never felt the need to discharge nervous strain in such ways as this, watched uncomprehendingly. Then he said, "What did you think of him?"

"Odell? Zeal of a reformer. I wouldn't be surprised if he does about what he says he's going to. Let's go, if you're ready." The coffee cup had served his purpose and he pushed it away.

"Go where? Back to the school?"

"That stinking place? Not on your life. That smell sort of clings to the inside of your nose and I've been smelling it with every bite I've been eating. Let's go to my place— I've got some whiskey there. That might fix it."

"All right. Sure, I'd like to."

To their surprise and to the pleasure of both, they discovered that they were living in the same house. The rooms, however, were vastly different, for Edward's was on the first floor, and large, with an alcove for the bed. It had once been the parlor of a fine, tall house before the edge of the city had encroached with the building of streets, a small ore dock, a wartime hospital and the medical school.

As Matthew saw at once, when he looked around admiringly, this was clearly the best, and no doubt the most expensive, room in the house. It was high-ceilinged and airy, with a fireplace that looked serviceable, and comfortable though shabby furniture.

"Gosh! Aren't you afraid of getting lost in such a big place? You should see the one I've got. You brought a lot of stuff with you, didn't you? Is that a fiddle in that case?"

"A violin."

"Do you play it?"

"After a fashion."

While Edward was at a washstand in the alcove pouring the drinks, Matthew wandered around, picking things up and putting them down again. He was a little awed by an array of personal possessions that was quite beyond his experience. When he came to a tall chest of drawers he stopped to admire some silver-backed brushes and a small clock that seemed to be inside a lump of crystal. Then a small framed portrait in pencil and wash caught his eye, and he bent to examine it. He saw a woman in a low-cut gown who at first glance, in the poor light, seemed to bear a striking, even a startling resemblance to Edward. She had the same dark hair, the slim black brows above a face as thin as his. The eyes were wider, deeper, like pools at night, secret and sad.

Perhaps because he felt he held in the portrait a clue to the strangely faceted character of Edward, Matthew carried it to the window where he could see the silvery pencilings and delicate tints more distinctly. He had become so absorbed that he might have been alone when Edward spoke sharply.

"Put that down."

"What? Oh, sure. Excuse me."

Matthew hastened to return the picture; then he walked away across the room. Edward set down the drink he was holding, then went quickly to the chest of drawers, picked up the picture and readjusted it on its easel, as though by doing this he could take away the profanation of a stranger's touch.

Matthew saw this with surprised indignation. He said "Sorry" in a tone that had no regret in it, and realized it was not the first time that he had apologized as a result of some unforeseen attitude of Edward's. The word stayed like an echo in his mind. This perfunctory apology Edward ignored and Matthew noticed with astonishment that he was white and trembling. He limped away to get his own drink and brought it back to the fireplace, where he stood with his back to the room, taking big swallows, and letting the whiskey's sullen fire assuage him.

He ignored Matthew, but there was something about the bent back, some emanation of despairing loneliness, that made Matthew feel that he did not want to be left alone, or to have his mood resented, and that after a moment he would want to talk. It was like an appeal by a hidden Edward that the Edward who was moodily staring into his whiskey glass was far too proud to countenance. Matthew's reaction to it was to scrub in a self-deprecating way at his bronze curls with both hands and then to give Edward a look of extraordinary clarity.

Dr. Hurd would have understood both the gesture and the look, and been warmed by them. He had seen them often enough to recognize in them a struggle between resentment and a compulsion that had seemed to the doctor one of Matthew's most endearing traits, that was a kind of obligation Matthew seemed to feel to see the other side. In this brief struggle the other side—Edward's side—won. Matthew did not signal the victory in any obvious way, for he was not aware of it as such. He merely hesitated a moment, then picked up the drink that Edward intended for him, carried it to a green-covered cot that did duty for a sofa, and sat down to wait.

Presently Edward tossed off the last of his whiskey and went, rather noisily, to pour himself more. When he came back to the fireplace he did not again turn his back, but stood there a little stiffly, gazing at a spot on the carpet. Matthew watched him and knew that this was the transition from the dark mood of a moment ago. With entire good nature he was willing to let Edward accomplish it in his own way, at his own pace.

After a moment Edward gave him a swift, searching glance and set his drink on the mantelshelf as though what he had to say could not appropriately be said with it in his hand.

"That is a picture of my mother, as you probably guessed. She's dead. My father killed her."

Matthew absorbed in silence the shock of this statement and stared openly at his friend. The dartlike line was back between Edward's narrow brows and he looked pinched and pale. After a moment he sighed, found his glass and took a drink, but not greedily, as before. When he again looked at Matthew it was half shyly.

"Don't take what I said literally," he said. "My father didn't shoot her, or stab her or poison her, but he was just as surely responsible for her death. Perhaps someday I'll tell you what happened, perhaps not. She meant a great deal to me. I'll tell you this much because the air is thick with your questions. My father has money—lots of it. But I wouldn't touch any of it. I'm here with the very little my mother left me, which will see me through until I start earning my own. I hate my father. I mean it. I hate him. He's a very successful doctor, mostly with women. He's pompous, prideful, stupid. He's a big bull of a man with a loud voice and he can focus his huge personality on a woman patient like a burning glass. I hope we'll never have to talk about him again. I wouldn't now, but . . . look, I know I'm not easy to get along with, but . . ."

What happened to Edward's face then was not a smile, for no muscle visibly moved. It was more like a disappearance of the strain that tightened it, leaving only the slightest marks behind. The result was a smoothed-out look, candid, disarming, almost boyish. Matthew was much moved by it.

"Matt, just take me as I am, will you? Which you've seemed surprisingly willing to do so far."

Matthew made no reply and did not even realize he was silent. The effect of this change in Edward was to make Matthew see in him a far more complicated character than Matthew had supposed him to be—a much younger young man whose hidden self was sensitive and seeking, perhaps lost. Matthew's own broad simplicity of outlook prompted him to look on these things as a handicap. Sitting there on the edge of the cot with his half-finished drink in his hand and looking at Edward with these thoughts in his mind, Matthew was unaware that his own expression was one of warm and open friendliness.

It was in this moment that these two really met. Then, because it was also a moment of threatened emotion, Edward said briskly, "Here, let me get you a drink. I'm one ahead of you."

After that they were able to pass the time until supper in satisfying, commonplace talk. Matthew sprawled on the cot, relaxed and careless. The neck of his shirt was open, his sleeves rolled up. Edward sat neatly in a chair, one thin, dangerous-looking hand resting on his knee. By the time the landlady's nine-year-old daughter rang the supper bell, their minds were misty from drink but they were quite satisfied with themselves and life in general, and they had acquired a considerable knowledge of each other.

CHAPTER THIRTEEN

The next morning, in accordance with Odell's advice, Matthew and Edward went to the school early to pre-empt a dissecting table with a good light. They found the front doors closed but unlocked. There was no one in the hall and the building gave them the impression of being empty, which they found to be disturbing and oppressive. They spoke in whispers because they were both feeling uncertain and like intruders, and as they climbed to the floor above, their footsteps on the wooden stairs made a hollow, resounding sound.

When they reached the dissecting room they found that windows on two sides had been left open and a brisk breeze from the lake was blowing in. "Doesn't improve things much," Matthew said. "Just stirs up the stink." He went to one of the windows on the lake side and stood there looking out. The school had been built almost on the edge of a bank back of the stony beach against which, in a storm, the waves would beat. There were no waves now, though out at a distance the heaving surface of the water was broken by short whitecaps that rose, ran forward and subsided in endless repetition. Under them the water was lead-colored. The sky hung low, a covering of gray clouds so thick they seemed to have piled together into ridges and deep valleys. It was an unquiet, sullen scene without beauty. Matthew, knowing it would be the background of his life for months to come, sighed and turned away.

He found Edward holding a piece of chalk he had taken from the trough below the blackboard standing by a table just behind him.

"How's this one, Matt?"

"How should I know? Looks all right to me."

"Window right near it; north light; that's what artists say is best. In a corner so no other table's too near. Here, put your name on your side."

Edward held out the grubby piece of chalk to Matthew, who took it and scrawled his name in big letters on the uneven zinc. Then Edward took back the chalk and wrote in a hand that on a better surface would have been precise, "Mine. E.C."

The pockmarked zinc with the chalk writing on it looked somehow lewd and unwholesome. Matthew, following the thought it gave him, said, "It's not going to be anything like what it was in the war."

"What on earth do you mean?"

"We saw plenty of dead ones but we didn't have to take 'em apart. It seems sort of indecent when you think about it. My God—what's that?"

They heard a sound like a groan, protracted and horrible. It grew louder until it seemed to fill the room, and the two young men listened in frozen stillness. The sound seemed to rise from somewhere beneath, and another sound, a grinding metallic noise, mingled with it. There followed a thud and after that, stillness.

The groan and the metallic sound had seemed to come from everywhere; the thud distinctly came from a windowless side of the room, and quite near. They both turned to face in that direction and Matthew said, "Christ, what is it?" in a low, tight voice.

On the wall they were staring at there were two doors, squat and wide, like an oddly shaped cupboard, and Edward said, "It's there, behind those doors. It stopped there."

"It sounded like something mechanical. Do you suppose we dare go look?"

"Wait. I think someone's coming."

The room was quiet now, and listening intently, they could just hear distant sounds that might be the rasping of footsteps on stairs below the flight that they had used. The steps came nearer, growing more distinct, until they became unmistakably someone walking in the hall below, then starting to mount the stairs to the floor they were on. The two young men waited in fascinated silence. In a moment there came through the door a man they had not seen before, a short, thickset man of middle age who had a bold face with something hard and disillusioned in its expression. He stopped short when he saw them, looked them over, taking his time about it in a way that belongs to authority. Then he spoke in the rough voice that might be expected from his general appearance.

"Well, young fellas. What you doing here?"

Matthew started to answer, found his voice was not working very well, cleared his throat and said, "We came to pick out a table." Edward said, "Who are you?" and it sounded as though he intended to be rude.

"Name's Czerny. Joe Czerny. You're going to know pretty well who I am soon enough. I'm janitor and I'm in charge here. I keep the Material. That's bodies—we call 'em Material. Sounds better. Let's see what you been doin'."

Czerny started to cross the room toward where the two were standing and Edward said, "What was that noise we heard just now?"

"You'll know in good time. I wanta know what you been doin'." He stood beside the table, thick arms hanging by his sides, and read their writing with moving lips. "What's E.C. stand for?"

"Edward Chisolm."

"You got the best table in the room. You'll be lucky to keep it if some second-year fella has a mind to it."

"What if we won't give it up?"

"Depends on who's toughest. Pretty rough lot we got in this school." He spoke as though he were proud of the fact and began to move heavily toward the doors in the wall, speaking over his shoulder. "There's a lot of sights in this room ain't so pretty if you're not used to 'em. Seems like at first and maybe for a long time the boys can't handle themselves quite natural." He had reached the doors and turned around to finish his speech. "Most gets sick and some can't get over it and has to leave school." He turned his head round toward Edward. "Seems like you might be that kind."

"Well, I'm not."

Czerny answered this with a derisive sound and went back to his lecturing, which he seemed to enjoy. "Then there's others the sights affects different. Gets kind of above themselves, these do. Throws things around—bits and pieces. Plays low jokes, this kind does. Disrespectful to the Material. I been at this long enough so's I can tell just looking at a student how he's goin' to be when he has to start handling the Material." He turned toward Matthew. "Seems to me you're the kind it makes get loud and roughneck. You watch yourself, young fella."

"I was in the war," Matthew said.

"Was you, now? That ought to help. Now, I can't bother with you two no more. I got work to do. This here's the dumbwaiter from the storage room in the basement."

Czerny put his big hands on the wooden knobs of the two doors and pulled them open. "This here's the first one," he said and stepped back, grinning, to let Matthew look inside.

On the platform of the dumbwaiter there lay as in a niche the body of a woman. She looked perhaps older than she was, for she was worn by illness. Her mouth was open wide as though she had died shouting for help, and the cavernous opening gave the body the appearance of emptiness, as of a hollow shell. Under the half-closed lids the eyes were like black pits. Above a wrinkled forehead the sparse gray hair was tangled and damp-looking. This might once have been a woman of normal size, but wasting illness had shrunk her so that her skin had become like a loose sack, too big for the bones and muscles inside. It seemed no longer to be attached to them, and the act of pushing this poor body into the dumbwaiter had twisted it around her in folds.

Matthew stared, unable to take his eyes away, unaware that he would never forget a single detail of what he was seeing. A part of his mind noted that Edward was making for a window, pushing aside stools that were in his way, and that when he reached it he leaned far out, vomiting.

"See?" Czerny said, with a widening grin. "Like I say, they can't stand it. You feel like being sick too, young fella?"

"No," Matthew said shortly.

"Thought not. Like I say, I can always tell. I'll admit old Dolly ain't pretty to look at."

"Dolly? You didn't know her, did you, for Lord sake?"

"Not to say know her. Not the way you mean. But she's been here a long time—one of the longest—lying there on her blocks of ice. Going in and out of that room a lot, as I got to do, you get to feeling you do know some of them, know what they're like, get to feeling sociable, like they was real people. I got to thinking of this one like her name was Dolly. You like to work on her maybe?"

"What do you mean?"

"I'm bringing up five bodies for the class. You and your friend got your name on a table. We work two to a body here, as you seem to know. You may not believe it, but you get kind of attached to the one you're working on."

"I don't believe it."

"Wait and see. The first day all you got to do is clean your body up. We keep 'em in the basement in a room lined with blocks of ice cut off the lake there. Naturally they get kind of damp. Some of 'em's got moss on 'em. Dolly here's not so bad. But what I say—first day, all they make you do is clean 'em up and cover them up good. You want to take old Dolly?"

"All right. It's all the same to me."

"Then the next one you do's got to be a man. Here, give me a hand lifting her, will you?"

Together they laid poor Dolly on the table where she seemed to wait with indifference. There were sounds in the school building now; then they heard someone coming up the stairs, and the second-year student named Preston entered the room.

137

"Hullo, Pres," Czerny said. "Thought it was about time you showed up to give a hand."

Preston glanced at Matthew without greeting and said to Czerny, "It's early yet. I was looking for you down cellar."

"All right, come on. We got lots of work this morning."

They went out together and Matthew, watching them leave, thought that he now knew something about what Preston did to earn his way through school. Then it occurred to him that it was time to go and look after Edward.

It seemed impossible to cross that room through the forest of stools without having to shove them out of the way. He knocked one over and let it lie where it fell. Edward had gotten to his feet and was leaning against the wall adjusting the sleeves of his coat. He did not look at Matthew, but kept his eyes down as though ashamed.

"Come on, Ed, let's get the hell out of here."

They went out and down the stairs in silence and stood together in front of the building, grateful for the pale early-morning sunlight, drawing deep breaths of fresh air. After a moment Matthew said, "You all right?"

Edward nodded abruptly, as though the question irritated him.

"Want to go back to the house and get some breakfast?"

"Christ, no."

"Look, you can't work all morning on nothing. Even if you just have some coffee . . . how about that place we ate in yesterday?"

"Shut up, will you? Leave me alone."

Matthew stood still. He might have made some angry reply but Edward had gone limping on, taking, however, the direction of the restaurant, and after a moment Matthew followed. Edward appeared to be aware of this for he was struggling fiercely to conceal the limp, every line of his body betraying the effort he was making. Matthew could not simply let him go, for he was incapable of harboring resentments without taking prompt action to relieve himself of their burden. Edward was not far ahead and with a few long steps Matthew had caught up with him.

"Say, what the hell's the matter with you?"

Edward stopped and turned a face toward him that was so white and drawn that Matthew was shocked by it. "All right," he said. "Forget it."

They walked on side by side, Matthew silenced by the

realization that Edward's outburst had not been directed at him but at Edward's own self. And Matthew marveled at the intensity of hatred that Edward felt toward his own lameness.

Inside the dim and smelly little restaurant Matthew hesitated, however, for he was not sure of Edward's feelings. Edward had pulled out a chair at one of the tables and was sitting down. Then he looked around and indicated to Matthew with an abrupt gesture the chair at the other side of the table. Matthew pulled it out and dropped into it. "How long we got before class?" he said, hoping the commonplace remark would launch the talk into smooth channels.

Edward pulled out his watch. "Three quarters of an hour—a little more. What's the first class about?"

"Haven't the faintest. They'll post it somewhere, but I have a fear it's going to involve a closer acquaintance with your friend Dolly."

The lone waiter wandered toward them, gave the table a perfunctory wipe with a damp, grayish-colored rag, and waited.

Ed spoke to him with averted eyes. "Just coffee."

Matthew said, "Same here," out of consideration for Edward though he was feeling a real need for food.

After they had each drunk a little of the coffee and were beginning to feel its benefits, Edward said abruptly, "What made you want to be a doctor, Matt?"

Matthew received the question with some surprise. "Why, I don't know. Things just sort of worked out that way, and I thought I'd like it."

"Didn't you have some noble idea about dedicating your life to helping suffering humanity?"

"Lord, no." Matthew laughed heartily, drank the rest of his coffee, set the mug down and looked at Ed with interest. "Did you?"

"No, and of all the reasons for choosing medicine as a life work my guess is that's the least common. I guess if I had to tell in one word what got me into this, I'd say curiosity. I'd like to discover things about illness and the human body—things nobody knew before. I don't care a nickel's worth about suffering humanity."

Matthew studied Edward thoughtfully and in silence. Then, as was his way when he found something beyond his comprehension, he grinned with self-deprecating good nature. He pushed his chair away from the table. "Let's get back to that stinking place. Dolly's waiting for us."

CHAPTER FOURTEEN

When they went back together into the dissecting room, they found that it was full of students but—perhaps because of Dolly—their table had not been pre-empted. A group of youths, all of them second-year students, were standing around one of the tables near the front of the room watching someone at work, and Matthew went closer to see what was going on.

Looking over the heads of the others, he discovered that the lone worker was Preston. His sleeves were rolled up, he was wearing a blue butcher's apron, and he had already begun to dissect the upper arm of the body on the table. The watchers were silent as Preston bent over his work, the only sound in that part of the room being the occasional click of an instrument laid down on the zinc tabletop. Matthew could not see well enough to follow the details of what Preston was doing, but he received a strong impression of skill and sureness that recalled Odell's comment that Preston was a surgeon of real ability. His mind occupied with the thought, which was new to him, that personality traits and ability are not always on the same level, Matthew reluctantly left the group around Preston. Edward had found a pile of butcher's aprons like the one Preston was wearing and, having hung his coat on a peg, was slipping the neckband of one of them over his head.

"Was that Preston showing off?"

"It was Preston." Matthew too hung up his coat and reached for an apron. "Maybe he was showing off, but I guess he's entitled to. He's good."

"He's a bastard."

"Maybe he's that too."

As they went back to their table there was a general movement in the room, the group around Preston breaking up and the students taking their places on their stools. Matthew, looking for the reason for this, saw that Dr. Zsokay had come in and was standing on the platform. Czerny was there too, in clean trousers with stains on them that had survived many washings. He was letting his heavy frame down carefully into a sitting position on the edge of the platform and looking around the room belligerently.

Zsokay had hung his cane on a chair back and had come forward to support himself with a hand resting on a small table. He too was looking around, waiting for the commotion to die down.

He prolonged the waiting a little longer than necessary, and there was a calculated effect, and even something stagy in the pause. Matthew watched with interest, for the man fascinated him. It came to him that Zsokay's handicap in his profession was no doubt the ugliness of his distorted body and a rasping, though possibly brilliant, personality. Patients would not be attracted to such strangeness, and this Matthew guessed to be the explanation for his presence in this school. Then, with no real reason for it that he could have put into words, Matthew suddenly felt himself very lucky indeed to be here where he could have contact with such a man. The room had grown quiet and Zsokay began to speak in a strong but slightly hoarse voice.

"Gentlemen, you are here to learn what each one of you is capable of learning about the human body. It is a far more intricate and marvelous creation than I suspect any of you has realized. After centuries of study we are still very far from knowing all there is to know about its parts and their functioning. Discoveries are constantly being made, and each one reveals that there is much more than was suspected still to know. I don't expect that any of you will contribute any new knowledge, but I hope you will come to have some appreciation of the great wonders hidden in the body lying on the table in front of you, and I tell you that your future worth as doctors depends to a large extent on what you learn in this room."

Dr. Zsokay paused and looked around at the faces turned toward him, seeming to study and judge them individually. His eyes lingered on Preston, who, being a second-year student, had heard this lecture before and was taking some pains to make his boredom evident. Zsokay's dark brows drew together and he seemed about to say something, perhaps in deprecation of a system that made the second year an exact repetition of the first. He made no comment, however, but the glance that lingered on Preston was not without sympathy. Then he made a gesture with his long, plum-covered fingers, as though he would dismiss what he saw.

"There will be no dissecting today. . . ."

At this there was a general murmur of relief, and some of the students slid off their stools, eager to escape from the foul atmosphere of the room. Zsokay held up his hand to detain them and they settled back reluctantly in their places.

"Wait, please. That does not mean that you don't have work to do. The first-year students will have this morning, and this morning only, in which to conquer the fear and horror of a dead body that I can see in your faces most of you have. The second-year students will be expected to maintain an attitude of tolerance toward these novices. You will work in pairs, cleaning the body assigned to you. It must be thoroughly washed, then treated with chloride of zinc to preserve it, and Mr. Czerny will be here to show you how that is done. You will find pails by your tables and you can fill them at the sink over there in the corner. You will finish by ten o'clock, when you will come to Room Five for a lecture on dissection of the forearm, which you will begin tomorrow.

"Now one word of warning. An untreated corpse contains poisons that are dangerous. The virulence of the poison is at its height a short time after death, when decay is beginning to set in, and slowly declines, but is always present so long as there is undried tissue adhering to the bones. If you have any cut on your hands, or any break in the skin, however small, then do not touch a body, for blood poisoning will result. If you cut yourself accidentally while working, then at once, without delay, wash the cut under running water, encouraging it to bleed. When you have done that, apply glacial acetic acid, or deliquesced carbonic acid, both of which are kept on the shelf above the sink."

Zsokay paused while all the first-year students turned their heads to look. Then he rapped the table sharply with his knuckles. "That is a solemn warning. Heed it for your own safety.

"Now, we have here cases of instruments you will need to use in dissecting." He reached his hand down and Czerny gave him a flat, oblong box that he took from a basket filled with others like it, which was standing on the floor near him. Dr. Zsokay held it up for everyone to see, opening it to show the instruments on their velvet bed. Then he laid it on the table beside him.

"I want to say something about instruments in general. You should prize them, for as your hand is an extension of your arm, they are an extension of yourself. They carry out your thoughts; your ability depends on them. When I am not holding an instrument I am only myself, not able to accomplish any of the thoughts and ideas that are in my mind. But when I hold an instrument I am more than myself. Therefore I respect them.

"These instruments belong to the school and will be loaned to you. As soon as possible you should acquire your own and learn to know them better than you know your own hand. Ask Mr. Czerny how to care for them and, most important, how to sharpen those that have blades, and keep them sharp."

He paused a moment as though to give the students time to think about what he had been saying. Then he took a step closer to the edge of the platform.

"Now one last word. You will treat the body assigned to you with respect, and you will do this for two reasons: first because a body is the most intricate and the most delicate mechanism any of you has ever seen, and second because that body was once a human being."

Having finished what he had to say, Dr. Zsokay unhooked his cane from the chair back and let himself down from the low platform with an awkward lurch. He stood there for a moment, turning his head from side to side, for the first time looking directly at the students, one by one, seeming to estimate them. Some received his glance nervously, some appeared stimulated by it. Edward took it with straightened shoulders, Matthew with a light smile. Then Zsokay appeared to smile, though the smile was more an impression than an actuality, and seemed to come from a grim amusement at their plight. After that he left and Czerny was on his feet, saying, "Now, young fellas, if you'll step up and put your names in this book I'll give you each a case of instruments. Like Dr. Zsokay said . . ." The rest of it was lost in noise as the students, Matthew and Edward among them, shuffled forward. When they returned to their table, Matthew turned to Edward, intending to offer to do alone the unpleasant work of washing Dolly, but he found Edward staring at the body with so set and grim an expression of determination that he gave up the idea. Saying instead, "I'll get the water," Matthew reached under the table for the pail.

In the normal course of things the hour like the one that followed is likely to be the hardest in the life of a medical student. During it he must conquer many revulsions, face disturbing realities and receive impressions at his nerve and finger ends that build up in him a changed concept of human life. All this was less difficult for Matthew than for Edward since, as he was growing accustomed to explaining, he had been in the war. Nevertheless, the wartime sense of emergency was lacking, and in the absence of those pressures he had difficulty in regarding Dolly as merely so much carrion clay.

The second-year students were working along with efficiency or bravado, according to their natures, most of them wearing hats because the room was cold, almost all of them smoking. Quite a few of the first-year students were in distress. Since Zsokay had left, Preston had been steadily working, with skill and assurance that verged on bravura, and Matthew, catching sight of him, remembered a remark of Dr. Hurd's to the effect that some surgeons never felt themselves right with the world until they had a knife in their hands. He seemed now to have completed whatever task he had set himself and he was sitting easily on his stool surveying the room. He caught Matthew's eye and smiled slightly. Then he saw Edward and his face darkened into a look of such intense hate that Matthew, startled, continued to watch. The look of hatred gave way to introspection, and he seemed to be meditating something, but after a moment he slid off his stool and bent over the table again, and Matthew lost his momentary interest and returned to his own work. As a consequence he did not see various signals and an apparently casual gathering of the second-year students near Preston.

What happened then took place so fast that in Matthew it paralyzed thought. Suddenly the room was full of noise, yelling and shouting, and the second-year students, now a tight group, all had objects in their hands and were flinging them. Something struck Matthew on the shoulder and fell to the floor. Looking down, he saw a severed hand, which he pushed under the table with his foot. Then he stooped and picked it up and dropped it into the pail.

When he straightened up he saw that Edward was freeing himself from a long strip of putrid flesh and liquefying fat that had hit him squarely in the face. He was almost blinded by it, unable to see through the loathsome mess the thing had left behind. Matthew took him by the arm.

"Steady, Ed. Come over to the sink and wash yourself." Gripping Edward's arm, he steered him toward the sink in the corner and, glancing over his shoulder, saw Preston sitting on his stool in the midst of the melee, staring at them, and had no doubt that it was Preston who had flung that particular missile. "Christ, what a thing to do," he said, and pushed Edward toward the sink. Edward was sobbing. Matthew turned the water on. "Here, Ed." He pressed Edward's shoulder to make him bend over.

Edward cupped water in trembling hands and dashed it into his face. Matthew watched him anxiously.

"Did any of it get into your eyes?"

"I don't know. I don't think so. I'm going to be sick."

"Don't. Hang on to yourself, Ed. There's some on your hair. You'll have to wash that too."

The riot behind them was dying down, though a few of the more resentful first-year students were retrieving bits of ammunition from the floor and hurling them back again. Czerny was standing in the doorway, shouting. Edward, still leaning over the sink with the water running full, said something that Matthew bent down to hear. He thought it was "God, I'll never feel clean again." Then Matthew remembered something and went back and cleaned up as best he could the place where Edward had been standing when he was hit.

Preston was still sitting on his stool darkly brooding, not paying any attention to what was going on around him. Matthew glanced back at Edward, saw that he was drying his face on the roller towel and so presumably was all right for the moment. Reassured, Matthew shouldered his way to Preston and stood in front of him.

"Preston."

"Yeah?" Preston glanced up but did not move. He looked exhausted, played out, without any of his customary domineering air about him. He seemed to be almost at peace.

"I'd like to know—I'm curious. Why would you want to do a thing like that?"

An odd look came into Preston's eyes, an unstable look like the flame of a candle tossed in an air current, but he made no reply. Matthew continued to stand there, vaguely trying to recall what it was that Odell had said about Preston. After a moment Preston got off his stool and walked out of the room.

CHAPTER FIFTEEN

The brief spell of damp, cold weather ended. Then a pale sun shone and the water of the lake, heated by summer, gave back its warmth. Tranquil day followed tranquil day, the sky was a pale but cloudless blue, the surface of the lake, gray-blue like polished steel, dazzled if gazed on too steadily. On the shingly beach there were no waves, but only a gentle lapping motion. In the vineyards along the shore the vines, their branches stretched and tied to wires, had lost all but a few large, golden leaves. The few misshapen bunches of grapes left by the pickers had dried and turned to gritty raisin sweetness. After long days of this the black cold came, suddenly and in the night, sweeping in on wind from Canada. Waves dashed against the shore, the spray freezing before it fell, and far out on the lake a long gray continent of ice began to form.

Before the cold came, the young men of the school had enjoyed the warm air at noontime, standing on the path in front of the building or sitting on the hitching rail to absorb what they could of the pale sun. When the cold settled in, there was no more pleasant loitering. By this time the routine of the school had established itself, and Matthew tried to fit himself into it. He discovered, in a whispered conversation with Czerny, that there was a "house" not far away where a good many of the students went on Saturday nights, and he mentioned this, rather hesitantly, to Edward, who said, "Not for me, thank you." Matthew went alone.

He was shown into a parlor where someone was playing a jangling, out-of-tune piano while eight or ten girls, their hands on each other's shoulders to form a circle, were moving languidly but more or less in time with the music. They were nude, their breasts sagged, and the soles of their feet were black with dirt. They stared at him with tired, bored eyes. A number of Matthew's fellow students were sitting or standing around watching this dreary dance, among them Preston, who was noisy and already very drunk. Czerny was there and his greeting of Matthew made it plain that he had some sort of official connection with the establishment. He presented Matthew to an unspeakably evil-looking little woman who had a curious odor about her so that Matthew left her as soon as he could and went to join the watchers.

He did not stay long. First he found the gyrating girls pathetic, something that had never occurred to him when he had been in similar places with other soldiers. Then, looking at his fellow clients, he found it all disgusting. He left as inconspicuously as he could, and on the solitary walk home began to wonder whether he might not be becoming a prig. But then his thoughts went back—as they unfailingly did whenever he was alone—to Cissie. He never went back to that house or sought any other such diversion.

He often had spells of desperate unhappiness about Cissie. These times of missing her came to him at night when he was alone in his little room at the top of the house. Then he would throw his books aside and pace around the restricted space in torment until Preston, who occupied the room across the hall, would shout at him to be quiet. He was surprised at the force of his own emotions, for they were more intense than he had suspected while he was in Haddon and they seemed to grow no less. He told Edward about his trouble, leaving out that part of the story that concerned Sue, and Edward was interested but not inclined to take Matthew's romance very seriously.

Finally Matthew wrote to Cissie, a letter that he worked over alone in his room for many nights. After that the most important thing in his life was the pigeonhole box in the hall of the school, where mail for the students was kept. When he entered the building, his eyes traveled to it at once. He could identify his own pigeonhole from a distance, and whenever he came down the stairs he looked there first of all, but the space was always empty.

Finally he gave up hope and tried to lose himself in his work, but this he did not find easy to do. The lectures bored him, as they did Edward, for the very good reason that they bored those who delivered them. Not one of their teachers had himself been a student in a medical school, except possibly Dr. Zsokay, about whom nobody knew anything with any certainty. Several were tired, defeated old men who were failing in private practice but who nevertheless thought this means of piecing out a living was beneath them. One was an egocentric old duffer, tabacco-stained and muzzy from drink, who liked to tell slightly lascivious stories in which he appeared a disreputable hero, and as his subject was diseases of women, his prurient mind had a wide field. They were a sorry lot—all but Zsokay, who was brilliant, erudite beyond the capacity of most of the students to appreciate, often cruelly sarcastic, but with the born teacher's ability to make a certain amount of what he taught take root.

His talent, his fire, his insistence on a high level of performance were wasted on all of the students but Matthew, Edward, Odell and Preston, though Preston lacked the powers of comprehension of the others. These four, but especially the two friends and Preston, were, however, enough to satisfy Zsokay and to give him a degree of what, in a less complicated and savage nature, might have been happiness. He drove them hard, in class and out. If he met one or the other of them by chance in the halls, they could seldom escape without being carried off to his office, where some new bit of knowledge was hammered or mesmerized into them.

He had no hesitation at all in showing his favoritism; and though it did not draw Matthew and Edward any closer to Preston, each in his way felt the self-importance of being one of the elect. Odell excepted, the rest of the student body, like the other teachers, were a sorry lot. They came from small homes that were for the most part located no more than ten miles distant from the school. Their fathers were small tradesmen or farmers or "ore people" who had prospered as a result of the war, and who were attempting, in the American way, to better their sons' stations whether the sons had it in them to be bettered or not. Some of them had only had three or four years of schooling, and as they were quite incapable of taking notes in lectures, they borrowed notebooks from the few who could keep them. Preston too failed here, though he made an effort and did succeed in filling a few pages in a bold, unformed hand. Matthew, Edward and Odell were looked on by all the students and most of the teachers as wonderful exceptions. In fact they would have been so in all but five or six of the best schools in the country, where many students had little more than an ability to read and write.

No textbooks were used in any of the courses, since the

greater number of the students were unable to cope with them, and the lectures were held down to the level of the stupidest and least able. Zsokay's lectures on anatomy were the exception in that they were illustrated with charts and engravings of anatomical figures, some of the latter taken from a late edition of Vesalius, and the beauty of these fascinated Matthew, though he knew nothing about their history. In the classrooms of other teachers there was nothing at all to meliorate the lecturer's tiresome drone. The school owned not one Bunsen burner, not one microscope. By the end of the first week in all classes but anatomy, surgery and dissection, Matthew was bored into somnolence, Edward into chronic irritability.

This state of affairs was made worse by the ill-ventilated classrooms. When the cold weather came, the windows were kept shut, and as almost everyone, including the teachers, smoked incessantly, these rooms were filled with a heavy blue haze from cheap cigars. The building had no furnace and each room was heated by a potbellied stove that gave out heat enough to roast those in its immediate vicinity while leaving the far corners chill and damp.

Matthew stood these hardships fairly well, but they told on Edward badly, and at the end of the third week he said, "This is the last time. I'm never going to sit through one of those lectures again—except Zsokay's. Never."

They were walking back to the boardinghouse and Matthew stood still with surprise. "How do you expect to pass your exams if you do that?"

"Easy. I'm going into town tomorrow and buy some medical books and read them in my room, and at the end of term I bet you I'll know more than anyone else, teachers included. And you'll be a fool not to do the same."

They went into the city the next day and discovered that the only medical books to be had were in a secondhand store, but among these they found some they thought would meet their needs. Edward made the selection and Matthew, looking them over, said, "I suppose you realize that all of these were written before the war and the chemistry quite a while before that?"

"I know. It's too bad, but it won't matter. I don't believe our honored professors have ever read anything even that recent."

They found the new system worked well, so well, in fact, that they began to take an interest in subjects that heretofore had bored them. Then one day when they were studying in comfort by the fire while icy snow tapped against the windows, Matthew said, "You know, it's pretty surprising . . ."

"What is?"

"I thought when you studied medicine you'd learn how to cure people, but there's nothing I've found so far that can really be called a cure. It's all just stuff that the doctor hopes may help."

"The doctor alleviates; nature cures. That's what it amounts to."

"Then why aren't the fellows who wrote these books honest enough to say so?"

"I suppose because most doctors, when the patient gets well, fool themselves into thinking it's they who have done the job."

Matthew stretched his feet toward the fire and thought about this for a few minutes. Then he said, "It's hard to believe. Aren't there *any* cures?"

"We're talking in generalizations and it depends a little on what you mean by a cure."

"But the whole purpose is to cure."

"The purpose is to help the patient get over what ails him, which isn't necessarily the same thing."

"And apparently the doctors don't agree on the best way of doing that. I suppose medicine advances by finding better ways."

"And the best way of advancing, I suppose, is to find out more about disease, which is the only part of it all that interests me in the slightest. The word 'cure' ought to be banned."

"The guys at school toss it around pretty freely."

"That's because they're dishonest and stupid. Have you found the word used in any of these books?"

"No, come to think of it."

They went back to work after that, and for a long time they were silent and intent while the wind tore at the house and snow blew in across the lake.

One day toward the first of December, when they stopped by the bulletin board in the school hallway to see what had been posted there, they found a notice saying that tickets for conducted hospital visits were now on sale. They bought theirs at once and joined the first group under the guidance of the professor of medicine.

The hospital was a big, gloomy brick building that had tall, narrow windows like a prison. It had been built toward the end of the war to care for the permanently disabled, who would wear away their lives here as though the hospital were in fact a prison. It was five blocks from the school and had been built so close to the lake that reflected light from the water shimmered and danced on the ceilings of all the rooms on the northern side. The visits, which were called "grand rounds," took place in the afternoons, but the wards still smelled of the morning's bedpans, mingled with the odors of bedding and disease.

There were about fifteen students in the group that shuffled along after the professor and clustered around him when he stopped beside the bed of a patient, who might or might not be one of his. At each stop the professor, after a jocular greeting to the patient, expounded on his case to the students, described the treatment, and discussed the chances of recovery as though the patient were deaf. Some of the students listened with real interest; there were always one or two who, bored, slouched in the background, and one or two who found repulsive stimulation in the sight of suffering. The grand rounds had the faults of all such visits, which is to say too many students and instruction that was too irregular, so that often the students saw a patient only once or twice and never knew the outcome of the case. Matthew and Edward joined in the rounds less and less frequently.

The hospital tickets also gave entrance to the operating theater, where a student could go by himself if he wanted to and watch from the tier of seats that half circled the room. This was a dreary place, located on the top floor on the lake side of the building. A huge window that lit the room with a bleak glare from the water made it cold in winter, and to counteract this there was a stove with an immensely long stovepipe that went out through the high ceiling. Before an operation someone was supposed to put out the fire in the stove so there would be no danger of the ether exploding, and Zsokay always made an inspection himself to see that this had been done. With the fire out the room grew cold in a matter of minutes. Spectators wore coats and sometimes their hats, and Zsokay a thick vest under his spotted operating-room frock coat. On really bitter days he added a long knitted muffler which he wound around his throat with the ends thrown back over his shoulders to keep them out of the way. This custom of his of wearing a frock coat instead of an apron while he operated was looked on as a European affectation by other

151

doctors on the staff, for such a costume was worn only by prominent surgeons in the great hospitals of the East.

Zsokay operated with the speed and style of the European-trained surgeon who never forgot that whatever else surgery might be, it must also be a good show. Preston was the student chosen to assist him, and it was here that Matthew was able to see the real quality of Preston's work. This was even better than he had been led to expect. He was not an imitator of Zsokay, for though he was bold, he was not by nature a virtuoso. He was deft and he could move his big hands with surprising speed when necessary, but speed for its own sake was not a part of his technique. Matthew had the impression that he worked as he did as a result of choice, and it began to dawn on him that this big fellow, for all his noisy overconfidence outside the operating room, was carefully and thoughtfully working out for himself a mastery over his art.

When he tried to say something about this to Edward, he encountered an attitude toward Preston that surprised and disturbed him. "Haven't you forgotten that first-day business yet?" he inquired.

"No, I haven't, and I'm not going to."

"Listen, Ed, what Preston did to you was bad, I grant you, but that was weeks ago. You can't go on being sore at him forever."

This was on a Sunday morning and they were working by themselves in the deserted dissecting room. Edward stopped what he was doing and there took place in him one of those strange, almost frightening changes that Matthew had learned to recognize as the outward sign of extreme anger. He grew pale, his lips and his brows drew into thin, parallel straight lines, and when he spoke his voice, which was normally low and quiet, was harsh.

"Keep out of this. What Preston did to me is my business and I'm going to handle it in my own way."

"What do you mean, handle it? You can't do anything to a guy built like a bull, and for God's sake don't try."

"I said keep out of it. I'm going to make him pay in my own way, so shut up, will you?"

"As you like, only don't get yourself killed or maimed for life."

"I'm already maimed for life. Now will you please shut up?"

Matthew went back to work, and because Edward had stirred up some resentment in him, he did not raise his eyes for some time. Consequently, he did not see that Edward was sitting quietly, not working, and that his hands were shaking. After that Matthew did not again bring up the subject of Preston, though little things that happened made him think that Edward's anger was not cooling, and for Edward's sake this troubled him.

The dissecting room continued to be the focal point of their lives. Nothing else was so interesting or rewarding, nothing so demanding of stamina and perseverance. They both did more work here than was required of them and they kept notebooks, though the other students did not. They propped these open between Dolly's thigh and the raised edge of the table and entered in them anything that seemed to them important. Matthew, discovering that he had an aptitude for anatomical drawing, filled his with curiously vivid sketches. Edward, who worked more slowly and to a finer detail, filled page after page with his thin, steeply slanting script.

They did not exactly grow fond of Dolly, as Czerny had predicted, but she ceased to be "Dolly" and ceased to be the subject of the crude jokes that concealed feelings they were unwilling to acknowledge. As they explored her body they came to regard it first with wonder, then with awe, and Czerny's remark was so far true that they never again attached the same degree of value to any body they handled.

During the regular hours, Zsokay spent his time going from table to table, sometimes instructing, sometimes merely standing still and watching with black eyes that were like pools of hot tar. Clumsiness with a scalpel always lit his anger; an incision that was not precisely or purposefully made, a nicked tendon or a slit artery was apt to produce a frenzy of rage. Muscles must be cleanly exposed for their entire length, their attachments laid bare in a way that proved knowledge. Nerves and blood vessels must be traced to their finest possible branchings. Anything else was unbearable to him.

Listening one day to a tirade at a nearby table, Matthew said to Edward in an awed undertone, "Damned if he doesn't think a leg without the skin on is beautiful."

"Well, isn't it?"

Matthew looked down at his own work for a thoughtful moment. "Yes, by God, you're right!"

Zsokay came oftener to their table than to any other, usually gesturing to them to go on with their work while he watched in silence. Now and then he talked to them in a low voice, pointing out to the fascinated pair this or that wonder of the body that had not been touched on in his lecture. He never praised their work, but they knew that, like Preston, they were favored students because their work was good. He seemed to do little more than give them occasional light guidance, but he watched their progress with absorbed intensity which they were aware of and for which they were grateful. It might almost be said that he loved them, and yet their relationship with him never grew closer, and only on one odd occasion, which neither of them ever forgot, did he use their first names.

This happened one day in the dissecting room when he was standing at the head of the table observing their work. He stood there for some time but he had made no comment of any kind until he said, "Matthew!" in a sharp, rough voice. Both young men looked at him, instinctively jerking their scalpels upward so that the startled jump of their nerves would do no damage to their work.

"Matthew, in later life you should work always with the living. You, Edward, always with the dead."

He left them then and they worked on in silence, each closed into his own thoughts. They never mentioned it to each other afterward, as though Zsokay had touched on something too personal for discussion.

Matthew spent somewhat more time in the dissecting room than Edward for he learned mainly by doing, but Edward spent more time with books. Matthew liked to go there alone on a Sunday when the evil room was empty, and to work as long as he felt inclined. He was there one Sunday just after the cold weather had set in. On all the tables there were covered mounds, and on his also, for he was working on a hand, which was all that protruded from under the edge of the sheet. He had been working a long time and the light had begun to fail, so that he sat on his stool bent over and sidewise not to block the little that remained.

After a time, exasperated and feeling very tired, he glanced resentfully at the graying oblong of the window and reached for a rag and cleaned the instrument he had been using. He fitted it into its slot in the instrument case with a sigh and moved the hand back under the sheet.

He had finished washing at the sink and was pulling the roller towel around, looking for a place that was reasonably clean, when he heard steps in the hall and Preston came in. He saw Matthew, shoved his hands in his pockets, and came toward him.

"Been working?" he said.

"Yes. Light got so bad I had to quit."

"I hear you work here alone a lot."

"Yeah, when I can."

Preston's manner was neither friendly nor unfriendly and Matthew was careful to show the same neutrality. Preston regarded him thoughtfully for a moment, jingling coins in his pocket. Then he said in an easier tone, "What you working on, Matt?"

"A hand. The palm, to be exact."

"Mind if I have a look?"

"No, if you want to."

Preston went to the table. "This is your side, isn't it?" He lifted the edge of the sheet and drew out the hand, maneuvering it delicately with his fingers on the wrist in a way that seemed practiced and sure. He tilted the skinless palm to the light, stooping to examine the details of the exposed anatomy.

"You should have followed that nerve through," he said, pointing. "Not cut it off there."

"I know. I lost it."

"Nerves and veins—even arteries—aren't always where you expect them to be. You'd be surprised how far out they can be sometimes. You just have to let them lead you along."

"I've had a little experience of that."

"Yeah, you were in the war, weren't you?"

Preston put the hand back under the sheet, wiped his hands on a rag and sat down on Matthew's stool. Matthew came back from the sink and sat on Edward's stool across the table. For a while Preston said nothing at all, but sat there, drumming with his fingers on the V-shaped segment of stool top between his spread legs. The fast-failing light had reduced his face to a pale oval on which all subtleties of expression were indistinguishable. When he spoke it was abruptly, with a return of the suggestion of belligerency that seemed to be his normal manner.

"Want to earn some money?"

"Depends. What you got in mind?"

Preston waved his hand toward the supine, sheeted figures. "Where do you think the bodies come from?"

"From 'afar.'" Matthew grinned. "Remember what the prospectus said? Ed's always quoting it: 'In our dissecting room these poor wretches vindicate their existence by contributing to science, a fact that no doubt counts in their favor when they stand for Judgment before the throne of the Almighty.' "

"That's shit. They come out of the nearest convenient burying ground. Anywhere handy, where there's been a burial so recent it won't be noticed if the ground gets disturbed afterward."

"Does Old Top Hat know it?"

"Sure he does. Tipped Czerny off just last year when the family of the departed, in company with the sheriff, came around looking for their dear one that mysteriously got lost out of his grave the very next night after they laid him in it. They didn't look under the coal pile, though. And the bodies they saw in the ice room were all so old they had moss on 'em."

"Are you suggesting that I go grave robbing with you?"

"Quick in the mind, ain't you? Yeah, got to be done before we get weather that will freeze the ground deep."

"I should think, from the feel of things, it would be frozen deep right now."

"Only a couple of inches or so. There's three new burials in that big burying ground between here and town. Ground all nicely loosened up so a pick and shovel will handle it easy, in big lumps. Want to come along?"

"I guess not, thanks."

"There's five dollars in it for you."

"I'm not that broke."

"Sure you won't?"

"Absolutely sure."

"Too bad. If you change your mind, let me know, will you? And keep your trap shut. You can see it's not the kind of thing to talk about. Especially don't tell that son of a bitch you pal around with—Chisolm."

"I won't—but you got Ed wrong."

"I don't like him, see? He's a snotty bastard. Also, he gives me the creeps—those thin hands of his. So don't slop to him. Well—sorry you won't join me. It's real work, alone."

Preston slid off his stool, pulled a match out of his pocket, struck it under the table and carried it to the nearest gas jet. The gas hissed and caught in a tall yellow flame, which Preston turned down until it became a quivering fan, blue at its base, pale gold along its ragged edge. Then without another word he left the room and Matthew heard his heavy steps going down the stairs.

CHAPTER SIXTEEN

Matthew kept his word to Preston and said nothing to Edward about their talk. They seldom mentioned Preston now and Preston, though he was not friendly toward Edward, had stopped actively persecuting him. Edward's resentment, however, had hardened into a cold, permanent anger. Matthew, whose angers flared into action, and so were dissipated, was troubled by Edward's state, but only vaguely, for the greater part of his thought and energy had to be given to the work of the school. Fortunately there was little occasion for Edward and Preston to be thrown closely together. Their dissecting tables were in different parts of the room, and at the protracted boarding-house meals Edward was always prompt, Preston unfailingly late.

One morning Matthew came into the dining room to find Edward was, as usual, well ahead of him and only three or four other early risers were present. They talked of this and that, reaching for food, eating rapidly out of habit. Edward finished first, rolled his napkin and fitted it into the ring. "I think I'll go along," he said.

"What's the rush?"

"Something I want to do in the dissection room."

Edward left and Matthew finished his coffee. It had been his intention to study for half an hour or more before going to the school, but the best hours of his day were spent at the dissection table, and if that was where Edward was he thought he would like to be there too. He got up, found his coat among others hanging on a long line of pegs in the hall, and was passing the stairs when he met Preston coming down. "Hullo," he said. Preston, morose with sleep, merely growled at him.

Because Edward's limp slowed him, he had only just arrived when Matthew caught up with him. They hung up their coats and went up the broad stairs together. The dissecting room with no living person in it but themselves seemed unnaturally quiet, and very cold. Matthew went along two sides of it, shutting the windows that had been left open during the night, and when he had finished he found that Edward was pulling off the sheet that covered the body on which Preston was working. Seeing this, Matthew said sharply, "Say, what do you think you're doing?"

"Come and watch."

Edward was standing in Preston's accustomed place and Matthew joined him there. The appearance of the body was not pleasant for Preston had been working on the opened abdomen, but even at a glance the skill of the work was apparent.

"He's sure good," Matthew said admiringly. "It's all his work, seems like."

"He won't let anybody else touch it. Look, the other guy's been working on a foot."

"Did you come over here at this hour to look at this? Preston would have let us see it, and without any urging, if I know him."

"No. This is something I've been waiting for. He's got to get his hands good and deep inside that body and he's going to be surprised at what happens to him. Right here and now is where I get even with that bastard and I'm going to enjoy myself."

"Ed, listen, for heaven's sake, don't go and tamper with his work. He'd—"

"Leave me alone, will you? If you don't like it, go away. Maybe you better, at that."

"I just don't want you to do anything to get you into trouble."

"Shut up, will you? I'm not going to do harm to Preston's precious corpse."

Matthew made no reply. Edward took a sponge from the pail under the table and began to soak up the fluids that had accumulated overnight in the depressions and cavities inside the abdomen. Matthew went around the table and sat on a stool, watching this. Edward worked swiftly, and when the inside had been cleaned to his satisfaction he laid the sponge aside, wiped his hands with a rag and took out of a pocket a tall, narrow green bottle.

"What's that?" Matthew asked.

"Croton oil."

"What's croton oil?"

"You don't know?"

"Never heard of it."

"And you pretending to be a doctor. Watch out, now.

You better move back a bit because you wouldn't want to get any of it on you."

As Matthew shoved back his stool, Edward uncorked the bottle and began pouring the liquid into the hollows inside the abdomen, where it stood in small pools that were not easily distinguishable from the liquids that Edward had sponged away. Matthew watched this with a worried frown.

"I wish you'd tell me what the hell you're doing."

"And spoil the fine scene there's going to be? Anyway, I don't think you'd want to know."

Edward went to a window on the lake side of the room and threw out the bottle and the sponge. When he turned back, Matthew was bending over the body, looking inside. Edward said sharply, "Here, help me put the sheet back up."

"Listen, Ed, I don't know what the hell you're up to, but I don't think I like the look of it. If you—"

"Leave this to me, will you please? Now let's get out of here. I don't want Preston to find us here when he comes."

Disturbed, but in silence, Matthew followed Edward out of the room.

They returned to find Preston, as burly as a butcher in his striped apron, in the act of stripping the sheet off the body. Six or eight students were standing about or pretending to work, and Preston was talking to them in his loud voice. Matthew and Edward stood under the row of pegs, slowly putting on their aprons and watching this scene. The sheet disposed of, Preston took out a cigar, bit off the end, spat it on the floor, lit a match and held it to the cigar. While he did this his eyes were on his work, estimating, studying. It was a thoughtful, intelligent look, and Matthew, watching, felt again an admiration, even a liking, for Preston that for the moment outweighed the distaste for the bully in him.

For a while Preston smoked in silence. Then he rested the cigar against the raised edge of the table and bent over the opened abdomen. A puzzled expression came on his face and he said, "What the hell?" He put one finger inside the body and held it to his nose, but apparently the smell told him nothing, for the puzzled expression remained. Then he stared all around angrily and said, "Some joker's been messing around here."

Several of the students wandered over to the table to see what was going on, and though Matthew had no intention of joining them, Edward laid a detaining hand on his arm. Preston was hunting for the sponge and, failing to find it, picked up a rag and used it as a swab. He was angry and so he took no particular pains about what he was doing and he used both hands in the work. The rag was soaked through in an instant and he tossed it aside and picked up another.

Suddenly he dropped the rag, straightened himself, and holding up his hands, looked at them back and front, saying in a surprised way, "That stuff hurts." The next instant he let out a howl of pain, used his elbows to thrust aside those who had gathered around him, and made for the sink. His hands were as red as though he had held them in the fire. He turned on the faucet and let the water run over them, but it appeared to give him no relief for he moved his big body from side to side, stamping and twisting under the force of the pain.

Matthew glanced at Edward and saw that he was watching Preston intently, the dartlike frown on his forehead and a muscle on his cheekbone twitching. The sight filled Matthew with sudden anger.

"What the hell did you do to him? That stuff burned him."

Edward turned on him. "It can't be all that bad."

All work in the room had stopped and the students were crowding around Preston, calling out advice or making remarks that were intended to be funny. Preston withdrew his hands from the stream of water and looked at them. On the red skin great blisters had begun to form and he stared at them as though he could not believe what he saw. Suddenly he said in a voice so loud that it startled everybody, *"Get Dr. Zsokay."* He did not wait for a reply but yelled at those who were crowding around him, *"Get out of my way!"* Holding his hands high above his head, he charged like a bull to the door and they heard his feet pounding down the stairs as he shouted, *"Dr. Zsokay, Dr. Zsokay."*

In the silence that followed, Edward limped to the sink, pulled out a handkerchief, wrapped his hand in it and turned off the water. Matthew went back to his own table and sat on his stool. He had no desire to begin work and when Edward came he did not look at him.

Edward said, "I didn't know it was going to be quite so bad as that, Matt. But Christ, think of the disgusting thing he did to me."

Matthew did not speak, and after a moment Edward

picked up his scalpel and began to dissect out the attachment of a muscle. Matthew watched him but without raising his eyes high enough to see his face. Edward worked as though he were alone, and in a little while Matthew got off his stool, pushed it back noisily and without a word left the room.

In the days that followed, neither one of them mentioned this incident again, though it remained embedded in their relationship. Zsokay addressed the class on the subject in terms of biting reproof, but that was all. Preston, with both hands bandaged, came occasionally to the dissecting room and sat for a while on his stool morosely watching his partner at work. Though he bristled with angry resentment because of what had happened to him, it was clear that he also did not know whom to blame, though he often watched Edward with what Matthew thought was a look of growing suspicion. By the following week, though he still had a small bandage on one hand, the class in general had more or less forgotten what had happened.

One night Matthew was in his room studying at the rickety table that was too small for him, his book and pencil and paper in the circle of yellow light from the student lamp, and all the rest of the room in darkness. It was nearly midnight and he was beginning to be bored and to let his attention wander. He raised his eyes from his book, ran his hands vigorously through his disheveled curls to rouse himself, biting back a yawn with a grimace that bared all his front teeth. Then he heard a sound below his window that had no relation to the normal sounds of the night. Any distraction was welcome, and he rose, opened the window as quietly as he could, and leaned out. The window looked down on a ragged, grass-grown driveway that led to a small barn where chickens roosted and tools and clothesline props were kept. At first Matthew saw nothing but the dark mass of the barn, though he felt that someone was there below him. Then a thin beam from what Matthew guessed was a dark lantern shone for an instant on the padlock of the barn door and moved in an erratic circle as the lantern was set on the ground. The faint sounds of someone putting a key in the padlock and the creak of the door came up to him. The lantern was lifted and for an instant a dim gleam showed a shovel and a pick lying on the ground; then these too were lifted by an invisible hand.

Matthew, grinning into the darkness, pulled the window

down as quietly as he could and went back to his chair. He sat there, one arm hooked over the back, listening, and after a while he heard the sounds he was expecting to hear. Someone, trying to make as little noise as possible, was coming up the stairs, then crossing the hall. After that the door of Preston's room opened softly and was closed again. In the morning Matthew, drugged with sleep and forced to hurry, forgot all about the night's disturbance until footprints on the stairs, muddy with yellow clay, brought it to mind again.

Matthew did not see Preston the next day or the next except at breakfast, when he seemed quiet and preoccupied, unlike his usual boisterous manner at this time of day. In the middle of the night that followed Matthew was wakened by someone rapping on his door. Struggling to throw off sleep, he groped on the bed table until he found a match and struck it on the wall where there were marks of many matches struck there before his time. The rapping had changed to kicking that was shaking the door, and Matthew, holding the match to the candle, shouted, "Come in, it isn't locked."

The candle flickered in the air current of the opening door, as Matthew shook out the match and looked around to see Preston in a nightshirt, haggard and wild-looking, with burning eyes, leaning against the door frame as if he needed its support.

"Matt, for God's sake, help me, will you?"

"What's the matter?"

For answer, Preston held up the hand that had lately had the bandage on it and Matthew was shocked by what he saw, for the hand and all the fingers were swollen to twice their size and the skin was an angry, burning red that looked dangerous to touch. Preston was grasping his elbow with the other hand as though he could not hold the hand up without this support, and where the sleeve of the nightshirt had slipped back Matthew saw that the redness had spread up the arm in long, burning streaks.

"My God, Pres, what's the matter with it?"

Preston made no reply other than a shake of the head that seemed dazed. He stared at Matthew blankly, breathing heavily through parted, swollen lips. Matthew started to get out of bed.

"Go on back to your room, Pres. I'll come over there."

Preston went without a word, and Matthew, his bare legs hanging over the side of the bed, groped with his feet for his carpet slippers. He tied a dressing gown around him and went across the hall to Preston's room. Preston was stretched on his bed, his poisoned arm lying at his side, his head tipped back against the pillow. His eyes were closed and he was breathing shallowly between parted lips. The room smelled of illness. Matthew moved the lamp on the bedside table so that the light would not shine on Preston's face and put his hand on his forehead. As he thought, it was burning hot.

"What happened, Preston?"

Preston's lips moved, but he made no sound, and as Matthew stood looking down at him, two drops of moisture glistened at the edge of Preston's eyes and retreated again under the lids. He made an effort that seemed to be prodigious, drawing in a deep breath that shook him.

"That body not properly embalmed. Beginning to rot. Bandage slipped while I was carrying it. Blister broke open. It's poisoned. Get Zsokay."

"Will you be all right while I'm gone, or shall I wake someone to stay with you?"

"I'll be all right. Hurry."

But as Matthew was turning away, Preston stirred and made a motion with his well hand.

"I know what it means, Matt."

"No you don't. You'll be all right, Preston." But Preston only shook his head and the moisture glistened again at the edge of the closed lids. Matthew touched his shoulder gently and went away.

Dr. Zsokay slept at the hospital, and Matthew, hurrying through dimly lighted corridors in which his footsteps echoed, feeling the restless quiet of the sick around him, finally located the room. His knock was answered by a grotesquely strange Dr. Zsokay clothed in a nightshirt that hung crookedly over the protuberance of his deformed hip, and a nightcap with a tassel that made him look like an illustration of a generation earlier. When Matthew told him about Preston he nodded and, leaving Matthew standing in the corridor, began to dress rapidly. Through the half-open door Matthew could see him lurching around the room like some huge monkey, the candlelight throwing his fantastic shadow on the wall. When he came out of the room, he was wearing a long overcoat and a muffler and carrying a black bag that Matthew had never seen before.

The climb up the long flight of stairs at the boardinghouse was difficult for Dr. Zsokay, and when, breathing heavily, he reached the top, he gestured to Matthew that he must pause a moment. He stood in the faint light that came through Preston's open door, rounded back bent so that his head was lower than his shoulders, one weird, knobbed hand curved around the newel post, shabby overcoat unbuttoned and hanging in the front almost to the floor. Then Preston called to them in a weak, anxious voice, and Zsokay, straightening himself, went inside, and Matthew, carrying the black bag, followed him.

There was little that could be done for Preston, and Zsokay told this to Matthew later, behind the closed door of Matthew's room. The night was ending by that time, and the dawn wind, erratic and unsteady, was blowing off the lake. Matthew was sitting on the edge of his unmade bed and Dr. Zsokay was seated on the only chair, a cup of coffee that had been made on Matthew's gas ring in his hands.

"Nurse him yourself, Matthew. I have an idea you'll be good at it and it won't be for long. Make him as comfortable as you can. Bathe him now and then to keep the fever down. I'll come back about suppertime, or any time you send for me."

"Hasn't he any chance at all, Dr. Zsokay?"

"Only by a miracle."

After that Dr. Zsokay brooded in silence for a while. Then he drank what was left of his cooling coffee and set the cup on the table beside him.

"I'm not going to ask you how this happened, Matthew, though I've been thinking about it, and I have an idea that you know. There is not much that I can do about it." He was silent again for a while and then the deep, troubled black eyes sought Matthew's. "Preston was the best surgical student I ever had," he said. "I'd rather it had happened to anyone else in the school, and I include myself." After that he went away.

Part of the time Preston lay in a stupor in which he seemed scarcely to breathe, but Matthew, watching closely, thought that he was conscious. At other times he was delirious, throwing his great body around in the bed and shouting. It was not always possible to understand where his delirium had taken him, but sometimes he seemed to be in an operating room calling for instruments. Again, he seemed to be on the ore docks, and Matthew could imagine him there, his powerful shoulders knotted by the weight of a wheelbarrow load of red ore, in the midst of shouting, quarreling workers like himself. Once, toward the end, when Matthew was dozing in a chair, he woke to see Preston looking at him calmly, with the light of reason in his eyes, and when Preston saw that Matthew was awake, he smiled. It was a feeble smile, but the light of it was in his eyes, and it was almost more than Matthew could bear. He got up and stood beside the bed and they looked at each other deeply and in silence; then Preston closed his eyes and appeared to sleep and Matthew went back to his chair. After that there seemed to be peace in the room.

All through the day students came to the door to inquire for Preston and to offer help. To each Matthew said that there was no change in Preston's condition, and as for himself he could manage all right but he would let them know if there was anything they could do. Then Odell came, made no offers and had very little to say, but installed himself as Matthew's helper. He was indispensable from the start, moving around the room with quiet efficiency while his glasses glittered with the light of his intelligence.

Sometime during the night that followed the first long day of Preston's illness Matthew went across the hall to his own room to make some coffee, and he found Edward sitting by the table. Edward looked up as Matthew came in, but he did not speak, as though he recognized that there was too much between them for words. Matthew went to the bed and sat there, feeling troubled and weary and, because of Edward, very sad.

Edward was the first to break the silence. "I want to do what I can, Matt."

Matthew considered this through the fog of his weariness, not clearly but in a slow progression of thought that seemed to advance but in the end got him nowhere. After a time he struck the bed a slight blow with the flat of his hand, rose and began to assemble cups and saucers and spoons. From the neighborhood of the gas ring he said over his shoulder, "Do you want some coffee, Ed?"

"Yes."

They were silent again until the coffee boiled, and Matthew filled a cup and brought it to Edward.

Taking it, Edward looked up into Matthew's face. "Matt, I've been doing a lot of thinking, and I want to tell you—"

"Don't say it, Ed."

For a moment Matthew stood looking down at his friend, seeing him a long way off like a figure on a remote stage seen through the wrong end of glasses. He put the heels of his hands against his eyes and rubbed them to rouse himself out of his fatigue, but he felt no more than the ache of his own tired muscles and a flicker of pain behind his forehead. "I'm sorry, Ed," he said, feeling that his meaning was vast but without knowing precisely what it was. Then he went back across the hall to Preston's room. When sometime later he returned to his own room, Edward had gone.

Preston died just thirty-eight hours after he had rapped on Matthew's door. Matthew and Odell were with him and it was they who carried his sheet-wrapped body down the stairs. Matthew, looking down and careful of his footing because of the weight of their burden, saw on the steps traces of the yellow clay that Preston's shoes had left there so recently and so long ago, and for just one short instant he knew and recognized the deceitfulness of time.

CHAPTER SEVENTEEN

When Matthew had recovered from his fatigue sufficiently to take up work again, he found on his dissecting table an envelope addressed in a bold, spiky, very black hand that he recognized as Zsokay's. Inside was a letter informing him that he was to take Preston's place as Zsokay's assistant in the hospital operating room, and that he was to begin at once. There was no pay attached to this assignment, but he would gain much valuable experience. Operations were performed three mornings a week, except for emergencies, which were likely to take place at any time. The time in the dissecting room that he would miss as a result of this would have to be made up as best he could, and after a few days of this new schedule Matthew realized for the first time the heavy burden of work that Preston had been carrying.

His relations with Edward since Preston's death had been

distant, for Edward had withdrawn into himself and Matthew could not conquer his aversion to what Edward had done though he tried to make himself take account of the fact that Edward could not have imagined such an outcome. Matthew knew that Edward, alone in his room at night, was drinking heavily. There were physical signs of this, and his work lost some of the delicate precision that had previously distinguished it. Matthew was aware that Zsokay observed these things also, as was inevitable, but he said nothing, though two or three times Matthew saw him studying Edward with a troubled look full of speculation. How much of what happened Zsokay put together in his mind Matthew never actually knew, but he made a shrewd guess that he weighed Edward's worth as a student against possible disciplinary action and felt it expedient to appear to know nothing.

Edward's work slowed for he often sat on his stool staring into space. Sometimes he would not appear in the dissecting room at all; and when Matthew, on his way to his own room at the boardinghouse, passed Edward's closed door, instinct told him that Edward wanted to be left alone. After the break in their routine that Preston's illness and death had caused they did not resume their habit of studying together. Though this was as much by Matthew's tacit consent as Edward's, Matthew missed the long evenings of work together, for he found that he had been more dependent than he realized on the stimulus of Edward's quick intellect and on his more practiced scholarship. Alone, Matthew had some difficulty in keeping himself to his books.

Matthew only once made any sort of reference to what had happened, and that was on a day when they were working opposite each other at the dissecting table. It was during the short Christmas holiday that both of them had elected to spend at the school; the room was empty, and all the bodies but Dolly's had been returned to the ice room in the basement. Edward was red-eyed that day, his skin had a grayish pallor, and his black hair was lusterless. He had lost weight; his thin body was stoop-shouldered and had a hollowed-out look. He seemed listless, as though his abuse of a none too robust physique had made him almost ill.

Matthew noted all this while he worked, but as he and Edward had not risked any intimate exchange of thought since Preston's death, he would have made no comment had he not felt that Edward was beginning to enter a mental state that he must take some action to block. Even though in these days they talked together very little, it was becoming too plain to be ignored that, with the help of the bottle, Edward was getting rid of his sense of guilt by transforming it into bitterness and self-pity. The atmosphere was becoming thick with it in some subtle, exasperating way that was not to be ignored. Matthew, trying hard to work, found it clogged his mind. When, one day, after they had been working in silence for some time, Edward drew a long, quavering sigh, Matthew at once laid down his scalpel.

"Ed!"

Edward raised lost-dog eyes and looked not at Matthew but through the window, far away.

"For the Lord's sake, come out of it, will you? Granted Preston wouldn't have died if you hadn't used that croton oil, but you didn't intend to kill him—or did you? All right, you acted like a damn fool and I blame myself for not interfering. But he was careless. . . . You know about that grave robbing business, I suppose?"

"Odell told me," Edward answered dully, in a tone that implied that nothing Matthew had to say could make any difference.

"He was careless, all right. He should have known better than to handle a body when he had a blister on his hand that might break. But the way you're brooding over it, Ed, isn't doing yourself or anybody else any good, so for Christ sake stop it!"

Edward looked at Matthew then, a hard, bright look, and without a word he put down the instrument in his hand and walked out of the room. He did not come back, and at the end of the morning Matthew, himself sighing heavily, cleaned up Edward's instruments and put them away.

The following morning Edward did not appear at breakfast, but when Matthew went to the dissecting room he found Edward already at work. He made no acknowledgment of Matthew's presence, but his appearance was much improved and the atmosphere was clearer. The old ease of friendship, however, was absent, and for this, perhaps, they were both to blame, though Matthew's new work as Zsokay's assistant kept him from feeling the lack as much as otherwise he might.

In the end it was Dolly who brought them together, a

Dolly who no longer bore any resemblance to her original whole, if rather raddled, self. But Dolly in spite of her present condition was a power, more of one almost certainly than she had ever been in life. As she yielded up the ever more marvelous anatomical secrets of her body, it was, after a time, impossible for the two fascinated young men not to discuss them. Eventually they had reached the point of talking without restraint, and after that it became quite natural for them to eat together once more and to spend their rare leisure in each other's company.

Dolly had served her purpose down to her bare bones, and these Edward skillfully articulated into a complete skeleton, which he kept for many years. To Edward, and Matthew also, these bones had a special meaning—almost, it might be said, a special value that no other bones ever acquired. And so it happened, though nothing in Dolly's life had warranted such a thing, that she after all achieved status, regard, and a kind of immortality.

When, after this piecemeal fashion, Dolly had departed, she was replaced by another body, but for Matthew and Edward this one lacked the intense interest that Dolly had aroused, for they knew much about the details of its structure in advance. That which it had to bestow on them was confirmation, not discovery, and in this the fine, sustained excitement was lacking.

In the depth of winter the lake grew silent, for no waves crashed onto the shore. As far out as the eye could see there was ice, great slabs and chunks of it piled up by the wind, gray under a cloudy sky, glittering in the rare sunlight. Three times Matthew, in company with Czerny and three other students, went out on this rough, frozen surface to cut blocks of ice for the room in the basement where the bodies were stored. Matthew did this more for the sake of being outdoors than for the two dollars the school allowed him for each expedition. He enjoyed himself, for the only time, day or night, when his nostrils were free of the sweetish stench of the dissecting room was when he faced the cold lake wind or worked in the ether atmosphere of the operating room.

One day Edward said, "School closes the first week in March, Matt. What are you going to do after that?"

"Work with Zsokay at the hospital, I guess. He expects me to. I thought I'd go back to Haddon for a couple of weeks when the good weather comes and things get slack."

"To see that widow?"

"To see if she'll let me see her. I'm afraid she won't, but I have to make a try."

"You can't forget her, can you?"

"No, I can't forget her, Ed."

They were in Edward's room, having a drink together, sitting on either side of the untidy hearth where a driftwood fire was burning. Icy sleet was blowing in from the lake, and from time to time a gust of wind rattled it against the windowpanes. Edward raised his glass and looked through it at the flames, admiring the bright golds and ambers and rich browns reflected there.

"I don't particularly want to go home this summer and I'm sure my father would just as soon I didn't. Your hospital work won't keep you busy all the time either. We might see if we could make a deal with Czerny to let us have some of his precious 'Material' to work on. What do you think?"

"Could be. In fact, it's a pretty good idea."

That became their plan, but Matthew thought more about his return to Haddon than about anything else. He wrote many a letter to Cissie in his mind. He even got so far as to begin some of them on paper. But the impossibility of giving his feelings adequate expression always prevented him from finishing them.

Sometimes he felt confident that Cissie really loved him and that, however hard it might be, he could win her back again if only he could see her. At other times, and these were far more frequent, he felt certain that she would never forgive him, and this certainty would for days be the gloomy background of his thoughts. The more he turned these things over in his mind the more urgent his return to Haddon seemed to be, and he became increasingly impatient for the ending of the school year.

In spite of his incessant thoughts about returning to Haddon, when the end of the school year finally came it seemed to him not only sudden and unexpected, but disrupting, for the routine of work had taken a firmer hold on him than he knew. Customarily the graduation exercises, which were attended by everyone, were simple enough. They were held in the dissecting room, which was the largest in the building. The tables were stacked at the back, the room thoroughly cleaned (the only good cleaning of the year) and folding chairs that had been rented from an undertaker set up in rows. Loops of bunting decorated the wall back of the platform and made a skirt around the small table beside which Old Top Hat would stand to make his speech.

On the great day there were only students present, for Old Top Hat wanted no parents asking questions and, as he put it, "snooping around" his school. A pyramid of rolled-up diplomas had been placed in the center of this small table, which left Dr. Burnett no place to put down the famous top hat. He stood there in his best frock coat, the one that was almost free of spots, with the hat in his hand, uncertain what to do. For a moment he seemed to consider placing the shabby hat on the floor at his feet, then it seemed he might put it back on his head. In the end he wrapped one arm around it and cradled it against his breast in much the way a man might cherish a jug of liquor, producing so ludicrous an effect that the students scarcely tried to suppress their laughter.

Old Top Hat, red in the face (which helped along the illusion of the liquor jug), his bushy eyebrows moving like two very animated caterpillars, stepped to the edge of the platform, took alarm at the brink below his feet, stepped hastily back a couple of paces, and cleared his throat. "Gentlemen . . ."

There was a hush in the room and a scratching of matches as the students lit cigars and leaned back, prepared to find what comfort they could in the undertaker's hard chairs. Matthew, in the last row, nudged Edward and winked, and Edward gave him his slow, sardonic smile.

Old Top Hat again cleared his throat and made another try. "Gentlemen. I call you that because the profession of doctor is a noble one and it entitles you to be considered gentlemen, and don't you ever forget it. I got something special to say to you this year."

His little eyes roved around the room and he seemed to be expecting applause for this statement. A few of the students nearest him obliged him.

"Well, gentlemen, as most of you probably know, I been away on a trip. I been East. I try to go every four, five years to try to find out what's new in medicine, because changes come along pretty fast nowadays, and I want to keep up. I don't say I approve of 'em—most of 'em I don't. But I sort of feel I ought to know what's going on. I haven't been there since the war, though—too busy—since a year before the war, matter of fact. And I can tell you changes has been coming along fast—mighty gosh-awful fast. And do you know—there's not one of them I'd want to offer for your consideration.

"The way you've been taught medicine is the tried and true way the doctors of your father's day practiced it, and are still practicing it, for the most part. Now, they were and are mighty fine doctors, and the best I can tell you gentlemen is to go out in the world and do just as they did. Don't be tempted by what's newfangled, because if it's new that means it ain't stood the test of time. So I say to you as parting words to take out into the world, beware of what's new. Makes sense, don't it?"

There was a small burst of clapping, and under its cover the student next to Edward spoke to him in a low voice. "You believe that?" he asked doubtfully. He was a short young man in whom it was easy to see the future practitioner. Portliness would overtake him and he would soon learn to disguise the worry of his uncertainties with a pompous manner. Edward looked at him with disgust. "Hell, no," he said, and returned his fascinated attention to Old Top Hat.

"Most of the things I heard I don't even need to bother you with," Old Top Hat was saying, "other than to give you a general idea, so to speak. People are looking through microscopes a lot more than they used to, and the things they claim they see would surprise you. They claim to see live things in the human body that are so small the human eye can't see 'em. They don't say what they're doing there or *how* they got there, but they seem to think they affect a living person in some way, though they can't say just how. One of two fellows I met thinks they might be responsible for sickness, but when I asked him how that figured, he couldn't answer me.

"Now, I've been practicing medicine or teaching it for forty years and I ain't never looked into a microscope in all that time. Why should I, I'd like to know, or why should you? And what's more, if someone put one down in front of me I'd refuse to look down it. I'd refuse. And why? Because it don't make sense, that's why. How could little animals live inside the body? But suppose they do, which is pretty crazy, how could anything so small you can't see it have any sort of effect on a human body? Well, I guess that's all I need to say about the nonsense of microscopes.

"But here's another thing I'll tell you about just so you can see how far some of these ideas go. Now, there's one thing every one of you in this room ought to know something about by this time, and that's dead bodies." There was a general laugh and Old Top Hat smiled in return. When he smiled, his sandy moustache thinned out into separate, aggressive, outward-pointing hairs. "Well, there's some that's been saying for the last thirty years, about, that these same little animals is what makes bodies decay. But all of you here know, I hope, that decay is just something that happens in something that's died. It's sort of spontaneous; it's the way things are.

"Cold will slow up decay, or even stop it for a while, but that's perfectly natural too, so why go looking for a cause when there ain't any but nature itself? Decay is catching, we know that too. Put one rotten apple in a barrel and before you know it the whole doggone barrel's gone bad. But do we have to go scientificking around for a cause? We do not. That's the way things *are*.

"But now they tell me that there's some fellow in France that's claiming that bodies don't just naturally decay, that it's these little animals he calls microbes doing it and that these microbes aren't made by the body, as some think, but they come out of the air and settle on a body like dust and get right to work causing decay. Now I ask you! And that isn't all—listen to this, now—he thinks that *if you could keep these microbes away from a dead body it wouldn't decay!* It wouldn't decay, he claims, no matter how old the body got or how hot it was. I think that's darn near the funniest thing I ever heard in my life, and he must be the downrightest fool in the world to believe a thing like that. He isn't even a doctor, either. He's some sort of a minister, a Pastor, they call him. And what's a minister doing messing around with things like that, I'd like to know? So, gentlemen, all you got to do in future to keep your Material smelling sweet's a daisy is to just chase away those little microbe animals. Now that's something, ain't it?"

He paused for a laugh, and got it. When it died down he stood there broodingly, his face muscles working, his moustache combing the air, and his very red lips making smacking motions as though sampling the air's quality. Then he shifted his hat to the other arm and continued.

"I guess I don't need to say any more about this Pastor and his crazy notions. It just emphasizes what I said at the beginning—beware of the newfangled. Stick to the old and tried, and nobody can criticize you and you can't go wrong. Them's my sentiments and I pass 'em on to you in parting. Now it's pretty nigh dinnertime, and so I'll begin passing out these diplomas, and as I do, you be ready to give me the twenty-dollars fee that you owe me at this time."

The famous hat had again become a problem and he looked around vaguely for a place to put it. And as before, he found none, so he put it on the back of his head, gave it a jerk to anchor it, and picked up the first of the paper rolls. Students were beginning to stand up, to shake down the legs of their trousers, and to make remarks to each other. The room was full of the racket of the flimsy chairs being shoved aside. Matthew rose and stretched luxuriously with a catlike elongation of muscles. Then he grinned. "Cracky, what an ass. Let's go eat."

CHAPTER EIGHTEEN

Peaceful days followed. With the students gone, Matthew and Edward had the building, most of the time, to themselves, and Edward worked there all day long, Matthew as much of the time as his duties with Zsokay at the hospital would permit. These duties he found to be utterly fascinating. Dr. Hurd's surgery, skillful as it was, had been confined to the repair of wounds and accidents. It had never occurred to Matthew that surgical techniques could be used in any other way, except for minor, superficial matters such as abscesses and tracheotomies and other small operations. Now he discovered that Zsokay used his surgical skills not only to repair but to cure, insofar as this was possible, and the concept, which was wholly new to Matthew, opened new horizons for him. He saw breast cancer removed, the chest opened, the abdomen invaded to remove ovarian tumors—bold surgery that Hurd would never have attempted and perhaps had not even read about.

Matthew worked hard but he enjoyed it all. He was on the wards day and night, tireless, a striking figure, bursting with sap and vitality, pleased with his own physical powers and the steady increase of his ability. His pride in his work and his own well-being brought to the fore the optimism that was natural to him. If the world was not actually his, he felt that all he need do was to continue as he was going and it soon would be.

In this mood he wrote again to Cissie, awkward sentences packed with feeling, and waited in unjustifiable confidence for her reply. Because his own passion was so strong, he simply could not believe that hers was not the same and that in the end she would not brush aside everything that stood between them and come to him.

No reply came and this time she had not even bothered to send his letter back. When he was finally convinced that he was not going to hear from her, he grew more and more impatient for the time to come when he could return to Haddon. This would not be possible until Zsokay took his own frugal vacation of two weeks, during which another surgeon, bringing his own assistant, would take temporary charge at the hospital.

Zsokay on a vacation was a concept that Matthew found hard to visualize. "What the hell do you suppose he finds to do with himself?" he said to Edward one day.

"Reads all day, probably. Where's he going?"

"A boardinghouse on the shore up the lake. I can see him sitting on the beach in his old frock coat!"

They enjoyed this joke as they did many others. In these long, quiet days, with the weather warming and the lake a vast diamond glitter in the sun, Edward began to throw off the depression that had followed Preston's death. He continued to work long hours in the dissecting room, sometimes with Matthew and sometimes all alone. He was becoming more and more meticulous, more and more skillful, succumbing wholly to the fascination of the difficult.

One gentle day in May the two young men, tired, warm, and contented, came back from the school to the boardinghouse to find a telegram propped up on Edward's mantelpiece. It announced the serious illness of Edward's father, Dr. Chisolm, and called Edward home. Before Matthew had time to grow used to the thought of Edward's departure, he had packed and gone, doing it with a concentrated hurry that made Matthew wonder if Edward's often-mentioned hatred of his father was perhaps not unyielding after all. Matthew was left alone with an empty, cheated feeling and the surprising discovery that a large part of the interest and intellectual stimulus of their life had been supplied to him by Edward.

Matthew had no word from him. Then one day when he came back to the boardinghouse he found Edward's door open and Edward, drink in hand, on the lookout for him. When they had greeted each other—noisily on Matthew's part and with real warmth on the part of both—and when Matthew had been supplied with a drink, they settled down to talk.

"My father's money comes to me," Edward said, "as soon as the lawyer gets through settling up, and in the fall you and I are getting away from this disgrace of a school."

"What are you talking about?" Matthew asked from the cot where he was lying full length, his hands behind his head, his drink on the floor within reach.

"You and I are going to a good school, my lad. Harvard, for choice, though there are others. No, shut up and let me finish. You told me Dr. Hurd left you money and you only came here because you didn't know any other school. Now you've found out what it's like, and I've got the wherewith, there's no excuse for either of us taking a second year here."

"Wouldn't a better school be more expensive? I don't want to get into debt." In saying this Matthew was thinking of Cissie.

"Probably it would cost more. And I'm not sure we'd get any credit for the work we've done here, but I've sent for prospectuses of several schools, and we'll see."

Matthew explained then that he would not be able to say certainly that he could consider this until after he had been back to Haddon and seen Cissie, especially if getting a degree would take more than two years. To this Edward said irritably, "Haven't you got that widow out of your system yet?" Matt's only reply was a good-natured grin and a momentary gleam of brighter gold in his lazy eyes. And so it was left that Matthew's decision was to wait until Cissie settled his fate for a second time.

That happened sooner than he expected, for one day he found a letter at the post office that changed his outlook about a great many things. Mail delivery had been discontinued to the school for the summer months. The nearest post office was a mile away and the two went there often, Matthew in the failing hope of hearing from Cissie, Edward because he had become a man of affairs and was in correspondence with his lawyer.

Matthew saw at once that the letter handed to him was not from Cissie. Nevertheless it made his heart beat in heavy thuds, for the postmark was Haddon. He ripped it open and looked at the signature. "It's from Stoner," he said to Edward, who was putting some mail of his own into his pocket.

"That banker fellow? If you're going to read it now, let's go outside."

They sat on the horse rail in front of the post office in the shade of a maple tree, and Matthew had only read a sentence when he said, "Well, for—The old boy's gone mad. Listen to this:

"'Matthew Chapin, Esquire.' Doesn't even call me doctor! 'I do not give you the title of doctor since I regard you as a disgrace to the profession. I find it in my heart to rejoice that my honored friend, Dr. Hurd, cannot know the tragic outcome of his benevolence or feel the hurt of your betrayal.'"

"Crickets," Edward said, "he's hot, all right. But he can't still have steam up about what you did to the widow, can he? That was months ago."

"I guess this is something new." Matthew read on:

I had believed, and congratulated myself, that your departure from Haddon closed a chapter that was so grievous in its conclusion to one so dear to me. I was horrified, then, when some months ago I discovered that you had left behind more than a memory of your disgraceful behavior.

"Ed, do you have the faintest idea what he means by that?"

"No. Go on."

The town shared my shock at the evidence of your depravity, and my beloved ward bowed her head in shame that in her innocence she let a scoundrel like you, sir, come close enough to touch the hem of her garment. When it became evident that that low woman, Sue Diggle, was with child, asserting that it was *your child*—

"Jesus," Matthew said and, lowering the letter, stared at Edward. After a moment in which it was evident that Matthew was struggling to understand the various implications of what he had just read, Edward said impatiently, "Go on. There's a lot more—read the rest."

"Ed, I can't believe it."

"Can't believe what? That the girl you rolled got pregnant? You must have left bastards all over the South. Why should this one upset you?"

"But—my God—think of Cissie."

"I doubt if she's as surprised as you seem to be. Go on

—finish the letter. Something else must have happened or it wouldn't be so long."

Matthew sighed, blinked at the pages in his hand as though he were having trouble bringing them into focus, and in an altered voice went on reading.

> —my dear ward, Cecilia, came to me. In what followed, my admiration for her Christian character has known no bounds. She begged me to recall you, that you might marry this fallen woman and so legitimize the child. I attempted to point out to her the folly of this, but to each of my arguments she cried out, "But it is *his* child. That's all that matters. It is *his* child."

Matthew stopped reading and sat staring at the dusty weeds at his feet, and this time Edward too was silent. When Matthew started again to read, Edward watched him, partly in sympathy, partly in speculation.

> Finally I yielded to her noble plea and drove out to see this woman, Sue Diggle. To my astonishment, she would have none of this marriage. "Leave him be," she said to me. "If he'd wanted to marry me he could have done, and I'm not marrying any man as doesn't want me." I begged her to think of the child, to which she shouted at me, in her coarse manner, "It's my child and I'll do the thinking for it. Now I'll thank you to leave me alone." I had done all that lay in my power, and so I left her.
>
> This took place five months ago. When her time came, no woman of good repute would go near her, and no doctor was to be had. When it became evident that the birth was to be far from an easy one and this woman was suffering great pain for her sinfulness, she sent her disreputable father for my ward, Cecilia, her nearest neighbor. I hope that you will realize the tribute that this poor sinner was unconsciously paying to the unselfish character and Christian pity of my ward.
>
> Cecilia went out into the night on this errand of mercy to the woman who had wronged her so grievously. Alone, except for the father, who to escape his daughter's cries went out to the barn and drank himself insensible—alone, I say, Cecilia struggled with the powers of Fate. After many terrible hours a child, a girl child, was born. It had scarcely uttered its first pitiful cry when, with a great gush of her life blood, the woman Sue died.
>
> Cecilia forbade me to tell you of these events, or to communicate with you again. I am violating her injunction not only to prevent your return to Haddon, which I am told by Cecilia you had planned to do shortly, but to make plain to

you the noble virtue of the woman who, through your own wicked folly, you have forever lost. The events of which I write took place two weeks ago. Cecilia has kept the child, and against my advice, nay, my *entreaties,* she insists that she will continue to do so and will raise her, along with her son Peter, as her own.

I hope that the harrowing tale of these events has entered your evil heart like the blade of a sharp knife. If it were in my power to cut off your inheritance from my noble friend, Dr. Hurd, I would do so, but, alas, it is not in my power. I shall never communicate with you again, my final injunction to you being never under any circumstances in the future to show your face in the town of Haddon.

In sorrow more than anger I remain no longer respectfully,

E. STONER

IV

Boston

CHAPTER NINETEEN

The Harvard Medical School occupied a building of some dignity and architectural pretensions on the level ground at the foot of Grove Street hill. The Massachusetts General Hospital was close by, and as these were the days before the expanding hospital had made it necessary to change the course of the river, that too was not far distant. On a crisp November day, the first Wednesday in November, 1866, a flag-flapping breeze was harassing the water into wavelets when Matthew and Edward came out of the school's porticoed entrance and stopped at the top of one of the two flights of steps that led to the ground. Each was holding a copy of the school's catalogue in his hand, and both wore serious, almost solemn expressions. Matthew spoke as he tucked his catalogue carefully away in an inside pocket.

"That was quite an experience."

"Pretty different from Toledo, isn't it?"

"Thing that strikes me is, we're going to have to work like hell. I've got to talk to some of the professors before I know how much credit they'll give me for last year's work. How about you?"

"Same. I don't expect any difficulty about anatomy or dissection, and you ought to be all right in surgery too.

Whatever they do, my idea is we're where we ought to be. Let's get out of this wind."

They started down the steps, still wearing their serious looks, for the experiences of the last two hours had awed them a little. From the moment they had presented themselves, as the catalogue had instructed, at Dean Shattuck's office, they found themselves in an atmosphere of almost grim endeavor utterly unlike the vacillating vagaries of the Toledo school. Many students were about, but there was no loitering and everyone seemed to know where he was going and why he was going there. Even their footsteps had a purposeful sound.

At first they assumed that the reason for this was the school's connection with the University, until they found that connection to be more nominal than real, and that the school was managed by its own faculty with little or no control by the University. Perhaps such an arrangement as this could not have worked so well in any city but Boston. However that might be, the faculty itself set the school's standards, designed its curriculum, and at the end of the school year divided their fees in lieu of salaries.

The Toledo professors taught because they had failed at everything else. Those whom Matthew and Edward encountered on this November day were dedicated men, dedicated as much to the training of their students as to the advancement and science of medicine. All of them were good teachers; two or three deserved to be called great. And so Matthew, after meeting these men, one after another, and sensing more than comprehending their stature, was led to say, "That was quite an experience."

"Now what?" he asked when he and Edward had reached the bottom of the steps.

"I'm going to find a place to live, out of the list of boardinghouses I got in the Dean's office. And you?"

"Go look at that minister's house where they give room and board in return for tending the furnace and other odd jobs."

"I think you're foolish, Matt."

"I can always quit. Let's meet back here at suppertime."

And so they parted, each with a sense of exhilaration. Matthew had not gone very far, however, when he came on a medical supply store, the first he had ever seen. He stopped and peered through the small-paned window at instruments and contrivances, many of a sort he had never seen before and a few of which he could not guess the use.

Wishing Edward were still with him, he pushed open

the door and went inside. The proprietor was sitting on a stool behind a counter reading a newspaper, a neat little man with the sort of secondary medical look about him that druggists, and others who are connected with the medical profession but not in it, seem to acquire. He looked at Matthew over his paper and gave him a half smile that said plainly enough that he was accustomed to students and expected only minor profits from them.

"May I look around?" Matthew said.

"Sure, sure."

The proprietor went back to reading his newspaper and Matthew wandered along the counter, peering through its glass top, until he came to a curious brass implement with a long, slanting tube and little wheels. It excited his curiosity and he stooped over to examine it.

"What's this dingbat?"

"A microscope. Haven't you ever seen one before?"

"Nope."

"You're at the school, aren't you? You'll find yourself using one before you're much older. You want to buy one of your own, the price is fifty dollars."

"Thanks, not today."

Matthew moved on. In the end, however, he bought a stethoscope and an ophthalmoscope because that morning at the school he had overheard a student saying he owned these things. He would have liked to buy a laryngoscope also, but he felt he had already spent a good deal of money, especially as he had no idea how to use these instruments, or even what their purpose might be. His purchases made a fine bulge in his pocket, and because he owned them he left the store feeling that his world had become better, wider, and a great deal more meaningful.

The Reverend Seth Brainard's house turned out to be large and almost new. It was boxlike in shape, painted a chocolate brown with much ornamentation done in the color of Jersey cream, and had clearly cost a great deal of money. The grounds were large, enclosed by a picket fence, and shaded by elms that made a canopy of their wiry twigs. Matthew was interviewed by the minister's wife, a massive, dominating woman who seemed determined to intimidate him and to whom Matthew rightly supposed the wealth belonged. To his surprise, this lady accepted him, and before dusk he was installed and was attempting to establish a relationship of good-natured raillery with the cook and housemaid, who were both Irish and took to him at once.

On the next day, in the late afternoon, Edward came here to find Matthew. He had gone to the front door as a matter of course, and given the bell an authoritative pull, but the housemaid in the long white apron who opened it told him severely that "them as wanted to see Mr. Chapin was to go around to the back and not be pulling at the front bell like as they was pulling it out." Smiling, Edward complied and was there met by the same girl, who let him in with an air of never having seen him before. She led him into a kitchen, where the cook turned away from the range to give him a hostile look, opened a door on a steep back stairs with treads scarcely wide enough for a foothold, said "He's up there," and shouted, *"Mr. Chapin!"* in a voice which made Edward's nerves jangle.

There were sounds from above, a door was thrown open hard enough to bang against the wall, and Matthew, with shirtsleeves rolled up and collar open, appeared at the top of the stairs. "Hey!" he said with the air of pleased surprise. "Hullo, you old son of a bitch, so you found the place? Come on up and I'll show you where I live, but watch those stairs, will you?"

The room was clearly meant for a servant. It was so small that to let Edward enter Matthew had to back up against the narrow bed. There was one chair, which Matthew offered to Edward with a gesture, a washstand scarcely large enough to hold its handbasin, a low bureau with drawers that could not be pulled out unless one sat on the bed to do it, and a single window partly blocked by the bed's headboard.

"Is this where you sleep? God, what a hole! That maid wouldn't let me in the front door—made me go around back."

"I'm surprised they let you in at all. Students are low characters around here."

"You going to stick it?"

"Why not? The food's good."

"Do you eat with the family?"

"Nope. In the kitchen with hatchet face and the other."

"But, my God, Matt, you can't study here. There isn't even a table and it feels like there's no heat."

"There isn't, but I've got all that fixed. Come on and I'll show you."

Matthew led the way to the stairs, clattered down them and waited at the bottom while Edward made a cautious descent. Then he plunged down a second flight, calling over his shoulder, "Watch out—don't hit your head on

184

that stringer beam," bent himself sideways to avoid it, and kicked open a whitewashed door at the bottom.

They came out into a large, well-lighted cellar which had many doors leading from a central room, and was filled with the odor of stored apples, squash and potatoes. At one side of this room a huge round furnace raised octopus arms to the ceiling, and from its interior there came a faint, breathy muttering. It had a look of mightiness, as though its arms alone held up the whole establishment.

"You have to tend that thing?" Edward asked, staring at the furnace.

"Yeah, but it's not as bad as it looks."

"It's nice and warm down here."

"Warmest place in the house. I'm glad you're here because I've got an idea. Why wouldn't this be a fine, comfortable place for us to study? We could rig up a workbench sort of thing out of that old lumber in the corner, and get a lamp and something to sit on, and we'd have a place couldn't be beat. What do you say?"

"It's an idea. Maybe a good one. Would the Reverend object?"

"Would Mrs. B. object is more to the point, but I bet she hasn't been down those stairs since the place was built. She'll never know. Come on, take your coat off and give me a hand and we'll fix it up right now, but let's be quiet about it."

They constructed the workbench out of planks laid on two packing boxes. They found a chair with a broken back in the room where the apples were stored, and Matthew made a clattering trip up two flights of stairs, returning with his own chair and an armload of books, paper and pencils. Then they took a glass lamp out of a wall bracket at the foot of the stairs and set it rather precariously on one end of the bench. The result was a very satisfactory place to work, and they stood looking at it with pride. Matthew, forgetting his own injunction to be quiet, tipped his head back and sang:

On the coast of Co - ro - man - del, Where the ear - ly pump - kins

grow, In the mid - dle of the woods, Lived the Yongh - y Bongh - y

Bo, Two old chairs and half a can-dle, One old jug with-out

han-dle; These were all the world-ly goods, In

mid-dle of the woods, These were all the world-ly goods, Of

Yongh-y Bongh-y Bo, Of the Yongh-y Bongh-y Bo.

He was drawing breath for the second verse when there was a heavy thumping overhead and they both looked up.

"The Reverend Seth Brainard?" Edward asked in a hushed voice.

" 'Fraid so. I forgot his study is about overhead."

"Sounds cantankerous. What's he like?"

"He thinks he's God's partner—the active partner—and that God couldn't get along very well without him. He's High Church, she's Low, so they hate each other and get a lot of enjoyment out of it. They have hymn singings on the first Sunday evening of every month for the Divinity students—and Medical School students, though I bet not many of those show up. You can come to one, if you like, and meet the Rev. Let's sit down, shall we?"

They settled down to their new surroundings like small boys who have just completed a tree house, and Matthew tipped his chair back against the wall.

"Why weren't you at Clin Med this morning?"

"Dr. Holmes was giving a special lecture on the microscope I didn't want to miss."

"You like that stuff, don't you? Slides and all that."

"If you had any sense you'd like it too."

"I'm a surgeon. I'll leave all that to you guys who want to be pathologists."

"And there you're wrong as hell. The opening up of

what Holmes calls the 'invisible world' by the microscope is the most important—and incidentally the most exciting—thing that's going on in medicine today. Maybe more important to medicine than the world we see."

"You believe that?"

"I do. Up to now a lot of medical practice has been based on speculation. Little by little the microscope will substitute knowledge for speculation." Edward laid his hand on one of the planks of which their desk was made. "Histology and microbiology are the sciences of the future. And I've settled in my own mind that there's where my real work's going to be."

"One lecture and you've chosen your life work?"

"You should have been there."

Matthew, at his ease, studied Edward a moment with bright, thoughtful eyes. Then he laughed. "Remember Old Top Hat?"

"I do," Edward said in a tone that disapproved of Matthew's levity. "Wait and see if what I'm saying won't come true someday. Is that coffee I smell?"

"Sure is. The maids are always drinking it. Want some? I'll bring it down here."

He went noisily up the stairs and there followed giggles and squeals of laughter that made it evident that Matthew was already a favorite in the kitchen. A moment later he came down again, grinning, and carrying a tin tray on which were two cups of coffee and two generous slices of cake.

After that it became a settled thing that they should study together here in the late afternoons and evenings. Because of Matthew's war experience and the extra work they had both done in anatomy and dissecting, both young men had a special and privileged standing in the school. Both took full advantage of the latitude allowed them to pursue their individual interests. Edward spent long hours with the microscope, learning to identify the normal so that he could recognize the pathological. He bought a microscope of his own and set it up at one end of the basement workbench. He began a collection of slides of his own that grew rapidly, and his eyes were often red-rimmed from strain.

Matthew began an intensive study of surgical procedures and techniques that opened his eyes to how fine a surgeon Zsokay was and led him to compare Zsokay's European methods with those he was encountering here. Every operating day he crammed himself into one of the narrow seats of the amphitheater on the top floor of the hospital to watch one or another of the attending surgeons at work. He went to autopsies, and these also interested Edward, though for different reasons.

He was in the dissecting room whenever possible. This was a ground-floor, windowless structure, built onto one end of the school and lit by a skylight. The school obtained its bodies legally, never by grave robbing, and so the supply of them was not plentiful. The dissecting was done by a demonstrator while the class looked on, though occasionally two of the students, working together, were allowed to do the demonstration. Matthew was a member of one of the first of these teams and worked with such skill and sureness that he was afterward regarded as one of the school's outstanding students.

Under this intensive, sharply focused work, both young men began to change in physical appearance and in the outward aspects of their personalities. Edward, thinner than ever, developed a hard, precise brilliance, an efficiency and direction of purpose that showed in his manner and in his curt, to-the-point speech. He seemed capable of concentrating his attention on his work, or on someone who interested him, with the intensity of a burning glass.

Matthew appeared to grow more powerful physically. He too developed an economy of motion, not Edward's taut, nerve-controlled purposefulness but the easy, relaxed strength of an animal that can respond in an instant with such perfect physical and mental coordination that there is no wasted or useless motion. The physical requirements of his chosen work were heavy. He was learning to meet them; and if techniques received a disproportionate amount of his attention, to the neglect of histological and pathological aspects of his work, it was perhaps only a phase of his youth.

Edward was aware, though perhaps not fully consciously, of the imbalance in Matthew's development and brought to bear a steady pressure to correct it. Sometimes he would insist on Matthew's looking through the microscope at a slide of a tumor section, and Matthew would say with good-natured resistance, "What the hell do I need to look at a magnified piece for? It's important to recognize the thing as a whole when I find one, and to know how to take it out. Can you tell me why anything else matters?"

At this time Edward could not answer him, but he continued to insist on the importance of his microscopic studies. In the laboratory, under the microscope, they watched the circulation pulsating in a frog's webfoot and the waving, rhythmic beat of the cilia on a fragment snipped from an oyster with a pair of shears. They looked at slides of pus in which they could see faint dots, usually in clusters like bunches of grapes, and saw strange, minute objects in the blood and tissue of the sick, but among their teachers there was little conviction and less agreement about what these objects might be. Microorganisms, said those who had been in laboratories in France and Germany. As to this, others reserved judgment, and some scoffed. They looked at red and white cells in the blood and knew in a general way what the proportion of one to the other should be, and that a change sometimes accompanied illness, but like much else in microscopy it was an observation without as yet any practical application.

Sometimes when the light was good and every condition favorable, Edward thought he saw other objects in the blood, oval or irregularly rounded shapes. They interested him, but they were so faint as to be on the borderline of reality and there seemed to be nothing he could do to satisfy his curiosity about them. He did not know that at about this time a doctor in Montreal named Osler was also interesting himself in these strange objects and he did not discover until years later that he was seeing the platelets, and that they were a third element of the blood.

Matthew's interest in the revelations of the microscope quickened a little as the weeks passed, but he never felt anything like Edward's profound fascination with these matters. He was, of course, young, and though it would have surprised him to hear it, he was very inexperienced. In time, however, he came to rely on the work of pathologists more than most surgeons of his day. He hated to cramp his big body over a microscope and he did his best to avoid any extra work involving what he considered the fiddling business of microscopy.

He was not greatly to blame, for the microscope that up to this time had been chiefly a fascinating tool of the naturalist had taken its place in medicine as a research instrument rather than as a diagnostic aid. The discoveries its lenses made possible were not so much a means to an end as an end in themselves.

Matthew was troubled without fully understanding why. The nearest he came to an expression of his dissatisfaction was when he said to Edward, "When you microscope fellows turn up something I can use in the operating room, then I'll be right there to grab it. Until then, that stuff's not for me."

"Don't you want to know when a tumor's benign and when it isn't?"

"Mostly I can tell by looking at it."

"No you can't."

"Suppose I can't. You find a tumor, you take it out, no matter what it is, so what difference does it make?"

And again, from his inexperience, Edward could not answer him. Nevertheless, Matthew good-naturedly brought back from the operating theater various bits and pieces of diseased tissue, portions of which Edward used to make slides for his growing collection. An incidental result of all this was that, during the winter, the Reverend Seth Brainard's old octopus of a furnace occasionally received some very strange fuel.

CHAPTER TWENTY

One day when Matthew was sweeping a light powdering of snow from the front walk of the Brainard house, he heard the heavy latch of the gate click and turned to see Edward coming toward him. Edward was carrying his violin case, and Matthew said without greeting, "What you got that thing for? You can't practice here. The Rev. would throw us both out."

"I'll do my practicing at my own place—if I ever get time for it. It's not my violin. I can't study with a dry throat even if you can."

"Oh, that's it. Well, go on in. I'll join you in a few minutes."

Edward, however, did not go, but stood there watching the easy swing of Matthew's shoulders as he began to sweep the snow from the bottom step. The thought came to him that Matthew's way of doing it lacked the touch of bad temper that seemed to be so necessary an ingredient of a woman's sweeping, and he smiled. It was an aloof smile that nevertheless held admiration, but then it faded, and as he watched the perfect coordination and muscular grace, a look of bitter envy darkened his face, a look he often wore but which he had never let Matthew see. Had Matthew seen it he would have been surprised, and in fact incredulous, for he was unaware that either envy or admiration had a place in Edward's mind. He did not, however, turn around until the gate latch again made its loud, curiously terminal sound, and in that instant the betraying look vanished.

Mrs. Seth Brainard, a lady of formidable proportions, was advancing on them up the walk. She was dressed in a wide brown skirt that extended beyond the walk to sweep the snow from the frozen grass on either side and looked as unpliable as she herself gave the impression of being. The skirt was topped by a pelisse of the same shade of brown, and trimmed with jet fringe that was in agitated motion as her bulk came majestically and smoothly onward as though on wheels. It was a dismaying sight and the two young men stood as though frozen in awe.

She came to a halt (a woman of such massive dignity could not be said to stop), shot a glance at Edward, whom she had never seen before, and, lifting her chin, looked at Matthew with tight-lipped inquiry. Matthew, who had been to a degree mesmerized, flushed and recollected himself with a start.

"Mrs. Brainard," he said, "may I present my friend, Edward Chisolm?"

Edward bowed stiffly and backed onto the grass to let her pass while Matthew took two or three hurried swipes with the broom at the steps to clear a way for her. She did not again set herself in motion, however, for the violin case in Edward's hand had caught her eye and she inclined her head toward it.

"You play, Mr. Chisolm?"

"A little, ma'am."

"Good, then you may come to our hymn singing next Sunday night and bring your instrument. Matthew, I noticed you were not at our first one. I shall want you to lead the singing. You can sing, I've heard you."

She turned to Edward with what she plainly felt was a gracious manner. "We shall be glad of your help, for our only music is a harmonium."

"Do you play it yourself, ma'am?" Edward asked in wonder.

"No, I ask some young friend. This winter it will be a widowed cousin of mine who has lately come to Boston to live. Mrs. Cecilia Ward. You can assist her greatly, I am sure." She smiled on Edward, nodded to Matthew, and began to mount the steps, the jet fringe quivering.

When the front door had closed behind her, Edward stepped back onto the path. "My God, Matt, could it be that girl you're so gone over? Is her name Cecilia?"

"Yes."

"Crickets! What's she doing in Boston?"

"How should I know?"

"What are you going to do?"

"Talk to her. Try to get her to see me."

"Do you think she will?"

"No, but I'm going to try." He was silent and thoughtful for a moment; then he said, "You're not going to come to the singing, are you?"

"Sure I am. You couldn't keep me away."

The three days that intervened before Sunday night seemed to Matthew to be outside the laws that govern time, for they both dragged interminably and passed with headlong speed. He yearned to see her, and was filled with apprehension. He did no studying at all, for when he opened a book he could not keep his mind on it long enough to comprehend the meaning of a paragraph. It was the same in class. When Dr. Holmes, who did not like to kill the rabbits he used to demonstrate in his anatomy lectures, asked Matthew to do it for him, Matthew did not even hear the request. Another student volunteered for him, and he only came to himself with the general laughter of the class. He missed all the fine points of an operation he saw. He barely ate his meals, and Edward, noting his state of worried abstraction when they were lunching in a dismal place up the hill on Grove Street, said, "Matt, pull yourself together!"

Matthew looked at him with amber eyes so glowing hot that Edward inwardly retreated and said a little angrily, "You can't be all that crazy about her."

Matthew pushed his plate away without reply; then he resorted to a gesture that was always, with him, indicative of despair in all its degrees of intensity. He ran his fingers in among his curls and scrubbed and tugged at them as though by physical hurt he could conquer mental agony.

Sunday morning came and it occurred to Matthew, as he lay on his back in bed, gazing at a map of cracks in the ceiling, that he might be able to have a preview of Cissie, so to speak, if he went to church and saw her there. Then he recalled that Cissie was a Congregationalist while the Reverend Brainard was an Episcopalian, so that she would no doubt attend some other, unknown church. He faced the day with a sigh. In the early afternoon Edward appeared and they went clomping down the cellar stairs to study. But Matthew was too restless to work and the heavings and twistings of his big body made it impossible for Edward to concentrate. He closed his book with no appearance of regret and they began one of their long, rambling, but to Matthew intensely stimulating conversations. They talked until Edward looked at his watch and said it was getting late and that he had better go back to his room and get his violin. "Not that I'm exactly looking forward to playing hymns," he said. "But at that, with the little practicing I get to do these days, it's about all I'm good for." Smiling his thin smile, he pushed his chair back and stood up.

He was at the top of the stairs when Matthew thought of something and jumped up, shouting, "Hey, wait a minute." He stood at the bottom looking up at Edward's slim, neat figure illuminated by the light from the kitchen. Sometimes when Edward was tired his face had a dusky look, like an Indian's, and his black eyes shone with unnatural brilliance. It was so now, and it gave him so alien, so almost foreign a look that Matthew, not very much in command of himself, merely stared.

"Well?" Edward said irritably.

"Look, Ed . . ." Suddenly Matthew looked miserable. A heavy, painful flush came into his cheeks and he seemed to be having great trouble finding words with which to finish the sentence. "Ed, listen, would you mind a lot going by yourself? I mean, going in alone, and I'll join you there? You wouldn't mind, would you?"

"What's the sense of that?"

"None, I guess, only . . . oh hell, do it, will you, and let me get my bearings by myself? Christ, I want to see her again more than anything in the world, and now I'm going to, I'm scared to death. You're more used to society affairs and meeting people than I am. It won't bother you. Just let me handle it my own way, will you?"

Edward laughed. "What a state you're in. All right, anything you like, I don't mind. But I can tell you I'm getting damn curious about this Cissie, especially as when you try to talk about her you don't make any sense at all." And with that he went his way.

After his departure a deep quiet descended on the cellar, the house, the whole world. Matthew stayed where he was, one hand on the wall, and vaguely wondered if everyone upstairs were lying dead. He wandered over to the makeshift desk and stood there for a while staring sightlessly at the downward sloping barrel of Edward's microscope. Then, with some vague thought that perhaps the furnace might need some attention, he crept wearily toward it and opened its door. After a few minutes he found himself standing there staring into the fiery pit without the slightest idea what it was he had in mind to do. He shut the door with a clang that made the whole silent world shudder, and pulled out Dr. Hurd's watch and looked at it without being able to comprehend its meaning.

It seemed to him that he was beginning to feel very queer, strangely weak in the legs and with an elusive but disturbing sense of something wrong in the region of his stomach. He thought he had better go up to his room and lie down on his bed, only he was feeling so very weak. He was not sure he could make the stairs.

He lay on his bed and wondered in a disinterested sort of way if he were really ill and what would happen to him if he were. He thought he didn't much care and that it would be the easiest thing in the world just to relax and die. Then he thought again of Cissie, or rather she seemed to float gently through his mind in a series of images that had no relation to sequential thought. Her grace so touched him that his own feelings of sweet sadness were unbearable to him and he was not surprised to find his eyes misting with what he was pleased to suppose were tears.

The room began to grow dark, and from the kitchen below came sounds of the preparation for supper, the rattle of cutlery and plates, the bang of stove lids. Presently a voice called up to him from the foot of the stairs that the meal was ready, and he answered in a shout that belied his feebleness that he didn't want to eat. He shut his eyes and tried to restore the beauty of his mood.

Then a thought, clear and sharp as a knife, pierced his melancholy. With the spring and elasticity of a perfect body, he rolled onto his side and stood on his feet all in one fluid motion. He yanked his best suit off its peg and began giving it a rapid but close inspection. A few hairs clung to it here and there. He snatched a clothes brush from the bureau top and brushed at them with fury. After that he went to the washstand and splashed water on his face with his cupped hands, and then he began slowly to array himself for the great event.

He stood in the doorway of the dining room and saw her, like a detail from some crowded, elaborate canvas, without being aware of anything more than a blurred, out-of-focus impression of many people in the large room. She was turning over the pages of a hymnal on the rack in front of her, preoccupied, her head under its lace cap tilted a little to one side. She seemed to him thinner and changed in some subtle way that he could not define, nor did he try to, but to him she was utterly lovely and she made a heartbreaking appeal to his tenderness.

He did not rush toward her, for the strange weakness had overtaken him again and he was almost trembling. For the moment the sight of her was enough. He had rehearsed their meeting many times, but now all that he had thought to say to her fled from his mind and he was overwhelmed by a sense of his own inadequacy.

He might have stood there blocking the doorway, unaware of his surroundings, for some time had not the Reverend Seth Brainard appeared behind him, wanting to pass. Reverend Brainard, as he was called by his large flock, appeared to be a militant man of God, an impression which he was careful to maintain. He was big, stern-faced, graying, and not so much hairy as bristly in an undisciplined-looking sort of way, like a dilapidated clothes brush. One saw him in a shaggy habit, sandaled feet trudging through the snow, cross thrust out before him, but in fact he loved the soft life, the social show that his wife's money provided for him, and he was impatient to shed his light on those gathered in his house. He laid a large, reproving hand on Matthew's back. "If you please, young man," he said in a hollow voice that brought to mind crypts and deep vaults.

Matthew started and moved aside, giving the Reverend Brainard an unfriendly look that caused the man of God to menace him with his bushy eyebrows as he passed on through the doorway. Dislodged from his anchorage, Matthew too moved away, drifting on the tide of his desire toward Cissie. She had found something in the hymnal that she liked, had flattened the pages with her palm, spread her skirts a little, and was trying a few breathy, experimental notes. Matthew, still oblivious of the groups of people and the noise of talking, moved forward until he stood beside the harmonium looking down at her.

She felt his presence and glanced up, and their eyes met. Her whole body jerked and a tiny spark of light flashed from a ring on her suddenly rigid hand. She grew pale, dead-white, staring at him with a frozen look. Then she made a movement as though to rise and he said *"Cissie"* pleadingly and touched her shoulder to keep her in her place.

She obeyed him, but she shrank from him and the frozen look turned to fright and a sort of wild horror of him that hurt him unbearably.

"Cissie, don't," he said, not knowing what he meant, but begging her with his voice, his eyes, the attitude of his body as he bent toward her. There was no one near them and he would not have cared if there had been. "Cissie, I love you. Can't you forgive me? What happened is terrible, I know, and I wouldn't have had it happen for anything in the world, but it doesn't have anything to do with the way I feel about you. Can't you forgive me, Cissie?"

"No." She spoke with her head bent, her eyes on her clenched hands in her lap. The paleness had given place to a flush, and her face was full of her suffering.

"Can't I see you? Can't I come and see you? I want to talk to you."

"No, Matthew. I don't want to see you—ever. Please go away now and leave me."

He did not go, but stood there in silence, looking down on her. He was too deeply moved for words, and the curve of her bowed shoulders, the way her head was turned away from him, told him that she was close to tears.

It was then that he was made abruptly aware of his surroundings, for Mrs. Brainard in all the magnificence of her spreading skirts and ironclad bosom was bearing down on them. Matthew gave her a distracted look of desperation, and saw that she had Edward in tow and that Edward was holding his violin.

"Cecilia, my dear," Mrs. Brainard said, "I see that you have already met Mr. Chapin, who is to lead the singing tonight. But may I present Mr. Chisolm, who will play his violin for us?"

Then Edward was bowing and holding Cissie's slim hand, not even glancing at Matthew, who backed away and stood, an awkward outsider, watching the scene. Mrs. Brainard was commanding like a general.

"And now, Cecilia, I think it is time to start. Here is a little list of the hymn numbers." She placed a piece of paper covered with bold black writing on the music rack. "Number 172, I think, to start with, don't you? 'Softly now the light of day'—Sweet. One of my favorites—'fades upon the hills away.' You know the words, Mr. Chapin?"

"No, ma'am."

"Then get a hymnal. There are plenty of them about. Number 172."

Matthew moved away and for the first time looked about him. The room was rich, almost sumptuous, but dark and forbidding, for Mrs. Brainard was one of those who believe that gloom is necessary to the religious life. There were many people in it, now at the moment all bent on finding places to seat themselves for the hymn singing. Most were men as young or younger than himself. Some he knew at the Medical School; others he had seen there, and the rest he rightly guessed to be students at the theological seminary. There were a few dowagers, plainly churchwomen, friends of Mrs. Brainard's, and six or eight young ladies obviously selected for their sterling characters and not for their ability to charm. Chairs were being brought forward for the ladies and they were settling into them with much ado about arranging their skirts. With all the seats occupied, the young men were making themselves as comfortable as they could, sitting on the floor close by the girls, or standing with their backs against the dark red walls. Though Matthew was expected to lead the singing, Cissie's coolness daunted him and he moved away. He maneuvered himself through the crowd and found a place for himself standing by the wall where he could see Cissie's back. Mrs. Brainard had retired now and Cissie and Edward were consulting, she looking up into his face, he leaning over her, violin in hand, touching a page of the hymnal with the tip of his bow.

The sight filled Matthew with a rage of jealous misery, and he was about to work his way back again to impose his presence on them when the music started. He stayed where he was and listened morosely to the clear, fine strains of the violin and the slightly wheezy notes of the harmonium as it came panting along in pursuit. Around him rose the ragged chorus of young voices. He did not sing though he imagined he felt Mrs. Brainard's sharp stare probing at him. Hymn followed hymn with only pause enough between for the two musicians to locate the next number and play the opening measures by way of announcing their selection. Once he saw Cissie look up at Edward and knew she had given him a quick smile, and he felt the agony of supposing that she had forgotten his presence. Once he saw Edward, helping to find a page in the hymnal, lean so close to her as to touch her shoulder, and he grew red with helpless fury.

It was the sight of the pleasure these two were so obviously finding in playing together that finally made him take a part. Cissie looked at Edward, questioning him, and he nodded. They began to play. Without taking his shoulders from the wall, Matthew sang. He filled his lungs and let his voice out.

> *Mine eyes have seen the glory of the coming of the Lord;*
> *He is trampling out the wine-press where the grapes of wrath are stored;*
> *He hath loosed the fateful lightnings of his terrible swift sword;*
> *His truth is marching on.*

Strong and true, the hymn floated over the heads of the seated people. At the first notes he saw Cissie stiffen and he sang the louder, knowing that the sound of his voice was bringing memories flooding back to her. Edward, hearing, half twisted his lean body around in acknowledgment, and out of the corner of his eye Matthew saw Reverend Brainard, seated with his great hands on his knees, bellowing in an aggressive bass.

The song ended and Matthew held the last note, held it longer than the violin, and knew that everyone was looking at him and he did not care. Before the note died, Reverend Brainard was on his feet, arms raised, his commanding voice almost, as it were, picking the note up before it ceased. *"In the name of the Father, and the Son, and the Holy Ghost, amen."* The timing was perfect, the effect full of drama. All over the room men and women were rising and bowing their heads, and with scarcely a pause but with a change in the level of the tone, the great voice went on: *"And now, the grace of our Lord Jesus Christ, and the love of God, and the fellowship of the Holy Ghost, be with us all evermore. Amen."*

A pause, and then a few people moved, a few spoke a word or two in subdued voices. Mrs. Brainard gave her husband a glance hot with resentment of his liturgical ending, and at once transformed herself into a smiling hostess. Talk became loud and general, the young ladies resumed their flirtations, and from the dining room there were sounds of sudden activity.

Matthew tried to struggle through the crowd to reach Edward and Cissie, but without having formed the least idea of what he would do when he got there. He had advanced no farther than the dining-room door when he met a barrier in the form of Mrs. Brainard with a large platter of fat ginger cookies in her hands.

"Well," she said, placing herself directly in front of him so that he could make no further progress, "you may at least pass these around." And she held the platter out to him.

Perforce he took it and began offering it mechanically to those who were near him. With so many people in the room there was little freedom of movement, and over their heads he could see that quite a few had gathered around Cissie and Edward so that he felt that there was nothing to be gained by attempting to join them. He concentrated on distributing the cookies, anxious to get rid of them as soon as possible. The young ladies were working their way in and out among the guests, bestowing cups of cocoa, pretending extreme efficiency and casting coy, sidewise glances at every young male and most of the old ones.

Suddenly Matthew was tired of the whole business, bored, weary. If he could not reach Cissie he wanted nothing—not in the way one usually wants nothing, but in a positive, aggressive way that made nothingness into a solid state. He put the platter, which still held six or eight of the puffy cookies, on top of a bookcase and retired into a dark corner where he hoped to be left alone. He was not. One of the smiling young ladies, assuming that his status in the house was that of guest, like the others present, thrust a cooling cup of cocoa at him. He accepted it with a sigh.

From his corner he could no longer see Cissie, and for the moment he was content to do nothing about it. He felt vaguely hungry, and this reminded him of the cocoa. He lifted the cup from the saucer, saw a thick wrinkled scum had formed on the surface, and lowered it again, took up the spoon and lifted off the scum. It clung to the spoon like a shroud, dripping dolefully. The sight revolted him and he hastily put the cup beside the cookies on the bookcase.

It was then that an idea came to him that banished his incipient hunger and galvanized him into action. The number of people in the room was lessening now, and the hall beyond was filled with the sound of departing voices. Matthew looked around him a little wildly, saw no sign of Cissie, and worked his way toward Mrs. Brainard, who was the center of a little knot of people, receiving their farewells with graciousness. As soon as there was any chance of securing her attention, Matthew spoke to her.

"Excuse me, ma'am."

She turned her bright public expression on him, but when she saw it was Matthew the brightness faded like the sun going behind a cloud, and disapproval took its place. She said nothing, but her skirts made an exclamatory rustle and Matthew felt himself reproved for his failure in singing and in cookie passing as effectively as though she had spoken.

"It occurred to me," he said, half amused, half annoyed with himself because of the small-boy feeling she gave him, "it occurred to me, Mrs. Brainard, that perhaps you would like me to see Mrs. Ward home."

Mrs. Brainard was one who presented her feelings of the moment, no matter how trivial they might be, as though they were the only ones she possessed. Now she became one vast monument of astonishment, making it clear to Matthew that anything like considerateness or good manners from him surprised her to the very core of her being. He grinned at her. "Why not?" he said.

"Why not? Because she's gone. She left a good five minutes ago."

"Alone?"

"Certainly not alone. The young man with the violin—your friend—is seeing her home. I asked him to, and he agreed most politely. He was looking for you before he left but couldn't find you, and Mrs. Ward had a headache and was anxious to get home."

The next moment Matthew found himself staring at Mrs. Brainard's back and he moved away. Then it occurred to him that Cissie and Edward had not yet had time to go far, that they might be walking slowly and that he might catch up with them. Dodging some people who were lingering near him, he precipitated himself into the hall, muttered apologies to those he brushed in passing, yanked open the front door and leaped down the front steps.

Not until he reached the gate did it dawn on him that he had no idea where Cissie was staying, and so had no notion in which direction she and Edward had turned. He went through the gate at a sober pace, stood on the walk,

200

and looked to right and left. Several couples and three or four lonely walkers were in sight, faintly illuminated by the yellow gaslight of the streetlamps, but though he could not see them clearly, he felt certain that Cissie and Ed were not among them.

He walked a little way down the street, not knowing what he intended to do, until the futility of going farther and the cold of the night brought him to a standstill. He did not want to go back to the house and pass the empty stool before the harmonium where Cissie had been sitting, or to risk encountering the Brainards, or to climb up to his miserable little room. There was nothing in the world that he wanted to do except to be with Cissie.

He had come to a stop under an elm tree and he left the path to lean his back against its trunk. The night air was clear and sharp with cold, and he hunched his shoulders and thrust his hands deep in his pockets. A little group of young men, the last of the guests, passed him and glanced curiously at him and were silent for a moment as they went by. Then one of them began to whistle the last hymn they had sung and they all swung along briskly, keeping step to the tune. After a while the front door of the house opened and Reverend Brainard came out to stand a moment in the spill of light from the hall. Matthew tensed a little, expecting to be called, but it appeared that Reverend Brainard had merely come outside to test the temper of the night, for he went inside again and the slam of the door echoed in the empty street. The light from the house began to grow dim as lamps and gas jets were extinguished one by one. Wearily, Matthew took his back from the tree and, plodding, made slowly for the gate.

CHAPTER TWENTY-ONE

On the first floor of the Medical School there was a common room, a place set apart where students could go in any short periods of leisure they might have. Perhaps there was no room anywhere dedicated to rest less tempting than this one. Harsh light came through uncurtained windows; the few pieces of furniture were battered and scarred. Charts of the venous and arterial systems hung on the wall, and an articulated skeleton, stained with much fingering, was suspended in a corner. There was nothing to read, nothing to please the eye, no comfort to be had out of the hard chairs, and yet at odd times during the day this unlovely place received a good deal of use.

It was here that Matthew went in search of Edward, having failed to find him in the basement microscope laboratory. He was here, and alone as Matthew had hoped, studying at one end of a long table with books and papers scattered in front of him.

"Hullo," Edward said, and laid his hand on his book in a way to indicate that he expected the interruption to be a brief one. Matthew made no reply but slouched on into the room, pulled out a chair beside the table and sat down. For a time he sat there without speaking, running his thumb nail along the edge of the table and giving it all his attention as though doing it were of great importance. Edward, his hand still on the open book, studied his face, his own face expressing nothing. Then Matthew moved his hand away and glanced sharply at Edward.

"You took Cissie home last night?"

"Mrs. Brainard asked me to. You don't object, do you? She wouldn't have gone with you."

"Just the same, you might have said something to me about it before you left."

"I did look around for you, Matt, but it was pretty plain that Cissie wanted to avoid you."

"Where does she live?"

"Off Charles Street."

"That's quite a way. Did you walk?"

"What else could we do? Did you ever see a hansom in that part of town on a Sunday night? Anyway, she said she liked to walk."

Matthew frowned down at the tabletop and when he asked his next question it was in an altered voice. "Tell me about her, Ed. Did she say anything about herself?"

"Yes, she did. I told her I knew quite a lot about her from you, and when she realized that, she seemed to want to talk. She's here with her own child and that child of yours that she's taken in. And if you don't mind my saying so, I think that's the most remarkable thing I ever heard of any woman's doing."

Edward paused, but Matthew made no reply, so Edward said, "Don't you think so yourself?"

"Certainly I do. Did she say how she happened to be in Boston?"

"She didn't know you were here, if that's what you're thinking. Her husband's father died and left her some money, though she's not what you call rich. Her parents came from here and she has relatives here."

"The Brainards."

"So I gather that when she took in that child, after that woman of yours died, the town was shocked. Her guardian, that she calls Uncle Something, was set against her doing it. I can imagine a small town could kick up quite a rumpus about a thing like that. Look, it's time for chemistry lab. We better go."

"To hell with chemistry lab. What else did she tell you?"

"Nothing much."

"Where does she live off Charles Street?"

"In a boardinghouse. She asked me not to give you the address. Come on, let's go." Edward began to gather up his book and papers.

"Listen, Ed, you can skip chemistry for once. This is important. I want to talk to you."

"That's all right with me." Edward laid the books down again.

Matthew sighed, and for a long time he said nothing. He sat with his head bowed and Edward watched him with a neutral expression, halfway between commiseration and unfriendliness. Finally Matthew looked at him and said, "I've got to make it up to her, Ed."

"You treated her very badly, you know."

"I suppose I did. I know I did. I didn't mean it that way. Did you talk about me?"

"Yes, we did. She seemed to want to. She was awfully upset by seeing you again."

"What was said?"

"She asked me if you had told me the story, though she must have guessed you had. I said I'd heard your side of it and she said, 'I really loved him. I really did.' And then she started to cry. We had to stop walking, she was crying so hard. I told her how sorry I was, and . . ."

"And what?"

"And I agreed with her that she'd had pretty shoddy treatment by you."

"That was kind of you, I must say!"

"It's true enough. You even admit it yourself. What was I supposed to do—plead with her to take you back?"

"It would have been a decent thing to do."

"Do you want to quarrel about it?"

"No," Matthew said miserably.

They were silent again for a while until Edward said, "Look here, Matt, you did what you did and you hurt her terribly. Now it's finished."

"Not if I know it."

"The kindest thing would be to leave her alone."

"Why? She ought to give me a chance to make things right again."

"If you want to know why—because she doesn't love you any more. I asked her and she told me. She told me to tell you that she doesn't want to see you any more, ever."

"Then why did she take the child?"

"Because she's a fine and good woman, and I suppose she didn't want to see the child of a man she had once loved turned over to the charity of the state."

"I've sent money for the child. It's always sent back again. I've got to see her."

"She won't talk to you. She said it in so many words."

Matthew made an inarticulate sound like a groan, and Edward said, "I'm sorry, Matt, but you asked for it." After that nothing was said for a moment until Matthew looked directly at Edward and spoke in a voice of anxiety. "Will you take her a message from me, Ed?"

"No, Matt. I'd rather not."

Matthew was thoughtful for a while, and then without another word he pushed his chair back, rose and left the room.

Edward did not appear in the basement study that afternoon nor in the evening, and Matthew, unhappy enough already because of Cissie, missed him acutely. The next day Matthew was afraid it would be the same. He had been studying for about an hour when he suddenly looked up and listened, for some part of his mind thought he had heard footsteps on the stone walk going past the cellar window. Then he distinctly heard the back door shut. However, when Edward came with a tentative air down the cellar stairs, Matthew was to all appearances hard at work. Edward pulled out his chair and sat down, and Matthew said "Hullo" but without taking his eyes from his book. Edward made an indeterminate sound in reply and he too set about making a pretense of studying.

It was no use, and after a moment he dropped his hands

on his open book and said, "I don't want to quarrel, Matt."

"Neither do I."

"There isn't anything to quarrel about."

"No, there isn't, actually."

"I'm sorry as hell about Cissie."

This time it was Matt who made an inarticulate sound in his throat. He moved himself restlessly in his chair, rested his elbows on the desk and his forehead on his two hands and willed himself to concentrate on the pages in front of him.

In the days that followed they appeared outwardly to have resumed normal relations. They sat together at lectures, studied together, ate together, but there was a new reserve between them. Matthew knew he was being unreasonable, that he was making too much of an unimportant incident, but he could not help himself. They spoke of Cissie only once.

That happened two or three weeks after the hymn singing when Matthew, tortured by his longings, abruptly said to Edward, "Won't you tell me where she lives?"

"No, Matt, I promised her not to." But as Edward said this his face, that rarely flushed, grew slowly red, and a flash of suspicion crossed Matthew's mind that Edward might have been seeing her. He put it away from him as being not only unworthy but unlikely, and so gave it no more thought.

He did what he could to find her, though in point of fact there was little he could do. He asked Mrs. Brainard for her address, and received so icy a look that he felt sure that lady knew part at least of his story. After this he rather expected to be asked to leave the Brainard house and was surprised that this did not happen. He went to the next hymn singing, though he had no real hope that Cissie would be there; and he went alone, for Edward refused to go with him. He got there just in time to see a strange young lady settling herself with much flouncing of skirts in Cissie's place before the harmonium, and the sight so outraged him that he left the room and went downstairs to his cellar study. Here he spent the evening, unable to work, and the sounds of the gathering above him came to him disturbingly.

His real effort to locate Cissie, however, was made in the vicinity of Charles Street. Whenever he could take the time, which was not as often as he wished, he went there to wander up one street and down another without any plan, merely hoping he might catch sight of her. He did this in all weathers, taking grim satisfaction in the cold, the rain or the snow, as making his devotion seem the greater. He asked for her in the neighborhood stores, describing her as best he could, but no one knew of her. He even canvassed as many of the boardinghouses of the district as he could find, and there seemed to be a great many of them, but a young widow named Mrs. Ward, with two children, was unknown in all of them.

All this disturbed but did not destroy him. His youth, his good health, and above all his optimistic nature made it possible for him, after a time, to lead a full and even an enjoyable life apart from his preoccupation with Cissie. This ability, or disposition, somewhat shocked Edward, who now and again referred to it in some way. "If you are as gone on the widow as you say you are," he said once after Matthew had done a dissection with a zest and display of vitality that had its effect on the whole class, "then how in hell can you get so much enjoyment out of life?"

"That's got nothing to do with it," Matthew had replied, and smiled with so much warmth and honesty and ingenuousness in his good-looking face that Edward was at least partially won in spite of himself.

There is no doubt that the two friends, at this time, were not as close as they had been and that, though the rift was small, it was Edward's attitude that was responsible. His manner to Matthew, during these days, was apt now and again to show a little prickliness and a hint of superiority. Matthew, not in the least recognizing that these things were in part symptoms of Edward's envy of himself, met this with bewildered good will, and finally, failing either to understand or to mitigate these intangible difficulties, he wisely ignored them and led his own life in his own way without troubling about Edward's incomprehensible moods.

All this time they worked very hard, but there seemed to be less and less opportunity for the recreation with which these two had more or less offset their labors. This seemed to be largely by Edward's wish, and Matthew didn't question it, but in this stretch of time life seemed to Matthew very grim. He missed the sparkle, the variety, the various forms of excitement that had always in the past seemed to be part of life and a means of discharging some of his superabundant physical energy. He missed, too, the intellectual stimulus, the unending fund of ideas, that had been the ingredient supplied by Edward in their easy give-and-take.

Then one day something occurred that did seem to hold out faint promise of some sort of interest to parallel his work at the school. He and Edward had gone on grand rounds together at the hospital, where they followed along from bed to bed, pausing with the others at each. These had the same inherent faults as the grand rounds in Toledo; in other words, there were too many students, not enough time for each case, and no way to follow each case through its several phases.

This day Matthew and Edward were standing on the fringes of the group where they could neither see the patient who was being discussed nor hear the professor, who was bending over the bed while he talked. In consequence, they were bored and idle. Matthew, sighing, let his eyes wander over the expanse of near-whiteness of the rows of beds. This not being a surgical ward, the patients in them had as little interest for him as bundles of bedding carelessly dumped, which in fact most of them resembled. They smelled like used bedding and worse. Trying not to think of the effluvium of illness that was poisoning the air of the ward, he gazed at the ceiling, which also was near-white, then out of the small panes of a window, where there was nothing much to see, then at the broad paneled door in the hope that someone might come through it to distract him.

To his surprise, someone did come through—a small nurse in a cap and big apron that were very much whiter than any of the whiteness around about. The sight of her astonished Matthew, partly because he had never seen her before but mostly because, unlike most of the other nurses, she was pleasant to look at. She attended to the shutting of the door and then came swiftly down the aisle between the beds, her feet in their large, serviceable shoes moving in that odd, prehensile fashion that seems to be common to most nurses.

As she came onward Matthew faced the aisle, his boredom for the moment all forgotten. The serviceable shoes made a soft *pat-pat,* her starched dress a papery rustle. When she was near him she raised her eyes, and in that instant he experienced a peculiar tightening sensation in his chest, for in a faint, slightly distorted way she looked like Cissie. She was shorter, the top of her body set on stouter hips. Like Cissie, her hair was blond, her eyes gray. The look of her eyes was different, however, for they were larger and of the sort that seem to have a special talent for sadness. The literature of the day would call them "speaking eyes," but there was something vigorous about her that belied the sadness.

Her mouth was not at all like Cissie's generous one, for it was short, full, and the upper lip arched itself. It seemed to be pursed at him, asking to be kissed in such a positive way that without thinking about what he was doing, he took a step in her direction.

At once she ducked her head and moved swiftly on. He turned all the way around to watch her. Then he remembered himself and faced the backs of the group of which he was supposed to be a part. He gave pretended attention to the lecture he could not hear. The group moved to the next bed, and he went with it, careful to keep on its outside, and watched the aisle in the hope that she would again pass by.

She did pass, not once but several times, and there was a heightened color in her cheeks. She seemed to be very busy indeed. Once she was carrying a pile of sheets, once a pitcher of water in which a single piece of ice clinked dolefully. She always hurried, and she did not look in his direction, but he knew by a sort of heightening and intensifying of herself that she was fully aware of him.

Then she passed him one more time, slowly. She was carrying a load of blankets that, in itself, showed that she was stronger than she seemed. She came up from behind Matthew and when she was opposite him she raised her head, her eyes just touched his, and the little pursed-up mouth curled into a faint, mischievous smile. She was gone while he was still tingling with the pleasure of this, hooking open the ward door with her facile foot and vanishing. Matthew knew he would not see her again that day.

The group of students was already moving on, following their leader to the next bed. In turning to go with them, Matthew, who had forgotten all about Edward, found he was being stared at with great intentness. The stare was not hostile, but neither was there any warmth in it. There was interest but no sympathy, a purely clinical look such as Matthew had seen him give some specimen that stirred his intellect but not his emotions. It made Matthew's skin prickle. He grinned against the look, waveringly and a trifle defensively, and in return Edward gave him a cold, glittering, and uncomfortable smile.

For several days Matthew thought that Edward would

surely make some reference to this incident, and the dread of it oppressed him. In his mind he worked up elaborate defenses. To exchange a glance and a smile with a cute little nurse meant exactly nothing at all. Nothing. So how could it tarnish in the slightest his great, yearning love for Cissie? Even if he saw this girl again and there came to be more than a smile between them, still it would have no effect on how Cissie made him feel. Even suppose—suppose a lot of things, there would be no repetition of the business about Sue. There would be no more Sues in his life, now or ever. He had learned his lesson there, and learned Cissie's true value. Cissie was a thing apart; his feelings for her were unique. Sacred. . . . But if he could only see Cissie once more! So Matthew prepared and elaborated his defense. Edward, however, never mentioned the little nurse.

CHAPTER TWENTY-TWO

In his long, persistent search of Charles Street and the neighborhood, Matthew had mistaken a number of women, seen from a distance, for Cissie. But when one day he actually saw her, though he saw only a part of her back and the whisk of her skirt as she went through a door, he knew her instantly. He felt sure she had not seen him, for he was across the street and half hidden by a van at the curb. He did not go at once to the house into which she had disappeared—he was far too shaken by the sight of her for that—though he was surprised by his self-control. He gave himself time to calm down a little, and to think about the situation while he continued to stand where he was.

From somewhere nearby a church clock began to strike, and a part of his mind counted the strokes. Then he verified the time by Dr. Hurd's watch, as though exactness were important. He did this almost mechanically, while on another level of his mind his thoughts were in a turmoil. The hour was noon, and as this was a Sunday, it was reasonable to suppose that when he saw her, Cissie was returning from church.

Even supposing he could get in to see her now, she would almost certainly be with the children, and Matthew wanted to see her alone. Then perhaps dinner would curtail his visit, and he had no idea whether she ate early or late. The sensible course—the course that might in the end gain him the most—would be to go away and come back at some later hour, perhaps three or thereabouts in the afternoon.

Still he could not bring himself to leave at once, but stood staring at the house front until it occurred to him that Cissie might chance to see him from a window. Then he sighed, turned his back on the house, feeling as though he were turning his back on her, and moved slowly away in the direction of the Brainard house.

The day was one of those deceptive, springlike days that sometimes arrive shortly after the middle of February. The sun shone warmly but through a mist rising from melting snow. In the road there were puddles and rivulets of water, and under Matthew's tallow-saturated boots the melting snow made a crisp, swishing sound. He passed a front yard where a man, who was hanging sap buckets on two large maple trees, received from him a humorous smile that acknowledged the folly of this optimism, and grinned in return. On the edge of the Common he stopped to watch a flock of sparrows quarreling noisily over some crumbs that someone had thrown on the snow. He scarcely saw the sparrows or knew why he had stopped, for he was in a dreamlike state, the active part of his mind still concerned with Cissie.

He ate his dinner at the big kitchen table with the Irish-women, but almost in silence and with none of his usual rousing banter, so that they grew disappointed and cross with him, and finally they too lapsed into silence. After dinner he went to his room, washed himself with his usual scrupulousness, and dressed in his best clothing. He reached the house that he had seen Cissie enter just as the church clock was striking three. By that time his dreamlike state of mind had vanished and he felt himself alert, vigorous, and determined that nothing should stand in his way.

The door was opened by a thin woman with a tired face who replied to his question by saying, "Yes, Mrs. Ward's to hum." The Vermont twang was unmistakable and it brought him an instant of nostalgia for the town he had been so glad to leave. He was pleased that Cissie had found, so to speak, a compatriot, but the woman had an unfriendly air about her and he hastened to reassure her.

"I knew Mrs. Ward in Haddon. I'm an old friend."

"Come in, then. Like she'll see you." She held the door open and Matthew entered a small, dark hallway. "She and the children's got the rooms upstairs. I'll go say as how you're here."

She glanced at the stairs in a way that expressed so much regret at the necessity to climb them that he said hastily, "No need to. I can just go up myself," and he smiled because this would suit his purpose so well.

The smile won her. "Well . . ." she said, letting the word hang, but giving him a look that confided in him all her fatigue.

He started up at once, thinking that his long failure to find Cissie when he had been inquiring about the boardinghouses in the neighborhood was explained by the fact that this was not really a boardinghouse at all. He guessed Cissie to be the only tenant, and now that he thought about it, this seemed a likely arrangement for her to have made. When he reached the top of the stairs, he looked about him with interest, but all there was to be seen was a small hallway like the one below, and several closed doors. He chose the door toward the front of the house and rapped on it lightly. From the room beyond he heard sounds of motion; then the door was opened and Cissie was there. He saw light come into her eyes, and saw it fade, and then something in their depths retreated from him, and she looked at him coldly and distantly, without any trace of other feeling.

"Cissie," he said, and found that he could not say any more.

"You shouldn't have come here, Matthew."

"I have to see you. Cissie, I want . . ."

She glanced toward the stairs, and he knew that she was thinking that the woman who let him in might be listening. He lowered his voice to a whisper. "Cissie, please let me come in."

"No. Please go away."

He moved a little so that she could not shut the door. "Don't do this to me, Cissie."

"Think what you did to me."

"I've thought about it more than you can guess. What happened was before——"

"I don't want to talk about it. Please go away."

He made no move to go, but stood there in troubled silence, staring at her. Then a thought came to him and he gave it expression without stopping to consider it, so what he heard himself saying surprised him.

"You can't refuse to let me see my own child."

The thought was obviously a new one to her, and its impact showed in her face as she looked up at him, for the moment forgetful of self, the idea occupying her whole mind.

"I want to see her, Cissie," he said, and found that he really meant it.

She hesitated a moment longer, and then without a word she made way for him to enter and, as he did so, shut the door behind him. He came in looking around him at a room that seemed to him pretty and comfortable. Misty sunlight from two long windows lay in oblongs on the carpet. On the windowsills geraniums bloomed, pressing their pink flowers against the glass. Two armchairs stood by a fireplace in which the embers of a dying fire glowed warmly. On one of the chairs a book lay open, face down, and on the floor beside the other a small toy wagon with spirited metal horses hitched to it lay tipped over on its side. Seeing this toy, Matthew said, "Where's Peter?"

"Down in the kitchen with Mrs. Hull. She keeps him while the baby's sleeping."

"She's sleeping now?"

"Yes, in the next room. I'll wake her for you."

"Not yet. What's her name, Cissie?"

"Sue."

"You named her that?"

"Yes. It seemed right because"—warm color came into Cissie's face and she looked away—"because the baby was all hers, though she never even saw it, Matthew."

They were standing constrainedly in the middle of the floor and for a while neither found anything more to say. Then Matthew again looked around the room, letting her see his interest.

"Are you happy here?"

"Yes."

In that small, tentative word there sounded many emotions—resignation, the hope of peace, a mature concept of what happiness can consist of. Matthew heard the tone without grasping its meanings, and without knowing the cause of his emotion, he was deeply moved. Faltering because of it, he said, "In the old days . . ." and had to begin his sentence over again. "In the old days you used to make us coffee and we would sit together and get to know each other. We're different people now, both of us. I wish we could do it again. Could we, Cissie? Could we sit together and get to know each other again?"

She gave him a look that was at first clear and then obscured by two tears that glistened in her lashes but did not fall. Then she bent her head and moved away, and went on out of the room, and he knew that she would be back after a while with coffee and that they would sit and talk and under the talk they would be trying to find each other. He knew that he must not hurry her, and he felt the strength in himself not to do so. He understood that if they could come together now, what would be between them would be fuller, better, deepened by all that had gone before. The room seemed misty, himself and everything around him a little less than real. He took a step toward the fireplace, saw Peter's toy and stooped to set it right side up, smiling at the motionless wild gallop of the metal horses. He went to the other side of the fireplace, picked up the book that lay on the seat of the chair, closed it and held it for a moment, then laid it carefully on a table. After that he sat down to wait for Cissie's return.

She came back carrying a tray with cups and coffee. He rose and set a small table by her chair, took the tray from her and put it down. He was thinking that in the past he had left these things to her, not bothering to help her, but letting himself be waited on by her. He stood in front of her while she arranged the cups and filled them. Her hands, moving to do these things, were trembling, and seeing this he made a small, inarticulate sound of sympathy.

They sat for a long time in silence, she resting back in her chair, not touching her coffee, he stirring the spoon in his round and round with a rhythmic, clinking sound. He sighed and swallowed some of the cooling coffee and said, "Cissie, I want to tell you, and I don't know how, what I feel about your taking the child. I think it was the finest, most unselfish act I ever heard of. I didn't know that anyone could—"

"Don't, Matthew."

"I want you to know how I feel."

"I've grown fond of her. She's good and nothing ever seems to trouble her. Small as she is, she seems to enjoy life. The way Sue did." And Cissie bent over her cup so that Matthew could not see her face.

"Cissie, I still have a good part of the money Dr. Hurd left me. I want to pay whatever it costs to bring her up."

"No, Matthew."

"I must, Cissie. I wouldn't feel right if I didn't. I won't have to take the full two-year course here to get a degree. They'll give it to me in a year and a half at the latest, and after that I can begin earning money almost right away. It isn't right for you to have the burden of her keep."

"I won't take your money, Matthew."

"Why not? It's my responsibility, and I want to live up to it."

"No."

"But why?"

"I don't want to talk about it."

"But . . ."

"No, Matthew. I love her. I want to bring her up as my own. She seems like my own—she did from the first night I took her home."

"It's a very wonderful thing for you to do."

"You don't know how dear she is. She couldn't be left in that dreadful place Sue lived in, and no one could think of just sending her away to a state orphanage. It's why I left Haddon—that and so Peter could go to a city school. No one here will know her story or who her mother was."

"If ever you need help—if ever there is anything I can do . . ."

"There never will be, Matthew."

The tone in which she said this distressed him more than anything that had passed between them so far, and he was silent under its impact. She seemed to have lost herself in her own thoughts, gazing sideways down into the glowing ashes of the fire. After a moment he came out of his preoccupation, sighed, and let himself study her face. She had grown thinner, as he had noticed before, but now that he looked at her closely he saw, or rather felt, since his feelings could hardly be called coherent thought, that the change in her went far beyond the physical. In some subtle way her spirit too seemed to have fined down, as though her sorrows had leached away what had been left of trivial youthfulness, of the false and unessential, of feminine delusions, so that what remained was bedrock. He had the illusion of knowing her more surely, of actually seeing her more clearly. And when she turned her head and looked at him with eyes that were more direct and open than he had ever seen them, he gave her back a look that, if not as direct and candid as hers, he at least attempted to make the messenger of his thoughts about her. To some extent he succeeded, for he saw her expression soften as she again turned away, this time to glance at the steeple clock on the mantelshelf.

"Four o'clock! Sue will have slept enough. Do you want to see her now, Matthew?"

"If I may."

She rose, her Sunday silk dress, the color of snow skies, rustling softly around her. "She's in the next room. Come with me, if you like."

The baby was sleeping on its face on a big bed, walled in with pillows and covered with a blue shawl. Cissie bent over her. "Sue, it's waking-up time." She pulled off the shawl and turned the child on its back. Sue responded with a baby sound of pure delight and began to wave her arms and pump her legs in so vigorous a fashion that Matthew laughed.

"She's as fat as a cabbage worm."

"Isn't she? Sue, do you want to come to Cissie? All right, then."

Cissie lifted her and held her with both arms wrapped around her, and Matthew said, "She's too heavy for you."

"No she isn't. I love to hold her. Would you like to take her?"

"I never held a baby in my life."

"And you calling yourself a doctor!"

Over Sue's head Cissie was smiling at Matthew, radiant and lovely, forgetting for the moment what had happened to them since she had last looked at him in that way. "Here, take her, but be careful."

Matthew took the warm little body, felt the child wriggle with pleasure, and he hastily sat down on the edge of the bed to keep his grip on her. "Got her!" he said, looking up at Cissie, and they laughed together in the old happy way. Then he looked down at Sue and said, "Hullo there," half seriously, half embarrassed. He propped her on one knee, disengaged one hand, and offered her a forefinger. She wrapped a small hand tightly around it. Feeling pleased and self-conscious at the same time, he grinned at the little fist with its plump fingers and tiny, perfect nails. "She's got quite a grip," he said, unaware that in these circumstances this was a standard remark.

The baby gazed up at him with solemn thoughtfulness and he studied her with much the same expression on his face. This Sue was a big and bouncing girl, as the other Sue had been. The baby features were too unformed to hold a likeness, but there was a look of Sue in the slightly broad lower part of its face, and the whole little being—the exuberance and vitality—recalled the other Sue in a way that was suddenly unbearable. *"Here,"* he said, looking up at Cissie in distress, and knew, as Cissie stooped to take the child from him, that she had understood his thoughts.

He stood by awkwardly while Cissie laid Sue back on the bed and fixed the pillows around her. Straightening up and brushing back a lock of hair that had come loose, she said, "I'm going to change her now, and put a dress on her." She spoke in a friendly, gentle voice, the clear gray eyes calm and without reproach. For no reason that he could have explained, Matthew felt himself growing red under this look. He watched her for a few minutes, then he wandered into the other room, shutting the door softly behind him.

When he turned around after doing this he found that Peter was standing in the middle of the room watching him with that air of serious dignity that can so readily make an older person feel ill at ease. "Hullo there," Matthew said, aware of this feeling and trying to sound friendly.

"What are you doing here?"

The child's tone was slightly shrill, slightly stern, and though Matthew knew that Peter was too young to comprehend the difficulties between himself and Cissie, still it made him feel vaguely guilty.

"I came to see the baby. I think she's very nice, don't you?"

To this Peter made no reply, but his scorn seemed to expand to include Sue.

With a touch of desperation Matthew tried another approach. "I found your wagon and horses lying on their side. I set them up for you."

Peter glanced at the toy with disdain. Then in silence and with, if anything, an intensification of his dignity, he turned his back, walked to a window and stood looking out over the geraniums. Matthew went back to his chair, where he sat waiting for Cissie's return. He was not entirely happy, for though he and Cissie had made what seemed to him a great deal of progress together, there still remained much uncertainty. On the other hand he was certainly not altogether miserable. By an effort of will he forced his feelings into a sort of neutrality, in the half-superstitious fear that too much hope would invite disaster.

When she came she was still friendly and she seemed to feel at ease with him, but it was perfectly clear that she expected him to leave. So he said, "I better go now, I guess," making it sound like a question, for he wanted very much to stay longer. To this she merely nodded. Then she called to Peter.

"Come and say good-bye to Dr. Matthew, Peter."

The boy came readily enough and when Matthew held out a hand he put his into it. Then, unexpectedly, he smiled. It was a radiant smile, very like Cissie's, and it seemed to readmit Matthew into their old intimacy.

"I'd like to come and see you and your mother again, if I may. And Sue. How about it?"

"Sure."

Peter spoke in an easy, offhand way that attempted to sound grown-up and succeeded very well. Matthew grinned, and then glanced questioningly at Cissie. Her eyes were smiling, but they grew grave again and he saw that she was about to refuse him.

"I want to see Sue," he said. "You can't say no to that."

"All right, Matthew, but you must understand how things are between us."

He said good-bye and as he was leaving before she shut the door, she smiled again.

CHAPTER TWENTY-THREE

When Matthew thought about his visit to Cissie, and he spent a large part of his time remembering, it was of her smile that he thought most. It overlay, without quite removing, her air of serious puritanism. It was not lavish and it gave little of herself away, as Sue's smile had seemed to do, but it was of value for just that reason. Behind the reserve it suggested intimacies, but intimacies that would have to be won and, if won, forever watchfully cherished.

He could not have said why the slightly frail, ladylike loveliness of this smile should so heat his blood. And now to this he was beginning to add a real knowledge of a character that, in point of fact, he had hitherto thought little about. When he considered her taking of Sue's child to herself, the strength of purpose, the independence of mind it involved almost awed him. Moreover, her attitude toward himself, her rigid adherence to her own principles though they were in conflict with her love, he could not help but admire, however much he might have to suffer because of them. Such thoughts were new to him. Formerly he loved blindly; now he was beginning to see reason in his love, or thought he was.

He was convinced that in spite of herself she loved him still. When this idea first took root in his mind, he felt in himself a great sweep of triumphant power, but then he at once realized that victory was a long way off and that he must move with caution not to lose the little, the very little, he had already won. But in spite of his warnings to himself his natural optimism came to the fore, and sometimes he felt completely sure that he would win. Then he wanted to shout, to do great deeds, to take the world into his confidence.

He could not even tell Edward, for though they were once more studying together and spending some of what little leisure they had in each other's company, there was still a shadow of reserve in Edward's manner. This puzzled Matthew, who was not himself capable of holding to a mood not involving cheerfulness and general good will for any length of time. It puzzled him, but since there seemed to be nothing he could do about it, he simply went on as though Edward's reserve were not there.

These were the subjects of Matthew's thoughts when he and Edward were studying together in the Reverend Seth Brainard's cellar—or rather, they were simulating study for each other's benefit. Presently Edward sighed and closed his book and gave Matthew a level, expressionless look.

"You've seen Cissie Ward."

Because concealment had been difficult for Matthew, the relief of finding that Edward knew was very great. He smiled broadly and with warmth.

"Yes, Sunday afternoon. And I saw the kid too—both kids." But then a thought struck him and he said with visible cooling down, "How did you know?"

Edward shoved his chair back raspingly. "Look here, Matt, I've been meaning to tell you, but I didn't know how without making too much of it, but I've seen Cissie two or three times since that night I took her home from the hymn singing—three, to be exact."

Matthew stared at him, his open face taking on a hurt, bewildered look, but he said nothing and Edward went on uneasily.

"I haven't been happy about your not knowing, and there isn't any reason you shouldn't. There isn't anything to hide, but I've just sort of found it hard to tell you. It's all over between you and her, and you can't expect her to stay in seclusion forever because of a lost love."

A phrase caught Matthew's thoughts like a snag in the river of Edward's words, and he said with some violence, "It's *not* all over between us."

"On her showing it is."

"Well, it's not, and you're going to see soon enough it's not. And I think you might have told me before sneaking off and seeing her like that."

He was shouting, and from overhead came the heavy thumping of the Reverend Brainard's boot stamping on the floor. They both gazed upward for a moment and then Edward said in a lowered voice, "I tell you, I felt badly your not knowing, and I started to tell you more than once, but your attitude's been so damn unfriendly lately—"

"It was *your* attitude that was unfriendly."

"Well, whatever it was . . ."

"Whose idea was it that you should go to see her—yours or hers?"

"Mine. I asked her if I could that night I took her home, and she said yes."

Edward said this with the bleached look of one confessing the truth at whatever the cost to himself, and when Matthew merely stared gloomily at the table without replying, he went on.

"I didn't intend to deceive you, Matt."

Matthew's only reply to this was a small, unhappy sound.

"I half believe that the only reason she said I could come to see her was because I'm a friend of yours. She's taken the breakup with you very hard, and she's not over it yet by a long way."

"She ought to have said something about your being there when I saw her. Did she tell you I'd seen her, by the way?"

"Yes, she did. I was there last evening and she told me

then. She asked me if you knew I'd been to see her, and I told her I'd been trying to tell you . . ."

Matthew gave Edward a molten glance that silenced him and they both fell into a brooding, uneasy mood. Then Edward said in an uncertain voice, "She said it was no concern of yours, really, but that she thought you ought to know just the same. I said I'd tell you without delaying any longer."

Matthew jumped up with a violence that threw his chair back against the wall. "Damn it, you sound as though there were something between you."

"There's not. You know there's not. How could there be when I've seen her only three—no, four—times in my life? What kind of a woman do you think she is, anyway? That's been the trouble all along, incidentally. You don't understand her."

Matthew shoved his fists deep in his pockets and began to stride back and forth as far as the limits of the cellar room would let him. He looked wild and distracted as he hurled himself along, and the sight of his very evident suffering began to trouble Edward more and more. Finally, when Matthew was striding by for perhaps the twentieth time, he said, "Matt," in a tone that made Matthew stop and glower at him.

"Look here, Matt, I won't go there any more, if that's what you want. Is it? Just tell me."

Matthew did not answer him at once. Instead he started to pace again, but slowly, the urgency gone. After a moment he came back and sat down, and Edward went on to elaborate what he had been saying.

"I wouldn't have gone there in the first place if she hadn't let me, and she only did that as a matter of politeness, or because she wanted to hear about you. I'd have told you too, except that—well, I might as well admit it—I got sore at you because of the way you treated her. That's all there is to it."

"Obviously it isn't all. You like her, don't you?"

" 'Like' is so vague a word. Maybe I'm a little bit in love with her, but I'm not sure how much I like her."

"Why not, for heaven sake?"

"Well, I'll tell you. She's stubborn. She's willful, and a trifle self-righteous, and not very intelligent."

"My God," Matthew said indignantly. "How can you—"

"I know that sounds uncomplimentary or worse, but it isn't, altogether."

"Including not very intelligent?"

"Yes, sure. All those traits are the result of having principles and sticking to them no matter what. That's a virtue, or so I'm told. But like all virtue, it's bound to be a little hard on other people now and then. Matt, let me ask you this. Can you remember a single time that she gave in to you on something she felt strongly about?"

"She nearly did once. I'm not going to tell you about it."

Edward smiled broadly. "I think I can guess. But be honest, Matt. Hasn't it been these rigid principles of hers that have caused all the trouble between you?"

"I suppose so." Matthew spoke a trifle sullenly. "But if that's the way you feel about her, why did you go to see her?"

"Because she attracts me. I imagine she'd attract any man. She's the most feminine-minded woman I ever met. She's entrenched in her own beliefs and interested only in her own affairs. She doesn't understand men or want to. I imagine she didn't understand her husband but that she served him well as a wife."

"Here, hold up a minute. You're making her sound too self-centered to love anyone, but you said yourself she was in love with me."

"On her own terms only—if what you've told me is true."

"But look here, Ed. You scarcely know her. How can you talk—"

"She's not hard to figure out and neither are you. But let me finish what I was saying about why she attracts me, will you? Her femininity is so self-sufficient that it's a challenge. It makes a man want to dominate her, force her to pay attention to him. That's more or less how she makes me feel, and if you're honest with yourself you'll admit she makes you feel that way too. No, wait a minute, Matt. Let me finish. Did you ever see a self-centered little lady pigeon ignoring a male with all his feathers spread, and driving him crazy by it? Same idea exactly. Cissie's the demure little gray lady pigeon and we're the males."

"Your ideas are disgusting."

"Not at all."

Matthew gave Edward a gleaming look full of doubt, sighed, put his hands in his pockets again and leaned his chair back against the wall.

"This is a hell of a life we lead, Matt. I haven't been inside a decent home since my mother died. You don't seem to miss it, maybe because that old woman who brought you up was strict and not very pleasant, but I do. There's something about the way she lives, that room with the fire and the flowers in the windows, and everything so neat and dignified, the way my own home used to be. It sort of got me."

Matthew thought this over for a few moments, then he said slowly, "I can see how that would be, I guess."

"You're a lucky guy, Matt. You've got everything, and I envy you. But you're also a damn fool, if you don't mind my saying so. But as I say, I won't go back there if you don't want me to, though what she could see in a guy like me to make you jealous is hard to imagine." And Edward shifted his lame leg a little, not blatantly but so slightly, so instinctively, that Matthew, who was watching him, felt he had done it without being conscious of it himself. It affected him all the more for that reason, and he said, "I don't want to tell you not to go there, Ed."

He saw Edward brighten and this troubled him, for it showed him more than anything that had been said how truly he valued these visits to Cissie's house. Then Edward smiled, the rare, boyish smile that so transformed his harsh, sardonic features.

"You're a hell of a good guy, Matt. I'll tell you what we'll do. We'll go together."

And so it was agreed. From Matthew's point of view the arrangement was less than satisfactory. On the other hand, Edward's presence prolonged the visits and kept them from being merely perfunctory calls to see Sue, at which Cissie might even decide not to be present. Cissie could not very well be stiff in her manner or display her resentment with Edward there, and though he foresaw the time when he would want very much to be alone with her, this plan seemed safest and wisest for the time being.

The visits, though not frequent, took on a pleasant, almost festive air. Edward did most of the talking, and did it with an ease and cleverness that Matthew envied. Most of the time Matthew was content to take little part, happy enough to watch Cissie and enjoy the knowledge that her feelings toward him were gradually growing warmer.

Sometimes the baby was with them, lying in a cradle with spindle sides which Matthew had bought for her. He had found it in a secondhand shop and lugged it to Cissie's parlor on his back, and the three of them made a pleasant business of installing Sue inside. And Sue had pleased them all by accepting the cradle with that easy cheerfulness that seemed to be her special quality.

Peter too was usually present at these visits. In his serious, grown-up manner, he seemed to regard Edward with special favor. He leaned against Edward's knee or sat on his lap, silent and content, with an air of recognizing a new and special understanding between the two of them alone.

Warmed by these influences, Matthew began to work seriously again, and as though his whole life had entered a new phase, he worked harder and to more purpose than before. He had, in a sense, found himself, as all medical students must do sooner or later if they are to become physicians in the fullest meaning of the word. The professors and his fellow students were quick to recognize these things. He became known in the school as able, reliable, and passionately devoted to the practice of surgery.

The rift between the two young men slowly healed, although, as in the case of all deep wounds, scar tissue remained, so that the relationship differed in intangible but important ways from the past. In the pursuit of knowledge, and teaching themselves fully as much as they learned in class, most of the spring term slipped away. "We ought to take the summer course," Edward remarked one day as he was cleaning some slides and dropping them into slots in their case.

"Sure, why not? We've nothing better to do." And Matthew thought that nothing would drag him away from Boston while Cissie was there.

But as it turned out, Edward alone registered for the summer course. One of the two house pupils who worked on the ward at Massachusetts General Hospital called Surgery East developed a serious infection in his hand, and Matthew was asked by Dr. Osgood, the surgeon in charge, to take his place. This happened in May, before the end of the spring term, but as Matthew had special standing in the school because of his war services, the arrangement was readily made. Dr. Osgood had chosen Matthew for precisely that reason. Ordinarily he preferred house pupils with less experience, and in fact they were not eligible by hospital rule if they already had a degree. But Dr. Osgood was a sick man, and Matthew's experience, plus the quality of self-reliance that might ordinarily have kept him out, now seemed a godsend to the ailing doctor. Osgood began at once to pile work and responsibility on Matthew, and Matthew delighted in it.

This appointment required that Matthew sleep at the hospital in a big attic room along with the other house pupils. The room would be stifling in summer, but there was a bathroom with a tub in it—the only other one in the hospital was next to the emergency ward—and this was a luxury denied him at the Reverend Seth Brainard's house.

On the last night of study in the comfortable cellar, both Matthew and Edward were uneasy and a little self-conscious, for they were aware that this was the end of a great deal. Matthew, with a book in front of him, which he was not really studying because he was wondering about the new life at the hospital, kept sighing and shifting his weight in his creaky chair. Edward could not get the lighting on his microscope to suit him and every few minutes moved the lamp this way or that. He was making notes in a notebook, slowly, as though his pencil were too heavy for him, when Matthew suddenly slammed his book shut and said, "Goddammit to hell," loudly and with passion. Edward put his pencil down and they sat in silence, not looking at each other. Then Edward leaned back, pulled out his watch, looked at it and dropped it back in his pocket.

"It's eleven o'clock."

After a pause, Matthew said indifferently, "Is it?" and they were silent again.

Edward put out the light under the microscope table, brought up the case from the floor beside him, and began to settle the instrument inside.

Matthew rose and stretched widely, with a deliberate pretense of enjoyment. "Well," he said, putting a hand on their improvised desk, "I suppose we'd better put this stuff back where we got it or the Reverend won't be pleased."

They carried the planks and boxes back to the lumber pile beside the furnace, opened the furnace door one last time, though there was no fire inside, and slammed it shut with force. Edward lifted the microscope case by its handle, and Matthew picked up the lamp and they moved together toward the stairs. "Well . . ." Matthew said, left the sentence unfinished, and started up.

The next day a new life at the hospital began for Matthew. The main part of the Massachusetts General Hospital was built (or rebuilt, since part of an older structure remained) by a great architect, Bulfinch, in 1821, and it was as nearly functional as the building materials and construction abilities of that early day could make it. Large, manageable windows let in sunlight and air, which made the building an exception to those which were being built in great numbers during and after the war. The men's ward called Surgery East was on the second floor, a long, wide room with a row of mosquito-netted beds on either side.

The ward seemed normal enough to Matthew, who had seen far worse during the war and, in fact, knew this to be one of the best. To Edward it was like the deepest circle of hell, and as in Toledo, he did his best to avoid any contact with operations and their aftermath. The sights, the sounds, the smells nauseated him; the screams of the sufferers during the daily probing of deep wounds filled him with terror.

To his mind, pain was degrading; illness and deformity, his own included, bitter reminders of life's cruelty. His was the egoist's need to feel himself exempt, advantaged, protected by his own worth, and when he saw flesh turn rotten and fall away from living body, he did not feel pity but fear and outrage. Every suppurating wound undermined him, every groan diminished his sense of his own value.

He never tried to convey any of these feelings to Matthew; in fact, they were so deep in his nature that to analyze them or defend them had never occurred to him. He recognized that he and Matthew were very different in these respects and he instinctively protected these feelings from Matthew unless some horror was so destructive to him that he could not keep silent.

After one of the ward visits which he was not able to avoid, he burst out to Matthew, "I wouldn't be a surgeon for anything in the world!"

"It's better than medicine," Matthew answered.

"Why, for heaven's sake?"

"It's cleaner, for one thing."

"Cleaner!"

"And most of the time you know what's wrong and just what you can do to fix it, or try to, which isn't as often true in medicine."

"But, Matt, the complications that follow surgery are so often worse than the original complaint! A patient is lucky if he leaves the hospital without having his constitution impaired for life."

"That's more or less true, I'm afraid. You've put your finger on the greatest difficulty. Find some way to prevent wound infection and the whole character of surgery will change."

When Matthew reported for duty he was told, to his surprise, to see a visiting surgeon in charge of another ward than the one to which he had been assigned. Matthew found him with sleeves rolled up and an operating apron on, ready to begin the morning's work. He was a large man, bald, but with a flourishing beard, and like so many bald man he had a habit of tenderly stroking his head. He did this now, as he stood talking to Matthew on the narrow landing of the stairs outside the ward.

"I have a note," he said, "from your supervising surgeon, Dr. Osgood, asking me to see you this morning. You are aware that Dr. Osgood has a heart ailment?"

"Yes, sir."

"He is not able to come to the hospital this morning, but he tells me you have had considerable surgical experience in the war. Do you think you can handle dressings by yourself?"

"Certainly." Matthew smiled broadly.

"Your teammate won't be much good to you, I'm afraid. Timid and inexperienced. You'll have to oversee his work. I'll come in when I get time to see how you're getting on."

As Matthew walked off in the direction of the ward to which he was assigned, he examined his hands carefully, back and front, looking for any small cut or scratch that would have to be protected against the infected wounds he must handle. He found none. Pleased, he pushed open the door of the ward and went inside. There he found the nurse waiting for him with the dressing cart that she would push after him from bed to bed down the long ward. He was amused to see that it was the little nurse with the prettily curving upper lip and the gray eyes like Cissie's who had once smiled at him.

"Hullo!" he said, pleased. "What you doing here, sister?"

"This is my ward, sir."

"Oh, it is, is it?" Matthew said this with so much enthusiasm that she blushed and, to hide it, bent over the cart, pretending to arrange the many objects it contained, making a show of industry but not really accomplishing anything.

"Where's the other fellow who's supposed to share this job?"

"I haven't seen him, sir. I think you do dressings alternate days."

"You got everything I need here?" Matthew bent over the cart so that their heads nearly touched. "Probes, directors, forceps, stick of lunar caustic—you shouldn't keep that lying loose. It will stain everything it touches. Bandages. Here, who ever thought these knives were clean? Take them." He handed them to her and stepped back to inventory the lower shelves. "Lint, towels, sponges. Where's the pus basin?" He looked at her severely, half meaning it.

"Oh!" She was all consternation, laying stubby fingers on her mouth. "I'm sorry, sir."

"Get one."

She hurried off down the ward, clutching the knives in her fist, and he watched her with amusement, noticing again the swing of the strong hips under her blue dress. Her long apron was fresh and stiff with starch, and on her head she wore an absurd round cap like a pleated pancake. She disappeared behind a screen, and waiting, he let his eyes rove around the ward. Most of the patients had pulled themselves up against their pillows, and all heads were turned in his direction. All the faces had the same look of fear of the pain they were about to suffer. Wanting to help them in some way but not knowing how, he smiled at them, a slight, apologetic smile, not directed at anyone in particular but at all of them together. Two or three of the men in the beds nearest him attempted to smile in return; others shifted themselves uneasily.

The little nurse, walking swiftly, came back with the bean-shaped pus basin and put it on the lower shelf of the cart.

"What's your name?" he said, speaking sternly because the look on the patients' faces bothered him.

"Hattie, sir. Hattie Fuller."

"All right, Nurse Hattie. These fellows are dreading this. Let's not keep them waiting any longer."

He strode the short distance to the first bed. She seized the handle of the cart and pushed it after him.

CHAPTER TWENTY-FOUR

While Matthew was working at the hospital, he had, in theory, one afternoon and evening in a week free of duties. The rest of the time, except when he was eating a hurried meal in a restaurant nearby, he was expected to be available both night and day. Another house pupil shared the work of Surgery East and the operations on its patients—a troubled, anemic young man whom Matthew believed to be more inefficient and untrustworthy than in fact he was. Dr. Osgood, feeling better, resumed his share of the operating schedule and supervision of the ward. On the whole, things ran smoothly. The work interested Matthew intensely, he knew that Dr. Osgood relied on him, and he was contented, but he looked forward all week to his free evening, for it was then that he and Edward saw Cissie.

She welcomed them with a smile that at first included Matthew out of politeness but very soon became warm and spontaneous. It was obvious that she liked these visits. She offered them minute glasses of port and pound cake conjured up out of her landlady's kitchen. She laughed at them and petted them, pretending to be much older and wiser than they. One night she welcomed them in a new dress of rose-colored silk, the first time Matthew had ever seen her in anything but black or the prescribed gray of "half mourning," and because its color made her shy and self-conscious, she seemed like a radiant young girl.

These visits never lasted long enough to suit Matthew, and it was always Edward who put an end to them by saying, "Well, Matt, tomorrow's another day. Don't you think we should be getting on our way?" Then they would all rise and Cissie would say, "Don't you want to have a look at Sue before you go?" She would make as though to pick up the lamp, but Edward was always there before her. Then they would all go quietly into the next room, gaze at the soundly sleeping baby for a moment and steal silently out again. Something about Edward's manner on these occasions revealed to Matthew a new facet of Edward's complicated and often seemingly contradictory character. He was honestly fond of children.

He and Matthew never discussed Cissie except for an occasional, carefully casual remark or two as they walked a part of their homeward route together in the soft spring night. Then Edward might say, "I thought Cissie was looking well tonight, didn't you?"

"Yes, but I'm afraid the children tire her sometimes, though she doesn't show it."

And then one or the other of them would make the remark with which these brief conversations always closed: "She's a wonderful woman."

So long as Matthew was in Edward's company he felt a constraint on his thoughts about Cissie, but as soon as they parted and Edward had turned off into the street on which he lived, Matthew let his feelings about her expand until they made him feel larger than himself, powerful, able to conquer Cissie, and his world as well.

One night, in some such exalted mood as this, he came near to the hospital where there was a strip of grass with some iron benches. On fine spring days the house pupils would come out here to smoke and soak up sunlight, tired-looking young men, pale from their winter's work indoors. Sometimes a pair of nurses would appear (they never came singly) to walk up and down a few times at a discreet distance from the young doctors. This night there was no one here, but on one of the benches Matthew saw what he took to be one of the long capes the nurses wore that had been dropped here and forgotten. He left the path, intending to pick the cape up and carry it inside to give to the Matron, but when he came close he heard a sound like a sob and he realized that what he had taken for a pile of cloth was in reality a person huddled up in the bench corner, weeping.

"Hey, what's the matter?" he said, and then, when a disheveled blond head was raised from the back of the bench and a wet face turned up to him, "My God, it's Hattie." He sat down on the bench beside her. "What's the matter, sister? What you doing here?"

Instead of answering she threw herself against him and wept the harder. He put an arm around her. "Listen," he said. Her hair against his face smelled of laundry soap, but a faint, fresh odor of lavender came from her dress, and it amused him to hold someone so small and stormy. "Look, come on, now. Tell Papa what's the matter. You got a handkerchief? Here." He thrust his rumpled one at her. She seized it and began to wipe her eyes with it. "Now, what are you doing out here all alone?"

"Aunt Mabel's gone, and . . ."

"Who's Aunt Mabel?"

She took the handkerchief away from her face and stared at him. "Don't you know? I'm the Matron's niece. She's my Aunt Mabel. I thought everyone knew that."

When she said this she was so childlike, everything else forgotten in wonder that he should not know what she thought her whole world must know, that he laughed. "Then I'd better not get caught out here talking to you, had I?"

Hattie took this remark quite seriously. "She's away, I tell you."

"And is that something to cry about?"

"I thought I'd have a good time while she was gone. She's been gone three days, and I thought I'd have a grand time with her away, but nobody's hardly spoken to me."

"You mean to say that with the whole Medical School and all these house pupils right here, a cute little thing like you has to sit out here all alone and cry? Must be they're all scared of her."

She thought about this for a moment, not sure whether his words should be taken at their face value. "I guess so," she said doubtfully. "But maybe it's just me."

He laughed again, liking her honesty. "There's nothing wrong with you, so cheer up, kid."

"I'm all right, now you're here."

He could not see the expression on her face but he felt her moving closer to him, settling herself. Then she leaned against him as simply and confidingly as Peter had on the rides in his buggy back in Haddon, and he wondered how old she might be. Quite young, he supposed—eighteen, perhaps—and he smiled down at her from the great seniority of his twenty-two years.

On the ward she was a quick and efficient nurse, concentrating on her work as she should, only occasionally showing a flash of the mischief of her sex. His response had been automatic and unthinking, and he had never until tonight considered her personality. Now she surprised him merely by being a person, and a stranger. Perhaps she sensed something of this, for when she spoke to him it was shyly, in a whisper which he failed to hear. "What?" he said, tightening his arm around her.

"May I call you Matthew?"

"Sure, why not?"

"I won't on the ward, of course, Matthew."

After that, leaning against him, she seemed to go off into a dream, and again he thought of Peter and the boy's long reveries. He was wondering how he might detach himself to go inside and get some sleep, of which he was chronically in need, when she turned her face up to him. By the faint light of the street-lamp he thought he saw that she was smiling.

"I like you, Matthew."

"That's good," he said lightly. "Keep it up." And feeling that all this had gone far enough, he pushed her away from him in order to get up. She resisted him by making herself limp and heavy against him.

"I like you best of all. The others are just boys, but you're older and you're so strong. You know just what to do if anything goes wrong on the ward."

"I like you too, Hattie. You're a fine nurse. Really, I mean it. But if we don't go in and say good night we won't either of us be any good at our jobs tomorrow."

"Matthew, wait. Matthew, please, I want to ask you something."

"What is it, then?"

"Aunt Mabel's so strict, Matthew. She won't let me have any friends."

"Why not, for heaven's sake?"

"She wants me to be a famous nurse, like Florence Nightingale. She has a picture of Nightingale in our room and it's almost like a shrine. She keeps telling me she would have been a great and dedicated nurse herself if she had started at my age instead of after her son went to war. And since she can't be, she wants me to be it. She's saving her money to send me to Kaiserswerth, where Nightingale studied and where nobody talks anything but German, and—"

"Here, slow up. What are you getting at?"

"I'm *telling* you! She won't let me have any friends, and she makes me sleep in her room with her so she can watch me all the time. And I *do* work hard, but I want to have a good time like other girls once in a while. That's only fair, don't you think?"

"It would seem so." Matthew spoke guardedly, not knowing where all this was leading him, but she seemed not to feel his hesitation.

"Oh *yes*. And now she's away and I have a chance . . . Matthew, won't you take me out some night?"

"I only have one night off a week, you know, Hattie, and on that night I always go to see a friend, a widow whom I've known for a long time."

Apparently the word "widow" called up an image far different from the reality, for Hattie only pouted a little and said discontentedly, "I suppose you have to." Then she brightened. "But that's night. Couldn't you take me somewhere—to the Common, maybe—in the afternoon if the weather's nice? My day off's the same as yours, you know, and Aunt Mabel won't be back until the day after that. Please, Matthew?"

"We'll see. Come on, now." He stood up, gave her a hand, and pulled her lightly to her feet, but she was not even yet willing to let him go.

"It's so nice tonight. Let's walk a little way—a *little* way, then we'll go in."

"All right, we'll walk to the Brick and back."

The Brick was a small brick building a short distance away where there were rooms for isolating cases whose wounds had grown too foul-smelling to be allowed to remain on a ward. Few who went to the Brick ever again saw the world outside, and Matthew and Hattie had no inclination to go close to this grim building. Streaks of light poured out of the windows on both sides of it, and the air seemed torn by cries and groans that these two imagined but could not in fact have heard. "Poor things," she said, turning away, and, their youth under a shadow, they walked slowly back to the hospital.

All that week he was conscious that she watched him, an expression of anxiety darkening her eyes, and he knew that she was troubled because he had not mentioned the excursion they had planned for his next free day. He wished, in fact, that he had not made this commitment, for, examining his feelings about her, he found he had no desire to know her better. He liked the little flirtation on the ward, her sly, meaningful glances, the self-conscious turning away of her head, and these things gave a lift to his spirits. He would rather not find out what sort of a person she was or have her make any claim on sympathies as she had done on the night they met by chance outside the hospital.

He might have pretended to have forgotten about the plans they had made had she not followed every move he made with an expression of such pitiable urgency. As it was, he waited as long as he could and then, just before leaving the ward at noon on his free day, said, "Well, what about this afternoon?"

The change in her was wonderful. She clasped her hands and looked up at him, all smiles. *"Oh, Matthew!"* Then, because she had used his first name while they were both on duty, she blushed and looked down, and he thought how inexperienced she was, showing so plainly every slightest feeling.

"I'll meet you out front in half an hour," he said, a trifle gruffly, and thought that he must first find Edward and explain why they could not spend the rest of the day together as was their custom. From the door of the ward he watched Hattie run up the spiral stairs on her way to the room she shared with her aunt. Then he saw the house pupil who shared the duty of the ward with him coming slowly up the stairs from the floor below. "Hullo," he said. "Just waiting for you to show up." Then he noticed that the young man was climbing the stairs as though each step were almost too much effort and that his face had a gray pallor. "Say, you don't look so good."

"I feel rotten. I hope to God it's quiet on the ward. Look, if I report sick tomorrow, do you think you could manage for a day or so?"

"Sure, I guess so. Excuse me, I forgot something." Matthew turned and went back into the ward.

He went directly to the second bed on the left, ignoring an elderly man with a stubbly chin who was sitting up in the first bed regarding him with hostile eyes. There was nothing to be seen of the occupant of the second bed but the top of a small head with mouse-colored hair mussed by lying on the pillow. Matthew approached cautiously for fear the child, a boy about ten years old, might be sleeping, but the youngster, hearing him, looked up and smiled. The smile was broad, ingenuous, with a touch of mischief in it that transformed the homely face into something irresistibly piquant and lovable.

"Hullo, Dr. Matthew."

"Hullo, Jimmie. How's the leg now?"

"It ain't so good. It hurts something awful."

"Try and sleep. You'll get some laudanum tonight. I just stopped to say good-bye."

"You goin' off with nurse Hattie?"

"None of your business, young fellow." Matthew bent down and arranged the covers around the child's thin shoulders.

Leaving the ward again, he did not hurry and he delayed further talking to Edward though he felt certain Hattie would be waiting for him. He saw her from a distance standing under a tree, and when she saw him she came hurrying forward. She had put on a dress of a rather bright blue that he suspected was her best and that she should not have worn it for a picnic on the Common. She wore a bonnet with a rose on it and, to his amusement, white cotton gloves. The dress was too bright a shade to go well with her eyes, and the bonnet threw an unbecoming shadow on her face.

"You look as if you were going to church."

"Much better than church. Oh, this is so nice."

She put her hand under his arm and walked beside him with such evident pride in being with him that he laughed at her, and she, understanding, laughed at him. He began to enjoy himself a little.

They bought bread and cheese in a store on Charles Street, apples that turned out to have brown spots inside from being packed too long in sawdust, some lumps of chocolate, and root beer in stone bottles that had been kept cool in a bucket down the well back of the store. They went into the Gardens first and he suggested that they sit down under a tree and eat their lunch, but she was too excited to think of food so soon.

She was eager to explore a path by the edge of the little lake, where she ran ahead while he followed slowly, watching her pick up stones from the path and throw them into the water. Each time she would stand and watch the widening rings on the surface until they disappeared, then she would turn back laughing and call something to him before running on again. She found a weeping willow on the low bank, seized a handful of the long trailers and, leaning out precariously, swished them back and forth in the water. "Look out," he called to her. "You'll fall in." She answered between shouts of laughter, "I only wish I dared." He thought that she was like a child that has been confined too long and, let loose to play, is a trifle above itself with excitement. Then she saw a swan sitting majestically on the water a little way from the shore and stopped to stare at it in silent wonder, so that without hurrying he caught up with her and stood beside her. "What is it?" she said in an awed whisper.

"A swan, I think."

She looked up at him, the gray eyes that held so much false promise of depth and sensitivity of spirit wide and solemn. He felt vaguely cheated without knowing why, so that he said abruptly, "Come on. I've carried this stuff long enough. We're going to eat."

She was a long time finding the spot that seemed to her just right. They crossed the road to the Common and found a slope with an oak tree at the top. Here the grass was long and the shade of the tree seemed pleasant to them both after the exertion of climbing the slope. He dumped his packages on the ground and she, carefully turning back the edge of her skirt, knelt and began to open them. She did this with a great show of housewifely care, enjoying the doing of it but serious about it, making it into something important, an offering to him as a man from herself as a woman.

He watched her tolerantly, but when he began to eat, his knees drawn up, a thick piece of bread and cheese held in both hands, he turned away from her and, eating, gazed off into the distance. Beside him she kept a meek silence. Strangely, he felt alone, almost lonely, and a little sad both for her and for himself because the strongest emotion she was capable of arousing in him was pity. He thought about this for a while, and then with no awareness of transition his thoughts were on a different plane, occupied with Cissie. For the first time he acknowledged to himself that Ed saw her more clearly and perhaps valued more highly the moral traits, the adherence to conservative attitudes, that heretofore he had regarded mainly as obstacles. Biting the cheese, his cheek bulging with it, he subjected himself to a critical examination in all his past relations with her, which left him feeling humble but oddly purified, and happier in his mind about her than perhaps he had ever been.

He felt that he must see her alone and try to explain his new feelings to her, and he thought she must certainly understand. It began to seem to him as though this had already been done, that what he desired had been accomplished, and he rested, at peace. He was conscious of the pleasant warmth of the day, of a little breeze, barely felt, that cooled his face, but he had literally forgotten all about Hattie lying in the grass by his side until she touched his sleeve.

"Matthew!"

He came back to an awareness of his surroundings with a start. She was lying on her back on the grass, her hands behind her head, smiling at him. The smile, the display of herself were a clear invitation to him, and he frowned at her, feeling in spite of himself her attraction. Illogically, he was a little shocked, though he felt that this blatant offering of herself came from instinct, not from knowledge. She should not be allowed to behave so. She needed to be protected against herself. He made an important business of taking out Dr. Hurd's watch and pretending surprise at how late it had come to be.

"Come on," he said. "Time we were getting back," and rising, he held out a hand to her.

"Not yet, Matthew. Please not just yet."

"Yes, now."

But she would not take his proffered hand. Pouting, she began very slowly collecting the remains of their lunch while he stood and watched her with growing impatience. Then as she got reluctantly to her feet, he took from her the package she had made and she threw her arms around his neck. She held her face up for a kiss, and he, feeling tolerant and pretending to be amused, stooped and kissed the tip of her nose. "Oh, you!" she said.

The words made an echo, and suddenly his mind presented him an unwanted picture of Sue smiling, rich as the earth, lavish as summer with her charms. "Come on, Hattie," he said roughly, and began to walk away.

She did not follow him, and after a moment he turned around to see what was keeping her. She was standing still, her profile toward him, gazing down the slope in the direction of the lake where they had walked together, an erect little figure, sturdy, lonely, full of longing, the bright blue of her dress a harsh note in the soft colors of the landscape. He watched her, thinking of the hard life she led among sights and sounds and smells that most men could not stomach, the long hours, the heavy work, the stern discipline to which her aunt subjected her, the absence of normal gaiety and laughter. Again he felt pity for her. He took her hand, noticing how roughened it felt, how hard the palm. "Come on, Hattie," he said gently. She let him lead her, holding back a little, to the exit from the Common.

CHAPTER TWENTY-FIVE

Reluctantly, Matthew took Hattie to supper, for she had looked so stricken at the idea of being returned to the hospital. He felt he could not bear to think of the lonely little figure going up the stairs to her empty room. He called himself a fool, for he had planned to eat dinner alone and quickly, in order to reach Cissie's house before Edward and so have a few words with her alone. It was a plan that, he felt, did not violate his agreement with Edward in any serious way, but as he led Hattie to a cheap restaurant far enough from the school so that he felt it not likely they would find Edward there, those few minutes grew in his mind until he felt there was nothing in life so important.

Hattie ate maddeningly slowly, trying rather pathetically to prolong their time together. "Come on, now," he said, "eat up. I have to go."

"Can't I have just one more cup of coffee?"

"You've already had two, kid."

"But I *want* another, please, Matthew."

He sat back from the table, his knees crossed, and watched in silence while she sipped it. Fresh air and pleasure had made her sleepy. She held the thick cup in both hands, elbows on the table, now and then giving him a vague, dreamy smile while he waited impatiently for her to finish and told himself that the whole business had been a mistake. "Look," he said, "you don't mind walking back alone, do you?"

"Where are you going?" she said, her tone suddenly sharp with suspicion.

"Ask me no questions and I'll tell you no lies," he replied in a heavy attempt at gaiety.

"Are you going to see the widow? Who is she, Matthew?"

"Someone I know. Will you please finish that coffee like a good girl?"

She drank the last of it in a gulp, and when she set the cup down there were tears glistening in her eyes.

"I didn't mean to be rough," he said, getting to his feet and waiting for her to rise.

She looked up at him and the tears rolled down. "I like you so much, Matthew."

"No you don't. You just think you do. We had a nice time, kid, and don't you go and spoil it now. Come on, get up, now."

She was meekly silent while he paid for the meal and he almost pushed her out the door ahead of him. On the sidewalk he said, "Cheer up, now. See you on the ward tomorrow," but she only sighed. Without looking at him and in silence she turned in the direction of the hospital and walked away. He watched her for a moment with compunction. Then, making a facile decision to keep clear of her in the future, he set off joyfully for Cissie's house.

A smiling Cissie opened the door for him. "Hullo, Matt," she said. "Where's Edward?"

"He'll be along. We didn't eat together tonight so I came by myself."

"You haven't disagreed about anything, have you?" She shut the door behind him and turned to look at him anxiously.

"No, not a thing. Cissie . . ."

The tone of his voice brought an attentive lift of her head, and the gray eyes looked at him with inquiring friendliness. He cleared his throat of the sudden choking off of his words and began again.

"Cissie, can't you forgive me for what happened? You know I've never loved anybody but you."

She put her head down and he saw color flooding into her face, but she stood there in front of him without moving and he thought, though he was not sure, that she was trembling.

Then she raised her head and gave him a wonderful, direct look that he felt all through him. He opened his arms and she came into them. She put her head on his shoulder and he held her close. He could not speak. After a while he began to stroke her cheek, lightly and with great tenderness. The emotion that was flooding him was too strong for words, too gentle for passion.

It was she who discovered that he was crying, for his hot tears had so blended with his feelings that he was unaware of them. "Why, Matthew!" she whispered, and put up her hand to touch a drop that glistened on the ridge of his cheekbone. A sound that was like a groan came from deep in him, and he held her to him so tightly that the breath went out of her and she struggled to free herself. Laughing with happiness, she held out her hands to him. "It's all right, Matthew."

"Cissie. My God, Cissie!"

"I'm glad, Matthew. I'm very glad. Only don't hurry me, will you? Let things just be as they are for a little while. Will you do that?"

"Anything you say."

"Then—" There was a light rap on the door and she caught her breath. "There's Edward."

She turned to go to the door but he caught her arm. "We've got to tell Ed."

He spoke in an urgent whisper and she answered him the same way. *"No, not yet."*

The evening that followed was like those that had gone before except for a heightened awareness of each other and, when Edward's attention was elsewhere, the exchange of deep and searching looks. If Edward felt any change in atmosphere he showed no indication of it and the only reference he made to the evening was while he and Matthew were walking home together, when, after a silence, he said, "That rose silk dress is becoming to Cissie, don't you think?" To this Matthew replied, "Yeah, it sure is," and felt a momentary renewal of excitement and joy of living.

On the ward the next day and in the week following he was formal and businesslike in his contacts with poor Hattie, overdoing it a little, which caused her to look at him every now and then with a hurt and puzzled expression. He was mildly bothered because she seemed to feel that their outing had established an intimacy between them which she was clearly determined not to relinquish in spite of his distant manner toward her. Except in these intangible ways she was not a problem to him, however, for her aunt, the Matron, had returned and was making her grim presence felt in a general tightening of the temporarily relaxed discipline throughout the hospital.

Matthew had all the work he could handle, for the house pupil who had been ailing was now really sick at the home of his parents in Cambridge. This left Matthew on call night and day, and, as had happened in the war, he was sometimes without sleep for thirty-six hours together. Dr. Osgood, having discovered that Matthew was both experienced and willing to take responsibility, seldom appeared on the ward, saving his strength for the weekly operating day. Matthew saw Edward occasionally at meals, which had to be eaten outside the hospital, but meals were uncertain in these busy days and occasionally had to be skipped altogether.

Then, after a week of this, the visiting surgeon of Surgery West discovered Matthew's plight and with unexpected kindness sent one of his two house pupils to relieve Matthew for an afternoon. Matthew left the ward in high spirits and found Hattie lingering under the trees in front of the hospital, clearly waiting for him to appear. He had forgotten that this was also her day off, but she came running toward him with such eagerness that he was compelled to stop and wait for her. Breathlessly she told him she had to go to the store for her aunt. "But we could go together, Matt, and we could walk back along the river."

"Sorry, kid, I've got something else to do."

"Oh please, Matt."

"Sorry. You run along. I'll see you on the ward tomorrow."

He went on his way, feeling annoyed with her and pitying her at the same time. He found Edward, as he expected, in the microscope laboratory, sitting at a worktable on which many objects were crowded together but without any effect of clutter. Edward glanced up when Matthew came in, said "Hullo" in a friendly tone, and went on with his work. Matthew sat on a stool opposite him, unbuttoned his coat and hooked his thumbs in the pockets of his trousers. He watched with mild interest as Edward shook out some emery powder onto a small slab of iron, added a drop of water, and stirred the mixture into a thin paste. That done, he took up a small oblong of glass and began slowly to grind the rough edges into the paste, testing them with his finger, and grinding them again. After perhaps five minutes of this Matthew said, "You've got more patience than I have. I never bother with the edges of my slides."

"You weren't made to sit still." Edward picked up a cloth, polished the glass, held it up to the light and polished again.

"What's this one going to be?"

"Blood from a patient with measles."

"Why go to all that work? It must have been done a hundred times before. What do you think you're going to find?"

"Probably nothing."

"Then why bother?"

Edward sighed as though this question were too wearisome to answer.

After a moment Matthew said, "This sort of stuff's not for me." Then, after another pause, "You're really convinced that microbes cause disease, aren't you?"

Edward raised his head and gave him a thoughtful look of pure intelligence. "What else?"

"Well, there's that guy who wrote the ward manual says it's a change in tone, or capacity of the capillaries, and—"

"Nonsense."

"But it doesn't stand to reason that things as small as that could really harm a body."

"Pasteur thinks they do."

"Pasteur. Remember Old Top Hat's speech?"

Matthew laughed and Edward gave him a feeble smile, unwilling to be amused with so serious a subject in hand.

"Ed, you don't have one scrap of proof."

"That's what everybody with a microscope is looking for—or if they're not they should be, and it's pretty damn exciting."

He spoke with a tone of finality, picked up a pipette, and with it transferred a drop of blood from a small bottle to the slide, smearing it around a little. Then he took another piece of glass, examined it, cleaned it and examined it again, dropped it neatly on the first piece, and prepared to fasten them together with sealing wax.

Matthew stood up. "Well, I've got to be getting back to Surg East where there's my kind of excitement."

Edward glanced up again, this time with a flash of irritation. "Why? It's your day off, isn't it? I thought we were going to eat downtown as usual and see Cissie afterward."

"Can't, Ed. You go see Cissie by yourself. That's what I came over to say."

"That wouldn't be according to our agreement."

"Never mind our agreement tonight." At Edward's look of doubtful astonishment Matthew laughed. "It's all right, Ed, I mean it."

"But what's up? What's wrong?"

"Not a thing. You know I'm alone on the ward. One of the guys on Surg West is covering for me, but he can only stay for a couple of hours, so I got to get back and work my ass off. Every bed in the ward's full."

"What you trying to do—run the place single-handed?"

"Just about. Osgood's so sick he's only doing essential operations—I told you that. Turns out the fellow who should be with me's got typhoid, so he won't be back very soon."

"Sit down and take it easy for a few minutes anyway."

"I mustn't. I don't know anything about this guy who's covering for me, and anyway—hell, it's my ward."

"No supervision to speak of from the visiting surgeon, no help, and you're enjoying it!"

"Sure. Why not? Except that I could do with some sleep. I haven't had more than two hours consecutively since the other guy got sick."

"You can't go on like that. Is anybody doing anything about it?"

"It's going to be hard to get a replacement this late in the year. Impossible, I should say."

Matthew wandered among the stools and tables over to a window and stood there with his hands in his pockets, brooding. Suddenly he turned around, his air of depression gone. "Say, Ed, I've got an idea." He walked quickly back and sat on the edge of the stool again. "Listen, you concentrate on this stuff too much. You need to broaden out, get more experience in other lines."

"What are you talking about?"

"You're getting round-shouldered. You need to get away from the micro, be more active. I think I could fix it for you to be temporarily house pupil with me on Surg East. How about it?"

Edward made a disparaging sound and went on with his work.

"I'm serious, Ed. How about it?"

"I wouldn't work in that slaughterhouse for anything in the world."

"You're wrong. Why not at least give it a try?"

Edward did not bother to answer this, and after waiting through a long moment of silence Matthew sighed and moved away, wandering around the laboratory, glancing without interest at various pieces of equipment as he passed. He was not one to linger with a disappointment, however, and presently he came back and sat on the stool.

"An interesting case came onto the ward the other day."

"Yes?" Without looking up, Edward reached for the microscope that was standing at one side of the table, drew it toward him and laid the slide he had been making carefully under the lens.

"He's a kid, ten, eleven years old. Came to us from our own children's ward. Bone abscess, or so they think. Leg. Those geniuses in Med think his leg should come off.

They're probably right, but—gosh—I hate to see him lose it. He's a cute little tyke called Jimmie, who smiles all over his face when he's not in too much pain. Everybody's crazy about him. What's interesting is that there's no fracture, as there usually is in osteomyelitis, no wound of any kind—what's the matter?"

Edward had pushed the microscope aside and was giving Matthew his full attention. "Go on, Matt. Tell me about it."

"Nothing much to tell. The leg's so sore he can't move it and the poor kid screams if you try to. The skin over where it's sore is shiny, swollen, warm to the touch. The muscles in that leg knot up in a spasm sometimes so as nearly to kill him with pain, but that's tapering off, seems like. On Med they tried painting it with some brown stuff, then they tried leeches. No good. I've just been using cold compresses and stalling for time, because I hate to see his leg come off, but I can't stall much longer, and he'll have to lose it next operating day, if Osgood's well enough to operate. If he isn't, I suppose I'll have to do it."

"When's next operating day?"

"Saturday."

"Three days. Matt, can I see this Jimmie?"

"If school were still open, you could get to look at him at grand rounds. You know you can't now. You'd get us into real trouble if you tried. Anyway, why do you want to?"

"For one thing, I want a blood sample."

"I can get your blood sample, but what do you expect to find? A pathological condition in the blood? Sure, there probably is, so what about it? You're certainly not thinking you can find something to cure the kid!" Matthew closed his hand around the barrel of the microscope and drew it toward him. "This thing never cured anybody of anything. It's a nice toy—it's interesting to see things the naked eye can't see. But I'm not convinced it has any practical use in medicine."

"It will have. I tell you that in a few years—"

"I know. I've heard it all before." Matthew rose and gave a lazy, powerful stretch. "I've really got to be getting back."

"Sit down."

"Can't. I've got to go."

"Sit down, Matt. This may be important."

Matthew sat on the edge of the stool and hooked his heels over a rung. "What's eating you?"

"I know something about what's the matter with that kid."

"Without seeing him?"

"Yes." There was suppressed excitement in Edward's manner as he pushed his chair back from the table as though preparing to talk. "Did the kid have any kind of injury—anything—anywhere on his body that he might have gotten in the last two or three weeks? Maybe something small that's healed up by now? Any way for microbes to enter?"

"I wasn't looking for anything like that. Microbes! I don't know."

"You don't know! You surgeon fellows make me sick. Anything you can't see or feel or use a knife on doesn't matter. You ought to know everything about him, every illness he's ever had, every accident. . . . Damn it, Matt, *find out.*"

"No bones broken recently, no cuts or bruises that show now. I know that much. Will you tell me what you're getting at?"

Edward got up abruptly and walked to the far side of the laboratory and back, his limp very apparent. He sat down again, crossed his legs and laid his hand on his knee. "What *do* you know about his medical history?"

"He's next thing to a waif. A priest carried him into the hospital about a week ago with chills, fever and vomiting. Sick kid. He said his leg hurt, but nobody paid any attention to that at first. It got worse fast and they thought it might be syphilis. Then they figured he had a bone abscess—osteomyelitis—though what could have caused it is a mystery. They figured if the abscess broke through to the surface and he lived, he'd be in misery all his life from an open sore draining pus, but they thought more likely he'd die of the poison draining out into his system. So they sent him to us to take the leg off above the knee. That what you want to know?"

"Part of it. Do you know what happened to my leg?" Edward put his hand around his calf, the pressure revealing the deformity of the leg normally hidden by his trousers.

"You told me you fell out of a tree and broke it when you were a kid."

"I say that when people ask me because that seems to satisfy them and they don't ask any more questions. I didn't fall or get hurt in any way. Same thing happened to me as happened to this kid—same thing exactly, Matt. All of a sudden I got sick and my leg got painful below the knee. Where does this kid's leg hurt?"

"Below the knee. Go on."

"It got so painful I couldn't bear to have anybody even put a finger on it, but they didn't take my leg off. Maybe my father thought I wasn't going to live anyway. Or maybe he didn't want a one-legged brat; I wouldn't put it past him. Anyway, after a while whatever it was broke through the skin in about six places and began to drain pus, then bits of bone worked out."

"I'm surprised you did live."

"The sores were slow in draining and slower still in healing. The poison from them got all through my system and I was in bed for months. I was anemic for years."

"Maybe that's why you're still so thin."

"I rather think so. When the leg healed it was shorter than the other and it doesn't feel like normal bone. Feels like new bone grew in sort of lumpy."

"You're just lucky you're alive and have still got a leg. Just lucky. The safest thing would have been to take it off."

"That's the surgeon talking. It's something of a miracle, I suppose, but if the pus could be gotten to drain faster, if the channels, the sinuses that the infection made to the surface, could have been opened up . . ."

"What was done for you?"

"Exactly nothing. The sinuses that opened drained for weeks and weeks. After a while those splinters of dead bone worked out and then the sores slowly began to heal. Look here, Matt, maybe you're right to take his leg off. Probably you are. But I'm wondering if there isn't some other way of handling it. If there were some way to clean out the infection better than the methods we use now . . ."

"As like what? You can go into the sinuses with a probe and open them up to drain, and half kill the kid doing it, and most likely he'd die anyway. I tell you, I hate to do it, but the best bet is to take off his leg and hope the infection hasn't weakened him so he'll die of the shock of the operation."

"Matt, I've got to see that kid."

"I never knew you to want to see a patient if you could possibly avoid it. What's eating you?"

"I don't know. I guess because I went through it myself."

"There's nothing you can do for him."

"I know. But, Matt, I feel I've got to see him. And get a blood sample."

"Which won't tell you anything, and get us both thrown out of school without our degrees. Ed, you're crazy."

"You're alone on the ward, aren't you? You could fix it if you want to."

Matthew, annoyed and a little upset by Ed's persistence and the unexpectedness of his attitude, began another restless tour of the laboratory. Once he glanced back and saw that Edward was not working but was merely sitting there, gazing at nothing, intent perhaps on memories of the sick child that he had once been. Something discouraged about his attitude touched Matthew so that he came back to stand in front of the table where Edward was sitting. Edward looked up at him with no attempt to mask his feelings, and for the first time Matthew really felt the bitterness that Edward's lameness caused him. And there passed through his mind the thought that Edward's corroding hatred of his father might also have had its origin here. He said, with none of the customary casual familiarity in his tone, "Why do you want to see this boy, Jimmie, so much, Ed?"

"I don't know myself."

"You don't even like children particularly, or I didn't think you did until recently."

Suddenly, with no warning, Edward was angry. He pushed his chair backward with some violence and put his fists on the table's edge. "Look, what the hell difference does it make how I feel? I've told you I want to see this boy for myself. Either you're willing to fix it up for me, or you're not. Which is it?"

Their eyes met and held, and Matthew made no reply. Then he looked away and said in the old, offhand manner, "Come over to the hospital a few minutes before nine and wait for me outside the front door. There's no use making this business any more conspicuous than we can help. I'll come and get you as soon as I can. And tell Cissie I'll see her next week—I hope." Without waiting for a reply Matthew went away.

CHAPTER TWENTY-SIX

At nine that night, Matthew and Edward climbed the stairs to Surgery East, walking quietly to keep their footsteps from sounding on the granite treads. Matthew had chosen this hour because Hattie would be on duty and she could be counted on not to report that he had brought an unauthorized visitor to the ward. There would be no one else there but Eph, the orderly, who was a good fellow and indebted to Matthew for a number of small favors. The ward was, in fact, Matthew's kingdom, and these two were his devoted subjects.

Outside the closed door of the ward Matthew put a hand on Edward's arm to detain him, but for a moment he said nothing. He was feeling the uneasy quiet that permeated the hospital at night, and through which he loved to move, being himself quiet, but feeling himself alert, very keenly alive, and believing in his own competence more than in the daytime. He smiled in slight deprecation of himself, a half apology for the moment's delay, and said in a low voice to Edward, "When we go in, you wait by the door a minute while I speak to the orderly." Then he opened the door quietly and they stepped inside.

The ward was lighted only by a single gas jet at the far end, shaded and turned low. Mosquito-net curtains had been drawn around some of the beds, turning them into dim, tentlike shapes, and from everywhere there came the sound of breathing, of sighs, of moans quickly suppressed. The windows were open, and a light breeze stirred up rather than dissipated the heavy smell of sickness, of sweat and suppurating wounds. As always, this smell made Edward a little nauseated for he tolerated the odors of the diseased living much less well than he did those of the dead. Matthew appeared unaware of the foul atmosphere. At the far end of the ward an orderly was sitting under the gas jet in a chair tipped back against the wall, and Matthew strode lightly toward him between the rows of beds; but halfway down the room he came on Hattie who was stooping over, a broom with a cloth tied over it in her hands, collecting dust from under the beds. She heard his footsteps, straightened up, brushed a lock of hair away from her face with the back of her wrist, and said, "Why, Matthew!" in a surprised voice just above a whisper. She realized at once her breach of discipline and amended it. "Sorry. I mean Dr. Chapin." She sounded as sulky as a resentful child and he grinned at her.

"Cleaning the ward at this hour?"

"It's the only chance I got all day."

In the dim light he could not see her very clearly, but from the droop of her shoulders, the way she was leaning on the broom, he guessed she must be tired. She had, after all, come on duty at five in the morning and she had still a half hour of work before her.

"Get any sleep this afternoon?"

"No. The doctors from Med East and West were having a consultation in the room because their nurses were sleeping in their room. Imagine!"

This garbled complaint Matthew knew meant that the room in which the surgical nurses slept two to the bed, when and if they could find time during duty hours, had been taken over for another purpose, a thing that happened frequently. "Tough," he said, feeling real sympathy, but not wanting to say more for he felt that tears of fatigue might be the result of kindness.

He moved away, thinking that in fact it was very tough. Through these long hours of hard physical work she had to endure the horrors of the ward, the dreadful sights, the suffering around her, and because of her stern aunt's ambitions she was denied companionship with girls of her own age. And for this she was given seven dollars and fifty cents a month and her meals, when she had time to eat them. True, he himself got nothing for hours as long and longer, not even food, though in his case there was a difference—freedom and status won at the end of it—while hers was a life sentence. Tough. Tough indeed. No wonder the afternoon away from the hospital had seemed to her like heaven.

All the amputation cases, and there were five, were placed together at the end of the ward, the beds in a semicircle, the bedclothes pulled up from the bottom to expose the bandaged stumps. An orderly was always on duty here all day and all night, watching for the appearance of a spot of blood on the bandages, the ominous sign of the start of a hemorrhage that, if not detected promptly, would end a life. When the orderly saw Matthew, he brought the front legs of his chair to the floor with practiced soundlessness, rose, gave his charges a quick glance, and advanced a little way to meet him.

"Hullo, sir. You got trouble? I thought everything was nice and quiet—for once."

"No trouble. I've got Dr. Chisolm with me. We want to take a look at Jimmie. Unofficial, so could you sort of forget to notice that you saw us here?"

"Sure, sure." All the orderlies complained about the house pupils, whom they considered not really doctors, but who tended to be more insistent on their modicum of authority than the full-blown physicians. Most of these youngsters, Eph felt, were ill-tempered because they were unsure, and anxious to put the blame on someone else if anything went wrong. Doc Chapin was something else again, a real doc, or as good as, and a great guy to have around if things started going wrong. So Eph's smile spread into a broad grin, and he said, "I ain't seen a thing, Doc, not a doggone thing."

Matthew went back to Edward who was leaning against the wall, waiting. "All set. I'll get us some light." A table with a collection of saucer-shaped china candle holders stood by the door, and Matthew lit two stubby candles of the sort called "short sixes" because they were sold six to a pound. They were given to sputtering and guttering and dying a quick death in a lake of wax, but they were one of the hospital economies dear to the Matron, and so all the wards were cursed with them. Matthew picked up both holders, saying, "Jimmie's over here. Come on," and led the way, two wavering ribbons of smelly smoke trailing behind him.

Jimmie was lying on his back on his uncurtained bed, and as Matthew's shadow fell across him, he turned his tousled head and opened his eyes.

"Hullo, Dr. Matthew."

"Hullo, Jimmie. Not asleep?"

"I heard you come in. What you doin' here nighttime, Dr. Matthew?"

The child's voice was thick from the dose of opium he had been given, his big eyes soft and lustrous. He pulled his hand slowly out from under the covers, and Matthew, setting the candle holders down on the night table, took it in both his own.

"This is Dr. Ed, Jimmie. I brought him to see you."

Sudden fear brightened the dulled eyes. "Is he going to cut my leg off, Dr. Matthew?"

"No, Jimmie. Where did you get that idea?"

"Mr. Toller said most likely they'd cut it off in the morning."

"Mr. Toller shouldn't have said any such thing." Matthew squeezed the hand he was holding and gave an angry glance at the next bed, where all that showed of Mr. Toller was the top of a bald head and a fringe of mouse-colored hair. "Aren't you going to say hello to Dr. Ed, Jimmie?"

"Sure. Hullo, Dr. Ed."

The smile, made sluggish by the drug he had taken, was nevertheless irresistible, and Edward, moving closer, responded with one of his own rare smiles. The limp in Edward's step attracted Jimmie's attention and he said, "Gee, you're lame too, ain't you?"

He gave Edward a look of comradeship that so moved Matt that he spoke gruffly.

"Dr. Ed wants to take a look at your leg, Jimmie."

In an instant the fear was back in Jimmie's eyes. "He won't move it, will he? It hurts awful. You won't let him move it, will you, Dr. Matthew?"

"I don't think he'll want to move it, Jimmie. He just wants to have a look-see. Here, let's get the covers off."

Edward stepped back to make room and Matthew turned the bedclothes back, exposing the wicker "cradle" over the leg that protected it from the unendurable weight of the bedclothes. He lifted off the cradle and put it on the floor by the foot of the bed. "I'll hold the candles for you," he said to Edward, and he too bent over the bed.

To Matthew the discolored flesh of the leg looked more distended than when he had seen it earlier in the day, and in the center the affected area showed more distinctly. He glanced at Ed sharply, but Edward was bent over, studying the leg intently. After a long moment of concentration he nodded as though satisfied and said to Jimmie, "That's all, youngster," and to Matthew, "Here, I'll help you put the cradle back."

When the bedclothes were in order again, Edward stood looking down at Jimmie with the expression of speculation so often seen on a doctor's face as he stands at a bedside, and Jimmie looked up at him with eyes that were large with anxiety. Then Edward laid a hand briefly on Jimmie's thin shoulder with a tenderness that Matthew had never seen him show before, and which he would not have thought him likely ever to feel toward anyone.

"Tell me, Jimmie," Edward said, "how did you get this bad leg?"

Jimmie, puzzled, stared up at him, and in the next bed Mr. Toller heaved himself in protest at this disturbance in the night.

"It just got sore," Jimmie said doubtfully, as though he were not sure that this was the answer expected of him. Then, speaking more brightly than he had so far and showing both interest and politeness, he said, "How did you hurt yours, Mister?"

Matthew laughed, but Edward said seriously, "I fell out of a tree when I was about your size. Didn't something like that happen to you?"

"Naw, I didn't fall offen nothing."

"Did you hit it, or get hit?"

"Naw, it just got sore."

"Did you get a cut somewhere? Even a little one? Try to remember."

Behind Edward, Matthew moved restlessly as though he failed to see the purpose of all this, and Edward half glanced at him and lifted one shoulder slightly.

"Jimmie, try to think. Did you cut yourself anywhere —even a little cut, a scratch, perhaps?"

"I ain't cut myself for a long time." Jimmie sounded a trifle resentful at this imputation of carelessness. "I don't never hurt myself anyways, or nothin' like that."

"Do you hurt anyplace else but in your leg? Is there any place where it's even a little sore when you touch it?"

"No, there ain't. Only I guess I'm goin' to get another risin' on my neck, but that ain't nothin'."

"*Another* boil? You had one before?"

"I gets 'em sometimes, same like anybody."

"Turn your head and let's see. Hold the candle, Matt."

A healed boil, so well called a "risin'," showed where undoubtedly a not very clean collar had rubbed the boy's neck, and there seemed to be another now forming. Edward glanced meaningfully at Matthew and said to Jimmie, "All right, kid. Thanks." To Matthew he spoke sharply. "Why didn't you tell me about that?"

"It couldn't have had anything to do with the other."

"You don't know that until we know what causes bone infections, Matt."

In the next bed the man named Toller heaved himself,

raised his head and said querulously, "Ah, shut up, please."

Matthew said, "All right, Toller. We're going now. That about it, Ed?"

"No, wait a minute." Edward leaned over the bed. "Listen, youngster, I want a tiny drop of blood from the end of your finger. It won't hurt."

He took out of his pocket two pieces of slide glass, wiped them carefully, and put them on the bedside table. Then he took a needle from the underside of his lapel and lifted Jimmie's hand. The boy looked up at him with wide, uncomprehending eyes, mutely aware of the imprisonment of his illness, like a trapped animal that has recognized the uselessness of struggle and accepts despair. The prick was swift, the drop of blood deposited on a piece of slide glass, a drop of water added to it from the point of a pencil, and the two pieces of glass bound together with thread. Matthew watched this, thinking how precise each motion was, and also how vitalized, as though all the intense force of Edward's mind were in what he was that moment doing. And for some reason unknown to himself, Matthew sighed.

Edward wrapped the slide he had made in his handkerchief and put it in his pocket. "I want to get this back to the mike lab while it's still fresh." He smiled at Jimmie. "We'll leave you alone now, kid."

Jimmie was watching as he moved away from the bed. "Does your leg hurt too, Dr. Ed?"

"No, Jimmie."

Matthew saw the sudden reddening of Edward's face, and, not to appear to have noticed, he bent over the bed. "Do you think you can go back to sleep now, Jimmie?"

"I guess maybe. . . . Dr. Matthew . . ."

The small hand reached up and Matthew put his around it. "Yes, Jimmie?"

"They ain't goin' to cut off my leg in the mornin', are they?"

"No, they're not. Forget it, will you? Close your eyes and go back to sleep." Matthew squeezed the hand and put it back under the covers. "You want your mosquito curtain down?"

Jimmie shook his head and two tears appeared at the edges of his closed eyelids. Matthew laid the back of his hand against the boy's cheek for an instant; then he picked up the candle holders and moved away. They had gone only a few steps when the light voice called softly, "Good night, Dr. Ed."

Edward stopped with a jerk, suddenly tense. Then he turned back to face the bed and the wonderful smile transformed his features once again. "Good night, kid."

From Toller's bed there came a martyred sigh.

CHAPTER TWENTY-SEVEN

The Matron's name was Mrs. Dunlop, but everyone, including the administrator, used only her title, for she had made herself into a symbol of unassailable authority. There was no precedent for this, for matrons who had preceded her had been mere dealers-out of sheets and towels, searchers for dust, housekeepers. The Matron had established her reign by her own character, and like any gifted monarch, she had pushed back the boundaries of her realm, fighting those who opposed her. As a result, her position was unique and now so firmly established that she was seldom forced to do battle for what she had defined as her rights.

She was in her middle fifties, thick rather than stout. She wore her gray hair, under the blackest of widows' caps, pulled back and knotted with angry force. Her dark eyes were hard, judgmatical and sometimes a little insane. Her dress of heavy black silk hissed when she walked, giving many a frightened nurse the illusion that the threatening sound emanated from the Matron herself. Her hands, carried at her sides, were always clenched.

She was good to her nurses after her fashion. She fought for them with the authorities and somehow instilled in most of them a pride in their work that made hers the best nursing staff of any hospital in the country. There was no formal training of the nurses and she herself had had none, but out of her store of common sense and from what she had read of Miss Nightingale's methods, she succeeded in teaching them, and herself, a great deal.

The house pupils were another matter. She did not like them. Perhaps it would not be too much to say she hated them, and for no other reason than that they were young and alive while her own son filled a grave at Gettysburg. Matthew, because he was the most blatantly alive, one who possessed a positively animal vitality, she simply detested. Later, when she came to know Edward, she pitied him because of his lameness, and if he did not warm her heart, she nevertheless felt a degree of partiality for him.

Fortunately for the house pupils, her authority over them did not extend beyond general disciplinary power in matters of behavior. This, however, she used to the full, and she never forgave an offense. Because a former generation of house pupils had misbehaved themselves in a manner forgotten except in the resentment of the Matron, meals were no longer served to these young men in the hospital. The alternative was a choice among several cheap and miserable eating places nearby, but the favorite was a place halfway up the hill on Grove Street. This was a restaurant bigger and cleaner than Pete's in Toledo, and serving better food, but it could boast these advantages by a not very great margin.

In one respect it was much worse. The almost constant breeze off the lake had kept Pete's comparatively free of flies, but there was seldom such a breeze across the Charles, and unfortunately there was a livery stable near, where they bred in swarms. The owner of the restaurant did what he could to control them. Sheets of sticky flypaper, always peppered black, hung in the windows and on the inside of the screen door, but in spite of this the flies buzzed in a dark mass under the ceiling, crawled on the tables and lit on the plates of food the instant they were set down. The diners resisted them by constantly waving their hands over their food, the effect produced being like a room full of demented people.

It was in this place that Matthew found Edward waiting for him shortly after noon the next day. Edward was seated at a table, one elbow resting on it, his hand mechanically fanning the air above a plate of bread. He was frowning and so deep in thought that he started when Matthew spoke to him.

"Hullo. Been here long?"

"Not very."

Matthew dragged a chair out and sat down. "Gosh, I'm tired. Been on the go since six this morning and I almost didn't think I'd get away to eat. What's in the package?" He indicated a brown paper parcel on the seat of the chair next to Edward's.

"Tin soldiers for the kid. How is he, Matt?"

"Not good. I wish the infection would come to the surface or near enough to locate it and get it to drain, though I don't think that would help much. He's a sick kid. What did you see under the microscope on that slide you made?"

"Nothing. Not a thing. Not one damn thing but red cells and white cells. I tried it under Dr. Holmes's microscope, which is stronger than mine, and there were some vague, oval things just visible. But when I talked to Holmes about it in the morning, he said they've been seen before and nobody knows what they are, but he's sure they're not bacterial."

Edward leaned back, silent for a moment, contemplating with discouragement the limits of knowledge. Suddenly he banged his elbows on the table and put his hands on either side of his head. "God damn it, there's *got* to be something there, if we could only see it."

"Why?"

"Why does there have to be something in the blood we can't see? Listen, Matt, this kid has an abscess on the bone of his leg, hasn't he? You're sure of that?"

"Yes, it's fairly common."

"All right, how did it get there? An abscess is an infection, isn't it? An infection doesn't just happen—it's caused by something. We know that much, even if we don't know by what. But how does an infection get to a bone that is all covered and protected? It's got to be carried there, hasn't it? And how could it be carried except by the blood? And if it's the blood, why can't we *see* what's being carried?"

"I could think of quite a few reasons, including the one that there isn't anything to see."

"There's got to be. There's got to be some subvisible thing that gets carried in the circulation until it lodges and develops somewhere. That is, unless you go for that old stuff about humors in the blood."

Edward, tense in every muscle, was bent over the table, nervously shifting objects around, putting them down and picking them up again. From time to time he glanced at Matthew, a sharp, direct look, demanding and keen. Matthew, his chair pushed back from the table, lolled at his ease, thumbs hooked in trouser pockets, relaxed, his breathing deep and calm. His head was tipped back and to one side, and he wore an expression, habitual to him, that was not quite a smile but that indicated his readiness to be pleased if life gave him the slightest opportunity. When he spoke, his easy tone was in strong contrast to Edward's passionate anxiety.

"You're talking about microbes, I suppose. But how would they get into the blood in the first place? You heard the kid—he hadn't cut himself or . . . hey, do you mean the boil?"

"That's exactly what I mean. Pasteur thinks microbes cause boils and the like, because you find microbes in pus. Maybe some of them get into the bloodstream and lodge—"

"But if you see them in pus, why can't you see them in blood, for God's sake—if they're there?"

"I don't know, I tell you. I don't *know.*"

"Don't get excited. I can't see there's anything you could do about it if you did see them. Have you talked to anybody about this, or are you trying to be a hero of science all on your own?"

Edward frowned, the sudden appearance of the dartlike line on his forehead seeming, as always, to italicize his thoughts. "I talked to Dr. Holmes but he couldn't help, though he made a fine speech about the pursuit of knowledge."

Matthew lifted his shoulders impatiently and sat up to the table. "And in the meantime the kid dies. All right, all right. You're interested in causes, I'm interested in cures."

"That isn't fair."

"Yes it is."

"All right, maybe it is. You have to know causes before you can make cures, unless you do it by guessing and luck. So I'm interested principally in causes, and I'd give anything in the world to know the cause of Jimmie's trouble so we could save his leg, or try to."

"Do you think there's a remote chance of finding out?"

"No."

"But still you try!"

To this Edward merely nodded, and after a moment's silence Matthew said, "Where's that damn waiter? I can't stay here all day."

When they had ordered and the waiter returned carrying two plates in one hand and waving flies away with the other, Matthew started to eat at once, speaking with his mouth full.

"Suppose you did find microbes in blood, the same as you do in pus, what do you think you could do about it?"

"Nothing. Absolutely nothing. We wouldn't even know

that they were harmful. We're in the dark. I wish to God we had more powerful lenses like those they're making now abroad. But look here, Matt, the moment you open the kid's leg I want to make some slides of the pus while it's fresh."

"All right. But eat your lunch. I've got to get back."

For the next few minutes they ate in silence. When Edward laid down his fork, some of the food was still on his plate, but Matthew wiped up the last of the gravy with a piece of bread, put the bread in his mouth and shoved his chair back.

"Matt, wait a minute."

"Well?"

"I've been thinking—if you can fix it for me to be a temporary house pupil on your ward, I'd like to do it."

Matthew stared at him in surprise. "Because of the kid? He's really got next you, hasn't he? I told you I thought I could fix it. Didn't I see on the list that you're up to give ether next Saturday? You and I could both talk to Dr. Osgood then."

Giving ether was one of the duties the medical students took in turn, and Edward hated it. He frowned and said, "Am I? I forgot to look. But I won't do it if you decide to take the kid's leg off, and that's final. You'll have to get somebody else. And in that case you can also forget about getting me onto the ward."

"I can keep Jimmie off the operating list for this week. As I said before, I'd like to have you on the ward to help me, but since I mentioned it to you the other day I've been thinking about it, Ed. I'm not sure you're tough enough for surgical duty. You never were any damn good as a surgeon unless your patient had quit breathing." Matthew laughed at his own joke.

Edward remained serious, and when he spoke it was with some urgency. "I can take it—for a while, anyway."

"There's nothing you can do for Jimmie. We'll just have to wait, and we can't risk much of that."

"Will you try to fix it, Matt?"

"All right, I'll see what I can do. If you're through, let's go." They pushed back their chairs and stood up.

Had it not been for Edward's passionate concern, Jimmie's would almost certainly have been a routine case. Except just at first, the diagnosis was not in doubt; the procedure was well established and the risk not overly great as those things were calculated. Matthew's intense desire to cure would most probably have stayed within conventional limits. But Edward, pointing to the object lesson of his own recovery without the loss of a leg, was not easy for Matthew to disregard. The problem kept recurring to him as he went about his work on the ward, especially when he encountered the small boy's sunny smile. But then he told himself that Edward's recovery had been by chance, and that Jimmie could not be left to chance, which brought him inevitably to the realization that there was no alternative to cutting the child's leg off on the next operating day.

Again and again in the days that followed, Matthew told himself that this was the proper course, and that to attempt anything else would be almost certain disaster, not only for the child but for his own career. On Thursday he made up the schedule of operations for the following Saturday, with an extra copy to be sent to Dr. Osgood who was still resting at home. On it he put Jimmie's name last and came near to not writing it at all.

Without realizing it himself, all this put him under a good deal of strain, which he relieved by feeling annoyed with Edward for what he called finicking around with a microscope when he knew, and admitted that he knew, that no help could be had in that way. Since their lunch together he had not seen or heard from Edward, and he told himself that he was glad of it. The writing of Jimmie's name on the operating list, which represented a hard decision, had not brought any relief to Matthew's troubled feelings. He wrote it late at night, leaning over the table beside the door of the ward, with the smell of candle wax in his nose and the uneasy night sounds of the ward in his ears; and having written it, he did not go up to bed as he should have done. Instead, he stayed where he was, hunched over the table.

He sat there a long time. He ceased to think in any conscious, logical way, and his mind had stopped working on the problem of Jimmie. It was then that the stirring of an idea began. He did not at first know what it was, but only that his memory was awakening. He sat tense and still, waiting. While his memory groped, his mind began to experience vague recollections of other days that were more sensation than thought. He felt again the heavy air of the South, the hot scents of piney woods and road dust, and a mind picture of the broad, sluggish river. Then, with no transition at all, he was thinking intently, almost furiously, about something Dr. Hurd had sometimes talked about. "It's a funny thing, Matt, but I swear to God it's true. A wound that's got maggots in it don't get infected. The little devils clean it out better than a knife can do. They never touch anything but pus and dead tissue, but they go right after that good. Right down to the bone, sometimes. . . ." The thought burst like a star shell in his mind, filling him with a fierce desire for action. He saw that not only did he have no plan for using this wild idea to help Jimmie but there were many reasons why it was useless. He tried to calm himself and found that he could not, but he did get so far as to realize that he had hold of something that should be thought about, in fact must be thought about carefully and thoroughly. That was enough for the present. He was feeling a great elation.

He did his best to bring it under control, but he found he was still quite incapable of orderly thought. In the dazzle of his idea this seemed not really to matter.

He drew toward him the schedule of operations and picked up the pencil that he had left lying across it. With the pencil in his hand he hesitated again, and again found the turmoil of his thoughts beyond discipline. Then he made a compromise with himself that he could not have explained, though he found it extraordinarily satisfying. He drew a thin, light line through Jimmie's name, leaving it legible so that Dr. Osgood could see that it had been there and had been crossed out. He did this carefully on both copies of the schedule. After that he made his way, rather more soberly, to the top-floor dormitory where the other house pupils were sleeping, and in a short time he too was asleep.

CHAPTER TWENTY-EIGHT

The operating room was on the top floor of the hospital, a large room, partly semicircular with an oblong at its base. The semicircular section was surrounded by tiers of seats that rose almost to the ceiling. Above it a dome, fitted with shutters, let in light from all sides onto the operating space below. The rectangular part of the room contained dark wood cabinets filled with fine French surgical instruments, two or three chairs and a table for dressings and basins. It was a neat, clean, businesslike place, famous the world over, for a little more than twenty years earlier the first demonstration of ether anesthesia had been made here.

Now, in Matthew's time, though operations were done here only once or twice a week (except for occasional emergencies), the room was never wholly free of ether fumes. On this Saturday morning they were very heavy, for the operation that was now over had been so long that the anesthetic had to be given more or less continuously. Now Edward, who was the anesthetist for that day, had gone to prepare the next patient. Matthew, in a striped apron, his sleeves rolled high above his elbows, was bending over the table; he felt the heavy, sweetish odor clogging his nostrils and imagined that he must fight a creeping lethargy in his limbs. The patient, a woman of about forty, had been given a great deal of ether, indeed almost too much, and the extreme relaxation of her throat muscles was causing her to make continuous sounds, like gentle snores. She was nude to the waist, one firm breast pointing upward, but where the other had been removed because it was cancerous, there was a long and ugly gash, in the depth of which Matthew was suturing. A shaft of light from the open shutters of the dome fell on her, giving the scene the pictorial importance of a painted composition on a canvas. Matthew was working with swift efficiency, knowing exactly what he was doing, and with a certain lightness of manner now that the end of the long operation was in sight.

Opposite Matthew an elderly nurse was standing very erect, one hand resting on the handle of a dressing cart and on her face an expression so neutral that there was in it no trace of sympathy or even of interest. Dr. Osgood, who had performed the operation because he was known to have a special skill in cases of breast cancer, was in the other section of the room, washing his hands in a large white china basin. A few students, who had watched the operation from the tiers of seats, were leaving noisily, and the lightening of tension which always follows a long and difficult operation was perceptible in the atmosphere of the room.

Dr. Osgood shook drops of water off his hands, seized a towel and, walking toward the operating table, used it as he went. He was a short, round man who lacked the expression of easy good nature usually associated with that type of figure, and his complexion had the unhealthy pallor of illness. He stood by the table, using the towel on each finger separately and watching keenly the work Matthew was doing.

"Dr. Chapin!"

Matthew cut the suture silk with a pair of angled scissors, then looked up with a politely questioning expression.

"Don't close any nearer the surface than that. If you do, you'll just have to open it up when the pus forms, to let it drain out. But cover the sides well with flour so the air won't get at raw surfaces and make the daily dressing too much of an ordeal for the poor woman. Nurse!"

The nurse came forward with a flour shaker and held it out to Matthew, who gave her the suture needle with its remnant of silk. He began to shake flour and Dr. Osgood sighed deeply.

"I remember the day when surgical wounds like this healed, more often than not, with no pus at all. They still do in the country. Now any wound we make streams pus. It's the pollution of cities, I suppose." And Dr. Osgood sighed again in tribute to days gone by. "It's putting a stop to any further advances in surgery, just at the time that ether's given us new freedom. What's the next patient?"

"Man called Toller. Gangrenous toe."

"Didn't I see that child for a leg amputation down for today? But then you crossed him off. Why?"

"I'd like to talk to you about that, Dr. Osgood."

"When we've done with this next case."

Matthew was applying lint and pads to the wound, and Dr. Osgood watched him closely and with approval.

"Whoever taught you to do dressings, Doctor, did a good job."

"It was a Dr. Hurd, during the war. Dr. Osgood, I was wondering if you'd consider taking on another house pupil in Surgery East temporarily, until the man who's sick gets back."

"Working pretty hard, are you?"

"I don't mind that. I saw a lot worse during the war. The thing is, with every bed full the way it is now, it's hard to do a good job. Dr. Chisolm, who's giving ether today, would like to be taken on."

"Tell him to see me when we've finished. You're ready for the stretcher orderlies. Where's that nurse? Gone for them, I suppose. I think I'll sit down and rest until the next is ready. My God, what's that?"

From just outside the door of the operating room there

was sudden loud shouting, a thud, a crash, and Edward's voice, thin-edged with fury, saying something unintelligible. Matthew, looking toward the door, smiled broadly.

"I guess Dr. Chisolm's having some trouble putting Toller under. Toller's a tough. Maybe I'd better go lend a hand."

"Maybe you had."

Matthew strode to the door, pulled it open, and gave a shout of laughter at what he saw. This operating theater, having been designed before the use of anesthesia, had no proper place for its administering. Sometimes it was done inside the operating room, but when, as today, the schedule was heavy, the ether was given just outside, in a space at the top of the stairs. This arrangement could not be more inconvenient. The space was only about eight feet square, with a railing and the opening to the stairs at one side, so that there was little room for the anesthetist to work, and a careless backward step might result in a fall.

Toller, a big, heavy man, had been put in a chair to be etherized, but at the moment Matthew opened the door he was halfway out of it. Drunk with ether fumes, he was yelling and flailing the air with his huge fists. One of these powerful blows had caught Edward's thin body just under the ribs and he was sitting on the floor, the breath knocked out of him, his back against the railing and his ether apparatus with the open but unspilled ether can beside him.

Matthew, still laughing, lunged at the half-conscious Toller to push him back into the chair, caught one of Toller's wildly menacing arms, and threw himself on Toller to hold him down. Weakened by laughter, he tried to grab the other arm, and after several attempts, during which Toller nearly threw him off, he succeeded. What with the fighting and the laughter, Matthew was gasping.

"Come on, Ed. Get up, will you? Hurry up. I can't hold him forever."

Toller's big body was heaving under him. The man, befuddled by ether, seemed under the delusion that the war had closed in on him again, for he was shouting, "Come on, you yellowbellies, git the bastards. Git 'em!" Edward was groping for his apparatus and starting painfully to rise. At this point the nurse and two orderlies arrived with a stretcher, and as there was no room for them on the landing, they stood on the stairs watching this scene with delight and laughter.

Edward, having struggled to his feet, was red in the face

with anger and humiliation. He poured ether onto the sponge inside the cone, grabbed Toller's chin, forced his head back over the top of the chair, and slapped the cone down over his nose. The long, thin fingers of one hand bit into the oiled-silk cover of the sponge, and the fingers of the other into the skin of Toller's face.

Matthew felt Toller's body under him begin to collapse like air going out of a balloon. He stood up, straightened his operating apron, and looked down at Toller with interest. After a moment he said, "Easy now, Ed. Don't get carried away. How much has he had?"

"About an ounce, with what I just poured on."

"That should hold him for now. Let's have a look at him."

Edward took away the mask. Toller's head rolled and he snored gently. Edward smiled grimly, put the inert head in place and pulled an eyelid back. The eyelid did not quiver or the eyeball move. "That's it," he said, still angry. "I'll give him some more inside when he needs it."

"All right. Help me get him out of the way to let the stretcher by."

Together, with considerable effort, they dragged the big carved chair and the insensible Toller over against the banisters and themselves stood back to let the little procession of the nurse, the two orderlies and the stretcher pass by.

"This is barbarous," Edward said. "There isn't room to swing a cat."

"Wait till next month when the new op theater's finished. A special room for etherizing. An elevator. But my God, this is luxury, if you only knew it. You don't know what difficulties are. Try operating under an oak tree in a rainstorm with acorns falling on you."

"Oh, shut up." Edward pulled out his handkerchief and mopped his forehead. "I know you. You probably enjoyed it."

Toller's was the last operation of the day, and the atmosphere in the operating room had become one of resting quiet. Toller, minus a gangrenous foot and part of a leg, had been returned to the ward. The nurse had gone to other duties, and Edward was cleaning instruments. The shutters had been pulled across the windows in the dome, but the slats had been left open, so that light fell on the room below in alternate stripes of sun and shadow. The instruments, as Edward dried them and laid them on the cabinet shelves, made gentle clicking sounds.

Dr. Osgood was resting, with closed eyes, in an adjustable chair that was kept here for use in certain types of operations. His face was pale, his lips bluish, and a pulse in his neck above his opened collar was beating against the skin with irregular force and rhythm. Matthew, still wearing his striped operating apron, was sitting on a low stool nearby. He was anxious to be down on the ward to cope with the pugnacious Toller if necessary when he began coming out of ether, but the irregular pulse in Dr. Osgood's carotid artery worried him and he sat on, watching it, his hands, with the fine gold-bronze hairs on the back, hanging between his knees.

After a long silence Dr. Osgood sighed deeply and Matthew, knowing he had not been asleep, said, "Sir, aren't you putting too much strain on yourself? Can't you get someone to take the service for you until you're feeling better?"

Dr. Osgood seemed slowly to gather his energies; then he rolled his head toward Matthew and spoke in a voice in which his deep fatigue was evident. "You don't know the circumstances, Matthew," he said, and he shut his eyes again.

There seemed nothing to say in reply to this, and Matthew thought for a moment about probable faculty pressures and rivalries that might make Dr. Osgood want to conceal if he possibly could the extent of his physical disability. A little color was coming back into the doctor's face, and after a moment he opened his eyes again and looked at Matthew with the penetrating gleam that was their normal expression.

"Why did you take that child off today's operating list without consulting me?"

Edward looked up from his work and Matthew said mildly, "I had an idea last night about that case. I'd like to talk to you about it." He gave Edward a swift glance, trying to telegraph to him that this was something new that there had not been time to tell him about. Edward, a bloodstained bistoury in his hand, stood still to listen.

Dr. Osgood said, "Well?" The word sounded like a small, angry explosion.

"Something that happened in the war gave me a thought. You know how, when you got a wound with maggots in it, you used to pour a little chloroform on them and they'd climb out quick?"

"No I don't, thank God. What are you getting at?"

"Toward the end of the war Dr. Hurd, the surgeon I worked for, found out that if maggots stayed in a wound a while they cleaned it out so there wasn't any infection. Later we found out the Southern doctors, who didn't have enough chloroform to use that way, noticed the same thing."

"Maggots!" Dr. Osgood spoke in a tone of pure disgust.

"Well, I thought, instead of taking the kid's leg off, if we let the infection come to a head and open it up, and then put—"

Dr. Osgood raised his head with a jerk. "Are you suggesting that *maggots* be deliberately put—"

"Yes, sir."

"Good God!"

Dr. Osgood stared at Matthew long and hard. His chest was heaving, the pulse in his neck was pounding against the skin, and he was making a determined fight to control his anger. After a moment he pulled out his watch, opened it and stared at it long and thoughtfully, and Matthew, watching anxiously, knew as clearly as though he had spoken his thoughts aloud that Dr. Osgood was considering the advisability of having the child brought up to the operating room at once. He glanced at Edward and saw the same fear in his face. Then Osgood slipped the watch back in his pocket and bent his head, letting his hands drop inertly on the arms of his chair. The gesture was movingly expressive of the feeling of inadequacy that illness had forced on him, but he spoke with the decisiveness of anger.

"Put that child on the next operating list, Doctor. I'll have a look at him on the way out to make sure it can wait that long. If we weren't overcrowded and shorthanded I'd relieve you of duty. Now I want to rest some more. Get out of here."

Matthew rose with alacrity and, his back turned to Dr. Osgood, grinned at Edward and went with long strides toward the door. Edward dropped the bistoury in a basin of water and started to follow when Dr. Osgood, who was sitting up again, clutching the sides of the chair, bellowed at him, "Not you."

Edward jerked to a stop but Matthew went on out, left the door open a little way and, the grin still on his face, leaned against the wall to listen.

"What did they tell me your name is?"

"Edward Chisolm."

"Don't stand way over there. Come here. A first-year student, are you?"

"Second, sir." Edward thought this the easiest way to describe his own and Matthew's complicated status.

"That smart-aleck young scoundrel said you want to be taken on here as a temporary house pupil. Do you?"

"Yes, sir."

"Leg strong enough to stand the work?"

"Yes, sir."

Edward's face grew red and Dr. Osgood glanced at him sharply. "Sensitive about it, I see. Do you like surgery?"

To this Edward made no reply.

"Would you expect to do as you're told and not take things into your own hands?"

"As faithfully as I could, sir."

After a long pause during which Edward shifted his weight from his good leg to the weak one and back again, Dr. Osgood glanced at him and said, "Very well. I can't go into this as thoroughly as I'd like to in the condition I'm in. How soon could you start?"

"Right away. Now."

Dr. Osgood scrutinized him for a moment as though he found this amount of zeal suspect, and then, leaning back in the reclining chair, he seemed to let his disabilities overcome his doubts.

"All right. Tell Matron to prepare for you. Now you get out, too, young fellow. I want to rest a few minutes more."

Edward closed the door carefully behind him and turned to find Matthew standing with his feet wide apart, hands on hips, to all appearances as full of energy as though he had not spent a morning bent over an operating table.

"Matt, have you lost your mind or something? Maggots! You can't do that to the poor kid. He'd better lose his leg. Was that why you took him off today's list?"

"Look, we can't talk here. I've got to have a look at Toller and some of the others. Go fix things with Matron and we'll talk at lunch. Save us a table and I'll meet you there."

Matthew turned and clattered down the wedge-shaped steps of the curving stair, and Edward, careful because of his lameness and of the aching bruises that Toller had given him, followed with more caution.

They could not talk at lunch because the only empty chairs were at a table where two house pupils from a medical ward were sitting. They could not talk afterward for Matthew, his lunch half eaten, was summoned by an orderly to the emergency room to sew up the scalp of a drunken drayman who had fallen off his wagon. After that one of the amputees hemorrhaged and there were various other matters, all of them urgent, demanding his attention.

He stopped briefly by Jimmie's bed and saw that the child looked ill and feverish. Usually in the afternoons he was up against his pillows, watching what went on in the ward. Now he was lying supine, and when Matthew spoke to him, he opened his eyes and looked up in pitiful misery. The toy soldiers that Edward had sent were scattered over him and the bed around him. Matthew picked them up and put them in two neat rows on the bedside table. Then he rested his hand for a moment on the boy's hot forehead, untied the tapes which held back the mosquito-net curtains, drew them around the bed and went thoughtfully away.

At the far end of the ward he stopped to speak to the orderly who was keeping his watch among the amputees. "When you're relieved here, Eph, get nurse to help you and take Jimmie down to one of the isolation rooms."

Eph got hastily up from his chair. "The kid ain't that bad, is he, Doc? He ain't goin' to die?"

"He needs quiet and we need the bed."

"We're full, all right. We'll have to lay 'em on the floor next. I seen that too in my day."

"When you move the kid, be as careful as you can, will you?"

Matthew was busy elsewhere when the move was made, but he knew it was being done for he heard Jimmie's scream and his wild, frantic voice calling "Dr. Matthew. Please, Dr. Matthew, please . . ." The cries receded down the stairs. Matthew closed his mind against them and went on with what he was doing.

Around five o'clock there was a lull, and Hattie brought him a mug of coffee. He drank it leaning against the banisters on the landing outside the ward. His damp curls were plastered to his forehead, his eyes cloudy with fatigue. He still wore the striped apron he had put on to mend the drayman's bloody scalp, and, as always when he was hard at work, his sleeves were rolled up his arms as far as they would go. He drank in great gulps, head bent, looking inward at his own thoughts while Hattie waited and watched him with dim, craving eyes.

From below he heard footsteps in the unmistakable cadence of Edward's limp. He drained the last of the coffee and handed the cup back to Hattie. She gave him a smile that was meant to remind him that there was much between them. Matthew did not even notice it. "Thanks," he said, and turned to Edward. "Ready to go to work? I could use some help. I've been run ragged."

"Yes, but I'll admit I dread it. If it weren't for the kid . . ."

Matthew opened the door to the ward and Edward stepped inside, looked at once toward Jimmie's bed where the drayman's bandaged head now lay on the pillow, and stopped still.

"Where is he? Matt, he isn't—"

"I sent him down to an isolation room. We can't do what we're going to do on an open ward. It's risky enough anyway."

"Matt, I must talk to you about that."

"All right. All right. Later. Go down and see the kid if you want to," and Matthew walked off down the ward. His manner of doing this was of one wholly sure of himself, as though this were his own ground, his command, and the core of his life. Edward watched him for a moment, his expression showing that he had never understood these things about Matthew so clearly before. Then he left the ward and, gripping the handrail, went down the stairs slowly, yielding to his limp.

CHAPTER TWENTY-NINE

From the start it was evident that Edward was going to be of little service to Matthew on the ward. He had not the confidence that he could help the sick that he had in his ability to handle laboratory work, and so he was at a disadvantage in dealing with them. He had no aptitude for dressing wounds, and he could not, as Matthew did so easily, lend the strength of his personality to those who were suffering. He did not even make much of an effort to do his duties, accepting Matthew's competence and breezy self-confidence as more or less relieving him of responsibility. This did not disturb Matthew in the least. In fact he seemed to expect that Edward would spend much of his time with Jimmie in the isolation room, and he went about his work much as he had done before Edward came.

Toward five-thirty on Sunday, while Hattie was carrying around the supper trays, there was a respite from the intense activity of the day. As the patients settled themselves and began to eat, something like an atmosphere of pleasure filled the ward and Matthew took advantage of it to run downstairs to see how the child was getting on. There, as he expected, he found Edward, who had set a chair close to the bed and was sitting in it, holding Jimmie's hand in both of his. When he saw Matthew, Edward made a slight motion of his head to draw attention to Jimmie. A glance was enough to tell Matthew that there had been a change during the last few hours and that the child was very sick indeed.

Matthew bent over the bed, alert and concentrated, but on another plane of his mind he was aware that he envied Edward's closeness to the child. For just a moment he felt the loneliness of having no really close ties with anyone. And while he felt the child's burning face and put his fingers on the pulse in his wrist, impressions of Cissie that were little more than faint rememberings of his senses accompanied the conscious thoughts about Jimmie's changed condition.

"Let's have a look at that leg, youngster."

He turned back the bedclothes and carefully lifted off the wicker guard, aware that the child's dark eyes were large with his fear of coming pain. The leg below the knee was more swollen than it had been; the tight skin was as shiny as though it had been given a coat of varnish. Matthew studied it briefly and said "All right" in the tone a doctor uses who does not want just then to commit himself. He glanced at Edward and said, "A poultice. Back in a minute, Ed," and without replacing the bedclothes, he left the room.

His plan was to use the poultice to bring the infection to the surface where it could be opened and drained. For this he intended an old remedy of Dr. Hurd's, a mixture of strong brown soap and sugar worked into a paste with a little water, and he set about assembling these ingredients. That he was breaking a strict rule—that house pupils could not prescribe medication or treatments of any sort —did not trouble him at all. He was a natural responsibility taker and he assumed, with some justice, that he was not to be classed with the first-year students who were having their first experience with the sick. He returned to Jimmie's room with a small wooden bowl and a pestle in his hands, triturating the mixture as he walked along.

Jimmie stared at him with the eyes of a cornered animal. His hold on Edward's hand tightened, and Matthew saw, with a pang strong enough to make him annoyed with himself, that in the short time they had known each other Edward had taken first place in Jimmie's affections.

"What's he gonna do, Dr. Ed? What's he got there?"

Matthew answered him. "Something to cool your leg off a bit, youngster, and make you feel better."

"It won't hurt," Edward said. "Want me to do it, Matt?"

"If you want to, but why don't you go get us something to eat? Toller's not rallying the way he should. I don't want to be out of call."

Matthew began to spread the paste on Jimmie's leg as though he had not just told Edward that he could do it if he liked. Edward rose slowly and went out of the room.

When Matthew had finished he went out on the portico of the building and sat on the steps to wait for Edward. The sun's heat had penetrated the stone on which he sat. He leaned his back in comfort against the base of one of the stone columns, feeling his weariness and letting himself relax, deliberately making his mind a blank. Boston ivy covered the gray granite walls of the building with a close mat of glossy leaves, and behind them, hidden from sight, sparrows chirped shrilly. As the invisible birds hopped from stem to stem the big leaves jerked and trembled, and Matthew, enjoying the warmth of the sun, watched this idly until he caught sight of Edward coming around the corner of the building. He called out to him.

"What did you get?"

"What do you think? Ham. Where do we eat?"

"Right here."

"We'll get thrown out, won't we."

"If Matron's mean enough not to feed us, this is what she's got to expect. Here, let me take some of that stuff."

He reached up and relieved Edward of a newspaper-wrapped package, and Edward set a coffeepot and two white mugs down on the step.

"I had to leave a quarter as surety I'd bring those back. Here, help yourself."

They ate in silence for a little while and then Edward said irritably, "Well, aren't you going to tell me about it?"

"About what?"

"Maggots!" Edward spoke the word in much the same tone of voice that Dr. Osgood had used. "A simply disgusting idea if I ever heard one."

"You heard what I said to Osgood, didn't you? They eat all the impurities out of a wound. They go down into all the channels of infection and clean them out. They do a more thorough job than a surgeon would dare do, and a more delicate one. They don't disturb a wound as a surgeon would, and they never touch healthy tissue. Make a wound clean and it heals easily. Leave pus and dead stuff in and you're sure to have trouble."

"I've come to think the whole business of surgery is disgusting."

"Most of what's disgusting wouldn't be there if wounds healed, the way very occasionally they do, without suppurating."

"Let's go back to Jimmie. There isn't any break on the surface. The abscess is clear down on the bone."

"What happened in your case?"

"I told you. After a while the skin broke in four or five places and the stuff in the abscess began to drain out and bits of bone came with it. If it hadn't, I'd have died, of course, and I pretty near died anyway. . . . Oh, I see what you're getting at."

"Sooner or later the stuff will come to the surface on Jimmie's leg, and then—"

"It's a perfectly loathsome idea. I can't bear to think about it. And you've nothing to back it up but what your Dr. Hurd thought about it."

"It's that or cut off his leg, and he's so sick now he couldn't stand the shock."

"Perhaps we should take that chance, Matt."

"Whose side are you arguing on now? You were the one who wanted to save his leg. Shut up. Here comes that fellow from the medical ward."

They sat in constrained silence while another house pupil, returning from his meal, came toward them along the brick path. At the bottom of the steps he paused and said, "Hullo, fellows. Picnic? Matron will have your hides."

"Then she should feed us in."

"You surgical Johnnies think you own the earth. Got any gangrene on your ward? Surg West's got three cases."

"One I sent down to isolation because he'd begun to stink. I kind of suspect the man in the next bed. His wound's beginning to look kind of gray around the edges."

"You can have it. Well, I gotta get back to work. I hope Matron catches you."

Matthew and Edward smiled automatically at this, and the medical house pupil climbed the steps and went on inside. As soon as the door closed behind him, Edward turned to Matthew with no trace of the smile remaining.

"Has it occurred to you that you'd be taking a hell of a chance going ahead with this treatment for Jimmie on your own? Osgood didn't tell you to go ahead."

"He didn't say no."

"He said to put the kid on next Saturday's op list, which is the same thing as no. You could get fired out of the hospital and the school too. If the poor kid dies, that's certain to happen. What would you do then?"

"Be a country doctor practicing without a degree."

"You must think a lot of Jimmie to take that chance."

"Christ, it's not for Jimmie."

"Then, for heaven's sake, why are you doing it, Matt?"

"Because, damn it, I think I'm right. I think I happen to know more in this particular instance than Dr. Osgood does. And if I'm convinced I'm right, where is the excuse for *not* going ahead? Damn it, if there's anything at all to the guff they talk about the noble calling of medicine, it should be in doing what you think is the right thing for the patient, and to hell with everything else."

Edward was silent for a while and then he said fretfully, "I wish we could find out what really causes this sort of thing."

"That's your field." Matthew, who had not yet simmered down after his outburst, spoke almost angrily. "You stick to causes. I'll stick to trying to get the kid well. And now—"

A sharp voice behind them startled them both and they turned to see the Matron standing there, chin lifted in command, eyes hard with accusation. She looked formidable and, in her black dress, solid as a statue. She wore the widow's cap like a crown and a black sateen apron on which at some time acid had been splashed, leaving its mark in streaks of rusty brown. Her hands were clasped under the apron, pushing it out as though to draw attention to this evidence of her hardships, and her tight bosom heaved with righteous wrath.

"Pick up that mess and remove yourselves at once!"

Matthew rose obediently, grinning at her. "Sure, Matron."

"The front steps of this institution are not the place to hold a picnic. I'm surprised at you."

Matthew raised the mug he was holding and drained the last of his coffee, then he looked at her attentively for he thought he detected another emotion under her anger. He did not know what it was, and so he started to help Edward pick up the remains of their supper, but he found a feeling of pity for her disturbing him. Edward, holding the coffeepot, the mugs and the newspaper wrapping, limped off down the steps. The Matron watched him for a moment with hard, bright eyes. Then, not looking again at Matthew, she turned and went back inside. For a moment of uncertainty he hesitated, then he followed her.

She had begun to climb the stairs, moving heavily, and he leaped up the steps behind her. *"Matron,"* he said, and put his arm around her shoulders.

She made a sound, half startled, half angry, pulled herself away from him and backed against the banisters. *"Don't,"* she said. *"Oh, don't!"*

"Matron . . ." He held out his hand to her, not knowing himself what he intended. She shook her head at him and he saw that her eyes were full of tears. Still shrinking from him, she turned away and climbed on up the stairs, helping herself with a hand on the banister rail.

CHAPTER THIRTY

At night there were no house pupils regularly on duty. All six of them slept in a big room at the top of the building in beds well surrounded by netting, for the banks of the river were marshy and a great breeding place for mosquitoes. If, at night, a house pupil was needed below, a night nurse would come to wake him, not always an easy task and one that usually resulted in waking everybody in the room.

This night, when Jimmie's fever was very high and he was suffering great agony from his swollen leg, Matthew and Edward decided he could not be left alone. They would sit with him by turns. As Matthew had had a full and difficult day, Edward said he would be the first to keep watch.

"Can't we have some opium, Matt?"

"He's only allowed one dose a day."

"But he hasn't had it."

"I'm saving it for if I open his leg. I'll have to do it in the room, because we can't afford to get found out and reported, and I won't dare use ether for the same reason. Tell the nurse to call me if you see any change. No, I'll see her myself."

With that he went off. The night nurse, who had just come on duty, was a pink-cheeked young woman from a farm, who had probably recommended herself to the Matron because she looked as though she would never tire. Matthew found her on the ward and spoke to her in a low voice. "Nurse, come out in the hall a minute."

The smile she gave him was open and admiring, as full of warmth as a cornfield on a sunny day, and Matthew smiled in return. They stopped outside the closed door and Matthew said, "About that kid Jimmie down in isolation—"

"How is he, Doctor?"

"Bad, I think. He's burning up with fever. Sponge him off, will you? I'm going upstairs to sleep a bit. Dr. Chisolm will tell you if he thinks I should be called."

"I'll go right down there now."

"Thanks." Matthew, with his hand on the stair rail, gave her another smile that half confided to her his fatigue, his hopes and fears.

Close to midnight she came to wake him. His was the fourth bed in the line of six, and by that time all the other beds had sleeping figures in them. There was no light in the room, but in the hall there was a gas jet turned low which gave just enough illumination to see the stairs but not enough to shed any light inside the room. The nurse knew, as all the night nurses knew, which bed each of the house pupils slept in. She also knew that they took great joy in laying traps for the nurses who must grope their way into the room in the dark. This night it was a pile of shoes just beyond the door. She stumbled into it and said, "Oh, bother," in an angry whisper, for she was in no mood for a joke.

Someone laughed and made a rude remark, someone

gave a mock groan, and a voice from the far bed said, "Oh, shut up," in sleepy irritability. Matthew floated upward from the depths of sleep almost to the surface of consciousness. And then the nurse was pulling back the mosquito net and whispering urgently, "Dr. Chapin, Dr. Chapin . . ."

He rolled on his back and rubbed his face with both hands, trying to force his mind into a state to cope with what was being demanded of him. Someone nearby was making loud smacking sounds intended to suggest kisses. A voice said, "Matt gets all the pretty ones," and another voice called, "Come over here, nurse. This bed's softer." Matthew pulled himself up on one elbow and said in a voice thick with sleep, "What is it? The kid?"

"Yes. Dr. Chisolm thinks you better come."

He was out of bed at once, staggering a little from sleep, groping for his clothes. Like most of the house pupils, he slept in nothing at all, and the nurse, quite aware of this though in the dark she could not see him, made a hasty retreat to the dimly lighted oblong of the door.

The felt slippers that Matthew wore when he was called at night made no sound as he approached Jimmie's room, and through the open door Matthew saw Edward, unaware that he was being observed, sitting in a chair by the head of the bed. He was bent forward, knees crossed, both hands holding his damaged leg as though it pained him. His dark eyes stared at nothing, and Matthew was sure that he was not conscious of what he was doing, but the sight was suggestive enough of his troubled state of mind to make Matthew pause in the doorway.

Edward either felt his presence or heard some slight sound. He got up at once and moved the chair away so that Matthew could stand by the bed, but he said nothing, and Matthew, coming to the bedside, was silent also. Jimmie opened his eyes and looked up, but as though he saw Matthew from a great distance. It was evident that he had reached the last extremity of suffering. His lips moved and Matthew bent down to hear what he was trying to say, at the same time putting his hand over the small hand that lay clenched on the bed covering.

"What is it, kid?"

Jimmie tried again to speak with trembling lips, and two tears, large and disturbingly brilliant, stood for an instant in his eyes and then slipped down the side of his face.

"I guess you can cut it off now, Dr. Matthew. I guess you better cut it off now."

Matthew squeezed the hand. "Not now, Jimmie, but I just want to have a look at it. I won't even touch it, kid."

He straightened up, but before he turned the bedclothes back he glanced behind him. Edward, his back turned, was standing almost in a corner, with his head bent and his shoulders drawn in. He was suffering along with the child and making no attempt to escape or control it. He did not speak while Matthew was making his examination.

Matthew did it swiftly and he liked what he saw, for it seemed to him that the infection was making itself focal points just under the surface of the skin. He replaced the cradle and the bedclothes, gave Jimmie's hand a touch that attempted to convey reassurance, and said "Ed" in a low voice. Edward turned a tortured face to him and Matthew jerked his head toward the door as a signal to follow him out of the room.

When they were in the hall together Matthew said, "I'm going to open up that leg, Ed. Give him his dose of opium and we'll let it take effect. Then get the stuff together that I'll need. I'll be back in twenty minutes, half an hour."

Edward nodded without speaking and started toward the stairs. Matthew pulled Dr. Hurd's watch out of his pocket, snapped it open and looked at the face. When he put it back he stood where he was for a moment; then he sighed, walked slowly toward the front door, put his hand on the big brass latch, pressed it down as quietly as he could, and went outside.

This door opened on the ground level so that the portico with its eight fine columns was above his head. He walked out onto the grass and stood there, facing the river, feeling the moisture-laden breeze in his face. On his left the square bulk of the Medical School with its tall chimneys on each corner stood out darkly against the faintly luminous sky. Behind an upper window a single light was burning. In front of him the broad flow of the Charles slipped silently by. The night was so still that he ceased to be aware of the dimly lighted hospital near him and he was alone.

He felt himself very much alone indeed, and for the first time there came to him a full realization of the risks in what he intended to do and of the responsibility he was taking. It was not himself or the consequences to himself if he failed that occupied his mind, nor yet in a way was he thinking of Jimmie. As he walked slowly down the slope toward the water, he was finding himself lost in concepts of the value of human life that were far too large for him. And for the first time he experienced an awakening perception of the greater problems that inevitably a doctor must face.

Though these thoughts were diffuse, half formulated, he felt deeply moved, even exalted by them, but not once did he have any thought or memory at all of the two men in the piney woods that he had shot with deliberate carefulness. The nearest he came to a recollection of those days —and it was not very near—was a sudden and quiet intense longing for Dr. Hurd's presence. He felt this as a child might, wishing for his strength and wisdom, and understanding for the first time that the doctor had taken on himself every care, every responsibility, leaving Matthew free.

He was free no longer and he was beginning to know that he would never be free again. Standing at the edge of the marshy ground along the riverbank, he sighed. Then, scarcely aware of what he was doing, he pulled out the watch again, pressed the spring that opened it and tilted it to catch the faint light. He could not see the hands. He took a match out of his pocket, struck it with his thumb nail and saw that almost half an hour had gone by. The doing of this dispelled the vague visions that had been filling his mind, and though they had stirred him, he abandoned them with relief to return to the small doings of the normal world. Dropping the watch into his pocket, he started slowly back to the hospital. He walked faster and faster. By the time he reached the corridor that led to Jimmie's room, he was walking with a quick, decisive tread.

From that time on Matthew did not hesitate. He found that Edward had the dressing cart ready, glanced at the array of articles on its top and chose a knife with a narrow, thin blade. He held the knife where Jimmie, who was watching with opium-softened eyes, could not see it and waited for Edward to pull the covers back and lift away the wicker cradle. Then, still hiding the knife out of sight, he came close and touched the swollen leg lightly two or three times with the tips of his fingers. What he did then was done swiftly, and the relief from pressure was so instantaneous that the child felt only an instant's pain. He cried out sharply once. Pus welled out of the incision and ran in a yellow stream down the side of the leg. He caught it in a pus basin. Then, as the flow diminished, he substituted a towel for the basin and took a clean knife.

There were five channels of infection from the huge abscess on the bone that had become visible on the surface of the general swelling by the pushing upward of the skin. He opened them swiftly, one after another, and laid down his knife.

"All done," he said, smiling at Jimmie and looking around for Edward, who had retreated to the other side of the room. "We'll leave it as it is, Ed, and let it drain itself for a while." Then he pushed the cart aside and leaned over the bed. "All right, kid?"

Jimmie nodded and his eyes filled with tears, but he tried to smile.

"You did fine, youngster. It should feel better, now the pressure's off."

Jimmie nodded again more vigorously to tell them that he already felt relief, and Matthew said, "I'll just clean up this mess. I don't want to get the nurse in on it."

Edward was beside him now. "I'll do it, Matt. My God, I'll be glad to do something."

"All right." Matthew was suddenly very tired. He went to the washstand in the corner, poured water into the china bowl and washed his hands. While he was drying them he watched Edward, who was taking time to make some slides before cleaning up. He had laid out enough glass to make four slides and the sight suddenly irritated Matthew, though he couldn't have said why.

"You know what you'll find. Nothing."

Edward made no reply and Matthew threw down the towel. He went back to the bed and stood there looking thoughtfully down at Jimmie, who looked up at him with a misty smile.

"All right, Jimmie?"

"All right, I guess, Dr. Matt."

Over his shoulder, still studying Jimmie, he said, "You go on and get some sleep, Ed. I'll stay here."

"Thanks, Matt. You need it worse than I do. I'll stick around."

Matthew transferred his thoughtful gaze to Edward, hesitated, and unexpectedly gave him a warm and sunny smile. Then he went out of the room, down the hall, and began the long climb up to the house pupils' room under the roof.

The next morning a little after dawn, Matthew let himself out of the hospital and stood for a moment, drawn tight against the chill and feeling the sharp freshness of the air. Then he climbed the Grove Street hill as fast as he could swing along. His steps rang hollowly in the empty street. Outside the restaurant where the house pupils ate their meals he stopped. The door was shut, as he had hoped it would be, and behind the dingy windows where the speckled flypaper hung no light shone.

A narrow alley led along the side of the building to the back, and Matthew slipped into this, taking care now to walk silently. At the back corner of the building he paused to listen, for he thought he had heard from inside the sound of a slammed door. For a moment there was silence. An early fly lit on his nose and he waved it away. Then he heard faintly the rasping of a broom on a bare floor. He slipped around the corner of the building.

In the littered yard, by the back door, a collection of dilapidated garbage cans and boxes was grouped. On the top of one of the coverless cans a gray cat was perched, and as Matthew came into the yard it gave him a startled look over a skinny shoulder, leaped silently down, and vanished. Matthew went to the can and looked in, but unlike the cat he found nothing of interest. The rest of the cans had covers and he worked them off as silently as he could, one after another, but with a growing expression of disappointment.

Then he turned to the boxes, and in the first one he found what he wanted—a chicken carcass literally alive with maggots. He stood for a moment, watching with fascination the motion of the plunging curved white worms. Then he took out of his coat pocket a jar with a lid, squatted on his heels, put the jar on the ground beside him and looked around for a small stick. He found one that seemed to be a long splinter from a chair leg, and he grasped it as he might a knife. He picked up the chicken carcass and with the splinter he quickly manipulated a tangled mass of maggots into the open jar. This done, he put the lid on and stood up. For the first time he noticed the smell of the place, and as he stowed away the jar in his coat pocket he wrinkled his nose in disgust. By the time he was back on Grove Street the sun had risen, touching the windows of the Medical School below him at the foot of the hill, making the glass in their small panes glitter.

CHAPTER THIRTY-ONE

On the second day it seemed to Matthew that young Jimmie had at least taken no further turn for the worse, and that the industrious white workers were, in reality, cleaning the wound. When Matthew said as much, Edward agreed but looked so exhausted, so pale and shadow-eyed, that Matthew felt almost as much concern for him as for the child: "Get some sleep, Ed—and look, worrying isn't going to help any and it just takes it out of you."

For a moment Matthew thought Edward was going to be angry, but fatigue quenched the spark. "You can always sleep, can't you, Matt?" he said. "You're a cold-blooded bastard." But he said it hesitatingly, as though he realized that the statement needed qualification.

On the third day, which was operating day, Matthew went early to Jimmie's room. He found Dr. Osgood there, replacing the wicker cradle after having examined the wound. Osgood nodded to Matthew gravely, settled the cradle and pulled the sheet over it. "Come out in the hall a minute," he said, and Matthew stood aside to let him go first through the door.

Unconsciously they assumed the classic attitude and serious mien of the doctors' corridor conference, heads bowed and close together, Osgood with his hand behind his back, Matthew propping himself stiff-armed against the wall. Osgood, reluctant to begin, stood in silence for almost a minute, staring down at the red tile floor. Then he gave Matthew a sharp, appraising glance and said in a tone of cold formality, "Do you find the child's condition improved, Dr. Chapin?"

"I haven't examined him this morning. Last night he was certainly no worse. What do you plan to do, sir?"

Dr. Osgood made no answer to this, and another long silence followed during which it gradually came to Matthew that the doctor did not know how to answer. Matthew was tempted to plead that the maggots be allowed more time to do their work, but was afraid that the attempt at influence would have the wrong effect. He thought of Edward and was glad he was not here to have to endure the strain of waiting for the decision. He could not prevent himself from making a restless movement, a change of position, and felt at once that Dr. Osgood was aware of it and that it had put an end to his thinking. Nevertheless, when Osgood spoke, what he said was so far away from the subject in hand that Matthew had a moment's difficulty in adjusting his mind to it.

"I'd like to have known this Dr. Hurd of yours."

"Why, sir?"

"I'd like to ask him how in the name of heaven he put up with you." Dr. Osgood was standing straight now, facing Matthew. He had every outward appearance of fury. "Dr. Chapin, I wonder if you have even the slightest conception of the risk you are taking. The strange thing is, I have an idea you do. You're not a fool and so you must realize that now, this minute, your degree is in the balance. If you weather this crisis you might someday make a bold and competent surgeon, but you'd kill a few patients on your way."

The anger was still there. Dr. Osgood was red in the face with it, but under the anger was another emotion that seemingly the anger was meant to conceal. Suddenly Matthew responded to this with a broad grin of pure good nature and self-assurance. Dr. Osgood gave the grin a look as though it were something to reckon with apart from Matthew himself, looked quickly away again and said in the voice of a harassed and very busy man, "The wounds seemed clean around their edges. They're draining, but what may be going on below one can't say. Maggots! But as you say, we use leeches without being disgusted by them. You might consider giving the child a whiff of chloroform and opening the sinuses a bit more—make the wounds saucer-shaped. Where did you get 'em?"

"Get what, sir? The maggots? Out of a garbage can back of the restaurant up the street."

Dr. Osgood made a sound of protest. Then he sighed. "We've been keeping our operation waiting." He glanced at the stairs and let his eyes travel upward as though he were already feeling in imagination the fatigue of the long climb.

The days passed, and the wounds improved to such an extent that they could be left to heal without the help of the diligent little white worms. The poison was all through the child's system, however, and he was made so ill by it that for days it was uncertain that he would survive. This was a time of great strain and little sleep for Matthew and Edward. Dr. Osgood, making an effort that left visible traces, came in every day to see the child and there developed between him and the two young men a closeness and understanding that was more valuable to all of them than they realized at the time.

At last signs of improvement began to be noticeable, uncertainly at first but shortly not to be mistaken. It was then that Matthew became aware of how greatly illness had changed the child's appearance. Enormous eyes, deep with suffering, stared out of a wizened little face. The brow was drawn together by nervous apprehension that seemed never to leave him, even in sleep. Matthew, seeing these things, was filled with misgivings that he might have prevented the loss of the child's leg at the cost of an unhealable wound to his spirit, and for the first time in his life Matthew began to experience sleepless nights and tortured self-questioning.

One day Jimmie, who had become a silent child, spoke to Matthew unexpectedly. "Dr. Matt, I ain't gonna have my leg cut off now, am I?"

With compunction, Matthew realized that in their concern over the child's serious condition, no one had thought to tell him this important fact. "No, kid, you're going to keep that leg."

There was a moment's silence, then, "Will I be lame like Dr. Ed?"

Matthew drew a chair beside the bed and sat down. "I'm afraid you will be. Would you mind that, Jimmie?"

There was no answer, but emotion was visible in the pale face. Thoughts Matthew could not read made the delicate muscles under the transparent skin tremble. Deeply moved, he continued to watch, and then it dawned on him that what the child was feeling was pleasure. The lameness would be the symbol of his fellowship with Edward. Matthew sat on in silence, thinking about this and trying to avoid the hurt it made him feel. That Edward's character, acid, brilliant, and not wholly admirable, included a real love of children was, to Matthew, both mysterious and astonishing. Jimmie, and Peter too, had been quick to sense this, and by instinct to feel the mental suffering that his lameness caused him.

All at once Matthew was acutely aware that the afternoon was hot, the hospital smell oppressive. Below the window a cicada shrilled and the nerve-piercing sound was suddenly unendurable. He resented it with a blind rage that made it impossible for him to stay still. He rose, aware that he was inwardly trembling but unwilling to examine the cause of the hurt to his feelings. He looked down at Jimmie and saw that the child had fallen asleep and that, lying there, he looked resigned, vulnerable and terribly frail. Matthew sighed and left the room.

The days slipped by. The house pupil who had been having typhoid fever returned to duty, fainted within the first hour, and was sent home again so that Edward remained to fill his place. To what extent the story of the maggots had got around the hospital, neither of the young men knew. For days they expected to be summoned before some sort of faculty tribunal, and when this did not happen they were mystified.

"They can't have overlooked us or forgotten about us," Matthew said.

And Edward replied, "Of that I should think you might be entirely certain."

"Maybe Osgood, the old son of a bitch, has put in a word for us."

"More likely they're waiting to find someone to replace us on the ward. What do you intend to do when we are called up?"

"Fight."

More time passed, and the mystery remained. They could not know, since for the good of their souls Osgood did not tell them, that the council had already met. At it Osgood had been their advocate, putting forward many arguments in their favor without success until, angered, he asked this court what it was they expected of a doctor. Did they think that following rules was the best that should be asked of a physician or did they believe that the role required that he accept responsibility and have the courage to carry out convictions?

Osgood added that the responsibility in this case was brought about by the state of his own health, that if the convictions were somewhat bizarre—*"Maggots!"* someone ejaculated—nevertheless the child would recover with a useful, though slightly deformed, leg.

The disciplinary court could not overlook this fact, or the telling one that Osgood thought enough of these two young men to subject himself to unwise strain in their defense. In the end they shifted the responsibility to Osgood himself on the grounds of not wanting to interfere with him in the running of his service. Osgood took his revenge on the two young men with grim enjoyment by leaving them in a state of worried uncertainty.

Jimmie's improvement was steady. Not only was he out of danger, but Matthew had come to believe that there was a good chance his future health would not be impaired. Then one day Matthew met Edward on the landing outside the ward. "I was coming to find you," Edward said, out of breath from climbing the stairs. It was evident to Matthew that something was wrong, and he had no doubt that the alarm reflected in Edward's face had to do with Jimmie, for nothing else had the power to disturb him to this extent. His new-found feelings of security about Jimmie's health vanished.

"What's happened?" he said sharply. "Is the kid all right?"

"Yes, but that damn priest has been here."

"What priest?" Matthew asked, completely at sea.

"The priest that brought Jimmie to the hospital. Don't you remember?"

"Oh!" Matthew leaned back against the banisters in sudden weakness. "What did *he* want?"

"To take Jimmie to the church orphanage when he leaves here."

Matthew thought about this in silence, surprised to realize that in their acute day-to-day concern about the boy they had never given a thought to his future.

"Look here, Matt, we can't have that."

"What *is* to become of him?"

"I don't know. I haven't had time to think. But I'll take care of him somehow—send him to school, or something. I've got the money, God be praised. I'll see the priest and fix something up somehow."

They said no more at the time but later Edward said, "I'm going to write Cissie a note and ask her to come and see Jimmie on visitors' day."

"Good," Matthew said, wishing he had thought of this himself.

She came, and there was instant understanding between her and Jimmie. Matthew looked in the door from time to time and saw them playing a game Cissie had brought, the boy propped up on pillows, Cissie sitting on the bed, her skirts flowing around her.

The next time she came the Matron was there, and to Matthew's astonishment the two women took to each other at once. "She's a fine, hardworking woman," Cissie said later, "and she's lonely with only that niece close to her." On that first meeting they had tea together behind a screen in one of the nurses' rooms, and the result was that since Jimmie was still in a room by himself, Cissie was given permission to visit him when she liked. Perhaps the permission was not the Matron's to give, but it was plain enough to Matthew that in Cissie she recognized a kindred spirit, an understanding friend, and that in some way that was beyond his comprehension these two were a comfort to each other. Cissie took full advantage of her freedom to come and go, making herself useful in many ways that lightened the burden of the nurse, an elderly woman, stupid, hardworking and rough.

One early afternoon when Matthew entered Jimmie's room with an air of having wandered in, which was part of his technique when making rounds, he found Cissie already there. It was Jimmie who greeted him in a voice high and squeaky with excitement.

"Dr. Matt, Dr. Matt—I'm going home with Aunt Cissie!"

"You're not going anywhere until you're stronger, young fellow."

"I know, but then I'm going to live in her house. She says so, Dr. Matt."

Matthew, in amazement, and not sure that he was pleased, turned to Cissie and found her smiling.

"He's going to be my little boy," she said.

Matthew said little about this just then, but he managed to waylay Cissie as she was leaving the hospital. They walked out from under the shade of the portico together and into the burning sun. She raised a parasol with a rustle of unfolding silk and there was a small *plop* as the latch caught, and she turned to him, smiling.

"I'm so pleased about Jimmie. You can't help loving him, can you? It was Edward's idea, really."

"I'm not sure it's a good one. It's fine for Jimmie, of course, but you . . . Three children could be quite a burden."

"Oh, I shan't mind."

"Cissie . . ."

"What?" She let it sound a trifle willful. He stopped and they stood still, facing each other.

"Cissie, hasn't it occurred to you that you may have more children of your own?"

To his surprise, she was angry. "You don't seem to un-

285

derstand, Matthew. This is something I want to do. I think it will be good for Peter. He needs bringing out of himself, and Jimmie has just the sort of nature to do it."

"You may be right about that part of it, but—"

"There isn't any 'but.' Besides, you saw how excited he was. You couldn't be so cruel as to tell him no at this point."

She turned and walked on, faster than before, and he had to take several long steps to catch up with her.

"I just wish you'd talked to me about it first," he said.

She made no reply and they walked on in silence until they reached the corner. Then he said, "I've got to go back. I shouldn't have come this far. Don't be angry, Cissie. It's you I'm thinking about."

"And I'm thinking about Jimmie."

"Anyway, it's done, and it's fine for the kid, no doubt about it."

He managed a smile and their parting was friendly.

Hattie had been confined, by the Matron's peremptory order, to the ward upstairs, but she made a good many surreptitious visits to the floor below when she thought she might find Matthew alone with Jimmie. She knew nothing about Cissie's visits, but one day she burst into the room, all eagerness, to find Cissie in the chair by the bed and Matthew, smiling and at ease, talking to her.

She should have gone away at once, and that they expected this of her was plain on both their faces. Instead she came in, shutting the door behind her, and began to fuss officiously about the bed, forcing Cissie to make way for her. Hattie no doubt guessed who Cissie was, for her manner was pert, and Cissie surprised Matthew by showing toward the younger woman a severity he had never seen in her before. He watched this partly with amusement but also with a trace of the annoyance a man is apt to feel when women behave in these ways toward each other and he knows himself to be the cause.

After that encounter it seemed to him that Hattie was forever contriving meetings with him outside the ward. He found this exasperating, and on two or three occasions he was rough with her, though his habit of good nature made him regret this afterward. She, however, had a clinging persistence in the face of his roughness that showed a determination he half admired in spite of his desire to escape her. He said as much to Edward one day, to which Edward replied, "She's extraordinarily like her aunt, isn't she?"

"The Matron?" Matthew's voice showed his astonishment.

"Can't you see it? Same single-mindedness, same will power."

"But my God, she clings so—clings like a wet towel. You can't say the Matron clings!"

"I rather fancy the Matron did cling at one time in her life, though to possess and hold, not because she needed support. She's had her tendrils cut—the death of her son—so now she's standing on her own roots, so to speak. Hattie's young tendrils are reaching out to wrap around you, and you better watch out."

Matthew laughed. "Have no fear. But seriously, I see what you mean about their being alike, though I wouldn't have thought of it."

In his imagination he looked at Hattie down the long perspective of the years ahead and thought he saw her as she would become, strong, a little crude and coarser-grained than her aunt because of her rougher upbringing, self-reliant, reliable, dominating. "I wish to heaven she'd wrap her tendrils around somebody else and leave me alone," he said with some petulance.

The weather—that up to this time had been moderate and even pleasant—now turned hot and still. There was not enough air moving to stir the ivy leaves on the hospital walls; the sun shone down with steady intensity, drying the earth until it cracked, and crisping the grass. The hard-packed dirt of the roadway back of the hospital turned to dust that powdered the weeds and caked on horses' sweaty hides. The sky was a whitish glare that hurt the eyes, and the river seemed like a stream of molten metal flowing between heat-struck banks.

Within the ward the heat seemed to search out and intensify every smell, to roast the bodies of the patients until their pores dripped their impurities. There was no respite from the heat even at night. The house pupils in their sleeping room under the roof tossed on their damp beds or sought relief in the tepid river water of one of the hospital's two bathtubs. In the morning they appeared on the wards listless, hollow-eyed, fatigued before their work had begun.

On such a morning Matthew sat at the little table beside the door in the ward. His morning rounds were over, but he was still wearing the striped apron he had put on to do dressings, he was coatless, and his shirt sleeves were, as usual, rolled above his elbows. A notebook, in which he kept a record of cases, was open in front of him and he was turning the pages, not following the course of any one patient but thinking about the larger question of why so many of these patients developed infections and complications that were always serious and too often fatal. He was deeply concerned with this ever-present and apparently growing problem when the door of the ward opened and Edward appeared. Matthew stared at him in surprise, for he had a whole free day and he had left the hospital nearly three hours earlier. He had, Matthew saw at once, an air of suppressed excitement. He spoke in the peremptory tone he sometimes used when his feelings were intense.

"Matt, come out here on the landing a minute."

Matthew rose and followed him, and when the door of the ward had closed behind them he said, "What's up? What did you come back for?"

"I've had an idea."

At this Matthew merely grinned, making it an amused comment on the frequency of ideas in Edward's life, and the grin annoyed Edward a little. "Matt, listen. Exams for the July commencement are coming up in a few days."

"So what about it? We're not eligible for degrees yet, though I bet we could pass the exams."

"Sure we could pass them. That's just the point. When we came here they didn't know how to classify us because of the special work in dissecting we did last summer and your war experience. They never did come to a decision about it, and when we turned out to be so good—"

"What I admire about you is your modesty!"

"Shut up, will you? I got to thinking, sure we can pass those exams, so why shouldn't we? So I went to see Dean Shattuck. I've just come from there."

"I also admire your nerve. So what happened?"

"Well, he backed and filled for a bit but he finally came to a stand by the post and said, all right."

"You mean to say all we got to do to get our degrees is pass those exams? Twenty-minute orals in each subject, aren't they? Easy! I can't believe it."

"Wait, I tell you! We can take the exams. That's settled. He says what with your war work and Zsokay, and what you've been doing here at Mass General, he thinks you could qualify. Depends on Osgood, and Shattuck is going to talk to him. My case isn't so clear, but I pointed out that my father was a doctor, and sort of let it be assumed I'd read a lot of medicine with him."

"You've got a nerve, all right."

"Well, I'm not going to hang around here by myself after you've gone if I can help it. I'm short all sorts of clinical work, sure, but I told him I plan to be a pathologist and study abroad and I never did intend to be a practicing physician."

"I bet that impressed him."

"As a matter of fact, it did. He knew about the extra work I've been doing in the micro lab, and he said he'd talk to Dr. Holmes about that and consult with some of the rest of the faculty about us, but it's my opinion we're all fixed up."

"What about a dissertation? Don't we have to do one to get a degree?"

"Sure. They'll let us turn those in later. We won't graduate at commencement, but who cares? Probably they'll mail us our diplomas. Also, we have to finish our house-pupil duty, but that's only about a couple of weeks—I forget exactly."

"I'd like to do my dissertation on osteomyelitis."

"Well, don't. Take some of the stuff you did for Zsokay and enlarge on it a bit. Illustrate it with some of those sketches of yours. It will be better than anything that's been seen around here for a long time."

"And that's all we have to do—that and take the exams? I can't believe it."

"Shattuck said we were two very bright fellows—in Deanish language. He talked about the coming age being one of specialization, and said the schools should recognize this in formulating their requirements for the degree . . . I tell you, we're all fixed up."

"Imagine sweating through exams in this weather! But do you know what I think? I think they want to get rid of us."

"You could be right there. The way things have been going, they probably feel they have to give us a degree and get rid of us, or fire us in disgrace. No middle ground. Yes, you could be right."

Suddenly they were laughing with relief and high spirits and the ending of long strain. The laughter was like an attack out of their control, and it cracked the careful coating of maturity acquired in the last months. When it was over they at once became very sober, but they were happy and relaxed. Matthew stood with his feet wide apart, his hands at his waist, an easy attitude of which he had lately lost the habit. Edward leaned against the railing, on his face one of the rare smiles that had the look of disarranging the permanent set of his features, almost of inconveniencing them, and Matthew, returning the smile, felt the unfamiliarity of absence of care, and felt it with pleasure. They looked into each other's eyes, a long, deep look without embarrassment, and that too was strange to both of them. They had never been so close before. They would never be so again, but this they did not know.

CHAPTER THIRTY-TWO

The examinations, which were exclusively oral, were held at the convenience of the professors in various rooms at the school and the hospital. The Dean's office supplied a schedule of times and places, and when Matthew and Edward compared theirs they found that they were to be examined separately. They had been expecting this, but they were disappointed nevertheless. "But at least," Matthew said, "they've given us the same hour and a half to eat in. I'll meet you up the hill."

"My first is with Holmes."

"Mine's Osgood. Well, good luck."

They smiled at each other ruefully and parted.

Each examination lasted twenty minutes, and it seemed to Matthew that the individuality of his teachers had never shown more plainly than during that brief time. Dr. Osgood was terse and as businesslike as though Matthew were a stranger. Matthew soon saw that all the questions had to do with surgical techniques and procedures about which Osgood suspected him of holding unconventional views, and Matthew, amused, carefully gave the doctor the answers he wanted to hear. While this was going on, each read the other's mind perfectly, and at the end Dr. Osgood gave Matthew a shrewd, sharp glance of pure annoyance.

"Someday, when you've had experience, I suppose you may make a good surgeon, but for the next five years I'd hate to be a patient of yours." To this Matthew replied with a grin.

Dr. Holmes held his examination in the laboratory, and as he talked he moved restlessly around the room, picking up objects and putting them down again, glancing at Matthew only occasionally. Matthew was there for forty minutes, or longer, for Dr. Holmes taught, among other courses, microscopy, Matthew's weakest subject. The questions, which were sometimes hard to hear if Holmes happened to have his back turned, were elaborately phrased. None of them was factual; all called for conclusions that required judgment, and at the end of the first twenty minutes Matthew was thinking that there was a good deal more to the subject of comparative anatomy than he had realized, and this worried him seriously.

Dr. Holmes was putting much thought into each question, but he left one subject and began on the second without a pause, and Matthew had difficulty adjusting himself. After a few uneasy moments of struggle with microscopy, Matthew realized that Dr. Holmes was cleverly relating all the questions to surgery, and in the process bringing out a closer interdependence between the two than Matthew had supposed there to be. He was aware that he was not acquitting himself well, and was certain that his answers were less than satisfactory, when Holmes stopped the questions abruptly, studied him with his bright gaze, and came to sit on a corner of a laboratory bench, facing Matthew. Ten minutes of the allotted time remained, and Dr. Holmes used it to talk about the relation of pathology to surgery. The literary quality of this brief lecture escaped Matthew; the meaning did not. When it was finished he said, "Thank you, sir, I wish I'd heard you say all that a lot sooner."

"It's been implicit in all my lectures."

Matthew, distraught, ran a hand through his curls. For a moment he was utterly miserable.

Dr. Holmes was saying, "I think your chief fault is a common one. You tend to overestimate the value of fact, which causes you to underestimate the value of thought. I believe that as time passes, you'll find that thought is never wasted or wasteful, but a great deal of fact, that probably cost you much trouble to acquire, is useless."

Suddenly Dr. Holmes smiled a mischievous smile that revealed a vein of perennial boyishness. "Dr. Chapin, I firmly believe that if the whole materia medica could be sunk to the bottom of the sea, it would be all the better for mankind—and all the worse for the fishes." He slid off the laboratory bench and stood up. "Your ordeal is now over. Good morning."

The two other morning sessions were also unexpectedly difficult, even, Matthew felt, outrageously so. He met Edward in the Grove Street eating house just before one o'clock and found that, Dr. Holmes excepted, Edward's experiences had been similar to his own. They ate without appetite and cursed their teachers with nervous violence.

The afternoon sessions were possibly worse, and, tired and a trifle angry, each of them began to think of himself as being victimized. This was unwise, but there may have been a trace of truth in it, though it did not occur to either of them that the difficulties they were encountering might have been a deliberate attempt to shake their self-confidence, or that some of their teachers might have been affected by envy of their youth, their ambitions, and of careers about to begin When the trial was over, neither was sure that he had made a good enough showing to have earned a passing grade.

As some of the faculty had private practices, and so were not at the school regularly, two days passed before Matthew and Edward received the results of the examinations. They were miserable days, during which they tried to conceal their uneasiness from each other. To make their strain almost unendurable, the burning heat continued. They slept badly in the suffocating night, and by day the stenches in the ward were so rank that existence in that atmosphere seemed a monstrous wrong. By the time the news that they had passed finally reached them they had once more become immersed in the familiar routine of the hospital, and the idea of celebrating, which had once seemed good, no longer attracted them. They discussed it a little, and ended by arranging with two other house pupils to look after their ward so they could go early to Cissie's house and spend the evening there.

That evening did not seem like an ordinary one to them, but instead of being gay, they were quiet and even subdued. The heat, perhaps, had something to do with it, or perhaps they had not given enough thought to what would come after the examinations. They may have found themselves a little confused to discover that the feeling of freedom that they had anticipated was, in reality, a sense of uncertainty.

Their mood troubled Cissie, who did not fully understand it, though she was feeling far from gay herself at the prospect of their going away to work in other places. She pushed her hair away from her perspiring face, for she too was feeling the discomfort of the heat, and said almost reproachfully, "But aren't you pleased that your exams are behind you?"

"It just feels queer," Matthew said.

Edward, looking more pale and tired than usual, was sprawled in his chair as though he lacked the energy to sit up straight. Without raising his head, he said, "I suppose we felt there was some sort of security in the work itself. We've lost that, so we've got to start all over again and get working at something else that will make it possible to kid ourselves into feeling secure once more."

Cissie thought about this a moment, then smiled. "I know Ed will certainly go to study in Germany, but Matthew . . . Each time you've talked about what you'll do next it's been something different. Now that you really have to decide, what will it be?"

"More surgical experience, as long as my money holds out. Maybe on Blackwell's Island."

"Isn't that a prison in New York? That sounds simply dreadful."

"There is a prison on the island, but there's a big hospital there, bigger than Mass General. It's called Charity—a free hospital where the work is about as varied as anywhere you could find."

Cissie shut her eyes as though the idea pained her, and Edward said, "If you haven't written to them, you'd better pretty soon."

"Time enough. They take in new staff in the spring, unless there's an unexpected vacancy—which is what I'm hoping for. I sort of thought I'd go to New York and do my inquiring in person."

Edward sat up, suddenly alert. "Did you hear that? I think it was thunder. A good storm might cool things off."

They all rose and went to one of the windows. A blanket of black clouds was hiding the night shine of the stars, and a jagged streak of lightning tore the darkness. "That one was close," Matthew said, and they listened to the long roll of the thunder.

They stood there in silence watching the brilliant flashes. Cool air came through the open window and touched their faces, and the long torpor of the heat began to leave them. "Listen," Cissie said with an edge of excitement in her voice. "Listen, the rain."

They strained to hear, and at first there was only the

sensation of sound rather than sound itself, a feeling that in the distance there was motion. Then, with a rustling of leaves, the drops began to fall. The rustling changed to a drumming sound as silver lances of rain struck through the trees, and the air was damp on their faces, like fine spray. They backed away from the window, and Cissie said, "I'll make some coffee." Air currents were stirring in the room and they all felt as though a burden had been lifted from them.

When they had finished the coffee, Cissie went to the piano and sat down, arranging her skirts and pushing back the ruffles on her sleeves. Matthew and Edward followed her, and she said, "I wish you had your violin, Ed."

"I never practice these days."

Matthew was humming and she listened with her head on one side to catch the tune. She began to play and they sang:

Comin' through the rye, poorbody,
   Comin' through the rye,
She draiglet a' her petticoatie,
   Comin' through the rye.

Edward's voice was true but harsh, Cissie's thin and breathy, but Matthew, enjoying himself, sang out. At the end of the verse Edward muttered something, walked away, and threw himself down in a chair by the fireplace. Cissie watched him with an expression of surprise; then she looked at Matthew questioningly. Matthew shrugged and said, "Go on." Cissie began to play again and Matthew leaned on the piano and sang as though to her alone:

Gin a body meet a body,
   Comin' through the rye;
Gin a body kiss a body,
   Need a body cry?

It was too intimate and Cissie took her hands off the keys. Matthew laughed with pleasure at her confusion.

She ignored him and spoke to Edward. "Don't you want to sing any more, Ed?"

"No, go on. Don't mind me, please." He sounded sarcastic and irritable.

"But it's no fun without you. Please come back and join us."

"I just said I didn't want to sing. Will you please leave me alone?"

"We can't have so many more nights like this, Ed, the three of us together. Won't you . . ."

Edward took a volume from the table beside him, moved around in his chair so that his back was toward them, and opened the book at random. Cissie sat with the tips of her fingers on the piano's edge and watched him with a troubled expression.

Matthew began to sing softly: "The strife is o'er, the battle done . . ."

Cissie transferred her gaze to him, her hands over the keys. He stood turned away, as though singing to himself. She folded her hands in her lap and listened, her face raised to him, and gazed at him, her lips parted

He sang the hymn through to the end, and then said abruptly, meaning to forestall any suggestion of another song, "I think the rain's slackening off and we'd better be getting back before it starts again, don't you, Ed?" Edward put the book back on the table with a suggestion of a slam, and stood up.

But then quite suddenly Matthew was reluctant to leave. He was realizing the truth of what Cissie had said—that there could not be many more of these evenings with the two people dearest to him in the world—and it was causing him acute sadness. He stood where he was, one hand resting on the piano, lost to everything but his reluctance to have this part of his life taken away from him. Then Cissie moved and he came to himself, half smiled, and turned to see her standing near him, watching him with complete comprehension. His smile deepened. She answered it, and they looked into each other's eyes for a long moment. Edward said, "Well, come on," and she touched Matthew's arm lightly and swiftly. He sighed, and they moved away together to join Edward, who was waiting by the door.

The rain, in a way, marked the transition. When Matthew went onto the ward the next morning, a fresh breeze was blowing through the windows, enlivening those who had lain torpid for many days. As he tied around him the striped apron that he wore to change dressings, he saw Hattie preparing the dressing cart and smiled a good morning. She received this with so disconsolate an air that he knew she must have heard somewhere that he had passed the examinations and would soon be leaving. Her sad look annoyed him and he grew still more annoyed when they began the dressings and he found her inattentive, inefficient, and large-eyed with sorrow. Finally, exasperated by some small clumsiness, he spoke to her sharply and saw her bow her head to hide her tears.

They finished their rounds somehow, and afterward he ignored her, but later in the day she waylaid him in the hall.

"Matthew!" she said imploringly.

"I'm busy, Hattie. Don't stop me now."

"I have to know. Are you really going away? I thought you'd be here for another year, Matt. Are you going to go away?"

"Sure, when they release me here. I've got to finish my time as house pupil. Then I'm off."

She gazed up at him with a stricken look. There was, he saw, a beading of sweat on her forehead and upper lip; and a warm aura of body smell, the product perhaps of her emotion, surrounded her. He started to move away, but she clutched his sleeve.

"Take me with you, Matt."

"Are you crazy? Behave yourself, will you?"

"No, I mean it, Matt. I'd be a help to you. I'd do anything for you."

He pulled away and left her and she said in a loud voice, "I'm going with you, I tell you I am."

Walking away, he felt the back of his neck prickle, half expecting her to throw herself on him. He could all but feel her arms wrapping around him, holding him, and he had an absurd impulse to turn on her with violence.

After the storm the summer grew cooler and more dignified. Jimmie continued to improve, and a little color came back into his cheeks. Edward used every moment he could for work on his dissertation, filling sheet after sheet of paper with his thin, flowing handwriting. Matthew began his, but, unfamiliar with this form of expression, he found the recalcitrance of language almost too much for him. He relied much on his drawing, so that the finished product alternated brief, terse bits of prose with his sketches. He had made few drawings since leaving Toledo and he enjoyed doing them, unaware that they had a delicate beauty of line in addition to perfect clarity, or that they gave the dissertation a unique distinction.

He had not quite finished his work when he received notice that he was being transferred to duty in the isolation building called the Brick, where he would work for the time that remained of his service as house pupil. There was nothing unusual about this transfer, for house pupils frequently did duty there, but like so many other arrangements made by the school, assignments to work at the Brick followed no fixed schedule. Matthew had simply overlooked the possibility that, in the short remaining time, he might be sent there, and the notice came as an unpleasant surprise.

This assignment was the most disagreeable part of the house pupils' training. Two wards were filled most of the time with men and women, some with foul, suppurating wounds that would not heal, others whose flesh was slowly being eaten away by the infection known as "hospital gangrene." All had originally come to the hospital for surgery. In the course of recovery all had been attacked by one or another of these uncontrollable infections and had been brought here to hide the miseries of their dying. Few left this place alive. There was little hope for anyone but the hope for death.

On his first day of duty, Matthew entered the men's half of the building, breathing shallowly, his face the expressionless mask of one who attempts to conceal almost uncontrollable disgust. In the first bed lay Toller, the foot amputee who had by this time lost the rest of his leg by stages, bold strokes of the knife that had not halted the gangrene's creeping advance. Toller was ash-gray now, his breaths were gasps, but when he saw Matthew there came a brief, wicked gleam in his greenish eyes which died quickly, like a momentary point of light in a dark room. Without forcing the old fellow to rouse himself Matthew moved on, thinking with bitterness about the mystery of why what should have been a good, clean, and simple operation should have had such a result as this.

He made the rest of his rounds, mostly in silence, pausing here and there, marveling that these doomed people still clung to life, not perhaps by the mind's desire but with the body's instinctive resistance to death. *Vis medicatrix naturae,* Edward called this tenacity to life. Nature's indomitable will to survive.

He returned through the ward more swiftly, driven now by the agonizing frustration of having to see good surgical work destroyed by forces he did not understand and was powerless to control. In every bed there was a failure—his and every other surgeon's. In every dying face he read his own indictment and theirs. And for the first time he felt a compulsion to believe what so many fine surgeons held true: that surgery had found its farthest limits and could advance no further.

Perhaps he was seeing clearly for the first time this barrier across the path of his profession, if not clearly, yet with enough perception to create in him a deep depression. He did not realize that there was anything worthy about depression for such a cause, or that it linked him to the few dedicated men who were (so far without success) struggling to throw the barrier down. He did not recognize in it the evidence of his own maturity.

Weighed down and angry, he went to the room that had been allotted to him. This room, where the house pupil was supposed to sleep if and when he could, was in the corner near the front door, a small, square, cell-like place. He barely glanced at it, but sat down on the narrow bed. He sat there a long time, not thinking but enduring and unhappy.

At the end of half an hour he sighed, rose, and slowly crossed the room to the washstand, where he poured water out of a white china pitcher into the bowl. With his cupped hands he splashed the water into his face, and did this again and again but without feeling either clean or refreshed. Then he began to undress.

He had been asleep for perhaps three hours when he awoke, alert and fully in possession of himself, to the awareness of someone in the room. He lay motionless, listening, and some evidence of his senses told him that whoever it was had just come in and was engaged in some activity not far from the bed. He heard the sound of a step and soft rustlings, but nothing more. He propped himself on one elbow, said sharply, "Who's there?" and groped for the matches to light the candle by his bed. At the same time he heard a whisper so soft that he scarcely understood the words.

"Matthew, *shush*. Someone will hear us."

"*Hattie!*"

"*Shush, Matt.*"

He got the candle lighted and saw her standing near him, her cloak on the floor at her feet. She was dressed only in a nightgown with a ruffle around the neck that made her look young, almost childlike. She was barefoot, a shoe in one hand, the other lying on the cloak, and she was gazing at him, smiling a misty, rapturous smile.

"Hattie, for the love of heaven!" He threw back the sheet, remembered that he was wearing nothing at all, and reached for a robe he kept on the foot of the bed for emergency calls in the night. "Look here, you get out of here quick!"

Her misty smile never changed, and as he fought his way into the robe and got out of bed the thought occurred to him that she might be sleepwalking. The next instant she had thrown herself at him and was clinging to him, her arms around his neck.

"Matt, Matt, I love you. Kiss me, Matt, oh kiss me."

He tried to loosen her arms and she pressed her body against him. "Hattie, you've got to get out of here quick. No, don't do that." To his own fury, he was suddenly and terribly aware of her body pressed into his. "Look, somebody may come in and find you here."

"I don't care. I hope they do. Matt, I love you, I love you. I want you to marry me. I want to be your wife."

"That's nonsense. Let me go, will you?"

He pulled at her arms and got them away from his neck, but she fought to keep herself pressed against him. He struggled with her, surprised by her strength, hating her, hating himself. Whimpering, she fought him until she could resist no more. He held her by her arms away from him. She was an ugly thing there in the candlelight, trembling, gasping for breath, her hair straggling down around her face, her mouth distorted by her weeping. "What's the idea, for Christ's sake?" he said. "Just what do you think you're doing?"

"You're hurting me."

He realized that his hold on her was very tight, and, filled with disgust and anger, he released her. She put her face in her hands and wept noisily while he stooped, put her shoes side by side, and picked up the cloak.

"Here, put this on and cover yourself up. Do you realize what a dangerous thing you're doing? You could get us both in hellish trouble. You've got to get out of here quick and be damn careful no one sees you leaving." He hung the cloak around her shoulders.

She tore it off again and flung it on the floor.

"No, Matt, no. I've got to talk to you."

"There's no use, Hattie. There's nothing you can say that would make any difference. Where's your aunt? Does she know you're wandering around in your nightgown?"

"Of course not. I waited till she got to sleep. Matt, you've got to listen to me. You've got to hear what I say, and then if you want I'll promise to go away."

"There's an orderly and a nurse working in this building

right now. Either of them might have to come here to call me any minute and—"

"Just one minute. Just one more minute, Matt."

A wave of discouragement and fatigue rose up and engulfed him, leaving him stranded, all feeling but inertia drained out of him. Even the effort of standing on his feet seemed too much for him and he went back to his bed and sat down heavily on its edge. Instantly she followed him and threw herself on her knees in front of him.

"Matt, please, please listen and try to understand. I can't stand it here with Aunt any longer, I just can't. And if you went away and left me here it would be just simply horrible. I'd rather be dead. I mean it. I'd kill myself."

At the thought of so unlikely a thing he smiled slightly, but all he said was, "It's no use, Hattie."

"Yes, it is. I want to go with you. I want to be married to you. I thought if I came here tonight—"

"It was a very stupid and dangerous thing to do."

"Take me with you, Matt. I'll work for you. I can get a job and I won't be any expense to you at all. I'll do anything for you, Matt. Anything."

"It wouldn't work, Hattie."

"Why wouldn't it work? Why wouldn't it?"

"Because as soon as I get myself established somewhere, I'm going to marry someone else."

She stared at him for a moment, stupidly, as though she had not understood. Then she put her head down on his knees. She did not cry, but in agony she pressed her face against him, her arms wrapped around his legs. Her suffering touched him and he said gently, bending over her, "Hattie, please don't."

Her only reply was a moan and he put his hand on her head, stroking her hair. "I'm sorry, Hattie. I didn't want to hurt you."

"Matt . . ." She raised her head and put her arms around his neck, trying to draw him down toward her.

"Don't!" he said sharply. *"Someone's coming. Get up quick!"*

He had heard the outside door close. He pushed her away from him and realized that the door of his room was partly open. He shoved her and she was as inert as a bag of meal. *"Get up!"* he said fiercely in a whisper. The door swung wide and the Matron was standing there.

He sat where he was and Hattie collapsed in a heap on the floor, covered her face with her hands and started to cry. The Matron said nothing at all but came on into the room. His thoughts were paralyzed so that he could not think of anything to say or do, and yet some part of his mind noted and magnified trivial things, as though these alone were important. He saw, as the Matron advanced on him, kicking the hem of her skirt outward, that in her hurry she had only laced her shoes halfway. He saw that Hattie's hair had fallen down and that through it a white patch of scalp showed unpleasantly. He vaguely realized that the robe he was wearing had fallen apart, and clutching it, he pulled it tight around him.

The Matron did not look at him but, going straight to Hattie, seized her arm. "Get up!"

Hattie pulled her arm away and threw herself prone on the floor.

The Matron bent over her. "I told you to get up. Did you hear me?"

There was no reply but Hattie's stormy weeping. The Matron bent over the girl and, taking her by the arms, dragged her to her feet. There was a grim ferocity in the way she did it that shocked Matthew back to life and he got up from the bed.

"Don't hurt her. She hasn't done anything."

The Matron might not have heard him for she was intent on Hattie. The girl was standing in front of her, swaying as though she might fall, her hands covering her face. The Matron pulled the hands away and slapped her. The slaps were hard and they made a sharp cracking sound. Matthew said, *"Stop that!"* and took a step forward, with some idea of using force. Hattie began to scream, and the sound, shrill and piercing, gave him a sensation like prickling needles.

"Shut up," he said, then to the Matron, "Don't do that. Keep her quiet. There's an orderly in the next room." There was a sound of running feet. "Oh my God. That's done it!"

The orderly was in the doorway, a shocked and startled look on his face. "Get out," Matthew said. "Never mind. It's all right."

"I heard someone screaming."

"It's all right. Never mind, I tell you."

Matthew started toward the door and saw that the orderly was hungrily trying to take in every detail of the scene before he was expelled.

"It's nothing," Matthew said. "Hysterics. You can go back to the ward now."

The orderly gave him a knowing look that made Matthew flush with anger. He shut the door and turned back into the room. The two women were standing there motionless and it occurred to him as he stooped to take Hattie's cloak off the floor that, standing together and staring at him like that, they looked astonishingly alike.

He held the cloak out to the Matron, who snatched it from him. She turned on Hattie. "Now I hope you're satisfied. The whole hospital will know what's happened." She thrust the cloak at Hattie. "Here, put this on and cover yourself. And as for you . . ." She turned on Matthew. "This is the most disgraceful behavior I've ever heard of. I hope you realize it isn't too late to stop your getting a degree and I'm going to enjoy seeing it's done. Come on, Hattie. I'll attend to you too. I'll make you both sorry you were ever born."

Hattie was weeping into her hands again. The Matron clutched her by the arm and pushed her toward the door so violently that the girl almost lost her balance. At the door she struggled with her aunt, trying to turn back to Matthew, but the older woman was too strong for her.

When they had gone Matthew stood where he was for a moment. Then he sighed, went slowly across the room to close the door, then returned to his bed and sat rather limply on the edge of it, thinking. After a moment he said *"Oh, Christ!"* aloud and feelingly. Then he sighed again, blew out the candle, and stretched himself on the bed.

CHAPTER THIRTY-THREE

Matthew went on the ward the next day to do the dressings in a mood made up partly of uneasiness and partly of anger. He felt sure that the nurse, a flat-faced, unwholesome-looking woman with bright, accusing eyes, had heard some version of the night's happenings. In fact, it seemed to him that everyone he met looked at him in a way that made him think the story had circulated all through the hospital, though he knew there had scarcely been time enough as yet. He went about his work more silently than usual and he was thoroughly uncomfortable.

He knew that there was certain trouble ahead for both himself and Hattie, and his first reaction had been to hold her wholly responsible. But as the heat of anger cooled a little, the natural leniency of his disposition began to return, and he grew less sure of the justice of giving her all the blame. Should he not have seen earlier that she was close to desperation? To escape from self-blame he tried to revive his anger, and found he could not do this with any sense of satisfaction to himself, because, in spite of everything, he felt sorry for the girl.

Just as he was finishing his rounds the hospital messenger appeared with an order for him to go to the operating room at eleven o'clock. As this was not an operating day, and as house pupils on assignment to the Brick were not called for emergencies, he knew that the summons must come from Dr. Osgood and have to do with a complaint of the Matron's.

He found Dr. Osgood alone, sitting in the adjustable chair that was sometimes used for operations, turning over the pages of a medical journal. He glanced up as Matthew entered, giving him the familiar look of sharp appraisal.

"It seems to me," he said, "that you have an unsurpassed talent for upsetting this institution and inconveniencing me personally."

"I'm sorry, sir. You see—"

"We'll wait for the others, if you please—the Matron and the young lady. I arranged to meet here where we would be sure not to be disturbed. Sit down."

There were several straight chairs about the room and Matthew sat on one of them. Dr. Osgood resumed the reading of his journal. The minutes went by and Matthew tried not to fidget, but the quiet of this high room, the dimness cut through by a single shaft of sunlight that came from an open shutter in the dome, made him uneasy. For the first time he seriously considered the possibility that his career might be in danger, and the thought drove him to a kind of frenzy in which any sort of action would be preferable to sitting still in this quiet place.

After what seemed a long time, but was in reality less than five minutes, he heard steps on the stone stairs, then, as the door opened, the familiar, ominous rustle of the Matron's skirts. Hattie, timid and frightened, came in first. She had the appearance of being driven by the Matron, who was close behind her, and after one swift, suffering look at Matthew she stood with her head bent, waiting. The fact that she wore her bright blue dress, which Matthew knew to be her best, struck him as somehow portentous. Her eyes were red and swollen with weeping and one cheek was reddened from the angry slaps she had received.

Dr. Osgood's voice startled him out of these thoughts. "If you will bring up chairs for us, Chapin."

Dr. Osgood continued to sit in the adjustable chair which, with its footrest, looked like some outrageous throne, and Matthew set the three straight chairs in a rough semicircle facing him. Dr. Osgood dropped the medical journal on the floor.

"Now, Matron, what is this all about?"

"I told you, Doctor, and it's the most outrageous—"

"Tell me again."

"Last night I found my niece in this young man's bedroom. He was making love to her, and—"

"Wait a minute. How did you happen to know she was there?"

"We sleep in the same room. I heard her get up and go out. I knew she only had a cloak on over her nightgown. I got dressed as quickly as I could and followed her. Dr. Osgood, I want to say—"

"Wait a minute, please. How did you know where she had gone?"

Unexpectedly, Hattie spoke up, her voice sounding as sullen as a punished child's. "She's been spying on me!"

Everyone looked at her, and the Matron's face grew red with indignation. "She's a bad, wicked girl, Dr. Osgood. What happened is proof that she has to be watched. But I'm not saying the big fault is hers. It's his, Dr. Osgood. It's his."

She made an angry gesture toward Matthew and leaned back in her chair. She was breathing fast, her eyes flickering with anger. The turmoil of emotion in her was so strong and so shocking that no one spoke for a moment. Then she resumed in a thickened, unnatural voice that caused the two doctors to watch her, thoughtful and alert.

"He's to blame. He's to blame. She's not a good girl, that I know, but I could have managed her if it wasn't for him. He seduced her, he ruined her. He shouldn't be allowed in this hospital. I want him thrown out, I want him disgraced. Dr. Osgood, I appeal to you."

She gave a heavy, half-strangled sob, but the burst of weeping which this portended did not follow. She pulled a handkerchief out of her pocket and sat with it clutched in her hand, her eyes shut.

In the strange way that we see without seeing the surroundings in which an emotional disturbance has taken place, the look of this room entered Matthew's brain by some route other than consciousness and never left it. Years later he could remember every detail, the tiers of empty seats rising to the ceiling in a semicircle around the empty operating table, the shaft of sunlight filled with swarming motes that fell on the edge of the table and spilled into a pool on the floor. There was the harsh blue of Hattie's dress, the Matron's disapproving black, his own legs thrust in irritation out in front of him as far as they would reach, the keen, clinical look in Dr. Osgood's eyes as he studied the Matron.

For a moment the place was filled with the irrelevant noise of sparrows chirping and chattering outside the open shutter of the dome. Then Dr. Osgood sighed, smiled faintly, and turned to Matthew. "Did you seduce her, Matthew?"

The sigh, the use of Matthew's first name, were not a hint of leniency so much as a disparagement of the Matron's excessiveness, and this Matthew understood. "No, sir," he said with a good deal of emphasis.

The Matron opened her eyes. "He lies."

"Dr. Chapin, have you done anything to—well, I don't know what the word is exactly. Let's say, to entice this girl? You say you did not seduce her. Did you ask her to come to your room with some such thing in mind? I realize that to expect an honest answer to that question would be to expect a miracle, but I must admit I'm curious to see how you will deal with it. Well?"

Matthew started to deny these charges with some heat, caught sight of Hattie's pale, stricken face turned toward him, and at once realized that to deny that he was in any way implicated was equivalent to putting the whole blame on her, of accusing her of being the aggressor, of pursuing him, of being unwanted. For a moment he felt that he was angry enough to do just that. She had pursued him though he had tried to shake her off. And then the thought suddenly came to him that perhaps she had come to his room intending to be found there. The implications of this so startled him that, forgetting the question, he stared at her blankly.

Enough of these thoughts could be read in his face to make Dr. Osgood smile again. "Well?" he said.

Blood flooded into Matthew's face. He hitched his chair angrily and gave Hattie a glance of burning resentment, but he could not find any words to answer. The Matron was leaning forward, staring at him, and the pause grew heavy and too long.

Then Hattie startled them all. She jumped to her feet. She was in a state of tense excitement, her voice high and shrill, her words almost inarticulate.

"I'll tell you what happened. I don't want him not to get his degree because of me. That wouldn't be fair, so I'll tell you just exactly what happened. He's the only person around this place who's been kind to me, who's even treated me like a human being. He hasn't done anything wrong, and I haven't either. He's been *kind* to me. I thought he was in love with me, maybe. I hoped he was. So I went to his room to ask him to take me away from here. I went in my nightdress because I thought if he wouldn't promise to take me away, I'd get him to make love to me, and then he surely would, and we—"

Sometime in the course of this outburst the Matron had risen. Now she seized Hattie's arm and, jerking her around, slapped her. The slap was swift and wicked. For a second Hattie stood with a dazed, stupid look on her face; then she dropped onto the chair and burst into tears.

"Perhaps," Dr. Osgood said, "we're getting a little nearer to the truth," and he too rose. "However, I don't see that in this case the truth really matters as far as I am concerned. If, Matron, you feel that your niece needs disciplining, that matter is in your hands. As one of your nurses, she is out of my jurisdiction. As for Dr. Chapin—whatever it is that has really happened is not a medical matter, and so I see no reason at all why it should stand between him and his degree. And so now, if you will be good enough to excuse me . . ."

The Matron answered him. "Doesn't the good name of the hospital mean anything to you? Are you going to let—"

"Matron, so far as my authority extends I am going to exercise it as I see fit. Matthew, there's a case downstairs I want to discuss with you. If you will come with me, please."

They went down the stairs together, leaving the two women behind them. With a sigh Dr. Osgood said, "You've got about a week more of duty here, haven't you? Adn then you will have earned your degree."

"Eight days, sir."

"Eight days. Have you made up your mind what you're

going to do next? I should have talked to you about this before."

"I'm not quite sure, sir. I want to have more surgical experience before I go out on my own. Lots of it. I thought I'd go to New York and try for a staff job in one of the big hospitals, probably Charity on Blackwell's Island, if I'm lucky enough to get in."

"Short of working abroad, that's the best you could do. Are you prepared financially?"

"I guess so."

"If you find the going hard, let me know and I might be able to advance you a little. No, don't thank me unless I do it. Only eight days more here with us! Do me a favor, will you?" Dr. Osgood put his hand on Matthew's shoulder. "For those eight days will you, for the love of heaven, just try to keep out of trouble? Any kind of trouble? As a special favor to me?"

"Oh sure, sir. For you, sure I will."

Matthew grinned and the two doctors went downstairs in peace and sharing a considerable amount of understanding.

That evening as the last of the daylight was fading, Matthew was returning to the Brick from a hastily eaten supper at the Grove Street restaurant when he saw Hattie. She was sitting on some boards left there by the workmen who were constructing the covered passage to the Brick, sitting there with the childish bonnet on her head and the white cotton gloves on her hands, all too obviously waiting for him. Then he saw that there was a large wicker suitcase on the ground beside her and realized that this would have to be an uncomfortable scene of parting. He would have turned back without speaking to her but she had seen him coming, had gotten up and was standing there waiting for him. She was unsmiling but there was an air of determination about her. As he came toward her a long lock of her blond hair slipped down from under her hat and lay across her cheek and he watched her tuck it up with clumsy white-gloved fingers. She seemed to him pathetic but he saw with relief that it was not her intention to appear so. When he reached her she was the first to speak.

"I've been waiting for you, Matt. Aunt has put me out."

"What do you mean, put you out?"

"She says I can't work in the hospital any more. She's got another nurse for the ward already."

307

"That's too bad."

"Yes, and she says I can't stay with her and sleep in her room either—that if Dr. Osgood won't do his duty and put you out, she can at least do hers and rid the hospital of me."

"Sounds like her, I must say. What are you going to do?"

"I don't know. Find a room to live and get a job at something. If it were winter I could maybe get another job nursing somewhere else, but they don't need nurses much in summer. Anyway, she says if anybody asks about my character she'll tell them the truth—what she thinks is the truth."

"But look here—she can't just turn you on the town."

"Yes she can. She's done it. She's going to Gettysburg again day after tomorrow. She always goes when she's upset."

"Have you got any money, Hattie?"

"I've got all my back pay, or almost. She says she won't let me have it all at once, but she let me have four dollars to get on with for now."

"She's generous, I must say!" He hesitated a moment, and said, "I don't like your being shoved out like this. Maybe when you get settled you better let me know where you are. I've got to be getting back to the Brick. I hate to leave you here like this but there's nothing else to do."

"No, listen a minute. There's something else."

"What else? Seems to me what you've told me is quite enough. She isn't human."

"Matt, she's insisting that you have to marry me."

"We went into that before, Hattie. Now I've got to go."

"No, *please* listen. She says everybody will think we did —something. She thinks we did, but even if we didn't it wouldn't make any difference if people think like they do now, so either way you've got to marry me, Matt."

"Hattie, I'm going to marry Mrs. Ward."

"I hate Mrs. Ward. I hate her! Anyway, she'll think like all the rest, that you and me . . . Aunt went to see her this afternoon to tell her all about it."

"She—*what!* Your aunt went to see . . . My God, the damn bitch! Cissie Ward wouldn't believe her."

"Oh yes she did. Aunt says she cried and said something about something like this happening before, and that she'd been a fool to think she could trust you. She believed it, all right!"

Matthew did not wait to hear any more but, walking fast, went along the path to the Brick leaving her standing there by the pile of lumber with her wicker case beside her.

As soon as the ward grew quiet that night he wrote to Cissie. It was a long, impassioned letter, full of resentment against the Matron, saying that Hattie was a stupid little kid without any sense, and that he had never come anywhere near loving anyone but Cissie.

After that he wrote a short note to Edward asking him to come to the Brick as soon as he could. He sent the night orderly out to post the letter and deliver the note; then he undressed and threw himself on his bed.

CHAPTER THIRTY-FOUR

After a distressing hour spent on the ward, Matthew went to the front door of the Brick for a breath of unpolluted air and saw two men coming toward him on the path. The first of these was Edward; the second, walking behind but hurrying, was the ward orderly. Matthew said, "Hullo, Ed. Wait a minute, will you? I've got something to say to this guy." Then, as the orderly came up to them, Matthew turned on him with anger. "Just where the hell have *you* been?"

"Getting me some lunch, Doc. A fellow's got to eat."

"You got to do some work too now and then. Go get the orderly from the women's side and bring the green box."

"Gone, has he? I thought he'd last anyway till night."

"Get going! Come on in here, Ed." Matthew led the way into his own room. "Chirst, I hate to lose them sometimes. One little spot of gangrene on his toe and a nice clean amputation, and now he's gone with no leg left."

"Toller?"

"Yeah. And he shouldn't have died. The life in him was strong—incredibly strong. The poison got all through him, but still he didn't die. For the last week his breath stank so

309

you could hardly make yourself go near him. He was rotting inside but still he didn't die. The will to survive was fighting for the old bastard. The last words he said were to curse me for a fool. He's right, Ed. We're all fools if we can't find out why these men die."

Matthew picked up a book and threw it with violence into a corner of the room, then dropped down on the edge of his bed and covered his face with his hands.

"Take it easy, Matt. There's nothing you can do."

Matthew took his hands from his face and clutched the sides of the bed. "That's just it. We touch a knife to these people and half of them die, and there's not a goddam thing any of us smart doctors can do about it."

"You didn't get me over here to talk about Toller. What did you want, Matt?"

"I'm a prisoner here. I can't get leave during all the rest of my tour of duty. No substituting allowed in the Brick. That damn woman . . ."

"The Matron?"

"Yes, the Matron. She went to see Cissie, with whom she's been great pals lately, and kindly informed her that I've been with her niece."

"I know she did. I saw her."

"Saw who?"

"Cissie. She sent a note to the hospital by Peter and asked me to come and see her. So I got that fellow from Med West to cover, and—"

"You saw her?"

"Yes."

"Well, what did she say? She doesn't believe that old witch's story, does she?"

"Look at it from her point of view."

"Ed, she doesn't think . . . My God, she can't!"

"Be reasonable a minute."

"Reasonable? Didn't you tell her the truth?"

"I told her what you told me."

There was silence for a moment, and the air between them was charged with Matthew's amazement that hardened quickly into angry resentment. He gripped the edge of the bed and stared at Edward, who was standing in front of him.

It was Edward who broke this appalling silence. "Listen, the girl was found in your room, in her nightdress, in your arms, or obviously just had been—"

"It's a goddam lie!"

"Maybe. I told Cissie that's what you said, and that Osgood seemed to believe you. But, Matt, you'll have to admit that with Cissie your record's against you."

"What do you mean, my record's against me?"

"The baby's mother, Sue. You can't expect Cissie to forget that. To her it looks like the same sort of thing all over again. I must say I can see why she'd think so."

"I've got to see her."

"I don't think she'll see you, Matt. She's terribly upset. She says it's the end of the world for her and she doesn't care what happens now. She talked about taking the children and going away somewhere. Maybe she will. I don't know. But I don't think she'll see you."

"She'll see me. She's got to! God, I wish I could get out of this hell hole just for a few hours."

Matthew brooded in silence, his head between his hands, while Edward limped uneasily about the room. After a little of this Edward came back to stand in front of Matthew.

"Listen, Matt, there's something else you'll have to know."

"Well?" Matthew looked up with no friendliness in his expression.

"Cissie's alone in the world and—"

"She's got me."

"After what's happened she feels herself alone in the world, and you can't really blame her. She's got the children, and that's a big responsibility for a lone woman, and it's going to get more of a responsibility as they grow up."

"What are you getting at?"

"Matt, I asked her to marry me. I want to take her and the three children with me when I go to Germany to study. She—"

Matthew was on his feet, angry and menacing. *"Get out of here!"*

"No, listen a minute, Matt. She hasn't said she would. She said she'd think it over. She doesn't love me. I think she loves you, but it's all over with you. Believe me, it is. Washed up, finished, and—"

"I said get out of here."

For a short moment Edward stared at Matthew as though he had never seen him before, stared at the strong taut body, at the mass of bronze curls, the burning amber eyes, the thick forearms on which the fine hairs gleamed like gold. He looked, and at the same time was aware of himself, slim in his black coat, frail, a trifle desiccated, pale. Clever face, thin, nervous hands hanging by his sides, trembling slightly. He said nothing, but turned and limped away out of the room.

Matthew received no answer to his letter to Cissie, and after his talk with Edward he hardly expected one. But when the eight days were over he went at once, in the morning, to Cissie's house. The Vermont woman opened the door when he had let the big brass knocker fall two or three times. "She ain't here, she's gone," she said in response to Matthew's question.

"When is she coming back?"

"She ain't comin' back, and what's more, I don't know where she's a-gone, case you want to know that, Mister. But she's a-gone, her and the two children that's hers, and the other new one."

"I don't believe you."

"I'll show you the empty rooms if you like."

Feeling heavy with despair, he let himself be led upstairs into the rooms Cissie had occupied. They were in disarray, and their emptiness depressed him still further. Without her books and her little treasured ornaments the tables seemed bare. The house plants were gone from the windows; no toys of Peter's littered the flowered carpet. While the woman waited for him by the door he walked into the middle of the place and stood there stupidly gazing around him. He saw with pain that was almost unbearable the corner of the sofa where she always sat and the pillow still dented with the pressure of her body. Turning away, he was close to tears. As he moved slowly toward the door he saw something lying on the floor at his feet and he stooped to pick it up. It was a fancy bookmark, a rose worked in cross-stitch on stiffened silk. He put it in his pocket and kept his hand around it as he followed the Vermont woman down the stairs.

Out on the street, he stood in hopeless uncertainty until the thought occurred to him that at the Seth Brainard house they might know where Cissie had gone, and he turned in that direction. There he found Mrs. Brainard, who showed him so much severity that he had no doubt she had heard his story. "If I did know where she and the children have gone—and perhaps I do—do you think I would tell the very man she's trying to escape?"

That was all he could get out of the woman, and with great reluctance he took the only course left open to him, which was to find and question Edward. But Edward, who had also finished his work, could not be expected to be at the hospital, and he was not at his room. When Matthew heard that he too had packed and gone, and without a farewell, a feeling of hopelessness came over him. In desolation he dragged himself slowly back to the hospital.

When he reached the main hospital building the realization of his present status finally took hold of him. His work here was finished, his connection with the hospital where he had worked so long had come to an end. He had now only a courtesy right even to enter, and someone unknown was filling his place and doing the duties that had been his. Listless with discouragement, he sat down on the steps below the great stone columns and listened vaguely to the noise of hammering from the new construction. He gazed around at the familiar scene and it occurred to him that in his stay here there was much that he had missed. He thought about this sadly, with a passive, inert regret.

After a while he sighed, rose stiffly, and began to walk slowly toward the Medical School. He did not go in, but he walked all around the building, looking up at it and feeling a kind of wonder at the strangeness of the familiar. Now and again he met a student or house pupil whom he knew, and greeted him distantly with no desire to stop and talk. Others passed him whom he felt sure he had never seen before, and his feeling of detachment from the life he had led here grew stronger.

Presently his wanderings brought him to the path that led to the Brick, and here he met the orderly attached to the ward that had so lately been his. The man had no business here at this time of day, and when he saw Matthew a guilty look came over his face, but then he seemed to remember that Matthew no longer had any authority over him, and he grinned.

"Hullo, Doc. Say, there's a letter and a package for you over at the Brick. I put 'em in your room."

"Thanks. I'll get them by and by."

"And the new doc's there. He'll be wanting to move into your room, I guess, soon as you get your things out."

"He can wait a bit."

"Oh, and another thing. I nearly forgot. You're to call at Dean Shattuck's office over at the school."

"All right, thanks. I'll go there now."

"And good luck, Doc."

"Good luck to you."

The summons to the Dean's office mystified him since his work was done; his dissertation had been handed in, and accepted without enthusiasm in a brief note. He had seldom been in Dean Shattuck's office and so it did not have the depressing effect on him of the well-known places he was leaving. He found there a brisk young man who told him that the Dean had gone out, but that it did not really matter since there was something here for Dr. Chapin. The brisk young man hunted among papers on a littered desk, found a small roll and handed it to Matthew. Without feeling any particular emotion Matthew unrolled it and read the words that granted him a degree as a doctor of medicine.

He went out with the roll in his hand, thinking that, as it was midafternoon and he had not eaten since breakfast, he ought to be hungry, but he felt no desire for food. He thought of going one last time to the flyblown restaurant on the Grove Street hill and found no pleasure in the thought of being there alone, so he went slowly back toward the Brick.

In his room he discovered a strange bag and some books stacked in a corner, and on the chest of drawers a letter and a large flat package. The letter had only his name on it, written in Edward's spidery hand, and Matthew opened it first.

Edward wrote that he had called at the Brick that morning to say good-bye but found that Matthew had gone. "Perhaps you wouldn't have wanted to see me anyway." He went on to say that Cissie, with the children, had gone to the Reverend Seth Brainard's house and that he and Cissie would be married by the Reverend Brainard this same morning. They would then go to New York with the children, and they would take the first boat to Europe on their way to Germany. The letter ended with the words: "I will do my best to make her happy, Matt."

With a trembling hand Matthew put the pages down and went to sit where he had sat so many times before, on the edge of his bed. He felt numb and without energy even for grief.

He sat there a long time, and then he drew a deep, steadying breath and rose and went to pick up the package. On the outside was written "For Dr. Matthew Chapin from E. Osgood," and when he tore the paper off he found a large case of beautiful French surgical instruments. He stood there holding the open case in his hands. His eyes kept filling with mist and he kept blinking it away and the mist would come back again. Finally he put the case down, dragged his traveling bag out from under the bed, put the case carefully in the bottom of it and began to pile his possessions on top.

He was still busy with this when he heard his name spoken softly, and, looking up, he saw Hattie standing in the doorway. It seemed to him more than he could bear. "Oh *Christ!*" he said, then, sharply, "For heaven's sake, don't come in here!"

"It can't matter now, Matt."

"It does matter." He went to stand in front of her, blocking her way. "I think you must have lost your mind if you ever had any."

"I just about have. Matt, I've got to talk to you."

"You can't do it here."

"Then somewhere else. Matt, you've got to help me."

The sound of desperation in her words made him look at her with more attention. She was limp and bedraggled, wearing an old brown dress that needed ironing, without the gay little bonnet or the brave white gloves. It seemed to him that she must truly be in a bad way to let herself be seen like that, and his harsh feelings toward her softened into his former vague, troubling sense of guilt. Perhaps this showed in his face for her mouth began to tremble, tears blurred her eyes and ran down her cheeks. She sniffed, but made no attempt to wipe the tears away.

"All right," he said. "Go on outside and I'll be with you in a few minutes."

She left then without another word and he resumed his packing, not hurrying. There was not much to pack and when he had finished he dumped the bag in the hall where he would be able to get it without disturbing the new occupant of the room, and went outside to find Hattie.

He found her waiting near the lumber pile apparently oblivious to the hammering of the builders close by. He said, "Let's go where it's quieter," and discovered without much surprise that he had the beginnings of a headache.

They went past the Medical School and stopped at the bench where he had found her huddled and unhappy a very long time—or what seemed like a very long time—ago. She dropped dejectedly down in the same corner, and as he seated himself beside her it occurred to him that she was to be pitied, for she had truly led a hard life, quite probably from the time she was a child. "Now tell me what's the matter," he said.

"You're going away." She said it accusingly.

"You know that."

"Yes, but where?"

315

"New York."

"When?"

"Tonight on the six-o'clock. Earlier if I can make it. It doesn't matter, Hattie. I have to go."

"It does matter. Matt, you're really the only friend I have."

He thought that this, unfortunately, was true, but he said, "What about your aunt?"

"She's still in Gettysburg and she's not coming back until day after tomorrow, and anyway she hates me. You should know that. Matt, I can't get a job because I have no references, and my money's nearly gone, and they put me out of the room I got in the morning, and I don't know what to do."

"I could let you have a little money, I guess. Enough for a day or two till your aunt gets back. She has a little money of yours, hasn't she?"

"Yes, but I hate to take your money, Matt."

"Never mind. She'll have to help you."

"I won't beg of her even for what she owes me. I won't!" Hattie burst into tears. She seemed to have no handkerchief with her and her weeping was a messy business. After a moment he sighed, took out his own handkerchief and put it into her wet hand.

Presently she said, "Matt, is it hard to kill yourself?"

"Don't talk like that, Hattie."

"But I want to. I want to be dead and not have to live any more."

She started to cry again—heartbroken, desolate weeping such as he had never heard before. Hs sat listening to it and it seemed to be the only sound in the world and to fill all space.

He sorrowed with her, grieving for himself and the bitterness of his loss of Cissie. In a way their grieving was a bond between them which grew stronger until they were both aware of it. After a time her tears slackened and he touched her knee gently. "I've got troubles too, Hattie."

She raised her head and looked at him then, as though it had never occurred to her that anyone else but herself could be unhappy. Her wet cheeks were flushed, her lashes stuck together, but there was a dawning of concern for him in her gray eyes. Without speaking, she seemed to be asking a question of him and he answered it.

"She was married to Edward this morning."

"Oh, Matt. Then you're alone too."

She had gone so to the heart of his sorrow that he was

overwhelmed. He put his head down on his arm on the back of the bench and gave himself up to utter misery.

She watched him in silence for a while, and then she reached out timidly and took his hand in both of hers. He let her hold it, though he did not return the pressure of hers, and after a time touching her began to comfort him.

They stayed like that a long time, and then she leaned herself against him and whispered to him, "Matt, if you'll let me marry you I'll do everything I can to make it up to you. We're so alone, Matt—both of us."

He shook his head and sighed, but he put his arm around her and let her lie against him. The shake of his head was a refusal; nevertheless he gave in to the comfort she offered him.

He gave her money—not much, but more than he thought he should afford—kissed her on the forehead and watched her walk away, a dreary, defeated little figure. Just at the last she had been surprisingly docile and this had relieved him somewhat. He put her out of his mind with no difficulty, and at a few minutes before six he found a seat on the train, lifted his bag to the overhead rack, and settled himself as comfortably as he could on the dirty green plush.

Almost at once he was asleep, rousing only slightly when the train made a jerky start. He slept for close to an hour, and when he woke it was to realize that someone was sitting beside him. He did not open his eyes to see who it was, but he moved, stretching his legs, and was startled into complete awareness by feeling a hand on his knee. He knew who it must be without looking, and his instant reaction was to be furiously angry.

"Hattie! Have you lost your mind?"

"The conductor's coming down the car collecting tickets, and I don't have one, Matt, or any money either. I had to use what you gave me to pay for my room."

"Oh, for Christ sake! What did you do this for!"

He was prevented from saying more by the conductor, but when he had given his ticket to be punched and bought one for Hattie, he turned on her.

"Why did you do this?"

"What else could I do?"

"Stay where you belonged. And not make yourself a burden to me."

"You don't understand. Please, please Matt, don't scold me. I just can't stand any more."

She began to weep, not noisily but in a despairing,

hopeless way, as though she had indeed come to the end of things. His anger was not proof against it. He watched her for a moment; then he sighed.

"All right, kid. I guess maybe you're right and things can get pretty tough for a girl without someone around to help. I don't see why you picked on me, but you did, and here you are, so I suppose we'd better both make the best of it."

She took her hands away from her face, but still held them cup-shaped in front of her, and stared at him with such a ludicrous expression of dawning hope that he had to smile in spite of himself.

"Here comes the sandwich man. Are you hungry? Maybe we better start by eating something."

He held up a hand to stop the man with the big basket on his arm, and seeing Hattie's sudden look of pleasure, his smile broadened.

V
New York

CHAPTER THIRTY-FIVE

The months that followed remained, in after years, dim and confused in Matthew's memory, perhaps because there was little in them that he recalled with any pleasure. He and Hattie were married as soon as that could be arranged because, with his money dwindling, he did not know what to do with her. They took a room under the roof of a shabby old house not far from Bellevue Hospital, and both of them set out at once to find work that would pay for their keep. In these days the time when Matthew would become established as a surgeon seemed very remote indeed.

They quickly worked out a routine of living that had the advantage of taking them both away from their small, depressing room for the greater part of the day. In the mornings they set out separately to look for work, meeting back at the room for a cold lunch, and then went out again. They returned to the room for the evening meal—cooked, not very expertly, by Hattie on a gas ring that stood on a rickety shelf in the corner, and as the ventilation of the room was poor, the odors of cooking were apt to linger throughout the night.

The food was never good, but in this way they saved the cost of a restaurant meal, and both of them were beginning to be seriously concerned about their dwindling supply of money. Matthew said little about his worries, but Hattie lacked this sort of self-discipline and she had begun to feel guilty about being a burden to him. Often she would say, "If it weren't for me you wouldn't have to live like this, Matt." And he would try to grin and say, "You don't hear me complaining, do you?"

"But if I weren't here you'd maybe have all the money you need."

"Don't worry, we're not going to starve."

Their only table was, more often than not, covered with his books and papers and they would shove these aside to make room for their plates. She sat on their only chair, he on the edge of the bed, and afterward he brought water up from the sink in the hall two floors below for her to wash the dishes. She heated the water on the gas ring, but it took too long to get really hot and it seemed to him that their plates always had a film of grease.

She alternated between being overly affectionate and declaring with bursts of weeping that she was nothing but a burden to him, and he found both moods equally hard to bear. He knew that, in spite of the restraint he put on himself, they were coming closer and closer to a quarrel. Finally one day he faced the fact that if he did not find work soon he would have to borrow money from Dr. Osgood and perhaps, in the end, give up medicine to take any job he could get.

The strain was telling on him badly, and that night he could not make himself swallow the greasy stew and half-raw onions. When she saw him push his plate away she burst into tears. She wept, as always, loudly and without restraint, making no effort to hide the ugly contortions of her face. His hold on himself broke and he yelled at her, "Oh for Christ sake, shut up!"

He flung himself out of the room and walked the streets half the night until exhaustion calmed him and drove him home. In the morning he told her he was sorry and she forgave him in words; but their wounds had not healed, and they were distant and unfriendly toward each other. Another quarrel might have followed soon but that she found work, and this, for her at least, changed the whole aspect of life.

He knew the moment he heard her footsteps on the stairs that she must have good news, and he rose from the table where he was working to open the door for her. Before he could reach it she burst in, radiant, and threw herself on him, her arms around his neck.

"Oh Matt, I've got it! I've got a perfectly wonderful job!"

"Here, stop choking me and tell me about it."

He led her to the bed and sat her down beside him. Telling her news, she bounced up and down like an excited child. She was to be a nurse again, not just an ordinary nurse but a "sort of supervisor." She would work in an isolation building for smallpox—the pesthouse, they called it—out on Blackwell's Island in the river.

"And, Matt, think of it, I'll get two dollars a week more than at Mass General."

"I am thinking about it and I don't think I like it, Hattie."

"But, Matt, why not? They don't take anything but smallpox cases and I've been vaccinated. You can vaccinate me again to make sure."

"It isn't that altogether. Did you see the hospital?"

"No. The Matron came over to Bellevue—it's some way connected with Bellevue—to interview us, three of us. I'm the one she picked, think of it!"

"It's a city-run hospital, Hattie, that gets its patients from immigrants and the slums. You've never had to work in a place like that before, and you don't know how tough it would be."

"But I'll be supervisor, Matt."

"Did the Matron tell you who the nurses are? They're from the almshouse and from the women's prison—prostitutes, thieves, the sweepings of the slums, from what I hear."

"She didn't tell me that."

"I'll bet she didn't."

"But she's nice—little and gray-haired, and like a real lady."

There was a drawback to this wonderful job, however —from her point of view the only one—and she told him about it with a worried frown after she had drawn from him with a reluctant consent to her accepting the position. She would have to live at the hospital, and because of the nature of the work she would be practically cloistered except for one day and night a week.

"We'll have to make that day and night very special," he said.

"Oh, Matt, I love you so!" She threw herself again into his arms.

321

With Hattie paying her way, and perhaps a little more, the situation looked considerably brighter and what remained of Dr. Hurd's legacy could be made to last much longer. Matthew had not been able to get a staff position in any hospital in the city, but in the process of trying he had learned a good deal about the various institutions. He knew that the hospital where he would choose to work if he could was the city-owned hospital named Charity affiliated with Bellevue. This happened also to be located on Blackwell's Island, about a mile from the Smallpox Hospital on a different boat landing.

Matthew's reason for wanting to be on the staff there was, in part, that the surgical work would be varied, but principally because, rather astonishingly for a public institution, the requirements for a staff position there were so high that anyone fulfilling them would then be acceptable almost anywhere. The work would be harder than anything he had yet encountered, except perhaps for some of the days in the aftermath of battle, but if he could be accepted, and then manage to survive for a year, he felt that his future would be on a firm foundation.

He was not at all afraid of hard work, but the more he heard about the examination that he would be required to pass, the more he feared it would prove a barrier that he would not be able to surmount. Whenever he made inquiries about this examination the conversation ran along the same general lines.

"Are you a university man?"

"No, I'm not."

"Then don't try it."

"But why not? I have a medical degree from Harvard."

"None better, but you see the exam questions are not all medical."

He was told he would have to know the answers to questions in history, literature, science, and the arts. "And medicine?" he asked, and was assured there would be some questions in this field also—everything, in fact, except languages, an omission he found surprising. Why knowledge of all these subjects was necessary for a hardworking intern, half of whose patients would be nearly illiterate, and who would be too busy ever to read a book or go to a concert, was never explained to him.

Somewhere he picked up the information that there were several teachers in the city who specialized in tutoring those who were especially anxious to pass or uncertain of their ability to do so. Matthew got the names of two of them and went to see them. The first of these, when he heard Matthew's qualifications, or rather his lack of them, declined to accept him as a pupil; the second, a good-natured old gentleman with bright, lively blue eyes, was equally firm in his refusal, though somewhat more courteous.

These experiences should have made it plain to him that he would not be able to qualify for the staff position he wanted; but though he was discouraged to the point of hopelessness, he could not put his ambition out of his mind. He realized he must have some sort of paying work, and though his heart was not in it, he again began to look for something. Shortly after Hattie began nursing in the Smallpox Hospital he found it in the City Health Department. He was hired to be an "inspector," the work consisting, as far as he could tell, of poking into places where people didn't want him to go. "The job needs big, tough guys like you," the man who hired him explained. When Hattie came for her day off he told her about it. "At least," he said, "a medical degree qualifies me to lift the covers of garbage cans and look inside." She giggled but he was full of bitterness.

Before beginning the routine work of an inspector he was given a one-day assignment to help out in what appeared to be an emergency at Bellevue. The work to be done was the vaccination of over a hundred immigrants who were ill with a variety of diseases and were to be admitted to the hospital. Matthew never fully understood what caused this emergency, for these people were customarily sent to Charity Hospital on Blackwell's Island, but he supposed that two or three shiploads of immigrants had arrived together, overtaxing the facilities of Charity.

They were a filthy, pathetic, degraded mass of humanity, huddled together in terror of their surroundings, all emaciated, all large-eyed with fright. They were herded into line by policemen, and as they came up to the table where he was standing, some chattered protests in unknown languages, some were silent and trembling. All were crawling with lice.

Into this batch of foreigners had somehow been mixed some others. One of these was an old fellow, wise in the ways of the wards, who regarded Matthew with the impudent eye of experience. Every city hospital knows him and his complaining all too well.

"I been here five times with my liver," he announced,

"and would you believe it? They vaccinated me every goddam time."

"All right, Pop, get ready for the sixth."

Another of these who seemed to be there by accident was a little colored boy dressed only in a sort of breechcloth. He was a skinny youngster with shifty eyes, an object of wonder to the immigrants. He was looking about him furtively for a way of escape, and—as Matthew discovered when he grabbed his arm—he was as slippery with sweat as a greased pig. When Matthew took a hold on him the youngster turned and sank his teeth in the back of his hand, and so got free. Perhaps he did escape, for he did not show up again. Matthew left his work, found the nearest sink and washed the bite again and again with strong yellow soap.

That night, in the solitude of his room, he spent an hour with a lighted candle hunting lice in the seams of his clothing and burning them. Later, he awoke from heavy sleep with the thought whole in his mind that the brat might have had syphilis, and for some time he lay in the dark sweating with worry about this.

When he became an inspector he found the work uninteresting, tiring and somewhat dangerous, and the nagging thought that he should instead be doing something constructive about his future career made it additionally burdensome. His assignment was to patrol the docks, the newly arrived ships, nearby hotels, and seamen's boardinghouses, on the lookout for cholera and typhus. And there was always a chance, though a fairly remote one, that a case of plague might find its way to port. He hoped that he would be able to recognize these diseases if ever he came across them, but he had no confidence about this. He was resented wherever he went, sometimes with blows. Once in a fight his hand closed on a knife, resulting in a cut on his palm that, had it been a little lower and a trifle deeper, would have put an end to his career as a surgeon.

He had to write weekly reports on his work and deliver them to the Health Department where he might also receive new instructions. This duty annoyed him because he disliked the bureaucratic atmosphere of the place. At the office he always had to wait, which he had never been able to do with any patience. One day, when he was sighing on an uncomfortable chair, idly watching people come and go, he saw, to his surprise, a familiar face. "Odell!" he said loudly, getting up.

"Matt Chapin! What on earth are you doing here?"

Odell's glasses glittered at him with a friendly light, and a smile appeared on his round face.

They sat down together and Matthew said, "Now tell me."

Odell explained that he was, in a way, doing just what he had intended to do, producing a crusading medical journal. It was called *Medical Meditations,* circulation about two hundred but rising, and Odell was owner, publisher, editor, and often chief author as well. "It's a start," he said, "and on the whole I think a good one."

Matthew then told him about his own affairs, though, for some reason he could not have explained, he omitted all mention of Hattie. He talked a good deal about his desire to become a staff member of Charity Hospital, and dwelt on his disappointment that the examination did not seem practicable and his consequent uncertainty about how to make a move toward a future career.

"You've missed this fall's exam," Odell said, "and there's not another till spring, but you'd need plenty of time anyway. Maybe I can give you some information that would help. Medical education is one of my subjects, you know. Let's have supper together some night. Here, I'll give you the office address and you come around after work, any time you like. I'm almost always free." He wrote the address on the flap of an envelope, tore it off and gave it to Matthew. Then he shook hands, smiled broadly, and went on his way.

The little encounter was briefly cheering to Matthew, but his mood in these days was generally one of settled gloom. He felt he was not only wasting his time in his job, but possibly retrogressing, through lack of practice, in his surgical skills. At night, alone in the dreary room, he was tired, bored, and though he did not admit it to himself, he was lonely. At first he made an attempt to cook his own meals, as Hattie had done, but he hated the work of it and the economy was not really necessary, so he gave it up and went to one or another of the eating places in the neighborhood.

The aimlessness of this life depressed him so that in desperation he laid out a course of study for himself. He worked diligently for a while, but the knowledge that he was not working to serve any particular end undermined his determination and dulled his interest.

When Hattie returned for her weekly visits he made an effort at cheerfulness, and under the conditions of his life at this time he was truly glad to see her. She was always excited by her return, and very loving, sometimes too much so, but her eager pleasure in their life together rather touched him and he did his best to be good to her.

She always had a great many things to tell him about her work, which she liked better than she had her duties on the surgical ward, and at which, in consequence, she worked much more conscientiously. She was given responsibilities that filled her with pride, and Matthew saw that these things were making a change in her. She seemed to him to regard her work with new seriousness, and to look on what she was doing not just as a job but as a career which she was creating for herself. Her appearance too changed subtly, her face began to lose its roundness and to fine down. Her gray eyes grew more thoughtfully observing, her carriage straighter, her walk more suggestive of purpose. Any stranger seeing her at this time would have guessed her to be a highly competent young woman.

She had swiftly acquired a little air of authority which she practiced on him, and this amused him but, because of the present lack of progress in his own affairs, also discomfited him. In consequence, he became more and more reticent about his own affairs, and was a little hurt when she failed to notice this. He did not tell her about his chance encounter with Odell, or mention it to her when he looked up Odell at the office of *Medical Meditations*.

The office was in an old building at the top of four dusty flights of stairs, and there Odell sat in the midst of the litter, happy, energetic, and convinced that he had a message for the world. "Hullo, Matt," he said. "Is this the night we eat together?"

"If you're not too busy."

"I'm always busy, but never too busy for a good talk. Just let me finish this piece I'm on. It will only take a few minutes. There are some journals over there. Sit down and make yourself comfortable."

Matthew wandered across the crowded room to examine the pile of medical journals on the table. Some of them were old, some recent. The one he chose was *The Lancet* for September 1867, for he had never seen an English medical journal before. He sat down and started to leaf through it while Odell's sharp pen scratched busily. After a moment he looked up. "Who's this guy called Lister?"

"Lister? You got the article on 'The Antiseptic Principle in the Practice of Surgery'? Read that. I'd like to know what you think of it."

Matthew had only read a paragraph or two when Odell said, "Well, that's that for tonight. Shall we go?" Matthew was so deep in the article that it required effort to bring his mind back to the present.

"Look, can I borrow this? I haven't read half of it yet, but it's fascinating."

"Sure, take it along. It's nothing we can use for the *Med. Med.*—or at least not until it's clearer if there's going to be a reaction to it and what it is. Surgery's not my line of country, as you know, but I'd like to hear your views. Come on, let's go."

Odell shut the door behind them, turned a key in an inefficient-looking lock, and they clattered down the long stairs with the expendable energy of youth. At the bottom, Odell said, "There's a place up the street that's not too bad. Remember Pete's?"

"Sure I remember Pete's."

"It's one of my few durable impressions of the school year."

They ate steak and fried potatoes and tore pieces off thick slabs of bread, and when the first edge of their appetites was dulled Odell took up the subject in hand.

"So you want to work in one of the big hospitals, preferably Charity, on Blackwell's?

"Yes, and I'd heard the exam was tough, but I thought it would be all medical. I didn't know about this other stuff. History, and so on."

"Didn't you talk to anyone about it?"

"Yes, Dr. Osgood, the surgeon I worked with. I think he ought to have told me."

"Probably he didn't know, but the Dean or somebody should have. One of the lesser troubles with medical schools—even the best of 'em—is that when they've given you your diploma, they're through with you. They should advise and help until you are practicing for yourself. Matter of fact, our whole way of looking at medical education is wrong. It's not something you finish and get through with. Until both the schools and the graduates realize that education, learning, has to go on all through a doctor's life . . . But let's not get started on that. I think I know a man who could get you through your exam, but you'd have to work like hell."

"That doesn't frighten me. Who is he?"

"Dr. Briggs. He runs a cram quiz course to prepare about twenty students for the exam. His course for the spring exam should be starting about now. It's expensive —a hundred dollars for six months. You got that much?"

"Yes. Tell me more about it."

"He's got questions from exams for years past printed up in big, paperbound books with the answers in the back. You have to learn them by heart. You got a good memory, Matt?"

"I think so. I never tried anything like that. Where do I find him?"

"He's on Thirty-eighth Street somewhere. You'll have to look in the City Directory. He's by far the best of the teachers and he picks and chooses his class, so you might have trouble getting in, I don't know."

"I can sure as hell try."

"Maybe he won't like you, and if so, you're in luck."

"How do you mean?"

Odell smiled his pleasant, sunny smile. "Wait till you see him and you'll understand. He's a real bastard."

"Bastard or not, I'll see him in the morning."

Matthew returned to his room with the borrowed copy of *The Lancet,* feeling as he entered that Hattie's personality in some way permeated the place. Odd as it might be, this was always his sensation, though she might in fact not have been there for some days. It bothered him and did nothing to alleviate his loneliness, and he thought of it vaguely as one of the aspects of her developing force. This night he made a conscious effort to dismiss her, so to speak. To an extent he succeeded and to that extent he felt free and comfortable.

He made himself some coffee on the gas ring and while it brewed he took off his shoes, set the lamp properly for reading and fixed the two limp bed pillows as a support for his back. Then he poured coffee, liking the way the aroma of it filled the room, and settled down to read. The cup of coffee stood on the table, cooling and forgotten, as he read on.

The article did not at first give him a feeling of discovery or of having arrived at a milestone in medical history. The concept of antiseptic surgery was too new for that.

". . . when it had been shown by the researches of Pasteur that septic property of the atmosphere depended . . . on minute organisms suspended in it, it occurred to me that decomposition of the injured part might be avoided . . . by applying a dressing capable of destroying the life of the floating particles."

Wound infection caused, like decay, by microorganisms

in the air! He read the paragraph again to be sure. Then, with a sort of mental start, he realized that he was being given here not only the cause of surgical infections, but the prevention.

". . . a dressing capable of destroying the life of the floating particles . . . a solution of carbolic acid in twenty parts of water . . . may be relied on for destroying any septic germs . . ."

Deep in thought, he lowered the journal to his knees. He was by no means convinced that this theory was correct, or that surgical infections could be prevented by any such means as those described here. He had never heard of Lister, but that his was a radical departure from current thought was plain. He realized, moreover, that all this would require a great deal of thinking about before its many implications were clear. The feeling grew in him that he could only settle the uncertainties in his own mind by experimenting, and this feeling developed into a passionate desire to be again in the midst of his own work. He thought for a long time, and with great bitterness, about his present idle state. Then he picked up the journal and went on reading.

". . . since the antispetic treatment has been brought into full operation, and wounds and abscesses no longer poison the atmosphere with putrid exhalations, my wards, though in other respects under precisely the same circumstances as before, have completely changed their character; so that during the last nine months not a single instance of pyaemia, hospital gangrene, or erysipelas has occurred in them."

CHAPTER THIRTY-SIX

Dr. Briggs was not hard for Matthew to locate for he occupied two floors of a wooden building on Thirty-eighth Street. On the ground floor were a consulting room and a waiting room, and upstairs was one large, bare classroom with a small platform at one end and a miscellaneous collection of chairs that looked as though they had been acquired at secondhand shops. It was here that Dr. Briggs took Matthew for an interview, as though the two floors represented two separate parts of the doctor's life that he did not care to mix.

"Sit down, young man," he said brusquely, and Matthew obeyed, taking a chair in what seemed to be an irregular front row. Disconcertingly, Dr. Briggs remained standing, and he put his questions to Matthew without once looking at him squarely.

"I suppose you've heard that this is the toughest quiz course in the city. What makes you think you're qualified to take it?"

"I'm not, strictly speaking, I suppose. But I want to pass that exam and I'm willing to work for it."

At this Dr. Briggs cocked his head on one side as though attentively, but he made a small, derisive sound and, putting his hands in his pockets, began to jingle keys. His manner was hostile and abrasive. It had been Matthew's experience that there was small profit in conciliating such a person and so he made no attempt to soften his own manner. Jingling his coins, the doctor took several steps toward the door, as though he considered the interview ended, and then came back again.

"University?"

"No."

"Medical School?"

"A degree from Harvard."

"Special interest?"

"Surgery. I need experience, as broad as I can get it. That's why I want a staff position at Charity."

"Do you realize that from all the cram courses in the city there'll be about thirty taking that particular exam and that there'll be openings for only the top four?"

"No, sir. I didn't quite realize that." Matthew tried to keep his voice from betraying the consternation he felt. There was a silence during which Dr. Briggs seemed to find great interest in examining the ceiling. He was a big, loosely-put-together man, sloppy in appearance, careless in his manner, but capable of sudden movements and sharp speech that fixed the attention. He made one of the sudden motions now, an impatient, outward gesture with both arms, as though he would sweep all stupidity, all inefficiency of the mind, out of his way.

"I don't want failures. This course has a reputation because it almost never happens that every man jack in the class don't land somewhere on the passing list and a higher percentage of my students wind up with staff jobs than any other school. What guarantee can you give me that if I take you, you won't let me down?"

"None, I'm afraid."

There was another silence while Matthew, tense and annoyed, waited and took care not to move a muscle. Abruptly, Dr. Briggs stepped up on the platform. There was nothing here but a swivel chair and the doctor threw himself in it, sprawling with legs wide apart and hands grasping the arms, and when he tipped the chair backward, the spring made a sound like a loud groan. Looking over Matthew's head, the doctor said, "Got a hundred dollars?"

"Yes, sir."

"I never take more than twenty students in the course. I got a waiting list, but classes begin day after tomorrow, so I can't be bothered picking a name off it at this late date. You're here, you get to fill the vacancy. We begin at two promptly. Bring the hundred with you."

When Matthew left he was carrying a volume bound in blue paper that contained the questions and answers. He went straight home, for although this was Hattie's day off, she—thinking that he would be working as an inspector —would not be expecting him until evening. His spirits were so high because of his success that he felt the need for action, and he decided to walk, though the November day was dreary. Because a thin, light rain had begun to fall, he carried the book pressed against him inside his coat. When he arrived Hattie, with her dress off, was washing her hair, which she did every week because she had vague ideas about carrying contagion. The room, cheerless in the gray November light, was stuffy and smelled of gas and the soap she had been using.

"Why, Matthew," she said in alarm. "Is everything all right?" She snatched a towel and wrapped her head in it, her eyes large with anxiety, fixed on him.

"Sure, sure." He tossed the book on the bed and hung his coat on a peg behind the door. "Hattie, I've got into a quiz school. I'm going to work for the exam!"

"That's nice," she said with vague affection, unwrapping the towel and beginning to rub her hair with it. "Would you like some coffee?"

"No, thanks. Yes, give me some."

She tossed her damp hair back over her shoulders and busied herself over the gas ring. He threw himself onto the bed where he sat propped up with the limp pillows, and brooded silently. Her failure to understand, or to be more than mildly interested in his success and his ambitions for the future, hurt and angered him. He thought he knew her limitations and could school himself to tolerance, but his need for understanding or even for sympathy was at the moment so great that he forgot this.

She brought him a cup of coffee saying, "There you are," in a tone that showed she was pleased with herself in this wifely role. Sulky as a child, he turned over on his side without touching the coffee, and without any such intention, he fell instantly asleep.

He awoke an hour later, relaxed and softened. She was sitting in a chair by the window mending something and he lay there, still inert with sleep, and studied her. She had dressed herself carefully and she looked fresh and clean, her hair bright from its washing. She had lately lost a good deal of the little-girl look and this interested him in a languid, sleep-laden way. "Hullo," he said, and she looked up and smiled.

"Have a nice sleep?"

"Yeah, but I'm a lazy bum, sleeping in the daytime."

He saw that, just as she had been unaware of the importance to him of having been accepted at the school, she had also been unaware of his resentment. He felt grateful to her, since this saved him from being ashamed of himself, and he thought that when he could find the energy to get up, he would go down to the Health Department to resign from his job, and on the way back buy a bottle of wine, which she liked to have with their supper, as a special treat.

The work of the quiz course was harder, even, than Matthew had supposed, and it seemed to him that there were two reasons for this. The first was that the work was an unrelieved task of memory alone. At the start he made the mistake of being interested in the answers to the questions, but he soon found that this would not do, for to let his mind loose in speculation was to cut down on the number of answers he could memorize. "What was the Hanseatic League? What were the Casket Letters? What is a fugue?" He found he must shut out thought and concentrate on learning and he discovered that the knack of doing this was itself something he had to learn

The second reason why the work was hard was that Dr. Brigg's personality made it so, for it seemed to Matthew that he lost no opportunity to be disagreeable. During class he sprawled in his groaning swivel chair, his long legs spread wide, and out of his own memory fired questions like shots from a gun. The student at whom he pointed his long finger had to answer without hesitating and with no more or no less detail than was supplied him by the book. Everyone hated the doctor and after a few classes Matthew realized that this was exactly what Briggs wanted. He took pleasure in arousing hatred. Antagonism stimulated him and fulfilled some need in him. A class was an almost orgiastic experience for him that in some unpleasant sense brought him relief. But though the doctor's taunting occasionally reduced the class to fury, Matthew saw that there was a certain value in this since the combativeness aroused the students to greater effort, and Matthew remembered Odell's saying that if Briggs disliked you, then you were in luck. He soon came to regard Dr. Briggs as a thoroughly disagreeable person, but also a teacher able to produce surprising results.

Two or three times, on Hattie's day off, Matthew asked her to help him by reading the questions to him. He soon found that this was not satisfactory, for she read badly and stumbled over the big words, unhappy and shamed by her ignorance. "In what year was Beethoven's Ninth Symphony first performed? Name the members of the first Cabinet of the United States. How is the speed of light measured?" The questions were so far outside her range of perception that they frightened her and made her look at Matthew with hostility because she was discovering aptitudes of his that were new and strange to her.

The strain of the incessant, irritating work mounted steadily. Occasionally a real row would flare up in class between some student and Dr. Briggs, and twice these resulted in the student's dismissal. Matthew managed to keep his temper though he felt, as perhaps every other member of the class did also, that he was the special object of the doctor's persecution.

He began to sleep badly, waking up frequently during the night with his mind full of questions. "Describe the viscera of the male pelvis. What was the gold snow rained on Rhodes? What sum was paid to what nation in the Louisiana Purchase?" Sometimes, awakened by the echoing of these questions in his mind, Matthew would get up and work by candlelight until the cold drove him to bed again. He ate with the book propped up in front of him. "What is an *aria cantabile?* What are the presenting symptoms of peptic ulcer? In what museum is the *Mona Lisa?*"

On two occasions he and Odell got drunk together, studiously and gloomily pursuing forgetfulness in a dirty saloon. But except for these two lapses, which happened early in the long ordeal, he kept himself more and more rigidly to his purpose. Three of his fellow students, unable to stand the pressure though they were university graduates, simply abandoned the course. Matthew's determination to see it through steadily hardened.

"It's a hell of a way to study medicine," he said one night to Odell when they were eating a hurried supper together. "When you're a medical student you get in the habit of thinking that the way to get to be a doctor is to get a degree. But really what medical school teaches you is how little you know. So here I am, still studying, and there's Ed in Germany still studying."

"It's a life sentence, Matt. You're just realizing it, is all."

The winter began to wear itself away and damp spring winds blew. Matthew was aware of the season's change chiefly because of the sparrows' chirp and chatter and the cry of gulls hunting for nesting sites among the buildings back from the river. In the brighter sunlight of spring Hattie seemed paler than her normal self, and tired. Matthew asked her about it.

"Are you all right? You seem a bit dragged out."

"The hospital's full—the spring rush, they call it—so there's no time to rest during the day. Matt, they've got some contagious cases that aren't smallpox there. Is that right?"

"I shouldn't think so. Overcrowding elsewhere, probably."

"And the spring seems to make the nurses from the prison restless. I hate to be scolding all day long. But don't worry about it. In a week or two it will slack up again."

When, early in the morning, she left to take the boat back to the island, he went to the window and stood with his hands in his pockets, looking down on her as she walked away. She was wearing the white gloves again, and she must have discovered a hole in one finger, for she bit at it with a nervousness he had never seen her display. He watched her out of sight, then he threw himself on the bed, sighed heavily, and picked up his quiz book.

What are the islands of Langerhans?

Who painted *The Last Supper?*

Define: 1, Dido; 2, Dado; 3, Dodo.

And what the hell, anyway? He flung the book into a

far corner of the room and, rising, began to pace back and forth in fury. All day long the questions filled the air around him. In class they flew back and forth like hard balls.

When the day of the examination finally arrived he was tired and jumpy, for the ending of the long routine was in itself unsettling. While he was cooking his breakfast, he broke a coffee cup and the trivial incident so unnerved him that he sat trembling on the edge of his bed for some minutes before he felt steady enough to go on with what he had been doing. He walked to East Twenty-second Street where the examination was to be held in a big house belonging to one of the hospitals. And as he walked he kept pulling out his watch and glancing at it with the unfounded fear that he might be late and so throw away the hard work of six long months. He arrived half an hour too soon.

The house had a yard in front of it, a pleasant place shaded by an ailanthus tree, with a bench by the fence. He sat there a while, watching other nervous students arrive, and then he rose reluctantly and dragged himself inside. He was surprised at the number of students waiting, for he had forgotten that other quiz courses would be represented here. He made a rough count and found there were more than thirty, all here for the Charity Hospital examination, all hoping to be among the four who would ultimately be chosen.

The room stank with the sweat of their fear and it was disgust at this and the sight of their anxious misery that restored Matthew's self-command. An official at the door began calling names, one at a time; for the examination, which was oral, was given singly by three examiners in separate rooms. The names were being called alphabetically, so Matthew had not long to wait.

The ordeal was less severe, on the whole, than he had expected. He missed three questions outright and he had no idea how many he might have answered incorrectly, but as a great many questions had been asked he could only hope that the number of errors had not been proportionately too high. He was told that the results of all examinations would be posted the next day at noon in all hospitals and medical schools, and as Bellevue was the nearest, he went there. He was early, and the lists were not yet up, but a good many anxious students were already waiting.

When a man appeared with the lists and began to fasten

them to the bulletin board there was a general rush that left Matthew behind so that he was not able to see over the heads of those in front of him. There was pushing and much shouting and he heard his own name called. "Chapin. Where's Chapin?"

"Here," he shouted, recognizing the voice of a man who had sat next to him in the quiz class.

"Matt Chapin! Congrats. You're third."

He would not believe it until he saw it with his own eyes, and even then it did not seem real to him. He walked away with his hands in his pockets and went slowly back to the room. He knew he should be feeling elation, and he tried to work up a feeling of enthusiasm, but the ordeal had been too long and hard. The room seemed stuffy, though the window was open. He took his coat off, then he sat down on the bed and pulled off his shoes. After that he just sat there for a while, his hands hanging down between his knees. Then he lay down, rolled over on his face, and slept.

CHAPTER THIRTY-SEVEN

Charity Hospital was a huge building, constructed about ten years earlier, of stone quarried off the island by the prisoners in the penitentiary nearby. It had a central portion with an L-shaped wing on either side and a regular bed capacity, which was often exceeded by overcrowding, of fifteen hundred patients. Matthew was taken for a long tour of the place by another member of the staff, a Dr. Watts, who was just finishing his year's internship and was to be replaced by Matthew. He was a dark-skinned, black-haired, troubled young man who wore a perpetual frown that, as it was constantly deepening or lessening, seemed to flicker on his forehead. "If it's experience you want," he said, "you'll sure get it here. There's not only this place but the prison hospital, the immigrant quarantine station, hospital for incurables, the Smallpox Hospital, and the insane asylum. You're supposed to work only here and in the prison, but I wouldn't want to bet you won't be in all of them before you're through."

"The equipment here seems old and a bit scanty."

"Well, it is. You know how it is with city hospitals—public funds get diverted to other things, and the hospital gets run down—until some politician decides to make political capital out of reform. We've been in a long period of neglect."

Within a few days Matthew learned that the condition of the hospital supplies would be a serious handicap in his work. There were not enough sponges, so that he had either to wait while one was washed after each wound he dressed, or use it merely squeezed out in a basin of water on the dressing cart, which was the usual practice. Sheets were darned by women in the workhouse so often that they were rough and lumpy, with the result that all the patients developed bedsores. In some of the wards and in the prison hospital there were no bedpans, and to replace them wads of oakum were pushed under the patients and often left there all day.

Instruments were old and clumsy. On his first day in the operating room Matthew was handed a scalpel with a nick in the blade. Angered, he threw it on the floor, and was reproved by the senior house man with whom he was working. "You better learn right now to take care of the few instruments we've got, Doctor. Otherwise you're going to find yourself operating with your own penknife." The scalpel, with a fresh nick in it, was retrieved from the floor and after that Matthew was more careful.

He found no friend among the members of the staff, most of whom were overtired and disillusioned. Some, like himself, were working for experience, keeping notes for future use and gradually coming to regard the patients as useful only for this purpose. Others, and these were all older men who were intending to make a career of what they called "city medicine," were cynical and hard. In the doctors' common room, on two or three occasions, he talked about the article by Lister that had appeared in *The Lancet* and tried to work up a discussion of the use of carbolic and the antiseptic technique, but he succeeded in doing nothing more than earning for himself the nickname of "Carbolic Chapin."

Finally one of the old-timers said, "Maybe you got something there, maybe you haven't, but there's something you've been overlooking. The way of treating wounds and doing dressings that you describe takes time, Doc. Time. And that's what we haven't got."

"But if every wound healed quicker, maybe most of them by first intention, in the end that would give you *more* time by reducing what they call the patient load."

"Now I ask you, have any of the medical advances of modern times, and there've been a lot of them, ever resulted in reducing the patient load? No. Just the other way, seems like."

He thought of using the antiseptic technique experimentally on two or three patients, but he regretfully decided that this was not feasible unless he and he alone had those patients in his charge. In the end he relinquished the project with the promise to himself to revive it at some future time.

He worked very hard and he was not paid, though his board and room and his laundry were free. Like Hattie, he had one day and night a week without duties, and she was able to arrange that hers should fall at the same time as his. They gave up their room across the river and spent their free nights in whatever place they could find not too far from one or another of the boats that ran from the island to the city. As the hospitals where they worked were some distance apart, they did not always take the same one, but arranged to meet at a certain time at a street corner convenient to them both.

She was almost always there ahead of him, standing in a doorway of an undertaker's establishment because there was shelter there from sun or rain. Sometimes he saw her before she saw him, and always her face in repose seemed unfamiliar to him, as though she were a woman whom he knew only superficially. This troubled him a little, for he knew that to a degree this was true. There were qualities and traits in her he had not suspected, and the life she was now leading was giving them room to develop. He saw with a vague feeling of guilt that the girlish look of her face had given way to strength; the extravagance of her manner had quieted into authority. He saw these things with a surprised, somewhat reluctant admiration, a feeling that she had grown away from him and that he was somehow responsible for the change in her.

He could always put an end to these feelings of his by calling to her, for when she saw him she smiled with pleasure and ran to him with much of her old eagerness. Then they would lunch and afterward begin the search for a room. For some reason she always found this hunt exciting, and she was always pleased with what they found, no matter how sordid it might turn out to be. And once the door was shut and they were alone, she would hold out her arms to him with a deep sigh of happiness. *"Oh, Matt."*

After this first kiss she would begin to undress with a frank eagerness that, in spite of his changing feelings toward her, he still found distasteful. Her lovemaking was eager and passionate but it left him with a sense of futility and depression. He would lie on his back, feeling remote and solitary, not wanting talk, as she did, his flesh quivering if she touched him.

Part of the trouble, he knew, was that she was earning money and he was not; moreover, Dr. Hurd's legacy was very nearly gone, and the day was not far distant when she would have to pay for their time together. The thought of that was intolerable to him. He did some figuring and it seemed to him that if they were to skip these meetings a few times, his money might be made to last until his internship had ended. He would then be eligible for a staff position almost anywhere as a junior assistant or, in view of his previous experience, perhaps a senior, as had already been hinted to him. To continue his staff work was something he wanted very much to do, but these positions also paid no salary and unless he could bring himself to accept money from Hattie, he knew he must relinquish his ambition. These unpalatable alternatives depressed him so greatly that he did his best not to think about them.

As a move toward economizing he wrote to Hattie saying he could not meet her that week as usual, though for reasons he did not examine himself about, he said nothing to her about money but gave the pressure of work as his excuse. She sent a reply by one of the hospital guards, but instead of the protests he had expected, she wrote only, "I'm sorry, Matthew," so he knew that she was hurt.

On that day and night they should have been together he spent an uncomfortable time trying to concentrate on some medical books he had borrowed. He had no idea what she was doing, and this worried him to such an extent that he would have gone to the Smallpox Hospital to find out, except that he knew there was no possibility of getting past the guards. By evening he was in a black mood of depression, and at this, the very worst of times, he received a long letter from Edward, forwarded to him from Boston.

He read it sitting on the edge of his cot bed, rustling the

thin sheets with nervous impatience. Edward was finding life interesting, for he had visited the laboratories of most of the men who were making German medical science famous, and had finally settled down to work in Leipzig:

> New knowledge about microorganisms and the microbe theory of disease is opening up so fast that the pursuit of it makes one feel breathless. We have a house, a strange-looking affair painted all sorts of colors on the front that have faded to pastel in the sun. There are carved beam ends and casement windows with diamond-shaped panes, picturesque, but the sewage runs in a ditch in the middle of the street.
> Cissie and the children are well. You would be surprised at how the youngsters have grown. Sue is going to be a buxom beauty, as they say her mother was. Peter is a serious, scholarly lad, showing signs of great intelligence, and Jimmie limps around as happily as though he had always been part of this family group.
> Cissie is well, but life has been hard on her, as you know. She loves the children dearly, but when you see her you must be prepared for her looking older, Matt.

See her! Matthew threw the letter on the bed and paced up and down his little room, feeling again all the agony of his love for her. For some days he thought about answering the letter, but Edward did not know that he had married Hattie and telling about this seemed so distasteful to him that in the end he made no reply.

The next week when Hattie was waiting for him under the undertaker's sign, the first damp feel of spring was in the air. Her greeting to him was friendly enough but without the ecstatic happiness of former occasions, and during their lunch the talk was desultory and a little strained. He knew he should explain to her his reason for not meeting her the previous week, but he did not do it for he felt he could not endure her protestations that she would gladly pay. Their time together was not a success, and he let some time pass before he again attempted to economize by not meeting her. He knew she was very busy for the hospital was crowded beyond capacity, and he hoped that the fatigue she must be feeling would keep her from missing him too greatly.

He had just received notice of his appointment, when his internship should have been finished, to the staff of Charity's affiliate hospital, Bellevue. Such appointments did not always follow a regular pattern of seniority, and so he was not surprised, though very pleased, to find that he had been chosen for the grade of first assistant in surgery.

With the appointment actually his he realized that his desire for it was so strong that for no reason at all could he bring himself to turn it down.

He wrote his news to Hattie, and then told her that he would not be able to meet her that week; he hoped that she would think the good news was the reason for the bad.

He had a little note from her in reply, brought over by one of the guards going off duty. Its tone made it evident to him that she had determined to conceal her disappointment. She said she was sorry they couldn't meet, and "better luck next time," and she was very happy about his appointment. "We'll have such lots to talk about!" She was, she said, very busy indeed, for the hospital had never been more crowded, and she was afraid that some of the patients with other contagious diseases might come down with smallpox too. Rules forbade the acceptance of these others, but in the face of necessity no one thought of rules. At the end of the letter she said, "We'll celebrate your big news next week."

When the time came, and he crossed the river to meet her, he was full of good resolutions to make their stay pleasant for her. To his surprise, she was not there waiting for him. He stood around for a few minutes, feeling faintly put upon; then he went into a saloon where he could watch the corner through the window, and ordered a glass of beer. The spring day was warm, the saloon dim and cool and restful, the richly odorous air soporific. He discovered that he was tired in every muscle of his body and glad of this chance to rest.

He finished the beer and she had not come, so he ordered another. He was not impatient, in fact he was quite content, and under the influence of the beer and his fatigue she began to seem slightly unreal to him, her coming vaguely improbable. He almost felt he could get up and walk away, go anywhere at all, and never concern himself about her again.

He let these half thoughts drift through his mind until the waiter came and asked if he wanted anything else, at which he shook his head and pulled out his watch. The discovery that more than an hour had gone by brought him to himself and he paid and went out into the street. He found a restaurant and ate a light lunch while he thought of all the things that might have happened to detain her. He was surprised not to see her waiting when he again went back to the corner, and it was obvious to him that now he must take steps to find her. Not knowing what else to do, he went back to the island and set out to walk to the Smallpox Hospital.

This was a large, square structure on a rise of ground without trees, cold in winter, hot in summer, and so ugly that it seemed evil. By the front entrance was a shed which served as a guardhouse, and it was here that Matthew stopped to inquire for Hattie. "Harriet Chapin," he said. "She's one of the supervisors. I'm her husband. Did she leave a note or a message here for me?"

The guard, an ex-soldier by the look of him, laid down the newspaper he was reading and got up from the battered chair he had been sitting on.

"Well now, it's a good thing you came along or I might have forgotten about it altogether." He began to rummage among papers on a shelf below the shed's single window. "It's here somewheres. She sent it out yesterday with a message, would I take it over to the big hospital on my way home, and damned if I didn't forget it entirely. Here it is. She's a nice girl. Shame she has to work in a place like this. You been married long?"

"No," Matthew said shortly and took the note outside to read. She was sick with a cold, she said. It was nothing, really, only she was afraid she would give it to Matthew. She had taken some of the funny little white pills called "A Hundred and Elevens" and she was feeling better already. She would send another note over by the guard in a couple of days.

Matthew went into the shed, borrowed a piece of paper, and wrote a reply which he took pains to make warm and friendly. He left it with the guard to send inside and wandered slowly back to his own hospital.

Three days later another note reached him. "I'm all right, so don't worry. I love you, Matt. Hattie."

The note did not reassure him and he went about his work heavy with depression. That night, when his rounds were finished, he walked back to the Smallpox Hospital and found another guard on duty. "My wife's sick," he said. "I want to see her."

"Rules says you can't. Nobody ain't allowed visitin', Mister." This guard was an old fellow with a gray beard stained yellow around his mouth, and he had about him a most unpleasant smell, so that Matthew kept what distance he could between them.

"Look, I'm not a visitor. I'm on the staff at Charity. My

wife's in there sick." He was shouting as though the man were deaf.

"And I say you can't. I'm real sorry your wife's sick, but it's that way with lots of folks and nobody can't see nobody. She should have got herself vaccinated."

Matthew started to reply to this, gave it up, and stood for a moment in thought. Then without another word he turned and walked rapidly up the steps and through the hospital door, the shout of the guard following him: *"Hey, Mister!"*

He went up a stairway merely to elude the guard, and down a long corridor to its end before stopping to take stock. There were three women here with scrub brushes, kneeling and scrubbing the pine floor with sand and water. "Where will I find the Matron of Nurses?" he asked. They stared at him. One was young and her expression so vague that he guessed she had only the intelligence of a child. Another, middle-aged, began at once to talk to herself in a rapid, dry whisper that was like the taking up of a never-ending tale of grievance. It made his skin prickle. The third had a look of evil and for some unknown reason she smiled, but to herself, not at him. It was quite clear that they were not going to answer him and he left them.

They were, he knew, from the lowest class of inmates from the women's prison, the better and more intelligent working as nurses. He should have been accustomed to them for prisoners worked at his hospital also, but he hadn't, up to now, considered them as they really were in terms of Hattie's daily life. The thought made him a little sick.

In the end he found the Matron because of a sign on a door. Without realizing it, he had been expecting to see a matron like Hattie's aunt, but instead he found a little gray-haired woman with sad, tired eyes.

"I can understand your wanting to see your wife," she said. "Our rules must seem harsh to you."

"I'm going to see her," Matthew said.

"I believe you don't know that she has scarlet fever."

"No. She wrote me—"

"She did not want you to know for fear you would worry. I was going to write to you myself, but she begged and pleaded until I promised not to. She is a fine woman, Dr. Chapin."

Matthew, thinking about this, said nothing, and the Matron went on.

"It's so very unfortunate. Sometimes we get cases that are not smallpox, and we have to take them, usually because of political pressure. We're a city hospital—but you know about that. We're not prepared for these cases, and often it is disastrous for the patients themselves, if they haven't had smallpox, and—"

"How sick is she?"

"She's very sick, I'm afraid, but we haven't given up—"

"Tell me where I'll find her."

The Matron hesitated, studying him, then she sighed as though she felt that this problem, added to all of her other burdens, was unfair. "If you will come with me, Dr. Chapin."

Hattie was in the last bed in a long ward, separated from other beds by screens. He saw at once that she was indeed very ill. She turned her head on the pillow and saw him. *"Oh, Matt!"* She smiled and two tears ran out of her eyes. She moved her hand a little, holding it up to him. He took it in both his and held it without speaking. Then he realized that she was trying to say something more, but her voice was weak and the words indistinct. He bent over her.

"Matt, don't get too close to me."

"To hell with that."

"I've got scarlet fever. Did they tell you?"

"Yes, Hattie."

"But I'm going to be all right." She was smiling and the tears were running out of her eyes at the same time.

"Of course you are. And then I'm going to get you out of here and you're never going to have to come back here again. I should never have let you come in the first place."

"Matt . . ."

"Yes, dear?"

"I'm so glad you came."

He found he could not answer. After a moment she made a little snuggling movement down into the pillow, like a child, and shut her eyes. He held her hand and presently he noticed that, with the heel of his own hand against her wrist, he was feeling the beat of her pulse. It was thin and light. Her hand in his was utterly relaxed. He watched her closely and saw that she had drifted into the facile, peaceful sleep of extreme illness. He stood there, holding her hand. She seemed to have put herself into his keeping, and he felt her to be very close and very precious. The Matron touched him on the shoulder and he came back from a long way off to realize that she was beckoning him to leave. He took his hand gently out of Hattie's relaxed fingers, saw that he had not aroused her, smiled softly, sighed, and quietly followed the Matron out of the ward.

CHAPTER THIRTY-EIGHT

A note from the Matron reached Matthew that night, delivered by the guard on his way home. Matthew gave the guard ten cents and opened the note with stiff fingers. His visit, the Matron wrote, had seemed to do Hattie good, though as he of course realized, she was still very sick. The purpose of the note, however, was to tell Matthew he must not, under any circumstances, come again. If he attempted to, it would be reported to the authorities in his own hospital. However, if there were any need to communicate with him, she the Matron would do so through the guard. In the meantime he must feel assured that his wife, who was very highly thought of by everyone on the staff, would have the best care the hospital could give.

This note lightened his anxiety a little but it did nothing to relieve his sense of guilt. The days that followed were crowded ones. The patients on his ward and on some of the others developed dysentery with diarrhea, colic pains and anorexia, which was thought to be food poisoning. As the weather suddenly turned chilly, most of the windows in the wards had to be shut and the air became as foul as an outhouse. The oakum under the patients and their beds were filthy, the men patients shouted and swore at the orderly, and some of them wept in their misery.

Matthew himself was affected, but he went grimly about his work with churning insides and a mind burdened with worry. He was surly and short-tempered with the other doctors and harsh with the patients. One of the orderlies was a lazy, impertinent fellow who claimed to have been given his job through some sort of political influence and was, in consequence, exempt from discipline. Matthew caught him in some miserable little cruelty toward one of the old men on the ward, remonstrated with him, received a reply that was both threatening and obscene, and promptly knocked him down. The orderly's political pull turned out to be unreal, for there were no repercussions, but the incident steadied Matthew a little and revived his self-control.

In the middle of the week a patient died who should not, by all the rules, have done so, and to discover the reason Matthew did an autopsy. He had to work at night, when he should have been sleeping, and alone. The deadhouse was a shed on a pier over the river where the corpses were stacked on wide shelves, their feet at the edge, identification tags tied around their ankles. Under the thin floor he could hear the water lapping against the piles.

By candlelight Matthew read the tags until he found the corpse he was looking for, tugged it out and dumped it on the long table in the middle of the shed. As he stood beside the table getting back his breath he looked down on the body with the tag swinging from one ankle and saw that rats had gnawed the face and one of the hands. Pity and disgust swept through him. The work was difficult, for the candle flame flickered in the draft that came in between the cracks of the board wall of the shed. The weather was still unseasonably cold and he worked slowly, alive to the danger of a scalpel in numbed hands.

The cause of death listed on the tag was pneumonia, written by Matthew himself but without conviction. Now he began a careful exploration of the lungs, and in a few moments he had laid bare an infiltrating tumor that had produced the pneumonia-like symptoms. He stopped work and stood looking thoughtfully down on this destroying invader. Then he took a pencil out of his pocket, went to the foot of the table, swung the tag around to rest on the top of the dead leg to get a surface to write on, crossed out the word "pneumonia," and wrote above it "pulmonary carcinoma." After that he hoisted the body back on the shelf, gathered up his instruments, and went away.

In such a life, under such conditions as these, he had little time to think about Hattie, and this suited him, for his desire was to escape his thoughts about her. The only other note he received from the Matron that week said that the disease appeared to be running its normal course and that Hattie was holding her own. This did not seem to him wholly satisfactory, and he promised himself that on his day off he would go to the hospital, insist on seeing her again and have a talk with the doctor, which he blamed himself for not having done the first time he was there.

When his day of freedom came he went early to the hospital. The guard called out a cheery, "Hullo, Doc. Got a letter for you. I was going to bring it along on my way home." He reached for it through the window of the shack and held it out.

Matthew hoped against all reason that it might be addressed to him in Hattie's own round hand, but the writing was again the Matron's. As he tore it open he turned his back on the guard and, walking a little distance away, began to read:

> DEAR DR. CHAPIN,
> It is with deep regret that I must inform you that your wife died during the early hours of the morning . . .

The words numbed him and he could not fully comprehend them. As he stood there his heart began to thump in his throat, choking him, and he did not seem able to get enough air into his lungs. The letter trembled in his hands. A feeling of weakness swept through him and he went to the steps and sat down. After a while he realized the guard was standing in front of him, watching him. He looked up, tried to smile, and said "Thanks" without knowing why he said it.

"You all right, Doc? I hope there ain't no bad news in that letter."

"I'm all right."

To shut the man out and keep him quiet he began to read again, the sense of the words coming through to him only in snatches:

> The sudden collapse which, as you know, sometimes occurs in this disease . . . We all liked her . . . I was with her when she died . . . She did not know . . . If you will arrange with an undertaker . . .

He knew where to find an undertaker. That thought alone had any reality for him and he tried to use it as a central fact around which to reconstruct his shattered faculties, but he could do more than picture in his mind the street corner where they had met so often, and for a while he could progress no further in his thoughts. He rose, once more said the meaningless "Thank you" to the guard, and walked away.

He walked rapidly for a minute or two without a clear

perception of where he was going, but then he found that he was very tired, so tired, in fact, that he felt that he must rest. Near him there was a short wooden dock jutting out into the river and he walked out on it aimlessly. He stood there for a moment, feeling the heat of the sun pouring down on him and listening to the sound of the water lapping under his feet. Then he went out to the end and sat down.

He sat there for only a few minutes before he remembered that he had not read what remained of the letter, so he pulled it out, smoothed the crumpled pages against his knee, and began to read where he had left off.

There was not very much more. The Matron wrote that Hattie had few personal possessions at the hospital and asked permission to have these destroyed as a health precaution. The body had been sealed in a coffin that was now in the hospital morgue. It would be released to an undertaker on written authorization from himself.

He folded the letter, preserving its original creases with unnecessary care, and put it away in an inside pocket of his coat. After this he sat with his knees drawn up, staring at the sunlit water. The current was swift and his eyes followed the flow of the bright water as far as they could without turning his head. Then they jerked back to move again with the current.

This went on for some minutes until he discovered he had a headache and that he could no longer look at the sunstruck water without pain. He stretched out on his back and lay there with his eyes closed but still feeling the brightness of the day through his eyelids. He realized after a time that, strange as it might be, he was resting and peaceful. For a while he let himself drift without disturbing this state, but then that he should feel so began to seem sad to him. The sadness grew and with it a perception of Hattie. She seemed to be with him and even all around him, encompassing him, but he knew that the sadness he was feeling was not true grief.

He saw clearly that this was so, and that he could approach no nearer to real grief, and this seemed to him saddest of all. He thought about her life, how hard it had been and how devoid of love. "Poor kid," he said aloud, and his own voice startled him.

He sat up again, sighed deeply, took a notebook and pencil out of his pocket and turned the leaves until he came on a clean page. He began to write: "This is to authorize the removal of the body of my wife, Hattie Chapin"—he paused, crossed out "Hattie" and substituted "Harriet," then went on with his writing—"from the morgue of the Smallpox Hospital on Blackwell's Island." He paused again, thinking, then he wrote rapidly: "Arrangements for the funeral will be completed later." He signed this, tore out the sheet, folded it and put it with the notebook into his pocket. Then he rose, and walking rapidly, he set out for the landing dock of the boat that crossed the river.

CHAPTER THIRTY-NINE

When Matthew went to one of the four surgical divisions at Bellevue Hospital as senior assistant he in effect skipped a grade. The authorities permitted this in special cases, in this instance because of Matthew's exceptional qualifications, and it always aroused envy and dislike among those of the staff who were not so fortunate. Toward Matthew these feelings were intensified by the unconscious impression he gave of competency and self-confidence, and also perhaps by his good looks, but as to what other members of the staff thought of him, Matthew was indifferent. He saw at once that there was a great deal of work to be done, much of it interesting.

His new position, which carried with it responsibility for three wards under the general supervision of a visiting surgeon, also gave him a good deal of authority over the junior staff members of his division. He did not hesitate to make use of this authority whenever he felt it to be necessary. He was fair but never lenient. He demanded long hours of work and worked longer hours himself. Stupidity on the part of one of his staff, whether a doctor, nurse or orderly, made him fiercely impatient. Laxness roused his anger to such an extent that the untrustworthy person never again escaped his vigilance. He made no friends among the doctors, but at this time he wanted none.

His relations with the ward patients were another matter. Suffering did not have the unreality for him that it has for many young doctors when it is remote from their own personal experience, though perhaps in the early days of the war this had been true of him also. He had escaped altogether the pretended toughness which causes some young doctors to close their minds to the human needs of the sick. He had learned compassion and the lesson had not come hard to him. But he had also learned not to let pity compromise his efficiency or interfere with his physician's duty toward his patients.

Perhaps he saw in the sick people a special need of love and he did love them, though he never permitted any of them the smallest intimacy with himself. He fought for them. He defended their rights as patients and their dignity as individuals; he helped them to live and to face dying, and they responded with such gratitude as was in their natures to give.

Matthew's immediate superior, and head of the Division, was a second-generation Irishman named Mike Moynihan, a big man, dominating and self-confident, and in the prime of life. His title was Visiting Surgeon, and in addition to his hospital duties he had a thriving private practice among wealthy people who preferred to have their operations in their own homes where the danger of infection was a good deal less. The inconvenience to the surgeon in this home surgery was considerable, but the fees were large. He had an assistant who had no connection with the hospital, two competent nurses, and an anesthetist, and he operated with all possible style. With this side of the big Irishman's professional life, as with whatever sort of private life he led, Matthew had no contact.

Because of the demands of Moynihan's private practice, Matthew, every now and then, found himself in command of an operating room for the first time in his life. This room was a big, well-equipped place with rising tiers of seats for visitors, of whom there were always several when Moynihan was operating. Characteristically, Moynihan referred to this as "my" operating room, though in point of fact it was not exclusively his. Operating on his own responsibility gave Matthew no uneasiness, for he was seldom handicapped by doubts or fears, and he was free from other considerations of self that sometimes weaken self-confidence and readiness to accept responsibility.

In these respects he resembled Moynihan, who as a surgeon was bold, swift, competent and sure, the chief difference between them being that Moynihan, having had more time in which to exercise these traits, had them in a larger, more emphatic manner. They, along with his physical bulk, produced the effect of his being somewhat larger than life. Matthew himself was already going in that same direction.

If Moynihan was dominating and sometimes unjust, he was never cruel, and he was capable of showing great gentleness toward a charity patient, as some of the doctors were not. A not uncommon sight on the ward was Moynihan sitting on a chair beside some bed, his big hands on his knees, and on his face a look of sympathetic tenderness that astonished those who had never before seen him in this role. It was wonderful to hear him reassure a frightened patient, speaking with a soft brogue assumed for the occasion. He never failed to leave with the patient the conviction of being the object of special solicitude.

Moynihan could be irritating at times for he had absolute faith in his own judgments about subjects such as music, painting, or world affairs, on which he was in no way qualified to have an opinion. About these things he was often naïve. In discussions about them he could not be talked down, and when, in the staff dining room, a loud argument broke out, Moynihan was usually to be found at its center.

When Moynihan met his new first assistant he looked him over with a cold, appraising eye, for he was mistrustful of first assistants, of their abilities and of their characters. "Your name Matthew Chapin?" he asked in the most unfriendly manner possible.

"Yeah," Matthew said. The Irishman's manner annoyed him and he deliberately made the single word sound rude and offhand.

Moynihan narrowed his eyes at him. "Want to show me you're a bastard, do you? Fine. I like bastards. The last first I had was a fool with no guts. Operating room in fifteen minutes. Breast amp. We'll see what you can do. I suppose you know which side of the table a first assistant stands on, don't you?"

He left the room laughing, without waiting for an answer. But far from being antagonized, Matthew felt stimulated by this exchange, and rather pleased.

During this first operation together they discovered to their mutual satisfaction that they were a perfect operating team. The similarities of character that at first tended to make near antagonists of them away from the operating table worked here to create a like approach to surgical problems and for similar modifications in techniques of the sort that produces individuality in surgery. They understood each other so well that at the operating table few words passed between them, for Matthew almost invariably had started to do what Moynihan wanted before words were necessary.

That the doings in Moynihan's operating room were regarded with a kind of startled awe by the other surgical services Matthew discovered during his first meal at the long table in the doctors' dining room. A staff man from the Second Division pulled out a chair next to his and sat down.

"You're Moynihan's new first, aren't you? Think you're going to be able to stand it?"

"Why not?"

"Seen him operate?"

"He did a breast amp for cancer this morning and I was with him. Pretty comprehensive job."

"I bet. A 'multilating radical,' as they call it, wasn't it? Good name for what he does, and he seldom does anything else."

"A fellow was telling me he gets better results with them that way than most."

"That's true, I guess, but they say around here that his operations are autopsies *in vivo*. You can have that sort of thing if you like it. It's not for me."

On the wards, and in dealing with the junior staff men under him, Matthew developed a grim seriousness of manner that his former associates would not have recognized. The amount of work to be done seemed to him formidable and requiring unremitting, arduous work lest it engulf him. No doubt he exaggerated this because of a need to expend himself to the point of exhaustion, for when he was idle there returned to him a stabbing sense of guilt for Hattie's death. In retrospect he saw her short life as hard, dreary, and unrewarding, cheating her of so much, and ultimately of the thing she wanted most, a kind of love from him that he had not given her. He thought of her now as brave, vulnerable and infinitely pathetic, and of himself as having been inexcusably, heartlessly indifferent. For him she worked in the pesthouse and he had, almost without a thought, accepted this from her. In the wakeful hours of the night, when there was no work against which to blunt his feelings, waves of remorse washed through him, leaving him weak and spent. In this way the crisis of his emotions would gradually diminish and as he lay on his narrow cot in his narrow room, a sort of peace would come over him.

It was after such storms of remorse, when he had grown calm once more, that thoughts of Cissie would, without his volition, invade his tired mind. He would see her then in familiar, lovely poses; sewing with the lamplight on her hair, or her pale oval face raised to the touch of the spring wind, or bending over her window plants, her little hand with the broad gold wedding band on it reaching out to pick a yellowed leaf. These memories of her weighed him down with sadness until he sank under them and was overwhelmed by sleep. But in the morning he awoke to feel once more the fierce compulsion to work and by this means to forget.

Here, as in Boston, he found himself surrounded by the agents of death that follow the surgeon's work to destroy it. Infected wounds, and the illnesses that arose from them, were so common that it began to seem questionable to him if surgery, even the simplest and most superficial, were worth the risk. He read somewhere of a surgeon giving up hospital practice because of a seventy-eight-percent fatality rate in his surgical wards, and the story affected him with something like the physical symptoms of a chill.

He made an effort to talk to Moynihan about his fear that, under present conditions, surgery could make no further advances and that some surgical practices, successful in themselves, might have to be abandoned because of the aftermath of infection. Moynihan listened with unexpected patience, then said, "Matt, it's the way of the worruld," speaking in the Irish manner, which he sometimes did when he wanted to soften for himself the harsh outlines of reality. "It's the way of the worruld, and there's precious little ye can be doin' about it, lad."

Matthew dug out of his trunk the article by Joseph Lister that Odell had given him, and read it again: ". . . suppuration in wounds is decomposition . . . properties of the atmosphere . . . minute organisms suspended in it . . ." He remembered reading somewhere that Pasteur believed that a microbe rode on every grain of dust in the air, or some such thing, but how the hell exclude air? The article answered him: ". . . by applying a dressing capable of destroying the life of the floating particles . . . carbolic acid . . . carbolic . . ."

Matthew brought up the subject of surgical infections with other members of the staff in the doctors' dining room. He discovered that some of the older men believed that erysipelas, which was prevalent enough to be given a special isolation hospital down by the docks, was caused by the east wind and could be prevented by keeping ward windows closed when the wind was blowing from that quarter. The younger men, in the absence of any strong convictions, relied on general cleanliness and considered themselves fortunate if the so-called "hospital diseases" remained below epidemic levels. Some of these younger men had heard about what they called the "Lister techniques," usually inaccurately. None had Matthew's passionate desire to experiment.

On one of his free nights, after he had been some months at Bellevue, Matthew and Odell were eating together in a chophouse and Matthew talked about his obsession.

"By God, the first chance I get I'm going to try it."

"Begin with a compound fracture, then."

"Why?"

"There are other articles. Didn't I show them to you? Lister had astonishing success without amputating. They describe the whole procedure."

"Give them to me," Matthew said.

They went to Odell's office and hunted until they found them—a dusty business. Matthew read them that night sitting on the edge of his bed, and read them again. One morning not long after this, when Moynihan was not expected at the hospital, his chance came—a compound fracture of the leg of a young man who had been involved in a street accident. The jagged ends of the broken bone, in pushing through the skin, had made a long tear, a kind of injury that experience had shown was so sure to develop infection that the standard procedure was amputation. Mike Moynihan, as most other surgeons did, liked to keep his mortality rate low, though he was far from being a fanatic on the subject, and Matthew well knew that had he been there he would have amputated without hesitating.

There was no more firmly established surgical practice than this, and so far as Matthew knew, no compound fracture in that hospital had ever escaped amputation. Matthew decided to take the risk, though he knew he was certain to be discovered the first time Moynihan made his round of the ward. He had found out that carbolic acid was kept in the hospital to pour down the old-fashioned and often offensive toilets. He brought a jar of it to the operating room, and while the intern was giving the injured man ether, Matthew poured some of the acid into a basin of water and washed his hands. He was about to dry them on a towel that the nurse handed him when Moynihan slammed open the door, producing the sense of turmoil in the air that his entrances usually created.

"What the hell's the stink? Carbolic?" He came across the room, sniffed and looked into the basin.

"I was washing my hands in it."

"Why, for God's sake?" Moynihan's laugh filled the room. "You'll take your hide off."

"It's not that strong."

Moynihan gave him a sharp look, went over to the operating table and looked down at the injured leg. "Nice mess." Then he looked again at Matthew. "What are you up to?"

"I'm going to reduce the fracture, treat the wound with carbolic and follow up with carbolic dressings."

"So you've been reading that stuff, have you?" Moynihan put his hand on the ankle of the injured leg. The intern with the ether cone glanced uncertainly from one to the other and said, "Patient's ready." Both Moynihan and Matthew looked at him blankly, as though they had failed to understand. Matthew said, "I've read about a new way of handling compound—"

"Yeah, I suspected that was what it was. I've read it too."

"Don't you think . . ."

"Fanciful quackery, that's what I think."

"I thought the experiment should be tried."

"Did you, now! There'll be no experiments in my operating room—except those I do myself. That clear?"

Matthew made no reply and there followed a long, uneasy silence. Moynihan was staring at Matthew but without seeing him for his attention was on his own thoughts. Matthew discovered he was still holding the towel and put it down. The nurse went to an instrument cupboard and began aligning the instruments on the glass shelves; when she moved, the soft soles of her shoes made a faint sucking sound. The intern shifted himself restlessly on his high stool.

Moynihan was capable of swift and unexpected action. Before anyone knew what he was about, he had taken a tourniquet from the instrument table and fastened it, then there was a knife in his hand, the leg was lifted and there appeared the red line of an incision completely around it. Seconds later there was only a stump where the leg had been.

It was a virtuoso performance of the old school with no flesh flap, a "guillotine" amputation that would probably give a lifetime of discomfort. Surgeons did this often, but not Mike Moynihan. Startled and shocked, Matthew felt that in some complicated way the performance had been meant as a reproach, as a kind of discipline directed at himself. Revolted, he tried to shut the idea out of his mind. Moynihan had kicked a stool up to the table and, sitting on the edge of it, was tying off blood vessels, working meticulously now and more slowly, as though the long, fierce knife strokes had released him from his anger. This was a part of the operation a senior surgeon never did himself, and after a few seconds of hesitation Matthew went slowly up to the table.

"Would you like me to take over, sir?"

Moynihan replied only by an inarticulate sound and an upward jerk of one shoulder. Matthew flushed, hesitated again, then walked away and took a place in the first row of the empty tiers of seats. He felt that Moynihan's doing of the routine work of the operation was meant, in some sense, as an apology, but this did not lessen his resentment.

He stayed in his seat until the familiar procedure was concluded, not bothering to watch but moodily indulging his disappointment. When Moynihan had finished he rose, stood waiting while the nurse poured a basin of water for him, and washed and dried his hands. Then he felt carefully around the bottom of his coat sleeves which he had not bothered to turn back—in itself a piece of surgical boastfulness. He found a small place wet with blood and sponged it off with a damp corner of the towel. He did this more painstakingly than he had done any part of the operation. Matthew climbed down from his seat, left the operating room and went on his way to the doctors' dining room.

This inconveniently located place was dreary, the air thick with odors of food and cigar smoke. The staff men, twenty-two of them, and such visiting doctors as could tolerate the cooking, ate here at one long table, not all at once but singly or in groups as their work would permit. Matthew found a place at the far end of it, and was eating without interest a slice of yesterday's roast and two boiled potatoes when the chair next him was drawn out noisily and Moynihan sat down. Matthew, after the first glance, kept his eyes on his plate and Moynihan called to the waiter, an old fellow with a bent back and cracked shoes.

"All I want's coffee, but see it's hot." He turned in his chair. "Now, Matt, look here. I don't blame you for being sore—or rather, I do because it's my operating room and nothing should go on there without my knowledge, and you must realize you're an annoying bastard. But I think I know how you feel. I shouldn't have handled the op the way I did either, and I should be at a meeting right now. All right. I want to talk to you. Shall we be reasonable?"

"Sure." The single word did nothing to conceal Matthew's resentment.

Moynihan did not at once begin. He lit a cigar carefully and glanced up as the waiter put a cup of muddy coffee in front of him. He looked surprised and faintly outraged, as though he had forgotten all about ordering it. Then he pulled the coffee cup closer, possessing himself of it in so emphatic and characteristic a manner that Matthew smiled a little.

"Matt, a lot of you young fellows seem to think what's new and different has to be good, and you assume nobody else keeps up on it. You're wrong, of course."

"Maybe," Matthew said grudgingly.

"Now it comes down to this, so far as I can see. This guy claims that microbes from the air get into a wound and cause infection. By God, if that were true we'd all be dead. There wouldn't even *be* a human race. It couldn't have survived. Make sense to you?"

"In a way. Yes, I guess it does. But the article is convincing, all right. He gives some cases."

"But look, Matt, suppose it's true that microbes ride in the air on bits of dust. It's dead things that decay, not living flesh." Moynihan sipped his coffee, found that it was far from hot, drank it all noisily and put the cup down hard.

Matthew said, "Maybe like he says, it's the blood clots that decay and infect living tissue, and if we could keep the air out—"

"Nonsense. Look here, Matt, you're going to be a good surgeon—you're one already. I don't want to see you spoil it by taking up fads and notions. Right?"

"I'd like to try this experiment."

"Not in my operating room you won't. You'd have us the laughingstock of the hospital in a week."

"But listen—"

"No, I've heard enough." Moynihan, his short patience exhausted, angrily knocked off the ash of his cigar into the dregs of his coffee, pushed the cup away from him and slapped his hands down hard on the table. "Now, Matt, I want you to understand this. A surgical reputation like

357

mine is hard to come by. You work for it, by God. I've had first assistants who've endangered it before now by being lazy, or inefficient, or just plain stupid. I've known what to do about them. Now, we're going to do good clean surgery and nothing else. Understand? That's for when I'm in the operating room and when I'm not. I laughed at you about that carbolic acid this morning. You do anything like that a second time and it won't be any laughing matter. I suppose you recognize an order when you hear one. This is an order."

Moynihan slapped the table again, shoved his chair back roughly and got up. He stayed there looking down at Matthew but he did not speak and his eyes behind the half-closed lids looked fiery. Then he walked away.

CHAPTER FORTY

The hospital employed as a messenger an ex-soldier, a battered fellow with wispy gray hair, whose duty it was to locate any doctor who might be wanted. He let it be understood that he did not like his job by appearing not to see anything around him as he plodded through the hospital on his errands. With this air of abstraction, brooding on his grievances, he pushed open the door of Mike Moynihan's operating room one day when Moynihan and Matthew were just finishing an operation. He stood there, shuffling uneasily, without so much as a look at what lay on the operating table, and Moynihan, hearing him, glanced over his shoulder.

"Want me, Charley?"

"No, sir. There's a visitor down in the waiting room for the doc there. A man."

"For me?" Matthew said, surprised. Visitors in the hospital were common enough. Relatives and friends of the sick came to the hospital in crowds on visiting day, and groups of sightseers made nuisances of themselves by crowding around the doorways to the wards, for Bellevue was one of the tourist attractions of New York. It was seldom, however, that any of these asked for a doctor by name. "All right," Matthew said, "tell him I'll be down when I finish here."

The waiting room was a dreary place containing chairs with sagging seats and on the windowsills a few plants, all of them ailing, that had been left behind by patients and rescued by the nurses. Weak, dusty sunlight was shining over them straight into Matthew's eyes as he opened the door, so that he did not at once see the visitor clearly. He was only aware of a thin stranger sitting in a corner who rose cautiously, as though he feared movement.

The doctor in Matthew saw the signs of illness before he was aware that the man was smiling, but when he spoke Matthew stopped short and stared unbelievingly with his eyes opened to the man himself. He had spoken only a single word, "Matt!"

"Ed! My God! Ed!"

In the first shock of surprise Matthew forgot the circumstances that had separated them and there were both warmth and pleasure in his tone. The next moment he remembered, and constraint came into his manner. "When did you get back?"

"A week ago. A little more."

There was a pause, uncomfortable for them both. Then Edward said brusquely, "I've got something I want to talk to you about." Matthew felt instantly relieved by the implication in these words that this was not to be a meeting, certain to be awkward or worse, over a dead friendship.

"All right," he said. "Let's sit down."

Edward, using the same caution he had shown in standing, let himself down into the armchair he had been using, and Matthew dragged forward another.

"What's on your mind, Ed?" But Edward did not seem to find it easy to begin. To help him, Matthew said, "You're not looking too fit. You haven't been having any sort of illness, have you?"

"Not an illness exactly, but I haven't been well lately. I suppose it's fairly obvious. Cissie wanted me to talk to you about it."

Matthew ignored the mention of Cissie, but he flushed a little and was angry with himself in consequence. "Didn't you see a doctor in Germany? I should have thought that of all places in the world that would be the best."

"Yes, I did. But Cissie insisted I talk to you. She absolutely insisted on it." Edward hesitated and then he said, as though it were something he had determined on saying ahead of time, "Matt, she's still in love with you."

"I doubt that. I doubt if she ever was."

"It's true enough, though she's done her best to hide it from me because she's kind. But I can't help knowing."

Matthew made no reply and Edward appeared to expect none. He was staring at his own hand lying on his knee, thoughtful and remote, as though the thin blue-veined hand were an abstract problem that required the focusing of pure intelligence. Presently he moved it away, seeming to discard it with regret in order to bring his attention to the subject in hand.

"Germany was hard on her, I think. The strangeness. Not knowing the language. Part of the time I was moving about a good deal to work with various men in their laboratories—a few months here, a few months there. That made it difficult with the children. She wants to see you, Matt."

Matthew sighed and turned his head away toward the beam of dusty sunlight, his mind dealing, but vaguely and without sequence, with all that had taken place in the years past. He seemed to himself no longer to have any connection with them, and this saddened him, but at the same time he seemed to have no difficulty in accepting this fate as inevitable. A phase of life had finished, as though a door that had been a long time in shutting had finally closed, and he felt it to be rather a pity that it had opened a little way once again. With some desire to convey this to Edward indirectly, he made an effort to be aloof and clinical. "Let's get back to you, Ed. What's the trouble?"

"Abdominal pain—colicky and intermittent. Not much at first, but it seems to be getting more severe."

"Where?"

"In the general vicinity of the navel, which I suppose means it's being referred from some other location. Constipation alternating with diarrhea. I feel worse after eating, so I've lost weight. I'm anemic, I suppose."

"And you talked to someone in Germany?"

"Yes, Thiersch, at his clinic at Leipzig."

"What did he think? He examined you, of course?"

"Yes, thoroughly. He couldn't feel any tumor and he said he was willing to rule that out, especially as I'm young for it. He thinks it's a band or bands that have formed, partially closing a segment of bowel. He used the word 'adhesions,' but he's inclined to think there's only one band causing the trouble."

"I've seen the condition at autopsy plenty of times. So have you."

"I have indeed. I saw one case over there where the abdomen was full of bands going every which way, over and under each other. There was a history of peritonitis, which probably accounted for it, and they seem to occur after surgery."

"Did you ever have peritonitis or any sort of abdominal infection?"

"I had an attack of inflammation of the bowels when I was a kid, but only that one."

"That might be enough to do it and you not know it until now. That's easily possible. What did he think should be done about it?"

"He wanted to operate."

"You know opening the abdomen's too risky because of the danger of infection—at least that's the conservative view around here. It would be a comparatively simple operation otherwise. Just open up the abdomen, feel around until you've located the band that's doing the restricting, cut it, and there you are. Any surgeon could do it as easy as we used to in autopsy. It's just one of a long list of operations we could do, but we don't dare, except to save life. And we don't succeed in doing that in about eighty percent of the cases. I'm very much surprised this German doctor suggested it, weren't you?"

"Thiersch has just begun to use Lister techniques at his clinic and the results are so good it's making them bold enough to try anything. You know about Lister's work, don't you?"

"Sure. I wish to God we were doing it here."

"Prejudices?"

"Yeah. Let's get back to you. How long since you saw him?"

"Six weeks—maybe a little more."

"Have you noticed any change in the condition since then?"

"I don't know. Sometimes I think it's worse, sometimes not. I keep to soft foods and that seems to help."

They had been talking easily, much as they had in former days, the interest of the subject overcoming the restraint between them. Matthew spoke now with the quick vitality of mind that had characterized him then, forgetful for the moment of the barriers between them.

"But tell me, Ed. Why did you come home? I should think that if there is any future likelihood that you ought to have an operation, you'd be better off in Germany at this fellow's clinic than anywhere else, unless you went to Lister himself."

"You're really sold on his method, aren't you?"

"Yes, from what I read about it. I've never seen it used. Yes, I'm sold on it."

"Somehow I thought you would be. Those were good days, Matt, there at Harvard. I wish we had known then how good."

"In a way we did know. But my God, how green we were!"

They were silent, both feeling the embarrassment of having brought the conversation back to the emotions of their relationship. "Well . . ." Matthew said, and let the meaningless word hang in the air between them. Away in the distance they heard the clanging of an ambulance gong and Edward turned to look without interest through the window. "Some poor devil," he said.

"We were talking about why you came home."

"Because of Cissie."

"She's all right, isn't she? Is anything wrong, Ed?"

"No, there's nothing wrong, except that she's more worried about me than she should be, but that's the way women are. But suppose it turns out that after a while an operation is unavoidable, and suppose it were to end fatally, as it very well might. Then if we had stayed in Germany she'd be stranded there with the children and no home to come back to here."

"And so you took a chance on having to run a greater operative risk in this country in order to get her home."

"I don't honestly think it's much of a chance. I very much doubt if an operation will ever be necessary, and she insisted that I see you, so here I am. She doesn't, of course, understand the problem or the considerations involved. I've been pretty careful what I've said to her about it. But she won't be satisfied unless you check me over, so we can have your opinion to put against that of one of the greatest surgeons in the world."

Edward smiled as he said this, the tight, secretive smile that Matthew knew to be inspired by irony or paradox, but never by humor. He said, a little distantly for he felt the smile to be more distasteful than he ever had in the past, "We'll go up to my room and do that, if you like. But first tell me why, aside from this ridiculous business of consulting me professionally, you're here in New York. You've been here more than a week, you say. You could have seen me and gone, by this time. You're not planning to live here permanently, are you?"

"We do intend to live here. I want to begin work in pathology and some teaching, perhaps, but certainly as much laboratory work as I can get. I think the best chance is in New York. I even thought I'd see if they'd take me on the staff here at Bellevue. Perhaps you could help me there."

"Perhaps. I'll do what I can, of course. We'll talk about it later. Let's go up to my room, shall we? Though I think getting an opinion from me, after where you've come from, is pretty silly."

They rose and were starting to leave the room when Matthew stopped short and said in a tone that was full of surprise directed at himself, "Say, I just happened to think. How did you know I was here?"

"You never answered my letter."

"I know. I'm sorry. I was having troubles at the time. Anyway, there didn't seem to be anything I could say."

"So I wrote Osgood. I thought he'd know where you were if anybody did. So he told me what's been happening to you—all of it. Cissie and I thought you did a fine thing in marrying that girl, Matt."

"He lent me the money to bury her, and enough more to see me through my staff appointment here."

"You know, I suppose, that he's not practicing any more."

Matthew replied to this with a nod. They went out of the room in silence, through the main lobby and up the stairs to Matthew's room under the roof.

Matthew's examination was gentle but thorough. Twice he stopped to say, "Am I hurting you, Ed?" and each time Edward shook his head. "It's tender, that's all." At the end Matthew sat down in a chair facing the bed, rested one leg across the other and put his hand around his ankle. "I think your German doctor's right," he said. "Your abdomen's distended some, but I can't find anything that feels like a growth."

Sitting on the bed, Edward began to put his clothes in order. "That's my own guess too. I'll just have to try to live with it. The trouble is that bending over a microscope seems sure to bring on an attack of pain."

"I appreciate your reasons for not having an operation in Germany, but just the same, I wish you had. I think the chances are very good that the trouble won't get any worse since it hasn't gotten markedly so already, but it's too bad to have to work under such a handicap."

They were silent for a few moments, Matthew nursing his ankle and frowning at his thoughts. Edward was resting comfortably on the bed. After a while he turned his head toward Matthew and said, "I'd hate to have it interfere in any serious way with my professional life. You've no idea of the interesting things that are going on in Germany in my field. Remember how we used to talk about whether there really was a connection between microbes and disease? In Germany they've felt certain of it for a long time—many years—and now it's proved, and work is directed toward discovering which germ causes which disease. I'll tell you about it in detail, sometime. Am I keeping you from something you ought to be doing?"

"I'm through operating for the day. The rest of the work can wait. As a pathologist, how do you feel about Lister's theory?"

"I believe in it absolutely—in the main, that is. I question some of the details of technique, but they can be modified in time, if necessary. I'm even willing to say it's one of the greatest of medical discoveries. I'd like to go over it all with you sometime soon. Cissie wants to see you. We're looking for a house, and when we find one we want you to come to evening dinner with us. She told me to tell you so."

Matthew frowned in thought. Then, as before, he turned the talk in another direction.

"Ed, we've both been assuming this condition of yours won't get any worse. I don't think it will, but suppose it did? I really wish to hell you'd had the op in Germany."

"You could do it here."

"I could, or Moynihan, my chief, could, but I'd certainly a good deal rather not."

"Let's both think about it a bit." Edward got slowly off the bed, moving in a way that told Matthew, who was watching him closely, that he was again being careful not to awaken pain. Matthew too stood up, and they went out of the room together.

At the bottom of the stairs Edward stopped and put his hand on Matthew's arm. "Look here, Matt, Cissie won't like it unless I tell her that you'll come to see us. What's past is past. She needs the kind of friend you could be to her."

"She's got you." Matthew spoke in a tone that was close

to anger, and he stepped back so that Edward's hand fell from his arm.

"I'm not right for her, Matt. I'm too introspective, too retiring for her. Not enough of a doer. She's never let me know she feels this. She's been sweet and dear, and as thoughtful as she can be. She's never let me know how she feels, but I know anyway. How could I help it?"

"Would you really want Cissie and me to be friends again, Ed? That's not like you, I think."

"I trust her absolutely. So I'm not jealous—or maybe I am. Hell, I don't know. Does it matter? She's not really happy and so I'm not happy either, and maybe it's absurd to think we could go back to old times, when the three of us . . . When I feel as awful as I do physically, I'd like a little solid contentment around me and not have to feel that she's hiding her real feelings all the time. I trust both of you enough to feel sure you wouldn't do anything behind my back, so why don't you come and we'll see how it works out?"

"We'll think about that, too, Ed."

Matthew began to walk slowly across the lobby toward the front door. He went out first and held the door open for Edward to go through. At the top of the steps they both stood still again. Matthew's hands were in his pockets and he was absently jingling coins. He stood there as though he were alone, looking out into the misty sunshine, across the river to the shabby outlines of Blackwell's Island. Edward, watching him, said nothing, but in these few silent minutes a great deal passed between these two. Both were fully aware of this, and aware also of all the past which neither of them could escape, or, at the moment, wanted to. Then abruptly Matthew turned to Edward. He was faintly smiling, thoughtfully, almost ruefully acknowledging the bond between them that could not be broken. Edward held out his hand and Matthew took it. Then Edward turned to the steps and went down them while Matthew watched.

CHAPTER FORTY-ONE

One noon, nearly two weeks later, Matthew walked into the doctor's dining room with a slow, almost shambling gait induced by fatigue and the knowledge that for the next hour or more there was nothing urgent waiting to be done. Almost all the places at the long table were filled, and he had stopped just inside the door to look around for an empty one when he saw someone at the far end signaling him with a raised arm. As before, he did not immediately recognize Edward, and when he realized who it was he felt a sudden depressing awareness of the long gap in their friendship, a gap he knew would in all probability never wholly close again.

Matthew started toward him, noticing once more as he drew near that Edward seemed much older, even worn. On his face there were traces left by experiences of recent years about which Matthew knew nothing, experiences which must have molded and changed him, making him to this extent a stranger. The long tan linen coat gave him a foreign look which, with his dark complexion and his extreme thinness, made him appear so different from the other doctors present as to seem not to belong among them.

Matthew pulled out the chair next to him and sat down. "Hullo," he said. "What's this all about? Don't tell me you've joined the staff?"

"I have. I'm an associate in pathology. I began the job this morning."

"I thought I was supposed to help with that. I didn't know you were ready."

"Actually, there was nothing to it. They found out I'd been working in Germany, and who with. . . . The prestige of German study over here is simply astonishing. And already, in a few hours, I can see things here are pretty far behind. Anyway, here I am."

"How are you?"

"Only fair, but anxious to be at work."

"What will your job be? Anything special?"

"Routine work mainly. Naturally, I haven't got into it yet. I spent the morning learning where things are kept, finding out the lab boys' names—things like that. The equipment's shockingly crude, by the way, when it isn't lacking altogether. I brought my own mike, and it's so much better than any these people have ever seen that everybody in the lab spent the morning fooling with it. But my real work, whenever I get time, is staph."

"Staph? Short for staphylococcus?"

"Yes. Remember when Jimmie had osteomyelitis?"

"You thought it was a microorganism in the blood, only you couldn't see it."

"I still think so, and I still can't see it."

"So what can you do about it? Just keep on not seeing it?"

"If I can find some kind of chemical that will color the microbes I'm after, and not color anything else, then I think I could see them. That idea isn't original with me, by the way. It's being tried in Germany, but so far without success."

"Where do you get the patience? I'd go crazy."

Matthew watched Edward dip a piece of bread in the bowl of soup in front of him and slowly eat it.

"Listen, Ed, is that all you eat? You can't work on that."

"It's all I can manage comfortably. Even this . . ."

Matthew sat frowning down at the table deep in thought until he realized that the waiter with the cracked shoes was wanting to set a plate of food in front of him. He moved to make room and glanced at Edward sharply. Edward seemed to him to have grown thinner in this little while since they had last met, but to have lost nothing of the nervous tension and the sharp intelligence on which the quality of his work had always depended. But it seemed evident to Matthew that the frail body could not support the demands and stresses of his active mind much longer. Matthew ate a few moments in silence, then pushed his plate away and turned to face Edward.

"Had you thought that we might do the op, using Lister techniques?"

"Yes. I wondered if you had."

"Moynihan's a fine surgeon."

"The man you work with? But not in sympathy with antisepsis, I think you said."

"No, he isn't."

"Then he couldn't be relied on to observe the rules in all the little details. No, you'd have to do it yourself, with somebody helping you, I suppose."

"I wouldn't want to, Ed. Anyway, that's out because I don't think house surgeons are permitted to operate outside the hospital, and you most certainly wouldn't want it done here."

"That reminds me—Cissie and I have found a house. We were lucky—some people going to Italy for a year, to Florence, where there's been a regular American colony for years. All we had to do was move in. I was going to look you up later in the day and give you a message. We want you to come to dinner tomorrow night."

"Don't you think it would be unwise?"

"Only if you make it so. I hope you will come, Matt, and so does Cissie."

The half-strange Edward in the foreign-looking linen coat spoke with sincerity, and also sadness, as though with regret for the loss of the past. Matthew felt both the sincerity and the sadness, but he had made up his mind, or thought he had, not to have any contact with the life that Edward and Cissie were living together. How could he without opening old wounds? He felt Edward's eyes on him and turned his head away to escape them. He was hurt and angry that Edward, and Cissie too, had so little understanding of his feelings as to try to force this on him.

He thought of making a refusal that would be also a reproach. He thought of getting up and going away without a word. He did neither. He bent over, shoulders hunched as though to protect himself and, picking up a knife, began slowly to incise long, parallel lines on the gravy-spotted tablecloth. He could not have spoken if he had tried.

He felt Edward's waiting and then Edward's hand was lightly laid on his bent back, and he heard the disturbing, unaccustomed gentleness in Edward's words. "Cissie wants you to come, Matt."

Matthew dropped the knife and jerked around to face Edward, about to speak, saw the pain, and much more, in Edward's eyes, and was silent. He laid his crumpled napkin on the table, clutching it, and shoved back his chair. Then he nodded his assent, rose, and quickly went away.

The next day at six o'clock they met in the lobby of the hospital. It had been warm, though this was still only April, and they stepped from the comparative coolness of the building into heavy, damp air that trapped and held the city's odors. Matthew said, "Where is this house of yours?"

"West Twenty-eighth Street. Too far to walk."

Three or four hansoms with listless horses and dozing drivers stood in a line, and when Edward signaled the first of these the driver roused himself and his horse and came toward them with a show of alacrity. The inside of the hansom smelled of the stable and of ancient leather, so that Matthew struggled with the strap that let the window down in the hope of fresher air. They made no attempt to talk on the uncomfortable ride over the jolting cobblestones, and when they arrived they stepped out onto the carriage block with a sense of escape.

Matthew's first impression of the house was of its unexpected grandeur. There had, in the past years, been occasion now and then to remember that Edward had inherited his father's money, but that it was enough to support the kind of life this house represented, he had never guessed. As he followed Matthew up the high flight of brownstone front steps, these thoughts produced in him a feeling of awkwardness, a sort of boyish shyness such as had not troubled him for years. Perhaps Edward guessed something of this, for as he put his key in the lock of the tall front door he turned to give Matthew his familiar sardonic smile, as though this were a humorless joke, not only on Matthew but on himself as well.

As he opened the door, cooler, fresher air came out to meet them and they went into a hall where gas was already lighted in a lantern overhead. The lantern globe, hung on thin chains, was made up of many small pieces of stained glass, and as it turned slightly in the draft from the opened door, droplets of colored light rained down on them, flecking them with ruby, green and amethyst. "She'll be upstairs in the drawing room," Edward said, and limped toward a carpeted staircase that rose into the shadows above.

Of the drawing room Matthew received little impression, except that it was large and rather grand, for Cissie had risen from a sofa near the windows and was coming forward to meet them. She came in a rustle of stiff silk, crying "Matthew!" and holding out both of her hands. As he reached to take them, it seemed to him that this was not really Cissie at all, but an older, more matronly woman with gray in her hair, lines of trouble on her face, and a grand gown of a fashion that was not familiar to him. He took her hands and they were Cissie's hands, their live touch familiar and dear, so that it was for him a moment of utter confusion. He felt himself growing red and he was both angry and ashamed. He looked down unbelievably at her hands and saw that the gold band which she had always worn had been replaced by another, topped by a ring with a blue stone. It looked strange and too heavy, as though it did not belong to her, so he let her hands go.

Edward was speaking in a voice a little too loud and artificially cheerful, saying something about a glass of sherry for all of them. Then he was guiding Matthew, with a hand on his arm, toward chairs by the fireplace. Through Edward's grasp Matthew felt the drag of Edward's limp, and tried miserably to remember whether he had said anything at all to Cissie, or merely clung to her hands in silence.

They sat down, Cissie lost for an instant of preoccupation with the elaborate structure of her gown, and then they were all unhappily, miserably silent. The silence was not to be borne, and Matthew, making a heroic effort, said, "I was so surprised to see Ed at the hospital the other day. I didn't know . . ." At the same time Edward got up, saying, "I'll get us the sherry," and Cissie said, "Matthew will want to see the children before their bedtime." Having all spoken at once, they all looked stricken; then Edward made a gesture of helplessness and left the room.

Matthew and Cissie looked at each other at once, deep into each other's eyes, and Cissie said softly, "You've changed a great deal, Matthew."

"And you've changed too, Cissie."

"It's almost hard to know each other again, isn't it? How strange!"

He nodded, lost and too unhappy to say more. He sat there staring down at the floor in front of him.

Then, a little more in command of herself than he, she said, "I was very sorry to hear about what happened to the girl you married, Matthew. Dr. Osgood wrote us. She was young, wasn't she?"

"Too young for what happened to her."

They were silent again for another awkward interval, and when Cissie spoke again Matthew knew by the intentness of her manner that she had only been waiting for a decent length of time to pass before speaking what was urgently in her mind.

"Matthew, how is Ed? Really, I mean. Please tell me."

"He's not well, and he's not getting any better, Cissie.

He has a band, or bands that are partly cutting off the function of his intestine at some point. If we dared, we could go in and cut the obstruction. How much has he told you about it?"

"All of that. I think he'll end by risking the operation. Matthew, I have a feeling that the trouble is more serious than you and Ed think."

"You've no reason that I can see to feel that way, Cissie."

From the back of the house there came sounds of turmoil and Cissie said, "Here come the children. I'd like to talk to you some more, Matthew. Could I come see you at the hospital?"

"Whenever you like." With that they both rose to meet the invasion.

Jimmie entered first, a surprisingly tall youngster, bright-eyed, turning his limp into a joyous prance. He was shouting, "Dr. Matt, Dr. Matt," and Matthew, stooping to receive the onslaught, felt two thin but strong arms tighten around his neck.

"Hullo, youngster. Say, you're strong!"

"You bet I'm strong."

Matthew got an arm around the active little body and held him pressed to his side. "Peter! You going to beat me up too? I can't handle two of you at once."

Peter, full of reserve, regarded Matthew with serious eyes; then he turned and asked a question of Edward in German. A brief exchange of understanding that went farther than words passed between them, which was evident enough to make Matthew remember that Peter had for a long time been closer to Edward than to himself. Then Peter turned to Matthew, regarding him gravely, in his manner the unconscious dignity of childhood that is almost always a reproach to elders. *"Guten abend. Wie geht es?"*

Cissie said, "Speak English, dear," and Peter said "How do you do, Dr. Matthew?"

"Very well, thank you." Matthew was smiling, faintly discomfited.

"Here's Sue." Edward set down the tray of sherry decanter and glasses that he was holding and touched Matthew's arm to draw attention to a nursemaid who was coming into the room, leading a plump, bright-eyed little girl whose head was covered by a riot of bronze curls. The curls seemed to Matthew so ludicrously like his own that he laughed aloud. He went down on his knees in front of her, holding out his arms, and she pitched herself headlong into them. He rose, holding her, and she gurgled with delight, beating his head with her fists. *"Hey, stop it!"* He laughed again, jouncing her. She sat easily on his arm, delighted and unafraid, and he turned to Cissie to share his pleasure with her.

Cissie was standing in front of the fireplace, watching this and smiling. The lines of care were gone; the hint of the tired matron in her manner was not there. He saw the old Cissie, radiant and lovely, and as utterly charming to his senses as she had ever been, and he forgot everything else. Holding Sue, but unaware of her, feeling suddenly larger than life, strong, and almost bursting with nearly uncontrollable animal vitality, he came up to her. He did not know how plainly all this showed on him. Color rose up into her face and she turned away, her dress rustling. Then Edward was saying, "Put Sue down, Matthew. It's her bedtime," and Matthew, shaken, made an elaborate business of setting the child carefully on her feet.

Nothing had actually happened, but all ease had gone because Edward had seen and understood. There was a small commotion as the children, herded by Edward, were sent off in the charge of the nursemaid. Sue clung to Matthew, her plump arms wrapped around his legs, and had to be pried loose, protesting tearfully. Jimmie said shrilly, over and over, "You'll come again, won't you, Dr. Matt? You'll come again?" until Matthew said, "Sure, sure," to silence him. Peter left the room without a word.

When Matthew and Edward, holding sherry glasses, returned to their seats, they found Cissie sitting near a lamp with sewing in her hands. She was still flushed, but the fresh loveliness had gone. Her face and throat were faintly blotchy, and her hands, holding her sewing, were trembling slightly. Matthew offered her his glass and she shook her head, smiling. Edward began to talk about his studies in Germany, a monologue, teacherish and detailed. Matthew listened in silence, from time to time raising his eyes to look at Cissie and quickly lowering them again.

He was having a strange and disturbing experience. It was as if the little woman sitting there quietly sewing, a woman prematurely entering middle age, who would soon be dumpy and gray-haired, was gradually, silently making herself known to him. And he found himself responding with a great feeling of liking, of gentleness and companionship, that was of a different and richer quality from anything he had felt for Cissie in the past. He was filled with contentment and with sadness.

He would gladly have stayed there with her like that for a long time, but a maid appeared to say that dinner was ready. Cissie put her sewing aside and Matthew rose and held out his hand to her to help her rise. Surprised by his gesture, she looked up at him, and then she smiled and gave him her hand.

They ate by candlelight while two maids moved efficiently around the table. Edward, making a pretense of eating some special food that was brought to him, talked on about Germany. Matthew and Cissie joined in now, as though the important thing which lay between the two of them had been settled and no longer distracted them. Edward was tense and nervous, and Matthew knew by little betraying signs that he was furiously angry still because of the unguarded moment with Cissie when the past had returned.

The anger was burning near the surface and Matthew found himself wishing it would blaze through, for he wanted very much to say to Edward that what he had seen was the last flare-up of the past, that the feelings of that past were dead, and that in the last hour something different, something better and more real, something far more reliable, had taken their place. He would have liked very much to let Edward know that the tie between Cissie and himself, though formed without words and in his presence, was more understanding and so closer than before, but unlike the old feelings they had for each other. They loved each other still, of that Matthew was newly sure, but love had deepened into maturity and wisdom. It would not now cause Edward unhappiness.

At the end of the meal, when the maids had left the room and Cissie was pouring coffee, Edward seemed suddenly to have talked himself out. He leaned back in his chair, bent over like an old man, and Matthew, seeing how his hands were tightened around the chair's arms, knew that he was in pain. He saw too that Cissie was watching anxiously. He laid his napkin on the table and pushed his chair a little way back. "Ed," he said, "I don't want you to feel—" He did not know what he might have said, or if he could have found the words he wanted. Edward's head jerked up and the look on his face desperately implored silence.

No one spoke. The candles fluttered in a sudden, mysterious draft and a soft patter of raindrops tapped on the window. Edward got to his feet. "I think, if you'll excuse me, I'll lie down."

Then they were all standing, and Matthew was saying, "It's late and I have to turn out early. I'd better run along."

Cissie, standing in front of her chair, said good night and gave him her hand. They left her there and Edward went with Matthew to the front door. With the door open Matthew hesitated, wanting to shake hands. A breeze from outside turned the lantern hanging above them, sending the flecks of colored light spattering over them in a wild dance. Edward's hands remained at his sides.

"Good night, Ed."

"Good night, Matt."

"See you at the hospital tomorrow."

"Maybe."

Matthew heard the front door shut behind him before he was halfway down the front steps.

CHAPTER FORTY-TWO

Matthew walked back to the hospital scarcely aware of the soft spring rain that glistened on the sidewalks and made a star of every distant light. He was angry with Edward, but at the same time filled with pity for him. He was angry with himself for supposing that a reunion of the three could possibly produce any of the pleasures of the past. He felt that he should have foreseen that Edward, ill, anxious about the future and at every sort of disadvantage in relation to himself, must inevitably be jealous. How can a sick man not envy a well man's health? How can he fail to be distressed by a display of vitality and well-being, in contrast to his own weakness, before the eyes of the woman he loves? Most of all, he thought of Cissie, who had so changed, but in changing had grown dearer. He knew he could never go to that house again, and the thought brought him great misery.

He made no attempt to see Edward in the days that followed, and he guessed that Edward was avoiding him.

Twice, when he went into the doctors' dining room, he saw Edward leave quickly by another door, and knew that his guess had been correct. Cissie did not come to the hospital to see him as she had suggested doing, and this did not surprise him, but he found that he was constantly expecting her, and her not coming was a burden to him. He tried to lose himself in the work of the hospital and grew irritable, tired, and beset by a feeling of the futility of what he was doing that, however unreasonable, had the result of making the work very hard to do. He had never before questioned the value of his chosen work, and in some ways this was hardest of all.

One night about eight o'clock, when the wards were comparatively quiet, he plodded wearily upstairs to his room and found Edward there waiting for him. Edward was sitting uncomfortably on the hard chair, plainly tired, but in the look he gave Matthew the spark of his nervous energy was still burning. "Come in, Matt," he said as though the room belonged to him. "I want to talk to you."

"What's on your mind?" Matthew said, letting himself down on the edge of his narrow bed. Edward did not answer at once and Matthew, watching him, noticed how sunken his eyes looked and how the dartlike line on his forehead, that once had appeared only in moments of anger or stressful thought, had now become permanent. He was so lost in thinking about the changes that time was making in all of them that he was startled when Edward spoke.

"I've decided to have the operation, Matt."

"I thought we'd decided to wait and see how you got along. What's brought you to this new decision?"

"I can't stand it any longer."

"What? The pain?"

"No, no. I can't stand being half a man."

Abruptly, Edward pushed himself out of his chair, limped to the window, and stood, his back to the room, looking out at the deepening night. "I can't stand it any longer. When I saw you and Cissie together the other evening, and you so . . . I want to be a man again or else I want to be dead. Sometimes I don't care which."

Edward spoke with passion, almost with violence, and Matthew, shocked but also moved by it, found nothing to say. After a moment Edward sighed, as though Matthew, by keeping silence, had somehow failed him, came slowly back to his chair and sat down.

"You can arrange to do it, can't you, Matt?"

"Me? You don't want me. There are plenty of more experienced surgeons, Ed. Moynihan, for example."

"Cissie wouldn't want anyone else." Edward produced his bitter sketch of a smile. "As a matter of fact, I feel that way myself."

"I think you're both very wrong. And there are lots of other reasons why not. In the first place, I don't believe house surgeons are allowed to do private work. I never heard of one doing any. But even supposing that part's all right, I'd need an assistant. I work with one of the other men occasionally for emergencies, when Moynihan isn't there, but there's nobody I work with comfortably, and I wouldn't want to undertake an op like that without being darn sure of the other man. No, Ed, you get somebody else."

"I tell you, I won't hear of anybody else. Neither would Cissie, and her peace of mind is as important to me as my own. Besides, do you know of any other surgeon you'd trust to use the Lister technique conscientiously and intelligently? I don't. It's you or nobody, Matt. You've got to arrange it somehow."

"I'll talk to Moynihan, Ed. That's about all I can do. I'm not even sure permission to work outside rests with him, and that doesn't settle the difficulty of the assistant anyway. No, you better think seriously about having somebody else."

"At least talk to him. My God, Matt, you can do that much, for Cissie if not for me."

The next day, over a late lunch with Moynihan in the almost deserted dining room, Matthew did bring the subject up. Both men were tired after a long morning in the operating room, not disposed to hurry over their second cups of coffee, and because their work had gone exceptionally well, Moynihan was in a relaxed mood. He listened to Matthew's story attentively and with real interest.

"One thing I have to say about you, Matt, you've got nerve. You're almost as good as me in that respect. Don't misunderstand me, now. A surgeon's no good unless he thinks he can do the job in hand better than anybody else. If he hasn't that sort of faith in himself, he's not to be trusted. Tell me now, boy"—Moynihan reverted to his not very authentic brogue—"tell me now, don't you in the soul of you believe you can do it foine? Better, perhaps, than me meself?"

Matthew laughed, but made no answer, and Moynihan said, "You want to do it, that I can see."

"I do and I don't. I'd like to do the op on somebody, but I wish it didn't have to be on someone I know so well."

"As far as permission to do it goes, that's not just up to me, but I can give you time off, and who's to know what you do with it?"

Matthew was silent for a few moments, adjusting himself to the idea that the project might not be so impossible as he had half hoped it would prove to be. After a while, having taken this forward step in his thinking, he said, "I'd plan to use the full Lister technique, both during the op and in maintaining antiseptic dressings afterward."

"Would you, now? I suppose you wouldn't like it if I came to watch? You don't have to answer that, but I'm getting curious about this business that's fired you up so much. Who are you going to get to assist, by the way? It wouldn't be wise to use anybody from around here."

"The op would be at Dr. Chisolm's house, of course. I thought of asking you about the man that usually assists you when you work outside, and I thought maybe you'd let me borrow your anesthetist too."

Moynihan laughed loudly. "So you really have been giving it a lot of thought? I guessed as much. You'll need a nurse. I've got some good ones."

"I'd want one after the op, not during."

"Why not during?"

"The Lister procedure's too complicated. She'd be an added chance of something going wrong, and I couldn't keep an eye on her all the time."

"Maybe you've got a point." Moynihan reached for the gray enamel coffeepot that was standing on a plate close by, filled his cup, and held the pot out to Matthew, who shook his head. Moynihan drank some coffee and set the cup down hard.

"They have the foulest coffee here of any place I know. Look here, Matt, how about me assisting?"

"*You* assisting?"

"Why not? It's a long time since I have, and I'd kind of like to do it once again. Humbling, and good for my arrogant soul, and for you it wouldn't be like working with a stranger. Besides, I admit I'd like to see this Lister business being worked."

"You're not by any chance serious, are you, sir?"

"Perfectly serious. Damned if I'm not."

Matthew laughed, not altogether comfortably. "It's very kind of you . . ."

"Do you want me, or don't you?"

"Sure I do!" Matthew, suddenly filled with enthusiasm, twisted around in his chair to face Moynihan, and gave the table a slap. "If you really mean it, sure I do!"

"You got these articles in *The Lancet* you been talking about? I've read 'em, but I want to see them again."

"I'll give them to you. The thing is, they don't make so much of details of procedure in the operating room as put reliance on post-op dressings. The implications of the idea are so far-reaching that they don't dawn on you all at once, but I've got some operating procedure ideas of my own. The thing takes a lot of thinking about."

"All right. I'll read 'em and think. Got a date in mind? We'll have to fix it to both be away at once."

"As soon as possible, I think. I'll talk to Ed."

"I want to see him myself, examine him. I may be only the assistant on this op, but by God, I'm not getting into it without making my own diagnosis."

"That's certainly fair enough."

"Send him to see me in my office—where I ought to be right now, by the way. Oh, and another thing. I've got a printed list of the things that have to be done to get a room in a private house ready for an operation. This friend of yours got a wife? I'll give you one to hand on to her. Now let's get out of here."

As they were walking up the stairs together, their shoes making a scratching sound on the stone steps, Matthew said, "I'm certainly grateful to you—very—but I'm damned if I really know why you—"

"Why I want to? I'll tell you. I don't go along with this Lister theory from what I know of it, but if there's anything to be learned out of it I don't want to be the one to miss it. I'll tell you something, Matt—if you don't know it already. A lot of doctors quit learning for good when they leave school, but any doctor worth a damn never stops. Learning is a doctor's lifetime job. Send your friend in to see me soon as you can."

Moynihan nodded curtly and swung away with long, easy strides toward the front door.

Before the week was out Moynihan had examined Edward, and agreed with Matthew's diagnosis of a partial occlusion of some part of the intestines by a band or bands. He was, however, a little less certain than Matthew had been. "You can't be absolutely sure," he said, "until you get in and see. However, what we think is a good enough working hypothesis. Now about the incision . . ."

"Midline, I thought."

"No, muscle midline. Make it to one side where there is muscle. It will be stronger when it's healed."

Moynihan also gave Matthew a copy of the list of preparations to be made, and Matthew, never having seen such a thing, read it with interest:

> The room chosen for the operation must be one that receives plenty of light at the time of day the operation is to be performed. However, if this room is on the ground floor, the bottom panes of the windows must be soaped to prevent the curious from looking in. Gaslight and lamps should be available should daylight fail.
>
> All furniture must be taken out of the room.
>
> The carpet must be lifted and taken out of the room altogether, along with the straw on which the carpet is laid. The room must then be thoroughly swept.

Matthew paused in his reading to think about that sweeping. Dust would be plentiful after such activity, and it would hang in the air a long time. Dust, the chief source, according to Lister, of the danger of wound infection. Matthew took a pencil out of his pocket, turned the paper over, and wrote, "The sweeping must be done two days in advance of the operation, the dust must then be allowed to settle, and the floorboards washed." He laid down the pencil and went on reading:

> Pictures must be well dusted . . .

He picked up the pencil, crossed out the last two words, and wrote "removed."

> Curtains, draperies, and lambrequins on mantel shelves must be taken away.

To this Matthew added "The fireplace must be cleaned out and left empty."

> A table must be provided for the operation. An ordinary deal kitchen table is best. This should be placed in a good light. A mattress, no bigger than the table, should then be laid on it. This mattress must be firm, stuffed with hair or straw. Feather mattresses are too soft and will not serve.

The mattress should then be covered with oilcloth and a clean sheet. There must be no covering on the floor under the table because of the danger of the surgeon's feet catching in it while he is at work.

Matthew thought about this paragraph for a moment, decided he had nothing to add, and went on reading:

There must be a small table, about the size of an ordinary parlor table, placed conveniently to hold two basins of water and the surgeon's instruments. This table should be covered with a clean cloth.

There should be a stool at the head of the operating table for the person who gives the ether.

The following items should be available for the surgeon's use: two basins, tin or enamel, a slop jar or pail, half a dozen or more clean huck towels, folded and placed on the instrument table, a sponge, well washed to remove all particles of sand or shell, a bowl of green soap, and two large pitchers full of hot water.

Matthew took up the pencil and corrected this to read "boiled water." He considered adding carbolic acid to the list and decided since this was all-important—the thing, in fact, on which the whole procedure depended—that it would be better to allow no room for error and bring it himself.

The list ended with a suggestion that if it seemed likely that, postoperatively, the patient would be disturbed by noise, the street in front of the house and for some distance on either side of it could be piled with straw.

About the hot water Matthew thought a long time. This would be used during the operation to wash the wound, the instruments, the sponge. Would the carbolic in the solution he proposed to use be strong enough to kill any germs that might have survived heating? Presumably so, since in this he would be following Lister's method to the letter. On the other hand, might it not be well to have the water heated a long time? Could microbes survive boiling? He did not know, though he thought it probable that Edward would.

Quite suddenly he was overwhelmed by uncertainty. The instruments and the suture silk he would use would soak in a solution of carbolic, but how about the towels or the lint that would be used around the edges of the open wound, if not in it? Would the final rinsing of the wound with carbolic solution before closing destroy any infection they might have carried? Again, the facts were unknown.

His own hands and Moynihan's would be washed, no, scrubbed, in as strong a solution of carbolic as the skin would bear, but what about the things he touched, the basins, the handles of the pitchers, the patient's skin? If microbes floated in the air did they not settle like dust on all these things? Was not an unknown source of danger here? Would not the very first stroke of the scalpel carry microorganisms downward into the tissues in spite of all? Unknown!

He was seized with a nightmare awareness of these dangerous, invisible enemies all around him, in the air he was breathing, coating every object in the room, on the paper and pencil in his hands, on his hands. . . . Would not the precautions he would take be futile and hopeless against such a host? Unknown! Yet people survived these dangers, so might there not be in the flesh itself protection against them? His mind repeated over and over again the key word of his uncertainty—*unknown, unknown, unknown*—like the tolling of a bell.

These thoughts were like an illness from which he did not, during the days before the operation, wholly recover. He did manage to put a stop to his more lurid and morbid imaginings. He told himself that he could only do his best without, perhaps, realizing that in doing this lies the ultimate peace of mind of all conscientious surgeons. Nevertheless the strain and a certain amount of unwholesome nervous tension remained with him.

He worried in a way that he never had before and knew that this was dangerous. But, more dangerous even than this, he began to doubt the extent of his surgical knowledge and his technical skill. He was as close to being afraid as he had ever been in his life, and he began to think of the operation as an ordeal. He was aware that if he did not conquer these feelings they would quickly undermine his ability. So greatly was he troubled by these fears that he spoke about them to Moynihan, who received the confidence with a mocking grin.

"And sure it's fair astonishin' if you've never felt the like before, me lad. If you can get over it, it's somethin' that's right good for a surgeon's soul, but get over it ye must." Then he dropped the Irish talk and said quite seriously, "Go over to the morgue and rehearse the operation, Matt. You've done that other times, haven't you? I'm surprised you didn't think of it yourself. Go this afternoon. I'll see that somebody covers the wards for you."

Before going to the morgue, however, Matthew called at the pathology laboratory, for it seemed to him essential that he have a few words with Edward whether Edward wished to see him or not. He found him sitting at a table with books and notebooks spread out in front of him. His back was toward the door through which Matthew entered, he was wearing his tan laboratory coat, and even though it hung loosely on him it did not conceal how thin he had grown. When Matthew spoke to him he started and got hurriedly to his feet.

"I won't keep you but a minute, Ed. There are just two or three things. First, Moynihan's going to assist."

"Moynihan!"

"He suggested it himself. I'd feel better about having him there. You don't object, do you?"

"You have to have an assistant and you ought to make a pretty good team. I don't mind."

Edward was leaning back against the edge of the table, looking directly at Matthew, but his eyes, Matthew noticed, had the appearance of seeing into some invisible distance, a look he had seen before in the eyes of the sick. And as he felt in his pocket for the list of instructions that Moynihan had given him, he thought again that the sooner this operation was over the better. He gave the list to Edward, explaining its source, and Edward glanced through it quickly. "I'll give this to Cissie," he said.

"Moynihan says either he or I ought to see Cissie and answer any questions she may have."

"That's not really necessary, do you think?" Edward turned as though he wanted to sit down to his work once more.

"Another thing I wanted to ask you, Ed. Can you kill all the microbes in water by boiling?"

"We work on that assumption, yes. Twenty minutes of actual boiling should do it, but it's only an assumption because of the limitations of the microscope. It seems to work, that's all." Edward smiled suddenly. "Have you forgotten already what we learned from Holmes?"

"Mostly, I'm afraid. At the time it didn't seem good for much."

Edward was still smiling, but absent-mindedly, and his eyes had shifted to the table where his work lay.

Matthew said, "Well, then," hesitated, then added, "So long," and went away. Before he reached the door he heard Edward pulling up his chair, and when he glanced back he saw Edward at his work exactly as he had seen him before.

Most of the time a morgue is a quiet place, and there is a quality in the quiet that is both profound and peaceful. Even such noises as may occur do not greatly disturb it. Sounds of a sweeping broom, the clank of a pail or footsteps echoing cannot penetrate deeply. They seem remote and the mind scarcely registers their meaning. Even the occasional autopsy or teaching session that takes place there does not disorder the surrounding calm.

On the afternoon that Matthew, carrying his case of instruments, walked up the ramp and pushed open one of the double doors, he found the place deserted, the morgue orderly absent. He stopped just inside, not wanting to enter a domain not his own without his presence being known, and though he was familiar enough with this place, he looked around him idly. The room was long and lighted by narrow windows high in the walls, and down the center of the floor space were two rows of zinc-top tables, most of them with sheeted figures lying on them. Two of the windows were open, causing stirrings of air that carried odors of disinfectant, soap and a soft, pervading smell that is not the odor of decay but often is the accompaniment of death.

Matthews nerves had begun to accept all this when through a partly open door at the far end of the room the orderly appeared. He saw Matthew at once and, unhurried, came toward him. He was a stooped man in his sixties, placid and a little gone to seed. He had never held any other job than this, and from long association with the dead he had taken on some of their yellowed, waxy look, their calm, and something of the dignity that so impartially invests those who have finished living.

He walked toward Matthew, smiling a little, though more in his mind than in the contours of his face. Through long habit he moved ploddingly, with his short body curved inward, his shoulders forward, as though he pushed an invisible stretcher cart in front of him. He brought his invisible stretcher to rest near Matthew and said, "Good day, Doc."

"Good day, Joel."

"Something I can do for you?"

"Yes. I want to do an op on one of them."

Joel considered this slowly. The request seemed to sadden him, for he sighed. "I hate to see them cut unless it's necessary, Doc."

"It is necessary."

"What kind you want? Man? Woman?"

"Man. Age doesn't matter, but I'd rather have a thin one."

"I got one. Ain't been with me very long. None of 'em stops here very long, you know that, Doc. But just the same, I get to know 'em. I'm their last friend, so to speak. I hate to see 'em cut. You've got to be gentle with the dead. But you're always good to 'em, you always treat 'em right. I think I'll give you Mr. Tenney. Come over this way and I'll show him to you."

Joel sighed again and began to push his invisible stretcher along the aisle between the tables. They stopped about halfway down beside a table that had a sign hanging on it, which read: JOHN TENNEY. 58. PNEUMONIA. NO RELATIVES. UNCLAIMED. Joel pulled back the sheet showing an emaciated man for whom life's struggles had happily ceased. "He all right, sir?"

"Fine," Matthew said.

"Then I'll leave you with him, if you don't mind, Doc."

"I won't need any help."

"That's what I figured." Joel did not seem in any hurry to go away, as though he would like to delay the work or, if he could, prevent it altogether. He laid a hand on one of the body's thin, ridged shanks. "You got to be gentle with the dead, Doc. You got to be gentle with the dead." Then he did go away, slowly pushing his invisible stretcher cart.

Matthew laid his instrument case open on the table. He took off his coat, laid it across the corpse's feet, and rolled up his sleeves. He stood for some minutes deep in thought, but aware with a part of his mind of sparrows twittering outside the open window, and of the quiet in this place. Then he went to work.

CHAPTER FORTY-THREE

On the day before the operation Dr. Moynihan sat on a stool watching Matthew close a long incision. Matthew was working steadily, meticulously, matching layer after layer with the kind of patient care Moynihan insisted on in others but hated to practice himself.

"You're a hell of a good assistant, Matt."

Matthew glanced up and grinned, but he made no comment.

"Damned good. And it's surprising rather, because you're not afraid to do things on your own. You're a responsibility taker and a fine surgeon in your own right."

This time Matthew did not even look up, but he flushed a little at the unusual and most unexpected praise.

"I know I'm a bastard to work for, and tomorrow, when I'm the assistant . . . You know, I'm looking forward to it. A lot. I want to see this new stuff you're so full of, and I want to see how you conduct yourself when it's on your shoulders."

Again Matthew made no reply and Moynihan at last sensed that the talk was not to his liking. He sat in silence for a while, listening to the soft snoring of the patient who was still deeply asleep from the effects of ether, and watching the movements of Matthew's hands. After a moment he laughed softly. "Speaking of assistants, I've had some beauts. Some of them have done things you wouldn't believe. There's the inattentive guy who daydreams, just isn't there, and stops pinching the artery just when you're about to tie the ligature, so the whole cavity you're working in is suddenly a lake of blood."

Matthew laughed. "How about the fellow that jabs around inside the incision with the scissors, trying to cut a suture for you, and nicks a major vein in the process?"

"God, I know him well. And how about the nervous guy who keeps talking to you through the ticklish part. 'Shouldn't we do this? Don't you think we should do that?' I had one like that once, and I . . . well, never mind what I did to him. I'm ashamed of it now. You're not drawing that too tight, are you?"

"No."

"All right. I can't see good from here. One assistant I had used to swoop down into the wound with a sponge, trying to be helpful, just as I got set to do something delicate. Every goddam time he did it, seemed like."

Both men laughed. Matthew picked up a pair of angled scissors, cut his suture and dropped the scissors clattering into the instrument basin. Then he began to pile lint onto his finished work, fastening it in place with a strip of cloth held down with adhesive. "I've met that fellow too," he said. "But how about the guy that leans over to watch you make the incision, and gets so interested he rests his hand on the skin just as you start, pulling it, of course, so the incision ends up a pretty zigzag?"

Both men laughed loudly again and Moynihan said, "The fellow I really can't stand is the one who tries to do the operation for you. I promise you I won't do that tomorrow. You through? Good."

A few minutes later they were walking down the corridor together, Moynihan's hand on Matthew's shoulder. "I'll pick you up in the rig tomorrow at ten, Matt."

"No need. I can walk easily."

"No, I'll stop for you. I'll have to teach you how to do house work in style. It inspires confidence in the patient's family. I sort of gather these friends of yours are carriage trade. You're bringing your own instruments, aren't you?"

"Yes."

"As I told you, I'll bring the rest of the stuff. My assistant keeps it packed up, but I'll check it over myself this time, so don't worry. The anesthetist's a nice kid. He can get there under his own power. So can the nurse. I know you don't want her during the operation, but I told her to be at the house same time as us anyway. Anything else?"

"I think we've covered everything."

"All right. Just don't forget the carbolic!"

Their laughter rang out in that grim place and Moynihan caught in the sound of Matthew's a note of strain. He gripped the shoulder on which his hand was resting. "Don't worry, Matt. You'll do all right. You'll do fine."

At ten o'clock the next day Matthew was waiting in front of the main building when a closed carriage, driven by a coachman with a cockade in his silk hat, drew up near him. The carriage glowed with polish, the horse was a beautiful bay, and the harness mountings were well-polished silver. Matthew was admiring all this when he realized that Moynihan was inside, beckoning to him through the door he was holding open. Grinning, he went forward. "You really do do it in style," he said, getting in and turning in his seat to survey an unfamiliar Moynihan in a Prince Albert and a tall hat.

"Good for business. You'll be doing it yourself in a couple of years. Matt, I never got around to asking you: Where are you going to practice when you're through here?"

Matthew half perceived that this question was intended

to divert his mind from the coming ordeal, and he was grateful for it. "I don't know," he said. "Here in New York maybe, or maybe in Boston. I just don't know."

"You still think you'll stay on another year as senior house man?"

"Yes, if I can afford it. I'll never get so much experience as here."

"My outside assistant will be setting up for himself by that time. It's something to think about, Matt."

"You bet it is!"

They talked about this for a few minutes more as the horse clattered over the cobblestones, and then they were in front of the house, stepping out onto the carriage block, and Matthew was saying, "Let me carry that bag, sir."

"I'm your assistant, remember?"

"Not till we get inside!"

Cissie was in the hall to greet them, Cissie in a dark blue dress that had long sleeves and a narrow white collar and cuffs. It made her look like a matron of some institution. Matthew could see strain and anxiety in her face but also the determination to bear herself well, and some antic action of his mind produced for him a picture of Cissie long ago, holding a lamp while he bent over the bed of her sick child. He vaguely wished that he had told Moynihan the story of that night. Then he remembered that he must introduce Moynihan and performed that ceremony. Cissie responded with an old-fashioned curtsy, then flushed as though she had not intended to do this and gave Moynihan her hand.

Over her shoulder Matthew saw, farther back in the hall, a nondescript young man was sitting on an uncomfortable chair with a bag at his feet. He rose and stood there as though waiting for orders, and Matthew assumed he was the anesthetist. Moynihan, expanded and magnificent in his formal clothing, was exhibiting to Cissie the full force of his personality, being at the same time the enormously reassuring doctor and the charming Irishman. It was, Matthew saw, a performance of note that half amused, half annoyed him to watch. Overwhelmed by it, Cissie appeared little and lost. In pity he intervened.

"What room do you want us to use, Cissie?"

She gave him a look of gratitude for her rescue. "Upstairs. It's next to the room that Edward will be in after . . . I thought, not so far to carry—"

"Good. Let's see it. The nurse is here, I suppose?"

"In the kitchen, I think."

They went in procession up the stairs to the bedroom floor, Cissie in the lead and the young man with the black bag bringing up the rear. The room was at the front of the house with sunlight coming through the windows.

"Excellent!" Moynihan said, but it was at Matthew that Cissie looked.

"It's fine, Cissie." His quick glance took in the table, the instrument table, all the items on the list set out with obvious care.

"I had the maids give it a last careful dusting just an hour ago."

"You shouldn't have done that." Matthew glanced up toward the ceiling as though he could see disturbed dust contaminating the air.

"Why not? Oh, Matthew, did we do something wrong?"

"It's all right, Cissie." He smiled at her and saw her gray eyes wide and full of trouble. "How about Ed? Is he resting?"

"Yes. He's worried, Matt. He wouldn't say so but I know because he's cross."

"Show me where his room is, but I won't disturb him just yet."

They went out into the hall and he was careful to shut the door behind him. She pointed. "It's there at the back."

"All right. We'll need the hot water now."

"I told them in the kitchen to bring it up as soon as it's ready. Perhaps I'd better go and see if I can hurry them."

She started to turn away and he laid a hand on her arm to stop her. "Wait a moment, Cissie. Will you tell the nurse I want her to sit out here in the hall while the operation is going on, in case something is needed?"

"I'll do it myself."

"No, I don't want you to. I don't want you anywhere near, Cissie. Where are the children?"

"I sent them out with Sue's nurse to have a picnic in the park."

"Good. Now another thing. I'm going to keep this door closed, and after the maids have brought the water I don't want anybody to open it for any reason at all."

"I'll tell them, Matt."

"And now about you."

He did not know that his manner was no longer brusque or that, as he spoke, the expression of his face greatly changed. He took her hands and saw that there were tears in her eyes. He said "Cissie" softly, and she lowered her head so he could no longer see the tears. She did not move, but she seemed to him to have come nearer to him so that he felt her to be in mind and heart very close to him. He did not speak until the shared moment could be prolonged no longer. He gave her hands a slight pressure and released them.

She said, "I'm going to Edward now."

"That's right. But when we begin I don't want you anywhere near this room, Cissie. We may be at it quite a while. I wish you would leave the house, go out and get some air."

"I couldn't do that, Matthew."

"Then find something to occupy your mind. I don't want you sick too."

"I'll be all right."

"I think you will. Try not to worry."

She started to move away, her head bent, and he thought that she was weeping. Then she turned back to him and he saw her eyes were dry, but deep and almost black with trouble.

"He wants so much to live, Matthew."

"He will."

Matthew just touched her shoulder and she went away down the hall toward Edward's room. With his hand on the knob of the door beside him he watched her until, without looking back, she went inside and closed the door behind her. Then he went back into the temporary operating room where he found Moynihan laying out instruments, some of Matthew's, some of his own.

"I'm putting them in the order you'll need them, but you know, I've clean forgotten what a lot of damn stupid drudgery goes with an assistant's job."

"You're wasting your time. All those have to be soaked in carbolic solution."

"By God, so they do. I'm too old a dog for these fancy tricks."

There was a knock on the door and when Matthew opened it he saw two maids, their starched aprons over their blue-and-white uniforms a little wilted, their faces red from the long climb up the stairs. Each had brought two ironstone pitchers that were now standing on the floor, vapor rising from them.

"Where would you like these put, sir?"

"Just inside here on the floor." Hard work, he thought, and wondered if they felt recompensed by the excitement of having an operation in the house. Perhaps so, for as each straightened herself after setting down the pitchers she gave a quick, avid glance toward the operating table before leaving the room.

Matthew brought one of the pitchers to the table where Moynihan had laid out the instruments and poured some of it into an enamel basin. Then he went to the bag he had brought with him, opened it and took out a large packet on which was written "Carbolic Crystals." He opened one corner of it and a stream of crystals rustled into the basin. The anesthetist, whose presence Matthew had wholly forgotten, rose from where he had been sitting in the corner of the room, came over to the table and peered into the basin as though he expected to see some active magic there. Seeing nothing, he went silently back to his corner and sat down.

Moynihan too was watching, with an alert, quizzical expression on his face. A strong smell of carbolic rose from the basin and he backed away. Matthew began gathering up the instruments and laying them carefully in the basin, the ends of his fingers growing red from the heat of the water.

"How do you know how much of that stuff to use?"

"I don't. I have to guess. Lister uses a twenty-percent solution in a wound, and I've got some measured out in a jar in my bag. I figure this should be quite a bit stronger, so I just dumped a lot in. And I don't know whether it kills microbes instantly, or whether it takes a long time, and if so, how long. Christ, I wish I did know. It's all guessing. All of it."

"You should get your friend to do some work with his microscope when he gets better and see if he could find out a few things."

"I intend to. I'll let these soak until we're ready to use them, and hope that's long enough."

Matthew finished laying the instruments in the basin, took up a piece of rag, dropped it in too and poked at it with his finger.

Moynihan said, "What are you doing now?"

"I'm going to wipe off everything we're likely to touch."

Moynihan, losing interest, wandered away, his hands in his pockets, talking over his shoulder. "You realize, don't you, that all this folderol takes a lot of time? It's all right under conditions like this, I suppose, if you really believe it does any good. But you'd never in the world have time for it in a busy hospital schedule. It would alter the whole procedure so much you'd have to have a new sort of organization in the op room."

Matthew was wiping off the handles of the pitchers, their rims, and various articles he took out of his bag, dipping his rag again and again. "If it succeeds it will be worth all the time it takes."

"You're not going to prove anything by this one operation, you know."

"I realize that. But if it does succeed you'd feel like trying it again, wouldn't you?"

"I want to see this thing through before I answer that, but I can tell you right now that I very much doubt it."

Matthew had a sponge in his hand, feeling it. He found a fragment of shell hidden in its depths, worked it loose and dropped it into the slop jar. The sponge he put into another basin and added the twenty-percent solution of carbolic. Then he stood there beside the instrument table, thinking deeply. Moynihan, aware of the silence and a feeling of tension, turned around and came back to the table.

"What now?"

Matthew did not answer at once; then he spoke slowly, as though he found the words hard to say. "I guess we can get Ed in here now."

To Moynihan's observing eye Matthew seemed suddenly to have become young and unsure. He said, "You through with all the fancy scrubbing, are you?" but the tone of his voice said something quite different. Hearing the unexpressed reassurance, the affection, the affirmation of confidence, Matthew looked at him and smiled, and answered on the level on which Moynihan had spoken.

"No, not quite, but it's going to take a little time to put him under and we can be finishing it then."

"Seeing he's a doctor himself, don't you guess we might work with our coats off? I wouldn't do it in a private house ordinarily. Gives a bad impression."

"Sure. It will be all right."

They took their coats off, laid them on a window seat, and rolled up their shirt sleeves, Matthew pushing his high above his elbows as was his custom. He could see the anesthetist wondering if he might take his coat off also, and deciding not to.

Moynihan said, "You want me to get him and bring him in?"

"I better do it. Christ, I wish all this were behind us."

"You're having your worst moment now, Matt. Go along and don't think about it any more."

When Matthew knocked on the door, Edward called

out, "Come in," his voice so familiar that for an instant Matthew's thoughts were complicated by the sensation of the past being the present and the real present having no reality. Edward, in robe and slippers, was sitting in an armchair with a pillow at his back, and Matthew's mind, erratic as the mind sometimes is under stress, noted that his dark hair, which was standing up in wisps at the back, looked thin and lifeless. The sight touched him. Cissie was sitting on the edge of the bed and he had the impression that at his knock she had straightened her back into rigidity.

"All ready?" Edward said, and rose as though with alacrity.

"All ready."

Matthew held the door for them to precede him. Edward, walking swiftly but shuffling a little, went straight to the door of the operating room and, without turning his head, opened it and went through. Cissie had stopped by the head of the stairs and was hesitating there. Matthew turned back to her. "I'll see you in a little while." She managed to smile and he gave her a smile in return, a little firmer but of the same substance as her own.

CHAPTER FORTY-FOUR

Matthew, after speaking with Cissie, returned to the operating room to find Edward arranging himself on the table in the middle of the room.

He put a hand on Edward's shoulder. "All right, Ed?"

"Sure. This place stinks of carbolic. I could smell it way back in my room." He smiled, and Matthew and Moynihan laughed loudly as though Edward had said something very funny indeed.

Moynihan was holding a folded sheet and Matthew helped him spread it over Edward. The anesthetist, having arranged a chair for his paraphernalia, was trying another for himself, and looking discontented because it was too low. Matthew, watching him, realized that he had not so far spoken one word, nor did he break his silence when

Matthew asked if he was ready. Instead he gave Matthew a look, and an eloquent one, that said his work had now begun, that he was quite equal to it, and that he preferred to be left alone to do it in his own way. Matthew received this look with a touch of indignation, Moynihan with a slight smile of amusement.

The room had become very still, the atmosphere suddenly businesslike, with the anesthetist's activities the focal point; Matthew and Moynihan were merely waiting. He put his hands on either side of Edward's head, long, thin hands with curling black hairs on their backs that seemed to have more personality than he himself. He moved Edward's head this way and that, adjusting it to suit him, settled it, and then tipped it back. Edward suffered this with closed eyes. The young man bent over him and said in a low voice, as though this were a matter only between themselves, "Are you all right?" Matthew saw the stretched muscles of Edward's throat move with his reply, but he could not hear the words. Then the ether cone was in the young man's hands and he was saying, "I'm going to put this over your nose. You must just breathe naturally."

Edward moved a little, a slight gesture of impatience. "I've given a lot of anesthetics myself."

"Just breathe naturally." The young man started dripping ether out of a can.

The next few moments were silent. The smell of ether was at first only noticeable, then all at once very strong. Street noises came into the room from the remote world outside, the sounds of children playing, the rattling of iron-rimmed cart wheels muffled by the bed of straw, and a knife grinder's bell. Matthew and Moynihan, at opposite sides of the table, stood motionless.

Abruptly, Edward stirred, attempted to turn his head, moved his hand under the sheet and said something loud and unintelligible. Moynihan put his hand over Edward's and held it down. The young man rose and bent over him, expertly holding the mask in place with his long fingers and clamping Edward's head with the heels of his hands.

After that there was no more motion. The young man remained standing, attentive now, and giving the impression of being alone with his patient. Silence, and for Matthew an oddly acute sense of time's passing. Then Moynihan said, speaking in a low tone that was nevertheless startling, "He's going under easy."

The young man shifted his weight from one foot to the other. "Too easy," he said. "There's no fight in him."

Moynihan went quickly to the head of the table and looked down at Edward. Then he slid his hand under the sheet, found Edward's pulse and held it a moment.

"Thin and rapid, Matt. When we get going we better not waste any time."

"All right. We'll finish up the prep so we can start soon as he's ready." He went to the instrument table, took a clean towel off the pile of folded ones, spread it out, began to take instruments out of the basin and to lay them on the towel. Moynihan watched him for a moment, then he said, "Hey, aren't you doing something wrong?"

"How so?"

"I know your own idea is that the germs in the air fall on the instruments, and you ought to get rid of them before they get into the wound, not afterwards. But then you lay the instruments down on a towel that for all you know is covered with them."

"It's a clean towel, for Christ sake."

"So were the instruments clean when you took them out of the case."

Matthew thought a moment, then he gathered up the instruments and put them back in the basin. He bunched up the towel and put it on top of them.

"You think you've thought of everything. You go over the whole operation in your mind. You think you've thought of every single precaution that should be taken. And then I miss a thing like that! Christ, what a fool I am!"

"You don't really know that it makes any difference. I don't believe for a moment that it does. And if I've got all this right, you're doing a lot of fancy things Lister probably never dreamed of. Don't forget some people have lived through this type of operation without benefit of any of this damn nonsense."

"Let's get our hands scrubbed."

Matthew took a brush, scooped up some green soap with it, rubbed it over his hands back and front, and handed the brush to Moynihan. After that he soaked his hands in carbolic solution and Moynihan, smiling with good-natured amusement, followed this ritual faithfully. With both hands immersed to soak in the solution, he said, "How long do we do this?"

"A minute, I should think."

"I feel like a goddam fool."

The anesthetist, addressing himself to Moynihan, said, "Patient's ready, sir." Moynihan took his hands out of the basin, started to reach for a towel, checked himself and smiled. "You're right. This is the damnedest thing to learn." He shook drops of solution off his hands. "You think it's only memorizing a few tricks, but it isn't. It's a whole new way of thought." Still smiling, he took his place at the assistant's side of the table.

The sheet still covered Edward to the base of his neck, and Matthew, his hands dripping, was looking down at it as though he were facing a dilemma. After a moment's thought he bent over, hooked his elbow under the top edge of the sheet and pushed it down without letting it come in contact with his hands. The anesthetist watched this with an expression of disdain.

Moynihan said, "You're certainly carrying this business a lot farther than Lister intended."

"That may be so. In fact I'm sure I am. But once you get it in your head that the air is full of germs you get to thinking they're on everything, and you don't know where to stop."

The room was filled with ether fumes and the smell of carbolic. Edward had begun to snore gently. The anesthetist struggled against a sneeze and then exploded loudly. Moynihan said, "One sure thing, we're all going to smell like polecats," and handed Matthew a scalpel. Matthew took it and with the handle he tapped the abdomen here and there, and found that the muscles were well relaxed.

"I'm going to work fast and tie off as much as I can as I go—arrest bleeding as it occurs."

"You can't have it both ways."

"I'll do my best. I want as dry a field as I can get."

They said no more. With the point of the scalpel Matthew marked on the skin where the incision would begin and end. Then he made several light scratches at intervals, and at right angles to the line the incision would follow, to be used later as a guide in closing the wound. When Moynihan saw them he smiled, for it meant that Matthew, not expecting pus to form, intended to close the wound tightly, and even for a tight closing no surgeon in a charity hospital bothered about such niceties of technique.

This done, Moynihan gave Matthew a small carbolic-soaked pad, which Matthew took in his left hand. He laid it on the skin, pulled upward to make the skin taut, and began the incision. As the incision lengthened he moved the pad, the tightness of the skin making it possible to cut

395

the incision straight and shallow. He worked swiftly, the red line appearing on the flesh as though by a magic unconnected with the knife.

The outer skin was strong and tough enough to dull the fine edge of a scalpel. Moynihan was already holding out another. This time the scalpel would go deeper, sweeping downward.

The problem now was blood flow, and Matthew began tying off the bleeding vessels as he came to them. Moynihan, helping with this, was showing a quizzical interest. For the sake of speed, in which he was a firm believer, he would not have tied off small vessels separately as Matthew was now doing, but would have shut off the larger vessels that supplied their blood. This did some damage, not only to the vessels but to the tissues, by depriving them of their blood supply, but it could be done in a fraction of the time. He knew that Matthew believed in the new theory that the careful preservation of tissues and their blood supply was more important than speed, but Matthew had never before carried out his theories when Moynihan was there to see, and it was almost too much for his self-restraint. Twice he started to speak, checked himself, sighed, and shuffled his feet in restless impatience.

Finally he could stand it no longer. "Matt, what the hell do you think you're—"

Matthew glanced up and grinned.

Moynihan said, "Excuse me. Forget it." He sounded half sullen, half amused.

After that the room grew very still, the only sounds being the gentle ether snore and an occasional click of an instrument. Both men were working smoothly now, their movements perfectly synchronized, both responding instinctively to the demands of the open wound.

Matthew worked with easy, fluid motions that occasionally approached the rhythmical. He did not look up and there was no necessity, for the instrument he needed was always held out to him, the used instrument taken away so smoothly as not to change in the slightest the pace of the work. Matthew seemed aware only of what he was doing, but this was not the case, for his mind was also keeping track of the action of the anesthesia. Moynihan too had this in mind, and he occasionally glanced at the head of the table where the silent young man, absorbed in his work, seemed to be guiding his patient in his unconsciousness.

The next step would be the fussy work of controlling

the bleeding in the fat layer, but Matthew had only begun to open this layer when Moynihan said sharply, "Here, hold up a minute. I don't like the look of this." He held the incision open and examined the fat. "Too yellow and too thin. That's always bad news, Matt."

Matthew looked at him with a worried frown, but he went back to work again without saying anything. He began to move faster, padding the sides of the wound with cloth soaked in salt and carbolic solution to keep them from drying out. Moynihan, approving this, relaxed a little, but he had a troubled look. The pads in place, Matthew straightened up and moved his cramped shoulders, for he was beginning to feel the strain of bending over the low table. Moynihan used the brief interval to rearrange some instruments, and when Matthew was ready to work again Moynihan was holding out a scalpel.

The work went on, through the muscle layer beneath the fascia. More blood vessels were ligated with fine carbolic-soaked thread. The deepest fascial layer now lay exposed, and below it the peritoneum, the membrane that is both cover and protection for the viscera, which many surgeons believed should never be opened.

They were working closely together again with an understanding of the problem that made words unnecessary. Both had toothed forceps in their hands and they used them to lift a small section of the fascial layer and membrane away from the tissue beneath. In this lifted, tent-shaped section Matthew made a small cut. Scissors replaced the scalpel in his right hand so swiftly that light flashed from them, and he nodded his head in acknowledgment of the perfect support Moynihan was giving him. He slipped one blade of the scissors into the opening and, blunt point angled upward in order not to damage what lay beneath, he enlarged the opening enough to slide two fingers inside. Another flash of reflected light and the scalpel replaced the scissors.

He used his spread fingers as a channel to enlarge the opening still further. Yellowish fluid was flowing out of the abdominal cavity. He pulled his fingers out and waited while Moynihan, with a rubber-bulb suction, removed most of it. Then he finished the incision and handed the scalpel back to Moynihan.

"That's it. We're in. I hope the band won't be hard to find. Give me a rag, will you? My hands are sweaty."

He stepped back from the table, wiping his hands with the carbolic-soaked rag. He did it carefully, back and front and between the fingers, all the time thinking deeply, and Moynihan watched him. He looked up to find Moynihan's eyes on him and he smiled slightly in self-disparagement and handed the rag back to Moynihan. "Well, here goes." He stepped close to the table again and carefully slipped his hand into the incision. He felt among the yielding intestines carefully, first to the right where, in his examination, he had felt a distention of the abdomen, then moved his fingers gradually to the left, then lower down. Frowning, he withdrew his hand.

"I can't find a thing, Mike, but it's got to be there. You have a try."

Moynihan slipped his hand in and, a little more boldly, a little less gently, he made his exploration. The soft intestines moved and slipped away under his touch. With his fingers high under the transverse colon, he hesitated, concentrating his attention. Then he withdrew his hand and looked at Matthew.

"I'm afraid we've got trouble here, Matt."

"Not a band? Something else?"

"You better enlarge the incision and we'll have a look."

Matthew went to work swiftly and silently, a worried frown again marking his forehead. When he had carried the incision downward, Moynihan slipped a retractor in the wound on his side to hold it open, and Matthew pulled back on his side with his fingers. Blood seeping into the wound obscured what was there to see. Moynihan took up a sponge, squeezed it out, and cleaned the inside of the cavity. They could both see plainly then the irregular gray mass of the cancer. It was pressing up against the transverse colon from below, on the left side, hard, restrictive, forcing the bowel to the right to dilate well beyond its normal size.

They both looked at the evil growth in silence. Then Moynihan said, "There was always this possibility, Matt. I was sure we'd find it when I saw the color of the fat." Matthew nodded but made no other reply. The anesthetist, guessing that something was wrong, got up from his stool and came around the table to see. Matthew gave him so angry a stare that he retreated.

Blood was seeping back into the wound, partly covering the growth. Moynihan again sponged the cavity dry. Then he picked up a forceps and with the tip touched the hard mass of cancer here and there. After a moment he held the forceps out to Matthew. "Look for yourself."

Matthew's examination was a careful one. Laying the

forceps aside, he felt with his finger around the growth, feeling for its attachments. He let Moynihan sponge the wound again, and again examined the wall of the bowel and the surrounding tissues.

Finally Moynihan stopped him. "It's gone too far for us to do anything, Matt."

"We could take out as much as we could."

"We couldn't take out enough to make any real difference. It's grown right into the artery wall and the wall of the bowel."

Matthew did not reply, but he made no further examination of the growth. He seemed dazed and shaken, and Moynihan said, "Do you want me to close?"

Matthew shook his head and at once began the long task of closing the wound, working swiftly, but neglecting no smallest detail. Toward the end, but without pausing in the rapid work, he said, "I'd like him to have a quarter grain of morphia before he's quite out of ether," and Moynihan left the table to get a hypodermic syringe out of his bag. When he returned, Matthew had finished the closing and was covering the incision with dressings soaked in carbolic solution. Over these he laid a long strip of tin. The bright gleam of the metal catching Moynihan's eye, he came close to watch. "What's that for, Matt?"

"Prevents the carbolic drying out. Hand me the adhesive, will you?"

Moynihan handed the adhesive and scissors across the table. Then he went to the head of the table where the anesthetist was sitting idle, watching Edward's breathing with a look of satisfaction. Edward had ceased to snore and his breaths were coming naturally, but he was very pale and he had the look about him of having withdrawn himself to a distant, secret place that is the accompaniment of deep anesthesia.

The atmosphere of the room had changed again. In spite of the tragic discovery they had made, tension was easing, as was necessary and inevitable. There was a feeling, if not of a return to normal, at least of the inescapability of presently making such a return. They were all three a long way toward succumbing to the irresistible force of the everyday.

To the anesthetist Moynihan said, "Have a look down the hall, will you, and see if the nurse has the bed ready. And leave the doors open when you come back so we can carry him through. Send anybody but the nurse away. Then come back and give us a hand with him. Not that he's so heavy . . ." And then to Matthew, "He's so far under I'm going to wait a bit for the hypo."

They carried Edward to his own bed, using the sheet under him for a stretcher, and returned to the room where the operation had taken place. Matthew went to a window and stood there, staring out but seeing nothing, his silence, the attitude of his hunched shoulders, making a barrier against any encroachment. Moynihan, understanding this, made no attempt to speak to him, but he stood at a little distance, silent and concerned, waiting for the moment when Matthew would find that he must come out of his solitude. The anesthetist was moving about, packing up his paraphernalia, getting himself ready to depart. He was not long about this business. He snapped shut the catches of his bag, first one and then the other, the sharp sounds making Moynihan wince. After that he did not so much leave as vanish.

Matthew continued to stand with his back to the room and Moynihan to watch him. After a time he said, as though it were a thing he had been turning over in his mind, "Do you want me to tell her, Matt?"

Matthew said nothing but laid his head on his bent arm against the window casing. Another interval of silence passed and Moynihan said in a different tone, "I'll go and see how things are coming along down the hall."

When he came back he found that Matthew had put his coat on and was wiping instruments and putting them in their cases. He looked at Moynihan questioningly. He seemed exhausted, the spark of his vitality, which Moynihan had never seen fail, all but extinguished.

His thoughts on these things, Moynihan said, "He came through it surprisingly well, as far as I can tell while he's still asleep. If you want to look yourself, I'll finish up here."

"I want to see her."

Matthew abandoned the instruments and went out of the room. He found Cissie alone in the living room, sitting in the corner of the sofa. She rose at once when she saw Matthew and went to him. Her motions, usually so graceful, were sudden and jerky, her eyes fever-bright, and he knew by these signs that during her long, solitary wait she had worked herself into an excited state of extreme nervous anxiety.

"How is he, Matthew? Matthew, is he all right?"

"He's still sleeping, Cissie."

"But he's all right, isn't he? You're sure he's all right?"

He could not tell her. "Yes," he said, and suddenly felt his eyes smart with tears. To hide them, he walked away from her. She followed him quickly, too anxious for the answers to her questions to see that he was suffering.

"But it's all over, isn't it? And he's got through it all right? Oh, Matthew." She held out her hands to him and he took them. "I knew you'd do it, only I've been so afraid."

Tears were running down her cheeks and she was groping for a handkerchief. He gave her his and she leaned against him, weeping, while he held her. After a moment, when it seemed to him that her tears had eased her a little, he said, "Come and sit down, Cissie," and he led her to the sofa.

He sat beside her and she clung to him. "I've been so terribly afraid. If anything had happened to him . . . Matthew, I've not been a good wife to him."

"I don't believe that, Cissie, and I know he doesn't think so."

"It's true. I've tried. I've really tried. I've done the best I can, but there's something he wants that I can't give him. And he knows I can't and it hurts him so. Matthew, he's so alone."

"Don't think of it now, Cissie."

"I must. I've been sitting here waiting and thinking. This has made me see it all so clearly. He's so *alone*, Matthew."

"We're all alone, I'm afraid."

"But not the way he is—alone where nobody can reach him. And he wants terribly not to be, but he's so proud. . . . It's taken this to make me understand, but now I do, and I'm going to do better now. Oh Matthew, I'm very, very glad he's all right. I've been afraid he might not get through this—he's so frail—and that I might never have a chance. Now I can, and, Matthew, I'm going to. I'm going to be so good to him and try so hard to reach him."

"Hush now, Cissie. You've had a long strain and this has been hard on you."

"But I *must* tell you, Matthew, I *must*." He was holding her hands again and she was gripping his with all her strength. He felt her arms trembling. "I'm so *glad*. I'm so glad, and I'm so grateful to you. Now I have another chance—"

"Cissie, you must try to be quiet now." She was near hysteria and he was frightened for her. "Cissie, you must be quiet. I know it's been hard." But she broke down once more into stormy weeping and he held her against him. He held her close, bending over her and stroking her hair, and little by little he felt the tension leaving her. When the tears stopped, he found his damp handkerchief for her, and when she made an effort to sit up, he released her.

She sat up and gave him her hands again, and he held them between his own.

"Matthew, it wasn't fair to him to marry him without loving him. But I'm going to do my best by him from now on. You understand, don't you?"

"Yes, Cissie, I understand." He sighed, wondering how he could relieve the tension in her that was building up again, driving her to say these things. She hurried on.

"You've given me a new chance, Matthew, and I'm so grateful to you."

He made a wordless, unhappy sound and released her hands, turning away from her.

Not noticing, she began to smooth her hair and straighten her dress, and when she had done this she said, "Can I go and see him now, Matthew?"

She spoke with an eager anxiety that was harder for him to bear than her weeping. He put his hands to his face and rubbed it; then he let them hang between his knees, conscious of his fatigue and of his heavy burden. A little of what he was feeling reached her, for she put her hand on his knee. He covered it with his own. Then he heard her last question echo in his mind, and he answered her, but without letting her see his face.

"You oughtn't to see him yet, Cissie. I'm going up there myself in a minute, and I'll tell the nurse to let you know when he's out of the ether enough to know what's going on."

She made no objection to this and he went away, climbing the stairs slowly, his steps heavy with reluctance for he did not want to meet Edward's conscious eyes.

When he came down again she was waiting for him in the hall. Her normal composure had almost returned and he felt at once that it put a distance between them; and though he knew that this was inevitable and necessary, it distressed him. She came quickly to meet him at the bottom of the stairs.

"How is he?"

"He's coming around. I told the nurse to call you when it's all right to see him, though it will be a while yet, so you should try to rest. But, Cissie, when you do see him
402

you must remember that he's been through an ordeal and that he's very ill indeed."

"I'll remember." Suddenly she smiled and held out her hand to him. "Thank you, Matthew. And please thank Dr. Moynihan too."

Matthew took her hand and let it go. He bowed his head, said a quick good-bye, and let himself out of the front door. He found Moynihan waiting in the carriage with the two bags at his feet. He got in and sat down without a word. When they had driven a block or two Moynihan said, "Did you tell her what we found?" Matthew shook his head and bending forward covered his face with his hands. After a moment Moynihan laid a hand gently on his shoulder.

CHAPTER FORTY-FIVE

Matthew saw Edward once before the night he died. Moynihan had taken on the duty of the house visits because Matthew was not free to leave the hospital, but when Matthew spoke to him he said, "Go ahead, Matt. You ought to. I'll see you're covered here and say I sent you if there are any questions asked."

"Thanks, Mike."

"But there's this. I haven't told them yet what we found. Your friend's been too sick to talk about it, though I have an idea he suspects, and Mrs. Chisolm . . . she's planning the future around him. Going to make herself the perfect wife from now on. I couldn't tell her she won't have the chance. I'm a coward maybe. I've been leaving it for you to do."

Matthew went on the afternoon of the second day following the operation, a fine, sunlit day with a breeze blowing off the East River and birds chirping in the trees, though in his present mood of sadness he felt remote from all such things. He walked from the hospital and when he came to the street where Edward and Cissie lived in their fine house, he found a wooden barrier partly cutting off its entrance. On the barrier had been chalked in crude letters: ILLNESS IN THIS BLOCK. QUIET, PLEASE.

Beyond the barrier the center of the street for its full length had been covered deeply with straw. And as he walked on the sidewalk beside it he thought how useless are most of our efforts on behalf of the dying, their real purpose being to solace ourselves, analgesics for our sense of inadequacy, soporifics for our guilt. A bird flew down to the ground in front of him, captured a piece of straw and flew away with it. A dog came from around the side of a house and gave him a friendly tail wag. Suddenly he was acutely, passionately aware of being alive.

When he reached the house he was told that Cissie had gone out for a short walk with the children, so he made his way upstairs alone. The nurse was with Edward but she rose and went away when Matthew came in and he took the chair near the bed in which she had been sitting. Edward's eyes were deep and soft from the opiates he had been given. He looked frail and exhausted, but Matthew's presence gave him obvious pleasure.

"How are you, Ed?"

"Well enough. Pain of course."

Matthew did most of the talking, and after a while Edward seemed to doze. Matthew sat on, lost in half-formed thoughts that moved through his mind in a slow procession, heavy with care. When, at the end of some minutes, he looked up, he found that Edward's eyes were on him, and with the feeling that he had been watched for some time, he smiled slightly. Edward responded with a ghost of his own old sardonic smile, no more than a momentary involvement of the features with an emotion so fleeting as scarcely to register at all.

"It wasn't a band, was it, Matt?"

Matthew felt his own body's prickling reaction to the shock of the question. With care he held himself perfectly still, taking time to consider. Then, without emphasis or any betrayal of emotion, he shook his head.

Edward shut his eyes and lay so still that he might have been sleeping. Then abruptly he gathered strength, or will, so that Matthew for an instant saw again and recognized the familiar nervous force.

"Where was it?"

"Under the transverse colon, just left of center."

There was another pause during which Edward seemed to drift away into a private place. Watching him, it came to Matthew that he was not unhappy there, that he did not want to be recalled. This realization soothed Matthew and to a slight extent he was comforted. In a moment Edward returned, sharply, decisively, and spoke in a strong voice.

"You weren't able to get any of it out, I suppose?"

"It had pretty well spread itself around."

"Does Cissie know?"

"I couldn't bring myself to tell her, Ed, and Moynihan hasn't."

"I'm glad of that."

Matthew, watching, could see Edward starting to drift away again and then with an effort bring himself back.

"Cissie," he said. Then, after a pause, "We weren't right for each other, Matt. It was partly my fault. I'm hard to live with—you know that. She did her best."

"I'm sure she did."

"I want to make sure you understand about her. She did her best, but she has a sense of guilt because we were never as close as we should have been. She has some ideal in her mind—she failed to realize it, and she's certain the fault is hers. Whatever happens in the future, Matt, I want you to help her over that."

"I'll do whatever I can, Ed."

"I feel sure you will. She'll be safe with you."

For a moment Edward appeared to be thinking. Then he turned his head toward Matthew and smiled. The smile was soft and bright and for Matthew nearly heartbreaking. A hand came out from under the covers and it seemed to Matthew that the long, thin fingers were about to reach for his touch. He half rose from his chair and the hand was withdrawn, quickly, as though to indicate that a show of emotion was reprehensible. Then Edward closed his eyes and Matthew watched, not the emaciated face but the scenes in his own memory. Edward's breathing grew easy and regular and after a time he seemed to be sleeping. Matthew waited until he felt sure of this, and then he went away.

Two nights later Matthew himself was asleep in his narrow bed at the hospital when he was awakened by one of the night orderlies who gave him a note that, he said, had just been delivered at the hospital. Matthew took the note to the door of his room to read by the light of the gas jet in the hall. There was only one line of hurried writing: "Please come as quickly as you can," and the scribbled signature below, "Cissie."

He dressed hurriedly, paused a moment to think, stuffed a stethoscope in his pocket, and ran down the dimly lighted stairs. As he walked rapidly through the empty, echoing lobby he glanced up at the wall clock and saw that it was two-thirty in the morning. Going outside was like stepping into another element, for the night was dark and thick with fog. By the blurred yellow light on top of the lamppost he saw the bulk of a hansom and smelled the rich stable odor of the horse. To his surprise, his name was called, and he saw dimly that the cabby was leaning toward him. So she had thought of this!

The sound of the wheels on the cobbles seemed to him loud as thunder in the stillness of the night, and the hansom rolled on without a break until they were stopped by the barricade at the end of the street. A red lantern had been hung there but the street was not fully closed off. "Drive round," Matthew called out, sitting forward on his seat, and now as they moved slowly through the straw the sound was a dry rustling like fall wind in dead leaves. A frightened maid was waiting to let Matthew in, her face and dress grotesquely speckled with colored light from the lantern overhead. Matthew ran quickly up the stairs.

Cissie, in a loose gray robe, was sitting on a chair drawn close to the bed, one hand resting on the counterpane close to Edward's hand. She turned her head when Matthew entered and he saw her anxious, frightened eyes.

"Matthew, he's breathing so strangely."

He went to stand beside her, looking down on Edward, who lay far beyond consciousness, peaceful and still. As Matthew watched him he drew a long, sighing breath, then for a long, long moment drew no breath at all. Another sighing breath lifted the counterpane over his chest and then again the too-long pause. Matthew put his hand on Cissie's shoulder and she looked up at him. All at once she understood and he saw it in her eyes and felt astonishment that she had not guessed before. Then she wept, her head on the counterpane, her hand covering Edward's, while Edward, undisturbed, beyond their reach, rested on.

Time moved slowly. She ceased to weep and stayed as she was, her cheek against Edward's hand. After a while Matthew took out his stethoscope, bent over the bed, and for a few minutes he was active. Afterward he went to Cissie and again put his hand on her shoulder. She raised herself and looked at him. Then she covered her face with her hands. *"No,"* she cried. *"No. Oh no."*

He took her hand. Her eyes were wide and dark, but he thought she saw nothing, nor did she seem aware of his touch. He led her out of the room. She went with him obediently, but he knew she was far from him, beyond thought or feeling. At the top of the stairs he held her arm for fear she might stumble, and guided her slowly down. She moved beside him, docile and remote.

He made no effort to recall her. Let her numbed mind and emotions rest, postpone their awakening as long as possible. He could put aside his own grief for her sake, but his heart was so sore that he felt he could not bear to see another person suffer.

He steered her carefully through the doorway into the living room and to the corner of the sofa which he thought was her accustomed place. But when he attempted gently to seat her there he felt her begin to tremble. He saw the light of awareness flare suddenly in her eyes. She looked once wildly around the room as though frightened to find herself here; then she clutched him. *"Matthew . . ."* Her whole body was shaking now and he put his arms around her to hold her. "Oh, Matthew—he was so alone. He was so alone and I never reached him."

She burst into a storm of weeping. He held her and she wept, not on his shoulder but bent over, her face hidden in the crook of his arm, as though bowed down by the burden of failure. He freed a hand and stroked her hair, making soothing, useless sounds over her.

He let her weep until the fountain was dried up. He was supporting her now, for she had exhausted herself. All her strength had gone out of her with her tears. She was almost too weak to stand but he knew that she was aware of him only as a strength to lean on, and this produced in him an ache of loneliness. He put her gently down on the sofa, helped her to stretch herself out there and fixed a pillow behind her. A knitted afghan hung over the back of the sofa and he spread this over her. She lay with her eyes shut, letting herself be cared for as though what happened to her scarcely mattered, indifferent alike to him and to what he did for her. He sighed, careful not to let the sigh be audible, and drawing an armchair close to the head of the sofa, sat himself in it.

He sat there a long time, watching her, his tired mind nearly blank. Now and again she moved a little, and when this happened he was instantly alert, but most of the time she seemed in a state neither taut nor tranquil, suspended between sleep and waking.

He himself was, for the time being, nearly at peace. Thought and action must come but in this present he could allow himself to rest.

He sat with limbs relaxed and let his mind dwell on her, not so much with coherent thought, but realizing her, comprehending her quality in a manner that was oddly impersonal. He felt her to be simple and good, clinging to the precepts she had been taught in her youth, but he saw that beyond these traits there was not very much of anything. A little innocuous culture, perhaps, and a gentle aptitude for homely music were about the sum of it. She had been brave once in her life that he knew about, and probably other times as well, but as a personality, beside Hattie, she paled almost into insignificance. And yet he loved her, loved her until he was weak with it. He was as certain as it is possible to be that he could never love anyone but this fading, gentle creature with the graceful ways and the gray coming into her hair.

Cissie stirred, opened her eyes and turned her head toward him. Instantly he sat up and leaned forward.

"Matthew . . ."

"Yes, Cissie."

Her hand came out from under the afghan and reached toward him. He held it in both his. She sighed and said, "Is everyone asleep?" And he knew by this question that while she was lying there she had begun to pick up the threads of life again.

"I think so. It's long past the middle of the night. If you went to bed now do you think you could sleep too? I could give you some opium to help you."

"No, Matthew, not yet. You understand, don't you?"

He thought that he did, that her renouncement of the comfort of sleep was a self-punishment, slight but immediately to hand, for the imagined guilt of her failure toward Edward. That she would find other punishments and use them on herself he had little doubt. He suddenly saw clearly that, left to herself, she might very well turn her future life into a perpetual penance. From that he would certainly save her.

He put the hand he had been holding back under the edge of the afghan and got to his feet. She was all anxiety in an instant.

"Matthew, you won't leave me?"

"No, I won't leave you, Cissie." He stood for a moment looking down at her; then he let the tips of his fingers rest on the afghan where her hands beneath it made a little mound. "But I'm going to make us some coffee. Will you be all right while I'm gone?"

She nodded, her eyes shut. Two tears slipped out from

under her closed lids and hung in her lashes, glimmering. He knew that the tears were gratitude, and he stayed there a moment longer as a silent acknowledgment. She seemed to him vulnerable and forlorn and infinitely dear. She touched in him so deep a love that it went beyond exultation into weakness, beyond joy into suffering. The pain of his tenderness brought a mist to his eyes and made his knees tremble. Not trusting himself, and filled with fears, but of what he did not know, he did not dare to stay near her a moment longer. He went quickly away.

When he came back with the coffeepot and cups on a tray, he found that she had pulled herself up on the pillow. Her mood had changed and her eyes had a bright and feverish look. Her hands were shaking again and she held her cup in both of them, like a child. He sat down on the edge of the sofa beside her and helped her to steady it. She drank all the coffee and when he took the cup from her she raised her head and looked directly, almost sternly, at him in a way that meant she was going to make herself say something that would take courage.

"Matthew, it was cancer, wasn't it?"

He nodded. Then he said, because he thought he ought to, "We didn't know until the operation."

"I think I knew all along. I think he knew, too. He was so alone, always. Matthew, why can't two people *reach* each other?"

"I don't know, Cissie."

"And now it's too late for everything."

She shut her eyes and let her head fall back on the pillow. Not everything, he thought, but he did not speak this thought aloud. The tears appeared in her lashes again, but they did not fall, and he watched her lovingly. He thought about telling her that Edward knew she had tried to love him and to be a good wife to him, that he understood everything and was truly grateful to her. Then he thought he would wait to tell her at some future time when the emotional strain would not be so great. There would be many things he would want to tell her someday and he let his mind wander off into the solace that thinking about that time brought to him. When, half ashamed, he looked at her again, he saw that she had fallen into the sudden sleep of exhaustion.

Careful not to awaken her, he rose, poured himself a cup of coffee and drank it standing beside the table. Then he crossed the room to a window, lifted aside the heavy draperies, and stepped into the space behind them. Here, though the lamplight was shut out, it was not quite dark, for the night had a grayish luminescence that lifted the weight of the shadows and paled the street lights to a golden glow. A brief, enlivening gust of wind rattled the window before which he stood. He put his hand on the glass, and it felt cool and fresh and, like the wind, enlivening.

His thoughts turned to Edward, lying now with a sheet drawn over his face and the nurse keeping watch or, more probably, sleeping in the chair beside him. His mind slid away from this mental picture into sorrow and a sense of loss. To his surprise he found that his grief was bearable, and he recognized the reason for this to be the unbreakable continuity of life's demands that allow scarcely a pause in the interest of the dead. Duties, many of them trivial but nevertheless exigent, would capture him as soon as morning came. He reminded himself that he must go at once to the laboratory and gather up the microscope and such papers and notebooks as Edward might have left behind. There would be much else to be done and these things would force themselves on him and on Cissie also. "In the midst of death," he said as though speaking aloud, "we are in life," and was unaware that he had remembered the quotation backward.

He merely rested until he perceived that the gray night was lightening. He reached in his pocket for Dr. Hurd's watch, but he held it in his hand without opening it, for suddenly he felt Dr. Hurd's presence near him, as though it filled all the air surrounding him. The feeling was oddly real, and comforting, giving reassurance and a strangely buoyant sense of the future. Matthew gave himself up to it until, after a long moment, it faded and was gone, and he found himself facing the realization that the youth he had been was also gone. He contemplated this thought for a moment with grave astonishment, but without regret. Then he let Dr. Hurd's watch, warm now from his hand, slip back into his pocket.

The window rattled again. The wind was blowing now in long gusts which swept through the street, swaying the treetops and rustling the bed of straw. A stirring within himself responded, recognizing the dawn wind, alive, premonitory. He turned his back on the lightening window and pushed aside the draperies. Walking quickly and quietly, he went to the sofa and stood beside it, looking down on Cissie.

She was sleeping deeply, her head half turned on the

pillow, her hand with its too-heavy ring resting on the afghan. The world shut out, she lay folded within herself; past sorrows, forgotten in sleep, reflected in her face; emotion mirrored in tranquility.

He gazed down at her a long time, not seeing her very clearly but feeling her throughout himself. Then, consoled and heartened, he turned away. Beginning light coming into the room through the open draperies had paled the lamp's yellow flame to uselessness. He turned the wick down until it flickered and went out. At once the whole character of the room changed, for though the sun had not yet appeared, the night was gone. He sat down in the armchair to await the full dawn.

Author's Note

The characters in this book are fictitious, with two exceptions. One of these is Dr. O. W. Holmes, who appears briefly in the story and is better known as the poet and philosopher, Oliver Wendell Holmes. The words he uses in his scene with Matthew are largely his own. The other is Jimmie, the small boy ill with osteomyelitis. When, as a student nurse, I was assigned to duty on a ward, I found Jimmie there. He was an attractive tyke of ten or twelve years, standing pain better than grown men, which is often the case with children. His eyes were bright with fever, he did not have a moment free of suffering, and yet when anyone stopped by his bed a sunny, irresistible smile would brighten his pinched face.

Like the Jimmie of my story, he was a victim of osteomyelitis, but whether or not maggots were used to clean out his infection I do not know. In those pre-antibiotic days, when osteomyelitis was common, especially among children, the "little white worms" were bred for the purpose, so it is likely that they were used in his case. If so, they failed. When I first met Jimmie, he had already lost his leg, but it was taken too late for he did not survive.

When Edward, searching for the cause of Jimmie's illness, made slides of blood samples he did not know for what organism he was searching or even if an organism was involved. Staphylococci cannot be seen in circulating blood by reason of their low numbers in that medium. The presence of microorganisms in pus had been noted at that time, however, and their pathogenic nature was suspected. Staining techniques had not yet come into use. In order to re-create the limitations under which Edward worked, slides relating to these problems were made and examined in a modern laboratory, using a microscope set at the magnification Edward would have used. Edward's failure was inevitable, but his determination was of the quality that in those days was giving impetus to scientific discovery, though another decade was to pass before the etiological role of staphylococci was established.

At the time Matthew operated on Edward, using the Lister technique as he interpreted it, Lister was convinced that wound infections were chiefly caused by pathogenic microorganisms in the air. Shortly after this he invented the famous carbolic spray to combat them, "Lister's teakettle," which was the cause of so much mirth to a later generation of surgeons. He underestimated such likely sources of infection as the instruments, the surgeon's hands, his breath, and his uncovered hair. Subsequently he recognized that he had overemphasized the dangers of airborne infection and he modified his earlier methods.

The time has come to acknowledge the advice, wisdom, patience and friendly concern of those who have been involved in the making of this book. Chief among them are Henry W. Simon, the editor, to whom the book is dedicated, and Dr. William H. Krause, surgeon and head of Windsor Hospital, of Windsor, Vermont, to whom I have turned many times with technical problems. His wife, Madeline, read the manuscript with a rare combination of mind and heart. Dr. Samuel Standard, Professor of Clinical Surgery, New York College of Medicine, gave much instruction and spoke many words of wisdom. Now as in the past Dr. Hugh Hermann, internist, Woodstock, Vermont, has given much assistance, as has Dr. George F. Egan of The New York Hospital in the field of ether anesthesia, and Dr. George A. Hindes, of The Royal Microscopical Society, who let me examine his fine collection of antique microscopes. I should like to add that such medical errors as may have crept into the text are wholly my own.

The Massachusetts General Hospital has kindly permitted me to use its library and to visit the operating room and the ward in the old Bulfinch building where much of the action of the story takes place. The library of the New York Academy of Medicine was literally indispensable. I want especially to thank Miss Gertrude L. Annan, Mrs. Alice D. Weaver, and other members of the library's rare-book room.

I find I do not want to be parted quite yet from the people in the book, and so I think that I will shortly go on with their history.

AGATHA YOUNG

THE BIG BESTSELLERS ARE AVON BOOKS!

☐	Autopsy John R. Feegel	22574	$1.75
☐	Shifting Gears George and Nena O'Neill	23192	$1.95
☐	Open Marriage George and Nena O'Neill	14084	$1.95
☐	Working Studs Terkel	22566	$2.25
☐	The Loo Sanction Trevanian	19067	$1.75
☐	Final Analysis Lois Gould	22343	$1.75
☐	The Wanderers Richard Price	22350	$1.50
☐	The Eye of the Storm Patrick White	21527	$1.95
☐	Jane Dee Wells	21519	$1.75
☐	Theophilus North Thornton Wilder	19059	$1.75
☐	Daytime Affair Joshua Lorne	20743	$1.75
☐	The Secret Life of Plants Peter Tompkins and Christopher Bird	19901	$1.95
☐	The Wildest Heart Rosemary Rogers	20529	$1.75
☐	Come Nineveh, Come Tyre Allen Drury	19026	$1.75
☐	World Without End, Amen Jimmy Breslin	19042	$1.75
☐	The Oath Elie Wiesel	19083	$1.75

Available at better bookstores everywhere, or order direct from the publisher.

AVON BOOKS, Mail Order Dept., 250 West 55th St., New York, N.Y. 10019
Please send me the books checked above. I enclose $_____ (please include 25¢ per copy for mailing). Please use check or money order—sorry, no cash or COD's. Allow three weeks for delivery.

Mr/Mrs/Miss_____

Address_____

City_____State/Zip_____

BB 3-76

THE TV NOVEL THAT'S ROCKING THE WORLD OF DAYTIME TELEDRAMA... THE NOVEL THAT REVEALS TELEVISION'S SECRET WORLD OF GLITTER, PASSION, INTRIGUE!

DAYTIME AFFAIR

Torrents of human emotion flame to life on the soundstage of the daytime TV drama, *Affair of the Heart*... and flood the private lives of the men and women who are actors, not just in this afternoon serial, but in all-too-real roles of ruthless ambition, raw lust, and explosive human drives. DAYTIME AFFAIR is the novel that sweeps across the soundstage, into the dressing rooms, and up through the very corridors of power of a major network!

20743/$1.75

Where better paperbacks are sold, or directly from the publisher. Include 25¢ per copy for mailing; allow three weeks for delivery.

Avon Books, Mail Order Dept., 250 West 55th Street, New York, N. Y. 10019